STORKS IN A BLUE SKY

Carol Anne Dobson

Appledrane

APPLEDRANE

Published by Appledrane 2008

ISBN   978-0-9558324-0-6

The characters in this book are entirely the product of the
author's imagination and have no relation to any person
in real life.

Printed by CPI Antony Rowe, Eastbourne
Graphic Design by Martin Jones
martin.jones@europa-i.eu
Acknowledgement to Stephen Burch for storks
www. Stephenburch.com

Appledrane
33 Carlton Rd.
Torquay
Devon TQ1 1NA
http://www.appledrane.net/

To Andy, Gareth, Rowan
and my mother.

1

Rain lashed the carriage as it jolted over the rough, stony tracks of North Devon. Wind howled across the burnt gorse and heather, screaming through bowed, spindly trees rooted precariously in moor-land soil. The road descended precipitously, clinging to the side of a cliff, and far below, waves thundered and crashed onto unseen rocks.

'What accursed country is this?' wondered Sarah, as the air's icy coldness clutched at her. The carriage lurched madly down the hill and she glanced in terror through the window at a sky and sea which seemed fused together in a swirling cauldron of witch-black fury. Lightning tore the heavens in vivid, staccato bursts, illuminating sheets of rain sweeping across a dark and violent sea. Water dribbled down the walls and streamed in ribbons across the pitching floor. With sweating hands, she nervously felt around her neck for her locket, whose miniature of a smiling, red-haired woman was her talisman against harm. She was sure the picture was of her mother, but had no idea how she had come to know that.

'Bastard! Slut!' The words still rang in her ears. The beatings were raw in her mind and the scars on her back and arms were a physical reminder of the kitchen.

At night, in her truckle bed, exhaustion almost overwhelmed her. 'I'm not long for this life,' she thought. 'Dear God, spare me. Let me be with my mother. She must be dead or she would not have left me in this state and with these people.'

She remembered the patterned hoar frost on the scullery window, its crystals sparkling in the November gloom. She was wearing a white apron and cap and ran her chapped fingers against the pane. She reluctantly climbed the back stairs and was pushed into a vast drawing room, its polished wood floor enlivened with red and gold carpets. Gold also gleamed on the gilded plasterwork of the ceiling and embellished the tapestry wall hangings and the brocade curtains at long sash windows. She found herself in front of a sharp-featured woman, whose powdered face was relieved of its death-mask quality by two, bright red circles of rouge on her cheeks. The startling whiteness extended downwards to her bosom which was caked with Briançon chalk, coloured with streaks of Prussian blue to emphasise her veins. Her hair, also a ghostly hue, its pomatum heavily scented with musk, swayed above her on a wire framework which she delicately scratched from time to time with a jewelled pin to dislodge lice. Her lace-frilled, beribboned, cerise silk dress was equally extravagant, its skirt enlarged by whalebone hoops, which made Lady Throgmorton appear nearly as wide as she was tall.

"You will be Lady Sophie's maid from now on," she said, her somewhat bulging, brown eyes reminding Sarah of those of the dead cod boiled on Fridays.

The soot-streaked pantry and kitchen were replaced by spacious, sunlit rooms, spared the noxious fumes from flyblown, putrefying waste heaped in the yard, suffered by the warren of servants' quarters at the back of the house. The Palladian mansion looked out over a park where cows grazed and riders cantered on horseback along the avenues. Sarah moved like a wraith, overawed by the resplendent furniture and decoration, trying not to dirty them by her unworthy touch. Her new mistress became the centre of her life. She loved her gentleness, her freckled face and her ginger hair, whose brightness could not be hidden, even by repeated applications from the powder carrot; the rainbow colours of Sophie's gowns entranced her and it was as though the dull monochrome of kitchen drudgery had been replaced by a brilliantly hued world.

Lightning repeatedly seared the sky and images continued to flicker through her mind, in a rhythm with the storm; Sophie's tears, her step-mother's malice, the beatings with hair brushes, sticks, almost anything that came to hand. Lady Throgmorton clearly hated and resented her step-daughter, whilst indulging her own children, who rampaged spoilt and unruly.

Her violence extended also to Sarah, but she had been so brutalised by servitude in the kitchen that the blows and pinches were trivial in comparison to her previous suffering. Her waif-like thinness disappeared; she became taller and more rounded.

At times she was disconcerted to find Lady Throgmorton's eyes on her.

'Why is she looking at me, a maid?' she thought and once even had the strange feeling she was gloating.

Standing at the spinet next to Sophie one day, she glanced up and saw Lady Throgmorton staring at them with such malevolence, that it made her flesh crawl, as though a loathsome cockroach was running over her.

' Why does she dislike Sophie so?' she pondered, wishing she could protect her. Then, as abruptly as she had left the kitchen, she found herself perched on a hard seat, clutching bags and boxes, in the Throgmorton coach en route to the wilds of North Devon.

"I'm sending you away. I'm finally getting rid of you, you wretched girl," Lady Throgmorton had hissed at Sophie, her face flushed with anger.

"Your relation, the Duchess de Delacroix, needs a companion. She's a lunatic and should be chained up in Bedlam! She will probably beat you every day, as you deserve! And her son's a brute! He's a savage! A Frenchie!" she shrieked. "You'll get your just deserts with them!"

Sarah's heart stopped beating. The world froze around her. Was she going to lose her beloved mistress?

Lady Throgmorton turned to her and she shrank in fright from the expression of naked hatred very apparent in her eyes.

"And you can go as well. We'll be rid of the pair of you. What a clumsy, useless maid you turned out to be! Now get out of my sight, you ugly, vile creature!"

As she spat out the words, in a shrill tone of near-hysteria, she yanked at Sarah's hair beneath the mob cap, making her yelp in pain, and then rained blows on to her with her hands. Sarah nimbly retreated backwards; Lady Throgmorton reached out to attack her further, and hampered by her unwieldy garments, fell awkwardly, beaching herself on the carpet, her dress held rigidly up in the air by its stiff underframe to reveal layers of silk petticoats and two very large, pink, satin-clad feet. Three footmen manfully attempted to right her and Sophie fled the room, pulling Sarah along with her.

Sophie cried all night and was still sobbing as they clambered up into the coach. She had coughed all the winter and was now finding it difficult to draw her breath after each spasm. Lord Throgmorton, his corpulent body concealed by a voluminous robe, a soft hat perched on his large head and a whiff of brandy still clinging to him from the night's disastrous card game, blearily looked at his daughter.

"Goodbye, m'dear. I hope your journey goes well." He peered short-sightedly at her, before glancing at Sarah, a puzzled frown spreading across his bloated face. She wondered if he was surprised that his daughter was accompanied by such a lowly servant and felt fearful that she would be told to return to the house.

The next minute, the carriage jerked and set off, joining a throng of other vehicles and sedan chairs making their way at snail's pace in the congested thoroughfare. Sophie leaned out of the window, tearfully waving to her half-brothers and sisters, before they were swallowed up by the swarming crowds always found on London's fashionable streets; the peacock-clothed wealthy and their liveried servants; the hawkers, trinket trays hanging from their necks; the ranks of tattered, gin-reeking beggars; all mingling with horses, dogs and even donkeys and goats, which were being milked and the fresh drink offered for sale as people surged around them. A strong smell from steaming manure on the cobbles blended with the bitter aroma of coffee from the coffee houses and Sophie swung her silver, incense-filled casolette backwards and forwards, to ward off unwanted odours. A sea of constantly changing noise, colour and scent flowing around her as she sat for the first time in a carriage, made Sarah's heart flutter with excitement. She did not know what life would bring, but she would still be with her mistress. She was not too sure what a Frenchie was, although in the kitchen everyone had thought they should be killed. And she had never heard of Devon. She was completely uneducated and signed her name with a cross.

She gazed in delight at the countryside as the coach trundled boneshakingly along. She had only ever seen the few streets near the mansion and stared at shire horses lumbering in furrowed fields, or pulling ramshackle, wooden wagons, overflowing with white and purple turnips and muddy orange carrots. Scarlet poppies and azure cornflowers studded banks of swaying grass, and red and blue slashes of colour cut across rippling meadows. Buttercups stretched in yellow waves to copses of ash and beech and the sun shone hot in a cloudless sky. The coach journeyed slowly over rutted paths, often deep with pot-holes, and the postillion astride one of the lead horses frequently had to crack his whip to make them advance through the dusty pits. They passed people trudging along, some of whom were well dressed in breeches, coats and tricorn hats, whilst others were barely covered by dirty rags, sometimes carrying their shoes to save the leather, their bare feet bleeding. She was sad to see women and children tramping dejectedly with their men and presumed they were all looking for work. White drifts of daisies were the backdrop to a skeletal gibbet, where three corpses hung motionless in the hot, still air and the stench of death travelled with them far down the road.

Various nights were spent at drab inns, where the fleas were the most lively part of the stay and several days later they changed coaches at a large city, called Bristol. The air was heavy with smoke like London, the streets were dirty, and dogs ran everywhere, pulling sledges. The new carriage surprised her, as it was extremely small and narrow, although luxuriously upholstered in a soft blue leather, and displayed a coat of arms prominently on the side. They had not seen the new coachman at the staging post in Bristol, but she could hear him now, shouting at the horses through the driving rain,

4

"C'mon, my booties! C'mon!" His speech sounded almost like a foreign language, but he seemed reassuringly in control.

Slumped limply against the corner of the seat, Sophie coughed and coughed and Sarah began to feel afraid.

"It's hurting here," Sophie moaned, touching her chest. Sarah bent forward to wrap a travelling rug more closely round her and her hair escaped from its cap, cascading down in fiery red curls.

"Your hair's so beautiful," whispered Sophie. " I wish mine was the same," and she unhappily brushed her hand against her own hair, which was a more orange shade of red and lay flat and damp on her head. She glanced at Sarah's oval face, her blue eyes, and her slim figure, so similar to her own.

"We've both been ill-treated," she murmured. "I only knew spite and loneliness until I met you. You're so kind and loving."

Sarah thought of how Sophie had helped her. She had shown her how to act as a lady's maid and had not laughed at her ignorance when she had first come from the kitchen. They had felt drawn towards each other, their fair complexion and red hair a common bond.

She had learned to imitate Sophie's voice and accent and had stopped speaking roughly. She had copied her manners, and after balls where she helped to serve guests with sweetmeats and wine, she would try and remember the dance steps and practise curtsying in her attic.

Another paroxysm of coughing gripped Sophie. She shuddered and Sarah cradled her against her shoulder.

"I think I'm dying !" Sophie muttered hoarsely. "The pain's getting worse."

"No, don't say that. Please don't say that," sobbed Sarah, unable to contemplate an existence without her young mistress.

"Don't worry," Sophie said. "If I die, we will meet in Heaven." Her chest heaved and a strange, rasping wheeze issued from her lips. Blood poured from her mouth and Sarah frantically tried to staunch it with a handkerchief, but it trickled down Sophie's neck, staining her bodice.

"You've been a true and good friend. You've helped me so much," whispered Sophie. "Now I want you to do one last thing for me." Her eyes were a pale blue, her face the colour of whey, and outside the coach the wind raged and rain droplets skittered against the window. Her breathing was now very shallow and rattled in her throat as she struggled to speak. "I want you to put on my green velvet dress."

Sarah's mounting sense of doom was briefly deadened by amazement. "But why?" she asked.

"Please oblige me," said Sophie, so quietly she could hardly be heard above the noise of the storm.

Sarah forced her fingers to fumble with the clasp of one of the leather bags next to her, as the carriage swayed and bumped.

' Is her mind wandering?' she wondered, as she finally managed to open it. 'Is she becoming delirious?' She unhappily pulled off her own, sober, navy clothes and trembled as she dressed herself in the velvet gown.

"Now take my ring and necklace," ordered Sophie.

"No, I can't. Why are you telling me to do this?" she protested in distress. "Please stop. Please don't make me."

Sophie clawed desperately at her jewellery and Sarah, not wishing to upset her, helped take off the ring and necklace and with shaking hands reluctantly put them on herself.

"This is wrong. This is sinful!" she cried, tears trickling down her cheeks.

She felt trapped in a nightmare; arrayed in such finery, whilst imprisoned in the ghastliness of a blood-soaked carriage battered by a storm, reminded her of the butterflies she had seen in drawers in Lord Throgmorton's study, their brilliance transfixed by the horror of pins skewering them to metal trays. She was frightened almost out of her wits to see Sophie fight for breath as each bout of coughing racked her body. She loved her and to feel her slipping away was more than she could bear.

"I think I'm going to die. Take my place. Be me," Sophie whispered.

Sarah gasped. "What are you saying?"

"No one knows me here in Devon. The Duchess is a distant relation and is insane. Her son lives in France and has never seen me. Dear Sarah, if I die, what will happen to you? You will be sent back to the kitchen. It was so awful for you there. It would kill you." She stopped, her face contorted in a rictus of pain.

"No, you're not going to die! No, no......!" Sarah cried.

"They will never know," Sophie murmured. "We even look like each other. Hold me. I think my time has nearly come."

Sarah clasped her in her arms, tears streaming down her cheeks. Sophie suddenly jerked frenetically with convulsions and she died.

The carriage juddered to a halt. She gently lay Sophie down, then stood up as the door opened. The world spun around her. She groaned and fell unconscious into the arms of the coachman.

. . . .

It was difficult to open her eyes. An enormous weight seemed to be pressing on her. She was lying on the yielding down of a feather bed. The room gradually came into focus and she saw oak beams across a low ceiling and furniture of the same dark wood. A tallow stub guttered in a dish and she became aware of a plump, red-cheeked woman standing next to her.

"There, milady. Let us 'elp ee. Ee've 'ad a gurt big shock," and the woman helped her to sit up. "Yer poor maid's daid, bless 'er zoul. There's nort us could do for 'er."

Her accent was so strong, Sarah could hardly make out what she was saying. But she remembered with terrible clarity, Sophie's death, and burst into tears.

"There, there, milady. God gives and 'ee takes away," the woman remarked sagely.

"Can I see her?" Sarah asked.

"Drink this, then us'll take you to 'er," she said, giving her a glass.

The brandy punch set her throat on fire, but revived her strength, and she allowed herself to be guided down wooden stairs. A door opened into a scullery and on a table, in the middle of the room, lay Sophie. Her body was covered in a woollen shroud, her red hair fell down onto her shoulders, her waxen face was calmly peaceful, no longer tormented by illness.

Sarah flung herself sobbing, onto Sophie's lifeless form.

"No, no," she whimpered. "Don't leave me."

"There, there, m' dear," the woman said, trying to comfort her, but she clung to Sophie, until finally, too exhausted to cry any more, she collapsed onto the floor. She was vaguely aware of strong arms helping her back to her chamber, where she tumbled half-fainting, onto the bed.

A watery sun gleamed wanly through the black-leaded, casement windows as she drifted briefly between sleep and waking. The bed was soft and comforting to her aching body. Her eyes hurt and she blinked as she attempted to make sense of the unfamiliar surroundings.

"Where am I?" she wondered.

The sharp memory of Sophie's death harshly jarred her feeling of warmth and well-being. She flung back the counterpane, jumped on to the wood floor and cried out in horror as she realised she was wearing the velvet dress Sophie had told her to put on. She guiltily realised she was also still wearing the diamond ring and necklace and suddenly recalled the innkeeper's wife calling her 'milady.' She had been too distraught to pay any attention at the time, but now panic gripped her.

"People will think I stole the dress and jewels as Sophie lay dying. No one will believe what happened. I'll be hanged! Even if I take off everything now, they will know how I was dressed last night."

As she looked frantically around her, she saw that there were not any bags or boxes in the room. There were no clothes to change into.

"Oh, Sophie," she moaned. "Where have you led me?"

She stood in despair at the window and looked out at the view, her eyes widening in astonishment at the sight of a cobalt-blue sea, its ferocious waves raking backwards and forwards across ridges of rounded pebbles. She watched, hypnotised by the power and frightening beauty of the breaking surf, before her attention was taken by the river flowing towards the beach, on the other side of a cobbled path. A river which was very unlike the placid stream in the park opposite the mansion, and which was surging along in swollen torrents of spewing foam, gouging and churning its way past giant, mossy boulders, as it escaped from wooded hills which rose up, almost sheer, into the morning sky.

She silently gazed in awe. Then she remembered her predicament and Sophie's words in the coach came back to her. "Take my place, no-one will know. You even look like me."

' I would prefer to die than to return to life in the kitchen. I have no family, the only person I have loved is dead. I am completely alone. What am I going to do? Sophie wanted me to be her. It was her dying wish. Perhaps it would be better to pretend to be Lady Sophie Throgmorton, even for only a short time, than to go back to my previous life?'

The idea took hold in her mind. ' Is it possible ? Would anyone guess? This wild country is so far from London, no one will ever visit and, in any case, Lady Throgmorton never wanted to see Sophie again. And it's true that I resemble her. We could have been sisters.'

Her cautious, timid nature was swamped by an onrush of impulsive thoughts, and she felt at the mercy of wildly fluctuating desires and emotions. She was crushed by a terrible sadness, and possessed by a gnawing, aching sense of fear, a fear that she would be considered a thief, that she had tried to steal Sophie's jewels. It even occurred to her that people might think she had killed her mistress and she was in no doubt what would be her fate if found guilty. Only the other day a seven year old girl had been hanged in Nottingham for stealing a petticoat. The servants had talked about it in tones of shocked disgust. Public executions were commonplace. She had many times seen condemned people, in their best clothes, the women in white with silk scarves, manacled to coffins in a cart, on their way to Tyburn, and she knew that justice in George's England was swift and not merciful.

She reached for her gold locket. She stood in the warm sun from the window and gazed at the miniature within it.

"Help me," she pleaded. As always, she tried to see the woman's features more clearly. Red hair framed an oval face. Blue eyes looked back at her and a pearl necklace gleamed against the cream of her skin.

'If this was my mother, she was dressed as a lady,' she mused, as she had done so many times before. ' Who am I? How did I come to be in the kitchen? Where are my parents?' As usual, she found no answer. 'I will never know who I am,' she reflected. 'Perhaps my name isn't even Sarah Durrant.'

The roar of the breakers disturbed her meditation and as she listened to the grating sound of the seawater running down through the pebbles, she realised that she did not really have a choice.

"I am not going to return to London," she said out loud. "And I am not going to be hanged for a thief or worse. Sophie placed me in this position and I will do what she commanded with her last words. She was thinking of me, and whether it is right or wrong, I will do what she wanted. And if fate treats me badly and I am discovered, I will end my own life before I am taken by the law. I will throw myself into the sea. I will not be buried at a cross roads, with a stake through my heart."

As she decided, a group of men on horseback clattered across the cobbles. Their uniform of black coats and hats brought a funereal morbidity to the scene and she shivered as she saw them.

9

'Who are they?' she wondered. ' I hope it's not an ill omen for the future.'

A knock at the door interrupted her bleak reflections and the innkeeper's wife came in, cheerfully beaming and carrying a platter of eggs and several rashers of bacon. Sarah seated herself at a round oak table and hungrily gulped down the appetising food, grateful to be alone in her room, where no one could see her.

"I must never forget I am Lady Sophie Throgmorton now," she told herself. She trembled as she sat, tense and nervous, the flame-red of her hair at odds with the whiteness of her face, her eyes watering with tears she was trying desperately not to shed. "I must not rush to do things like a servant. I must wait and ask others."

A fresh sea breeze blew in gusts across the bare churchyard. The low, dry stone walls were no protection against the onslaught of winds which had raced across the Atlantic and then been funnelled up the Bristol Channel. Tussocks of grass grew between moss-shrouded graves, and against a grey body of a church sheltered a dying yew, thick woody growths ridging its massive trunk, and so ancient it had witnessed pagan rites.

Sarah stood and watched as heavy clods of earth were shovelled into Sophie's grave. She had insisted on a good wooden coffin and had ordered a marble gravestone which would be erected later. The innkeeper's wife had protested at such an expense for a serving maid and Sarah had noticed her look curiously at Sophie's blood-stained, but very obviously expensive, dress, which she had insisted on taking with her.

'It's best not to leave anything to incriminate me,' she had thought. She paid for the coffin and the gravestone with coins from Sophie's purse and it had been a very strange and guilt-wracked experience being able to touch such a large amount of money for the first time.

The vicar's hastily intoned words were whipped away by the wind and she only caught snatches. Her mind strayed from the service, as waves of grief engulfed her. She felt so completely alone, standing there in the desolate cemetery. Her beloved Sophie would be abandoned in this grim place, so far from any life she had ever known.

'Perhaps I will be able to come back and visit her grave sometimes,' she wondered, feeling a sense of profound guilt that Lady Sophie Throgmorton was being laid to rest in this poor part of the churchyard, without any of the trappings that would normally be expected for her rank and status. The vicar seemed ill at ease, his cassock flapping against his ankles. He looked anxiously towards the church and as she followed his gaze, she noticed several horses tethered by the lych gate. Banging and knocking echoed from the building and she saw a man dressed in the black uniform she had seen that morning, come out of the main door. The vicar, visibly preoccupied with what was happening inside his church, rushed his last words and quickly made a sign of the cross.

She felt drained of emotion. It was almost as if she was floating away on the wind and looking down on herself. Her leaden feet carried her to the waiting coach, and dazed, she sat and looked back at the treacherous, winding ravine which led to Lynmouth. Dun-coloured cottages, beetle-browed with overhanging thatch, huddled in the lee of a hill, and barefoot children gaped with amazement to see strangers in this remote corner of Exmoor. The innkeeper had told her that the village on the top of the hill was Lynton.

"I must remember the name," she said to herself. " I want to return here."

The carriage rolled swiftly along, once past the hamlet, as the track became flat, caked earth. Moor-land stretched as far as a smudge of dark hills on the horizon. Charred swathes of land striped the pale green bracken; a singed odour tainted the air and curling wisps of blue smoke drifted across the barren landscape. A grass verge was bounded by prickly gorse with its lemon-yellow flowers, and by tall, tapering foxgloves, heavy with pink thimble bells.

She was pleased to have left behind the extreme steepness of the Lyn's wooded gorge. Far below the moor, the sea was a sombre blue and in the distance she could see a ship, its sails billowing out. Cumulus clouds, edged in black, served to deepen her despair and she sat hunched in a corner of the carriage, grief-stricken and afraid. She had arranged her hair high on her head, with curls on her neck, and it seemed very strange to be without her cap. She had chosen a plain gown in white muslin, and a blue cloak, and repeatedly smoothed and adjusted the clothes, trying to gain courage from the idea that, in a way, a little of her mistress was still with her.

All too soon, the openness of the moor was left behind. A sunken lane descended downwards, high hedges of elm scratching and banging at the coach's sides, and she now understood why it was so small. The sun was low in the sky and light slanted across the path. The banks diminished in height, medieval field strips could be seen in rows on curving slopes and whole plots of dark green hemp lay flattened and broken. A muddy brook, awash with twigs, leaves and even a dead sheep from the recent storm, flooded untidily across the valley floor and lapped against cob-walled cottages and a building which strangely resembled a house of cards. The coachman called down, "This be Combe Martin, milady, t'is not far now."

The coach rattled along, splashing through rivulets and pools of water. The stream flowed in full spate across a shingle beach, carving out the branches of a myriad channels. Fishing boats squatted untidily on smooth mud, and a low cliff, fashioned like the head of an animal, a stone Cyclops with one eye, jutted into a choppy sea.

The meandering track followed the coast, sometimes high on exposed headlands, sometimes careering down into sheltered combes, smothered with white-flowered may. The light was starting to fail. Evening was drawing in.

She took one last look at her locket's picture. " Give me strength for whatever lies ahead," she prayed.

Cottages appeared, some thatched, others roofed in slate. The path climbed almost vertically, then fell steeply seawards. A chapel lantern glowed dimly on a hill near the entrance to a harbour crowded with ships, and the jagged outline of a massive cliff loomed hazily in the twilight. The monogrammed coach trundled along Fore Street, past several ale houses, and people moved hurriedly out of its way. Inquisitive faces stared and a few men knuckled their heads.

Her heart was in her mouth. She nervously patted her hair and pulled the cloak tightly around her.

"What's going to happen to me?" she murmured. "Dare I do this?"

Woods replaced the town and the evening gloom blotted out the hills and trees, blurring the nearest branches into mysterious forms. Venus shone with a sparkling brightness in a darkening sky, eclipsing the neighbouring star-patterns still faint in the early night. Sarah felt shrunken and insignificant. A creature screamed and she briefly glimpsed the broad, flat head and powerful wings of an owl, silhouetted against a full moon. The country night terrified her, a terror made worse by the thought of her imminent arrival.

She noticed two lichen-encrusted pillars, surmounted by birds with broken wings and a chipped coat of arms, then the coach gathered speed along a beech-lined drive. It came to a halt, wheels crunching in the gravel, and she peered out apprehensively to see an imposing, grey stone manor house, its slate roof dotted with tall, rectangular chimneys. Candle light glimmered in several of the rooms and the smell of wood smoke hung in the air.

The wild countryside and Lady Throgmorton's chilling words had not prepared her for the sight of such a grand building. Her knees buckled, her heart pounded, her vision blurred.

"In the name of God! What recklessness is this! I can't be Lady Sophie Throgmorton !" she muttered.

But too late. She knew she could not draw back now. The trap she had helped to spring was tightening around her. The solid, brass-embossed door opened and white-capped maids ran down a flight of steps. The carriage door was unlatched and a footman in blue livery offered his hand to help her down. By a supreme effort of will, she forced herself to walk daintily, in Sophie's fashionable, high-heeled, pointed shoes, across the flat taddle stones, each rimmed by a circle of weeds.

A tall woman, her black dress blending almost invisibly with the darkness, but her white cap, apron and face eerily standing out as though disembodied, stiffly descended the steps and as she gave a perfunctory curtsy, Sarah could hear the clink of keys from the chatelaine hanging at her waist.

" Welcome to Wildercombe Manor, milady. I'm Mrs Yelland, the housekeeper."

Her tart expression and tone belied the words of her greeting and Sarah was almost shocked to find that her own fervent wish to be anywhere other than her present situation, appeared equally matched by a similar desire for her on the part of the housekeeper.

Momentarily nonplussed, she looked at the woman's bony face, which in the rapidly encroaching night reminded her of a pudding which had been rather too long boiled, with two sunken raisins for eyes. The housekeeper turned and walked away, leaving Sarah to follow in her wake, disconcerted by her rudeness.

As she climbed the steps she momentarily wondered how Sophie would have felt, arriving to this reception, then found herself standing in a cavernous, stone-flagged hall, mustily redolent of damp, and brought her thoughts sharply back to the present and her own predicament.

Candles fixed in brackets created flickering shadows over wood-panelled walls, revealing a wide staircase leading to a recessed landing. A chest, its front chiselled into fierce battle scenes, occupied one alcove, a black settle stood in another and she had an impression of stepping back in time; the hall and its furniture seemed relics of another age.

Mrs Yelland led the way in to a drawing room, lit by branched brass candelabras perched on tables and chests. More panelling reached to high, plastered ceilings and she noticed that an odd mixture of ancient, dark oak furniture and modern mahogany side boards and walnut-veneered tables, jostled side by side. She quickly saw that there was no sign of anyone resembling a Duchess and sat down cautiously onto a chair, next to an open hearth, where crackling logs were throwing out an overpowering heat into the warm evening.

Supper was brought by a footman and she was taken aback to see the ornate plates set on a table thick with dust. A general air of decay hung over the furnishings and it occurred to her that Mrs Yelland's sharpness did not seem to extend to her housekeeping practices. She ate as delicately as she could, attempting to remember Sophie's mannerisms, whilst trying to avoid thinking of her lying dead in the churchyard at Lynton. The footmen, the maid servants and Mrs Yelland were all openly staring at her and she nibbled firstly at a pilchard pie, baked in the shape of a star, and then at a plum tart with unusually thick, clotted cream; not letting her hunger lower her guard.

"Her Grace will see you tomorrow," the housekeeper said frostily. " She has already retired."

Sarah nodded, reluctant to speak, noticing that there was no suggestion the Duchess was a lunatic as Lady Throgmorton and Sophie had thought, and reflecting anxiously that she would quickly be found out if she was not insane.

"Have you no maid?" the housekeeper continued. "Have you come alone? We understood you had someone travelling with you."

"She died of an illness, two days ago at Lynmouth," she replied, her eyes filling with tears. " I thought it best to bury her there. She had no family."

If Mrs Yelland thought it odd, she said nothing, just pursed her narrow lips together.

The meal finished, she was taken to her bedchamber by a young maid called Jenny, who appeared as vivacious and friendly as the housekeeper had appeared sullen. Her cap was jammed onto glossy black curls and her brown eyes gleamed with mischief.

"Zour as a grab, ee is," she described Mrs Yelland.

"A grab apple," she explained, seeing Sarah's puzzled look.

She ran excitedly backwards and forwards, unpacking Sophie's clothes, exclaiming over the beautiful velvets and silks, in obvious pleasure at being a newly appointed lady's maid, and Sarah sighed with relief when she was finally left alone. She lay rigidly in a damask-curtained, four-poster bed. Sophie's nightgown clung to her and she saw again the windswept churchyard and the lonely grave.

"Sophie! Sophie!" she sobbed. "Help me!"

The spectre of the fateful meeting with the Duchess de Delacroix the following day haunted her thoughts and she peered out from the coverlet, trying to recognise the shapes around her, which seemed to be moving and creaking in a night as blackly forbidding as the River Styx. She jumped nervously out of bed and ran and pulled back a curtain, calming as the moon's silvery light revealed velvet-upholstered chairs, sturdy oak furniture and the thick damask drapes.

She finally managed to sleep and awoke to the warmth of sunlight and the crowing of a cockerel. She lay and watched dust motes sparkle in the rays streaming through the casement windows and felt a new sense of purpose and determination.

"I am Sophie,' she told herself. ' I will be her.' She superstitiously touched her locket and prepared herself mentally for the task ahead.

A welter of sensations and images flooded over her that first morning. The strangeness of servants helping her dress and waiting on her at breakfast, was unnerving, and she tried to speak and move with a slow dignity, so as not to reveal herself by a slip of the tongue or unsuitable behaviour.

Each minute waiting to meet the Duchess seemed an eternity and it was almost a relief when she finally followed the austerely dressed housekeeper along a corridor and into a dazzlingly bright drawing room. She blinked, her eyes temporarily blinded by the sun, and smelled the honeyed scent of flowers overlaying the odour of mildew and damp which pervaded the house. Her eyes focused first on red roses in Chinese patterned vases and then on a shrivelled doll of a person, seated on a green, brocaded chair by the window.

A clock in an oval glass case ticked noisily on a marble mantel piece. Her heart thumped, she tried not to tremble. As she approached the elderly woman she saw that the skin on her face was so transparent and lined it looked like parchment, her eyelids sagged, almost obscuring milky blue eyes, and on one cheek was a rather incongruous, black beauty spot. A white lace headdress was tied under her chin and her emaciated body was encased in a gaudy, pink and blue dress, adorned with a vivid purple bow on the bodice. Around her neck hung a gold crucifix, a ruby set in its middle, which the sun suddenly caught, making it glow with a deep redness.

'Like living blood!' she thought and almost took to her heels in panic, both at the grim association and at her first sight of such a religious symbol being worn as jewellery.

She clutched Sophie's favourite blue silk dress and executed an awkward curtsy.

"Lady Sophie Throgmorton, your Grace," announced Mrs Yelland curtly, then left the room, her keys clinking.

She jumped as a bony stick of an arm shot out towards her and grabbed her dress, thin fingers pawing at the silk. She forced herself to stand confidently still, as, far from appearing insane, the old woman looked as sharp to her as a new pin.

16

"You're…" she questioned, her cracked voice quavering.

"Lady Sophie Throgmorton," Sarah repeated the name.

"You're real!" she continued, in an astonished tone. "You're flesh and blood!"

Sarah eyed her nervously, at a loss to explain her words.

"Perhaps you would care to take a dish of tea with Lord Templeton?" and the Duchess nodded towards a stuffed owl in a glass case. "Lady Soustrans also joins me at this hour," she remarked, this time inclining her head in the direction of a fish mounted on the wall.

She suddenly realised imaginary friends were present in the room and almost exclaimed out loud in joy; for the first time since Sophie's death experiencing a stirring of hope.

The morning passed surprisingly quickly. The rigours of the past few days had emotionally and physically taken their toll and she sat quietly next to the stuffed owl, as the Duchess chattered to a social gathering so exalted it included King George, who appeared to be the orange at the top of a pyramid of fruit. She even felt bold enough to look about her and her attention was taken by two gilt-framed paintings. One was of a tall officer in military uniform, whilst the other was of a serious young man with very dark hair and eyes.

' Is that her son, the Frenchie?' she wondered. 'The Duchess is obviously English. If her son is French, then her husband must have been French.'

Her knowledge of the outside world was very limited, but she was well aware of the hostility directed towards foreigners in England and the talk in the kitchen had been angry and contemptuous towards them. For as long as she could remember, England had been at war with France. In the streets she had often seen foreigners spat on or beaten and French men were always a popular target.

Her thoughts wandered, tiredness making her light-headed, when the booming of a gong sounded from the hall announcing dinner.

Two footmen carried the frail old lady on her chair to the dining room and placed her at one end of a long table, whilst Sarah was seated at the other end.

She had no appetite and struggled to swallow a few mouthfuls of a roast lamb. Her hair was damp against her face, the unfamiliar clothes were suffocatingly restrictive. Her head swam from the heat, the wine she had too quickly drunk on an empty stomach and the mosaic of dark and light in the room; bright where the sun caught it and in shadow where it escaped its brilliance. The Duchess's conversation to make-believe people, echoed emptily around her and she felt an almost uncontrollable urge to laugh. She spluttered, clenched her teeth, and knew it was not merriment which gripped her, but the fragility of her mind, which was spinning like a hundred weathercocks, plunging her into a traumatised coalescence of past and present. The porcelain plates in front of her conjured up the mansion's kitchen and stacks of rancid-smelling, dirty crockery waiting to be washed; a blue-bottle buzzing on the fat-streaked lamb evoked the unsettling image of three dead men, swarmed over by flies, in a field of white daisies.

"Would you like more wine, Lady Athelstone?" the Duchess enquired and a footman hurried to fill yet another of the glasses lined up on the table, each of which had not been as much as sipped by the non-existent guests.

'Is madness catching?' Sarah wondered, and as she tried to concentrate on the already difficult task of being someone she was not, she attempted to stop her feverish ramblings and respond adequately to the unusual social demands being made on her. She attempted to give every person mentioned a body, to give substance to the elaborate game of imagination being enacted, but was horrified to realise that she had endowed each one with the characteristics of Lady Throgmorton. One lady enjoyed her prominent eyes, whilst another had pearl-bodied lice, like gem stones, draped through her hair. Sophie rose up before her, then tantalisingly vanished and instead her corpse grinned at her from the scullery table.

"Don't slouch at the table, Jean Luc, or I'll take the whip to you!"

She started in fright as the old woman's voice sharply changed from a mellifluous chatter to a harsh shriek. She sat bolt upright on her chair, the words slicing through her fantasies. She could feel again the hot stickiness of blood on her skin when she had been beaten, and revulsion made her nauseous. She unhappily looked at the Duchess, and as their eyes met, she was astonished to see the old woman almost crumple, and bow her head submissively.

"Please don't go," she begged in a piteous voice. "It's been so long. Please don't be cross with me."

"No, I'm not going," muttered Sarah, confused by her unexpected domination of the situation and relieved to see the Duchess's expression soften as she reverted to her previously pleasant manner. She briefly wondered about the identity of the unpopular Jean Luc, before eating a large portion of plum porrage, holding her spoon with a new-found confidence.

18

The Duchess remained silent for the rest of the meal. She ignored the port, biscuits and cheese proffered by the footmen and slowly closed her eyes, her head lolling forward. Sarah rose quietly to her feet and tip-toed to the door. She looked back to see the footmen emptying all the wine into the tappet hen, to be drunk later in the kitchen, and realised why they had rushed to fill all the glasses to the brim; then she escaped from the house and out into the fresh air of the garden.

She wandered along a gravel path leading to a lake, her dress smelling of the lavender which had accompanied it in sachets on the journey. She scuffed the bald patches of brown earth dotting the yellowing grass, and eddies of dust floated towards her. The sun did not filter through a haze-filled sky as in London; it shone fiercely down and each leaf, each flower, could be seen with a clarity she had never observed before; their bright colours were perfectly mirrored in the lake's glassy stillness and as she leaned over the water she suddenly saw Sophie again, staring back at her; her long red hair, her blue silk dress.

"Oh!" she exclaimed and held her breath. After the initial shock she was disappointed to realise it was herself, not Sophie, standing there, and she rippled the water with her hand to disturb the image, which distorted into a million pieces, elongating and curving beneath glittering points of light on the surface.

She turned her back on the lake and walked past regimented lines of clipped box trees, towards a high-walled garden. She stood in its arched doorway, breathing in the heavy fragrance of white, red and pink rose bushes, radiating outward from a stone sundial and training against wooden trellises; buzzing, brown-velvet bees were like dark eyes against the petals they were nuzzling, and a dragonfly's iridescent, fairy wings shimmered in the sunlight.

The sweet rose perfume followed her as she roamed across the garden and approached a wood. She peered into a tangle of trees and bushes, then resolutely marched along a path winding up the hillside. She had never walked in woodland before and found herself thinking of witchcraft and sorcery as the tree canopy grew more dense and twilight surrounded her. Vertical shafts of sunlight pierced the gloom, illuminating clusters of red campion and white stichwort, their brilliance accentuated by neighbouring banks of plants which had been plunged into thick darkness. Pale green shoots of wild garlic were everywhere, pungently scenting the air, and the black fungi of dead man's fingers projected from branches and rotting wood. The stone path was stained with orange growths, like little misshapen bowls and she weaved her way erratically to avoid crushing

19

them, gently touching overhanging ferns, and being fascinated by the brown symmetry of spores on the underside of their fronds.

Her magical world abruptly disappeared and she stood on the edge of the wood, blinking in the sun. In front of her an expanse of wiry grass was traversed by lines of bare rock which fell away in a dizzying descent to the shore far below.

She had not realised the house was so near the coast. She hesitated.

' Have I strayed too far? Perhaps I should have stayed in the garden?' she wondered. Then drawn irresistibly towards the sound of breaking waves, she scurried down the cliff-side path.

A tumult of sound and colour assaulted her senses as she reached the beach; a crescent of sand, between two headlands, glinted silver, contoured by black seaweed and bleached driftwood. A patchwork of sparkling blue stretched to the horizon; sunlight, clouds and currents irregularly shading the sea, whilst Atlantic waves were crashing down on to the shingle, raking the pebbles and flinging out flecks of foam to settle like snow on stones and rock pools. Salt spray was wet on her face and an intense joy seized her as she ran full-tilt towards the edge of the water. She stood for a moment, caught unawares by the rapid ebbing of the flow, which left her stranded far from the breakers. The next minute, the waves roared towards her and she was knocked over by the force of the surge. She scrabbled to her feet and was discomfited to not only find herself soaked, but also to hear laughter.

She looked towards the headland and jumped in alarm to see a man observing her. He had a mane of black curly hair and a beard and was wearing a patched greatcoat which hung loosely at his sides; it was one of the few times she had seen a man not clean-shaven and she took fright at being alone on this unknown beach, with such an odd-looking stranger, and hurriedly ran back towards the cliff path.

In the shelter of the woods the reality of her situation came forcefully back to her. "I must be more lady-like. I am sure Lady Sophie Throgmorton would not have gone out exploring by herself," she muttered.

She retreated down through the trees and timidly entered the house, leaving muddy marks on the flagstones as she squelched across the hall.

Mrs Yelland appeared from a side room and frowned at her dripping skirt and wet shoes.

"I'll send a maid to you," she snapped.

'Sour as a crab apple!' thought Sarah, remembering Jenny's words and trying to reassure herself that the housekeeper's ill-nature was not confined to herself and did not mean that she suspected her deception.

4

She spent the next few days in a jangle of nerves. Even the sight of her own shadow, close on her heels, was enough to make her jump.

"You foolish girl!" she scolded herself. "You can't possibly pretend to be Lady Sophie Throgmorton!"

She constantly walked backwards and forwards to the main gate, each time meaning to escape from the estate, but each time returning. She had no idea where to go, or what to do.

'There will be such a hue and cry if I just disappear. I would be caught and hanged!'

She wandered the house in Sophie's fine silk dresses, but felt naked.

'Everyone's laughing at me!' the refrain ran repeatedly in her head. ' They all see I'm really a rough servant girl.'

She was surprised to find she was happiest sitting each day with the Duchess de Delacroix. She posed with the contents of the fruit bowl on her head to represent a classical goddess in a tableau and discussed whether to hunt, or to visit the fountains at Versailles, a foreign-sounding place, whose name was frequently mentioned. It occurred to her that she was already masquerading as Lady Sophie Throgmorton and so it seemed only a small step to act out other roles in a fantasy which was less threatening to her than the real world.

The manor house overawed her. The thick stone walls muffled outside noises and the heavy quietness increased her anxiety. She restlessly roamed through the rooms, noticing again the slovenly manner in which they were kept.

To her amazement, no one denounced her. Her heart started to flutter a little less and the horror of the journey began to fade.

One day she managed to snag her dress on a broken piece of wood and tear the material. She was cross with herself for carelessly harming her clothes and was suddenly struck by the thought that she now considered the dress as being hers, not Sophie's. She realised that she had also stopped glancing through the windows to see if soldiers were coming to arrest her and that she had also curtailed her endless sorties to the main gate. It shocked her to think she was actually starting to feel that she was Sophie and she was also shocked to think that she was beginning to enjoy herself.

Her favourite room was the library where she always breathed deeply on entering to savour the satisfying aroma of paper and leather. She randomly chose books to leaf through at the oak desk in the window and tried to decipher letters and words, but was only rewarded by frustration at her ignorance. Pictures of incredible creatures, with long trunks or striped bodies, held her spellbound, and inspired by the illustrations, she took paper and drawing materials from a drawer and painstakingly copied the flowers, animals and stones she saw on walks in the estate.

The Duchess always retired to her bedchamber after an early dinner. Mrs Yelland also disappeared at a similar time and she was surprised to come across her, late one afternoon, emerging from the cobwebbed mustiness of the wine cellar, walking unsteadily and clutching two bottles of gin in her hand, and she began to understand why the house was so dirty and ill-kept.

She discovered a spinet in a side room and almost beside herself with excitement, attempted to learn to play it. She knew from watching Sophie, that the notes on the music sheets matched the keys. For weeks she only produced a faltering, tuneless sound, then finally found she could play simple melodies and sang to accompany them.

Every evening she sat in the library. On the wall hung a portrait of the young man she had first noticed in a painting in the drawing room. His eyes seemed to watch her, his face had a confident, determined look. On the table in front of her she placed her locket and indulged herself by imagining that the man in the painting and the woman in the miniature were her relations and that they were there with her in the room. Her aching desire to be part of a family was a powerful, persistent yearning which had possessed her for as long as she could remember. She had always been alone. She had always felt abandoned. And in the quiet of the library, even although she knew she had embarked on a reckless, foolish course, whose outcome she would surely regret, she experienced a sense of peace, a sense of wonderment, that for the first time in her life, there was no shouting and no violence and that, in a strange way, she had found a home where she belonged.

One afternoon she noticed an arched door half-hidden in a recess on the landing. She curiously pushed it open and saw dark, unwelcoming stairs, spiralling upwards within a narrow cupboard. She stood for several minutes, unsure whether to explore further. An almost imperceptible, sweet fragrance, wafted towards her through the blackness and she resolutely followed it up the twisting, turning staircase.

She guessed, rather than saw, that she had reached a door, and leaned hard against it. It creaked alarmingly and opened to reveal a sun - filled corridor, light flooding through glass panels in the roof. The fragrance teased her, stronger now, an exotic blend she recognised as partly of orange, jasmine and cinnamon. A choice of doors confronted her; she tried the nearest and found herself on a crenellated parapet looking out over the trees towards the sea. She was surprised that the coast could be seen from the house and watched a ship slowly tacking in full sail up the Bristol Channel and could even hear the shouts of the sailors on the deck. The wind whistled about her and she felt unsafe so high above the ground. She clung to the door jamb for support and as she glanced towards the end wall gasped in horror to see a row of brown bats hanging upside down under the eave. Huge ears looked grotesque above squashed, pug faces and she quickly retreated backwards.

The fragrance enticed her along the corridor and she pushed open another door and gasped again; but this time, it was from wonder, not disgust.

An Ali Baba's cave of treasure glittered in front of her eyes. Necklaces and rings spilled across carved, ebony-black furniture; paintings of Mary and her child were propped against a dingy wall and richly embroidered materials were thrown over tables; gold crucifixes gleamed a dull yellow, making her heart beat even faster by reminding her of her soul's certain damnation.

The furniture was of a foreign style, quite different in wood and design to that found in the rest of the house. It seemed strange that the jewels and paintings had been flung so carelessly and she stared, mesmerised, breathing in the heady perfume, which appeared to come from an overturned silver flask. She absentmindedly ran her finger over the glass front of a lantern leaning against the wall and then jumped in panic as she felt the unexpected warmth of a body behind her. Startled, she swung round and saw it was Mrs Yelland. Her black-button eyes were narrowed, almost to a slit, and the expression on her face was venomous.

"What are you doing up here?" she shouted.

"I'm just looking around," Sarah stammered.

"Stay downstairs!" the woman barked, as though addressing a servant and she was astonished to find herself almost pushed back down the stairs. She ran to the library, her mind still full of what she had seen and uneasy at how she had been treated.

'Has she guessed I'm not Sophie?' she asked herself over and over again.

The fear of being discovered returned to haunt her with a vengeance and she tried to keep out of the way of the housekeeper as much as possible and to anticipate any situation which might expose her.

When the first Sunday arrived she wondered how to avoid the dangerous ordeal of meeting the local gentry at church.

"Is there a service held at the house?" she summoned up her courage and asked Mrs Yelland, hoping the practice would be the same as at the Throgmortons.

"Yes, the priest comes here when he can," she answered rather vaguely, surprising her by the use of the word ' priest,' as in her experience, he was always called ' vicar,' or ' reverend.'

She saw him arrive on horseback, in mid-morning, shortly after the whole of the household, in their best clothes, had filed down the drive to visit the parish church in Ilfracombe; she noticed that he was not dressed in the usual black dress with a white surplice, but was wearing brown shoes, brown breeches and a worn, black coat.

"Do you want to attend the service, your ladyship?" asked Mrs Yelland and she nodded her head, thinking it prudent to do so. The housekeeper led the way to the west wing, to a door hidden behind a thick tapestry, which opened to reveal a highly decorated chapel, far removed from the plain church surroundings she was used to. The rich colours of a stained glass window played across the stone floor and walls; a gold crucifix gleamed on a red, brocaded altar and bouquets of flowers adorned every niche.

The Duchess was making the sign of the cross, an action she had never seen anyone, other than a vicar, do before, and as the unfamiliar service progressed, with clouds of incense floating around her from a silver ball swung by the priest, it slowly dawned on her that she was participating in an illegal event. It was not a Church of England service, it was Catholic. In the kitchen, the servants had often talked of Popish plots and dirty foreigners with their blasphemous religion and she shivered with an impending sense of doom.

'What's going to happen to me? I'm in the house of the Devil!' she thought, before remembering that her sins were now so great, Heaven would not be her destination anyway.

As the priest and his horse disappeared down the drive, she stood at the bedroom window, her thoughts racing in time with the clouds scudding across the sky's arching greyness. She felt as though she was in a dream-like trance, brought down to earth only by the cloying smell of incense still clinging to her.

'It is not only Sophie who has been left behind at Lynmouth,' she mused. 'Sarah Durrant has also been abandoned there.'

She had become someone else, a person who did not have a name. It was impossible to think of herself as Lady Sophie Throgmorton. She shied away from calling herself that. Lady Sophie Throgmorton was dead and lying in the cold churchyard.

'It's very quiet here,' she reflected, watching a bee bumble against the glass.   'Sophie would have hated it.' In London there had always been a stream of visitors, balls and social visits, and she gratefully reflected on the fact that so far, no one had visited the Duchess.

"Luckily, she's as mad as a coot. No one is likely to call," she muttered.

The idea now also occurred to her that the Delacroix family might be very unpopular in the locality. 'They are not only partly French,' she thought, ' but they are also Catholic.'

5

The summer was hot. Long, sultry days followed each other. The ground became even more parched and brilliant crimson sunsets flooded the evening skies. The beach fascinated her. Near the cliff, the pebbles were large and smooth, then became smaller and smaller, until only fine pale grains curved in a crescent across the cove. Her brown buckled shoes left a pattern of prints, crisscrossing the whiteness. One day she abandoned her stockings and shoes and for the first time felt the sand clinging to her bare feet. She wandered along the sea's edge and enjoyed the delicious sensation of a soft, damp roughness. The water lapped her feet and she gradually waded deeper and deeper, peering down at the seaweed swaying on the sea bed. She recalled Sophie's friends who had just returned from a town called Brighton, and had overheard one of them describe standing in the sea in a special bathing dress.

"It was so frightening. I nearly drowned. And some people could swim like this, like a fish," and she remembered her flapping her plump hands and breathing in short gulps.

The next time she returned to the beach she carried a chemise and in the shadows of a cave near the headland undressed and put it on. Feeling naked, she crept out into the sunlight, glancing around to make sure that the beach was deserted, then ran into the sea, crying out as the freezing water enveloped her. Exhilaration and fear swept through her in equal proportion. The numbing cold gradually lessened and she jumped up and down in excitement, before retreating to sit on the sand and kick her feet in the rippling shallows. The thrill of that first experience was repeated many times and by the autumn she had taught herself to swim and sometimes even dived down under the water and watched crabs scuttling over the stones.

The sea was a cleansing, healing force which soothed her anxiety. London and the Throgmortons now seemed a very distant, far-off threat and, for the time being, it seemed safer, and considerably more enjoyable, to continue as she was.

One day, as she reached the bottom of the cliff path, she nearly fell over a wicker cage. She looked up in alarm and saw the same shabbily dressed man who had laughed at her the first day. His eyes creased into a smile and her panic subsided.

"John Buzzacott, me lady," he announced, raising his knuckles to his bare head of black curls. He scooped up the lobster pot in an enormous hand and strode down the beach to a rowing boat, where she could see silvery scales glinting from a pile of fish.

She realised he was a fisherman and as she became more aware of the ebb and flow of the tide, always knew to expect him when the sea flooded high on to the beach. Like clockwork, he would arrive to fish in the cove with a thin line from his boat and proudly show her any lobsters or crabs he had caught in the pots.

"The vish'll be rinning vaur day," he told her one afternoon. "The parish lantern's gain be vull."

She was puzzled for a moment and as he pushed his boat across the shingle she realised he had meant the full moon and that 'vish' was 'fish'.

She spent her days roaming the estate, sketching and collecting stones and shells. Almost overnight, summer changed to autumn. Blackberries gleamed in thick Devon hedges and the perfumed lilac flowers on a tall bush by the beach had faded and were no longer covered in butterflies.

She followed the meandering paths through the half-light of the wood and was not surprised to find a fairy-ring of pink mushrooms. The leaves on the trees were more brightly coloured in death than they had been in life and an eruption of tawny yellows, oranges and russets replaced green.

She rarely strayed outside the estate's high walls, but one afternoon in early winter, when the sky was a monotonous grey and a brief rainstorm had left the drive awash with muddy pools, she turned her back on the stone birds guarding the entrance and wandered down the lane towards Ilfracombe. A sluggish trickle of water in a narrow ditch gurgled its way seawards; hawthorn hedges were red with haws and a yellow-headed, golden gladdi was singing what sounded like a 'little bit of bread and no cheese.' She suspected that the colourful name John Buzzacott had told her, was not the usual English word, but had no idea what it could be. She trudged along the track, apprehensive about venturing too far and smiling at the thought of the new Devon words she had learnt from Jenny that morning and thinking that 'drumbledrones' and 'appledranes' sounded far more interesting than 'bees' and 'wasps'.

She rounded a corner and almost bumped into an elfin child, his blond hair matted and dirty. He was holding a handful of grass and tearing at it with his teeth.

"No, you shouldn't eat that," she exclaimed. "It isn't good for you."

The boy looked at her, his pinched face reminding her of crushed egg shells, his swollen stomach the only sign of plumpness on an otherwise emaciated body.

"Are you hungry?" she asked.

"Yes," he whispered.

"Where do you live?" she enquired.

He silently pointed to a low, cob-walled cottage.

"Let's go and see your mother," she said, giving him her hand.

They walked together past rows of disease-blackened, stunted cabbages, submerged in a sea of groundsel, and came to the open door of the house. She waited in the entrance, peering inside and trying to accustom her eyes to the darkness. A rank smell made her wrinkle her nose and she saw that the floor was carpeted with brown ferns.

A thin, fair-haired woman, children clutching at her skirt, stared blankly at her.

"He was eating grass," mumbled Sarah, ill at ease and not knowing what to say.

" Us abn awt to eat," the woman said, her voice soft, but distinct. "Me man's daid and ee's left me with all zese boys to veed. The parish gees us ale and teddies," and she pointed to four small potatoes on a table, " but nowt much azides. Us're aiting dewsnails and snails. Us'll be put in Woodbine Cottage, the Poor Ouse, zoon," and tears ran down her cheeks.

"I'll go and bring some food for you," Sarah said, without a moment's thought, and letting go of the boy's hand, walked quickly back to Wildercombe House.

In the kitchen, she stood timidly on the door step. Food seemed to be everywhere. Pink hams, marbled with creamy fat, were hanging from hooks. A chicken was cooking on a spit, turned by a dog in a wheel, and on the table, an overflowing bowl of flour was surrounded by heaped dishes of raisins, lemon and orange peel, brown eggs, sugar and cinnamon spice. She recognised the head cook as she was wearing leather sleeves to protect her arms from the fire and on her head was a tall, snow- white cap.

"I would like ham, cheese, bread and apples placed in two baskets," she said firmly, addressing her.

"Yes, milady," said the cook and bustled around, giving orders to the maids.

Sarah was aware that there was no lack of food at Wildercombe House. Every day she had noticed files of donkeys loaded down with panniers of vegetables, meat and dairy produce, making their way from the farm gardens to the house.

"A small amount won't be missed," she told herself and knew that the servants could not easily question her orders. She prayed Mrs Yelland would not appear, and as soon as the food was ready, picked up the heavy baskets, declining the help of a footman, and rapidly retraced her steps to the cottage.

She did not linger and with Mrs Blackmore's heart-felt thanks echoing behind her, passed by the birds' stony stare and pensively walked back along the drive, saddened by the misery she had seen.

'I will go again with food to them,' she thought. 'It might not be quite the sort of social visit Lady Sophie Throgmorton would have made, but at least some good has come from my wickedness.'

Dandelion seeds blew in clouds past her, parachuted by the wind. She laughed to see them and danced merrily over the puddles, trying to catch them in her hands, and returned to Wildercombe House, her spirits completely restored.

6

Sometimes, on black, moonless nights, she heard the spirits of the wood stirring. Lights danced amongst the trees. Clanking noises, shouts and braying, as though from donkeys, sounded muffled and strange.

Late one evening, a freshening wind from the west was fast becoming a gale and she pricked up her ears as she noticed again the tell-tale, unearthly cries, sharply distinct against the storm. She had seen a fox for the very first time earlier in the day, and, in her excitement, had only realised when she returned to the house, that it had perhaps been a witch's familiar and not a real animal. Now she was certain of its true nature and retreated to the welcoming safety of her four poster bed.

On her pillow she placed a flower she had picked in the summer. It had originally been white, with a bright yellow corolla, but now was so faded and limp, it bore hardly any resemblance to its original state. Jenny had told her that such flowers were a protection against witchcraft and she always carried it with her when she roamed the wood. She slept restlessly, the Atlantic wind pursuing her into her dreams, chasing her across cliffs and graveyards. The nursery rhyme, 'Who killed Cock Robbin' somehow became woven into her disturbed thoughts and she felt herself fluttering helplessly, trying to escape the arrow coming towards her. She awoke in a cold sweat, still vividly recalling the dream and suddenly aware that she had heard a pistol shot, not the twanging of an arrow.

The storm had died. There was a stillness in the air. She sat bolt upright in bed, blood pounding in her head, and strained to hear if anything was moving outside in the gardens. Minutes passed and her fright was just subsiding, when two shots echoed again. She clutched the covers and became aware of a delicate clip-clop of horses' hooves slowly approaching the house.

Paralysed with fear, she awaited her fate.

'I've been found out! Somehow, someone has discovered I'm a fraud, an impostor!' the words hammered in her brain.

A thunderous knocking reverberated through the house. She half-fell on to the floor, then dragged herself to the door. She opened it a fraction and peered through the chink.

Black-coated men, carrying muskets and cudgels, their uniform similar to those she had seen at Lynmouth, were entering the hall and Mrs Yelland was running agitatedly towards them, her frilled night-cap frivolously perched above her plain face.

A man stepped forward. He removed his brown tricorn hat and she saw that he and the others appeared cold and wet. A gust of wind blew leaves across the stone slabs and the draught caught Mrs Yelland's night gown, ballooning it indecently to reveal her legs.

"We're chasing smugglers who were unloading contraband from a lugger down at Brandy Cove. One of the varmint's dead and we've winged another!"

She almost fainted with the blessed relief that she was not the prey. The man's words blurred across her consciousness. She vaguely heard, "Tubs... Frenchies.."

His face was angry, a weather-beaten red. His gaze swept the stairs and the landing, as though he imagined smugglers might be concealed behind tapestries or paintings, and she could see a bad-tempered aggression in his manner.

" If we see anything, we'll send word to you, Squire Connibeer," said Mrs Yelland. Her voice was chill and it was her face, and her demeanour, which suddenly frightened Sarah, not the blustering Squire, with his gun and his dark-clad Preventive Officers.

'There's an evil about her!' the thought came to her, as she watched the woman.

She shut her door and crept back to bed and was pleased when, a few minutes later, she heard the horses slowly pick their way back down the drive in the moonless night. The remains of her flower were crumbled into pieces which stuck fast to her hands and she fell asleep holding them to her cheek.

Next morning, the sky had a washed-clean appearance, an innocent blue. The ground, however, bore clear scars from the storm's fury and even from the house she could see statues overturned, plants and bushes flattened and an oak tree sprawling on the grass, its roots stumpy in the air. She decided to walk through the estate and see what other damage had been caused.

Her preparations, as usual, involved a lengthy deliberation over what to wear and the arrangement of her hair. She had never seen how ladies dressed in the countryside and so always wandered the estate in a state of attire it would be difficult to fault in the most fashionable London circles. She was aided and abetted in this by the Duchess, whose failing intellectual faculties had not diminished her passion for fine clothes, cosmetics and perfumes, and she and Sarah spent their happiest moments together experimenting with strange concoctions from almonds and breadcrumbs to improve the complexion, dabbing on exotically scented toilet waters and sticking extravagant beauty patches on to their faces. Her sole concession to the difficult paths and rocks she often scrambled over, was to wear Sophie's only pair of flat shoes, instead of the numerous, high-heeled, pointed ones which had accompanied her.

As she crossed the hall to leave the house, she noticed the door wide-open to a room which had remained locked since her arrival. Always curious, she stood on the threshold and saw that men were mending a window which had evidently been cracked by the storm. A long bench stood parallel to a wall and on it was arranged a varied collection of the most weirdly shaped glassware she had ever seen. Bulbous containers stood on three-legged stands and narrow pipes snaked at odd angles from one pot to another. Jars were filled with coloured powders and shelves were laden with untidily stacked books and papers. Dust covered every surface, a not uncommon feature of the house, and as she craned her neck to see more, Mrs Yelland came out and banged shut the door. Knowing the futility of asking the housekeeper any questions, she continued on her way, pondering the strangeness of what she had seen.

As she skirted the oak she glanced back at her bedroom window and glimpsed Jenny. She had been unusually subdued that morning, her eyes looked sore and swollen and she had wondered if she had known the smuggler who had been killed. Jenny had refused to say what was distressing her and so she had asked her to obtain beeswax to polish the furniture in her chamber.

'At least she will be free from Mrs Yelland's clutches,' she had thought, ' and my room will be cleaner.'

She left behind the lawns, untidily speckled with leaves, and entered the wood, experiencing as always a strong sense of communion with the natural world around her. Patches of sky could be seen high above, through bare, close-twining branches. Slashes of fresh brown earth revealed where a few of the smaller trees, such as ash and larch, had been uprooted and left broken at odd angles in the undergrowth. A thin black trail led over the white pebbles of the path and she bent down to examine it more closely. She decided that, very oddly, it appeared to be tea and smiled to think of a witches' tea party, although, in reality, she was coming to think that the wood was perhaps a frequent scene of a more human visitation.

A sudden baying of dogs and the heavy thudding of horses' hooves made her blood run cold. She felt exposed and vulnerable alone on the path and nervously shrank back against a tree trunk. The next minute, men on horseback came galloping up the hill and leading them was the same man she had seen the night before. He reined in his horse sharply when he saw her, surprise very evident on his face.

She was intimidated, as he leaned down from his saddle. She felt in danger of being trampled underfoot by his horse, but forced herself to regard him calmly, remarking that daylight did not enhance his features – his cheeks were even more redly hued than in the night and his eyes were almost hidden in creases of swollen flesh.

"Who are you, m' dear?" he bellowed roughly.

"I'm Lady Sophie Throgmorton," she replied, as haughtily as she could. "I'm staying at Wildercombe House."

She thought she caught an expression of distaste in his face as she mentioned the house and then was nearly knocked off her feet by two beagle dogs which bounded and leaped at her, their tails flailing the air, their jowls slavering.

She screamed and the rider behind Squire Connibeer jumped down and cuffed each animal hard and they slunk away, tails between their legs.

"Captain Vinnicombe at your service, milady," he introduced himself and she found herself looking at a tall, grey-eyed man, dressed in military uniform, whose red jacket was startlingly bright in the leaf-shaded wood.

She was glad she had powdered her face and her hair that morning and hoped she appeared suitably aristocratic. She also knew she was not the person being hunted, so had the confidence to attempt an imitation of Lady Throgmorton and sniffed disdainfully.

"We shot a smuggler last night," said Squire Connibeer. "And there's blood down by the beach. Have you seen anyone?"

"No, I have not, sir," she replied sharply.

He nodded briefly at her, in a manner she considered rude, and shouted, "Come on men!" and cantered off up the hill. Captain Vinnicombe acknowledged her with a bow, then swung himself up onto the saddle and followed the others.

She could hear the sound of hooves fading away into the distance, before the quiet of the trees closed round her again. She was unsettled by the unexpected intrusion of strangers in her wood and pensively followed the trail of tea.

The day seemed to have become dark and drab. She could hear shouting in the distance and the blood-curdling howls of the dogs. The winding black line petered out and she left the path and climbed over moss-covered boulders to search for the scarlet and white toadstools she

34

had found the previous day and which Jenny had told her were useful for repelling flies.

She felt a sense of disquiet. A weird, prickly sensation crept up her body and she had the strange feeling she was not alone. She hastily looked for the russet fox, but he was nowhere to be seen and she held her breath as nothing moved, not even a quiver of grass or leaves. She turned to go home, afraid to venture further, and noticed a remnant of ragged brown cloth hanging from a twig. It reminded her of someone and she balanced uncertainly on a rock facing a dense bramble thicket.

She was suddenly aware that eyes were staring at her through the briars. She squeaked, like a mouse, and nearly fell off the uneven stone she was standing on. She could see the outline of a face and whimpered in fear, riveted to the spot. Her gaze was locked fast on to the eyes and slowly she made out black curly hair and a beard.

"John Buzzacott!" she murmured in amazement.

He groaned in pain and she could now see he was hunched over, one leg stiff in front of him, his clothes dark with blood. She realised she had found the smuggler and stared at him in horror.

From the brow of the hill came the whinnying of horses and a crashing, tearing noise. She glanced upwards and saw the black-uniformed men beating the undergrowth with sticks. Squire Connibeer and Captain Vinnicombe were rapidly approaching her on horseback and the beagles were barking excitedly. She knew that even if the men did not find John Buzzacott, the dogs would quickly scent their quarry. She was only too conscious of her own precarious position as Lady Sophie Throgmorton, but had no intention of letting her friend from the beach be taken off to swing from a rope if she could do anything in her power to save him.

She grabbed the torn piece of cloth and stuffed it into a pocket. Her voice shaking, she called loudly towards the Squire.

"Call off your dogs, sir! They are frightening me! Please remove them!"

At that moment, the beagles' yapping rose to a frenzy as they flushed out a rabbit. It desperately zigzagged over the rocks, trying to escape, but one of the dogs caught it and with one bite broke the unfortunate creature's spine, making a sound like the snapping of a dry twig.

"Are you searching for smugglers, or poaching?" she cried, seeing the glimmer of an opportunity.

35

The Squire leaned down and snatched the rabbit from the dog's mouth and threw it violently into the bushes.

"You are trespassing, sir!" she called out again, surprised at her own audacity.

"I'm on the King's business!" he shouted back, his face almost purple with annoyance. " This estate's gone to rack and ruin. It's a hot bed of smuggling and God knows what else! Where's the Duke, eh? What side is he fighting on?"

She thought he looked as though he was about to have a fit of apoplexy and he cantered off to the path, bellowing, "Traitors! Papists!"

The men followed him and as Captain Vinnicombe turned away too, he raised his hat politely and gave her a broad grin.

She stood, amazed that she had thwarted them and waited patiently until she could no longer hear the horses and dogs, before parting the brambles.

"Thank ee, me lady. Thank ee," John Buzzacott whispered gratefully.

"What are you going to do?" she asked. "You're badly injured."

"I'll stop 'ere in the brimbles til dark," he replied.

"I'll come back, just before nightfall," she said, " and I'll help you."

"No, no me lady, I dith'n wan ee to do that. I will try and traipse down the ' ill by meself," he gasped, his teeth clenched in pain.

"I'd better go now," she said and pulled down branches to conceal him better, then set off back to the house, her mind feverish with what had happened and pondering the words of the Squire.

The bright afternoon was clouded by the knowledge that John Buzzacott was hiding in fear of his life in the wood she could see from her window. She knew she would be putting herself at risk of prison and perhaps even of death, if she was discovered helping him, but was determined to try and save him.

As the last fingers of sun vanished below the horizon, she slipped out of the house unnoticed. She followed the path through the wood, the pebbles softly white in the deepening twilight, her heightened senses on edge to every rustle or noise. A twig snapped and she jumped in panic, thinking it was a pistol shot. A snub-nosed vole scuttled across the stones and she waited for it to disappear into the bracken. She climbed the steep hillside, the bushes and trees twitching and jerking in the wind, and with difficulty located the bramble thicket where she had stood that morning.

A dark shape which seemed barely human was crawling crabwise across the ground, the injured leg hanging limply. She ran swiftly towards him and he looked up, startled.

"Yer dithn' 'ave come," he muttered.

"Let me help you stand. If you lean on me, you can perhaps get along." She bent down and tried to pull him up. He was almost too heavy for her, but she clung on and managed to drag him to a standing position.

"Hold on to me," she ordered.

"Naw, I cawn't, me lady," he replied in embarrassment.

She put her arm around him, smelling the sweat from his body and feeling the roughness of his coat. She was breathing with almost as much difficulty as he was, terrified someone would chance along. His breeches were torn and she could see dried blood on bare flesh. He moaned and she could feel him struggling to keep quiet.

She supported him as he hopped and they tottered together slowly down the path in a three-legged parody of a dance. A grey halo of light circled the moon, but under the trees it was as black as the rest of the heavens. They stayed in the shelter of the wood, skirting the avenue leading to the house and finally reached the main gates.

"Me 'ome's nair the 'arbor," he muttered. " But daw'n ee ' elp us gaw there. There's a cot nair yere. If I stape there, volk will 'elp me 'ome."

She knew it was far more dangerous to be in the lane than on the estate and bit her lip in anxiety as they lurched awkwardly along. They passed Mrs Blackmore's cottage and John Buzzacott indicated a thatched house on the other side of the stream. A dog whined as they approached and she could hear a man gruffly talking.

"Thank ee, me lady. Go now. Thee bist so gude. Go," he whispered.

She propped him against the fence, then knocked on the door. She did not wait, but gathered her skirts in her hand and rushed swiftly back to the lane. She heard someone say, "John? Bist ye urted?" and hoped he was now safe.

The ghost-face of an owl stared white from a tree and she fled, pursued by its mocking hoot as creatures scampered all around her. She reached the bottom of the wood and stopped to catch her breath. The damp clamminess of night held her close; a solitary star twinkled near the moon. She started to run again but her long skirt hampered her. Near London, highwaymen had roamed Hampstead Heath, robbing people, and she wondered if such ruffians were found locally. A horse whinnied, then another and suddenly horsemen appeared, holding lanterns. To her dismay, she recognised Captain Vinnicombe with a black-uniformed Preventive Officer.

"Well, demm me, it's Lady Sophie again!" he said in an astonished tone. "What on earth are you doing out here alone?"

"I lost my way," she said. "And it became dark so quickly." Even to her own ears her account sounded lame, but he dismounted and said chivalrously, "May I have the honour to escort you?"

"Yes, thank you," she replied graciously, more than a little pleased to have the protection of the dashing captain and also thinking that if he was walking her home, he was not pursuing John Buzzacott.

"Go off, Ezekiel. I'll meet you at the Cairn," he told his companion, then led his horse by the bridle, holding the lantern so that Sarah could see the ground more clearly.

She walked hurriedly to avoid conversation and Wildercombe House quickly came into view, appearing out of the blackness, as it had the first night she arrived. This time no candle light glimmered in the rooms and no servants came running down the steps and she could feel Captain Vinnicombe's surprise at seeing the desolate nature of such a grand house.

"Thank you sir, for helping me. I should not have been caught out so late in the evening," she repeated.

"Until we meet again. Good evening," he said and waited as she ran up the steps and pushed open the main door.

A single candle was spluttering its last, the hall was almost completely in darkness and in the distance she could hear servants talking and laughing. The smell of beeswax greeted her as she entered her bedchamber and dying embers smouldered red in the hearth. She stood quietly in the window and watched the flickering light from Captain Vinnicombe's lantern until it disappeared.

'I don't intend to see you again, sir,' she thought, recalling his grey eyes and handsome face and the way he had looked at her. 'I want my wood as it was before the storm and the smugglers. I want its magic back, its spirits and ghosts.' She shrank from the reality which had reached out and touched her that day and huddled against the cold window pane, wishing to remain as she was for ever.

7

She woke with a start in the middle of the night. From the hall came the roughness of men's voices, the trampling of boots and dull thuds. Wind gusted under the ill-fitting door, rattling the window panes. She listened intently, straining her ears to try and discover what was happening.

'Is it smugglers again?' she wondered uneasily.

She crept across the cold carpet, gently opened the door and cautiously ventured out onto the landing.

A scene of near-pandemonium greeted her. Candles flickered in the gale blowing violently from the wide-open main door, casting moving shadows over a thronging mass of men, bristling with pistols and knives and carrying crates and boxes. Their clothes appeared outlandish and foreign to her eyes. Rows of metal or gold buttons decorated waistcoats and coats, many of which were red. They all wore boots and reminded her of soldiers, even although they were not in uniform. Several were carrying wide hats of black felt, which they had evidently removed in order to enter the house.

A tall, well-built man with grey hair, whom she took to be the leader, was standing stiffly next to Mrs Yelland. He was holding a fur hat, his coat was also made of fur and he was looking dourly around him. She could see that Mrs Yelland was very flustered; her cheeks were blotched pink and although she was dressed, her night mob cap was still on her head.

Snatches of a foreign language drifted up to her and in a corner an animal was squealing and spitting aggressively. The rising sense of panic beginning to seize her was momentarily forgotten as she gazed at one of the strangest creatures she had ever seen. It was about the size of a large cat and had thick, grey fur. Its tail was ringed with black and white and its pointed, fox-like face had a broad black band across its eyes, which resembled a highwayman's mask. It suddenly shot across the hall and disappeared into the garden, pursued by several of the men. She burst out laughing and the man who had been kneeling next to it, stood up and turned towards her.

She abruptly realised she had been mistaken. This man was the leader of the group. His coat glowed a deep purple in the shadowy half-light. Rows of lace decorated his pockets and cuffs, and rings gleamed on his fingers. He looked up at her and she saw with horror the same dark eyes, strong jaw and aquiline nose she had so often noticed in the painting on the library wall. He stared at her, expressionless, and she trembled in her thin night gown, as the chilled air rushed in from the wintry night.

His familiar features blurred. The blood ran ice-cold in her veins and she clenched the wooden balustrade with both hands to keep herself upright. Her red curls were caught by draughts of wind and she felt an overwhelming desire to escape into the night, as the masked animal had done.

She stumbled back to her room and hid under the covers of her bed, realising that she was at least safe until morning.

Jean Luc, Duke de Delacroix, watched her go and for a few minutes continued to stare at where she had stood, an expression on his face almost of disbelief. Then he picked up a lantern and went outside to hunt for the raccoon he had brought back from Louisiana.

She tossed and turned restlessly throughout the long night, considering, over and over again, the questions which had tormented her in her first weeks at Wildercombe House.

'Lady Sophie Throgmorton cannot just disappear. I will be caught and hanged. In any case, where can I go to? I have no family or friends.'

It comforted her somewhat as she recalled Mrs Yelland saying that the Duke had only visited the house once since the war against the French had started and also as she recalled that he lived in France and had never seen Sophie.

She abandoned her bed and roamed backwards and forwards, oblivious to the cold and dark, her thoughts screaming at her. The room, which had originally seemed so forbidding, was now her sanctuary. She pressed her face against the window pane and gazed blindly out at the mysterious, magic wood. She reached towards the walnut dresser and ran her hands over her stones, shells and drawings, placed neatly in piles. In her heart she knew what she would do.

'Fate has smiled on me so far. I will keep calm and remain as Lady Sophie Throgmorton while I can and attempt to find a way out of my predicament. Hopefully this man will not stay long and I will try to see as little of him as possible.'

At dawn, she watched a twin sun and moon grace the lightening sky together and as she looked out at the garden a black and white striped tail, curled round a branch high up in the horse chestnut tree, caught her eye. "We're both fugitives," she murmured.

She summoned Jenny and questioned her about the visitors.

"Didn't ee know, milady? That's 'is Grace, the Duke. Ee's been praying in the chapel since before sunrise and 'as been out searching for that fox. They be saying the war with France has finished. Perhaps that's why ee's come. " She bit her lip as though unsure whether to say any more and muttered, "In Ilfracombe there be talk of the Delacroix family......"

Sarah was flayed by despair and hopelessness and, in an instant, saw her new life smothered just as it was beginning. For a fleeting moment she realised she knew almost nothing about her previously absent benefactor and wondered where he had come from and if he had now returned to live in North Devon.

'Will I be found out today? Will I be exposed ?' Her hand trembled violently as she chose a lemon silk dress to wear.

Reluctantly she walked down the staircase, trying to push images of capture and imprisonment from her mind. Her shoes tapped sharply against the stone steps, reminding her of the drum beat at executions. Her wasp-waisted bodice was choking the breath from her body; the lemon silk floating out around her, its frills and lace contrasting almost mockingly, it seemed to her, with the gravity of her situation. There had unfortunately been no more cosmetic powder that morning and she felt very much at a disadvantage with her own natural complexion and hair, unable to hide behind her usual white concealment. The months spent at Wildercombe House resembled a dream which was now shattering into a sickening, ghastly nightmare. Her sins had caught up with her.

Logs were damply spluttering in the fireplace of the dining room. A fine damask cloth covered the table and there was a bitter-burnt smell of coffee.

Jean Luc de Delacroix was standing at the window, surveying the gardens. He turned, as she entered, and her heart jumped as she saw again the painting transformed into a living person. He was taller than she had realised. His face was not pallid and blemished like the previous aristocrats she had encountered, his skin was clear and tanned by the sun, as though he had spent many hours in the countryside. He was fashionably dressed in a plum-coloured coat, cream breeches and black boots, not in a robe and cap as Lord Throgmorton had always worn at home, but his dark hair was again bare, as on the previous night and it struck her as very strange to see a nobleman without a wig or a hat.

He bowed. "Lady Sophie. I'm very pleased to make your acquaintance. I had no idea that you were living here with my mother, but I am delighted that your family has been so kind to allow you to keep her company." His deep voice was loud in her ears and although her limbs were locked into a frozen immobility, she forced herself to curtsy.

He regarded her gravely for what seemed like several minutes.

'Has he found me out already?' a voice shrieked in her head. Her vision blurred and through a ringing in her ears she heard him say, in slightly accented English,

"Please be seated and have breakfast. I've waited for you. Mrs Yelland said you generally eat at this time."

A footman pulled out a chair and she sat down as gracefully as her agitation and tightly-laced stays would allow. He sat down heavily opposite her, closed his eyes and prayed.

She was grateful for the respite and held herself very upright on her chair, trying to keep calm. Lady Throgmorton's words strangely echoed in her head, " He's a savage!" and she found herself glancing at him, whilst keeping her eyes half-shut, pretending to follow him in prayer; refusing, even in her present vulnerable state, to join a Catholic in his religion. She noticed he was somewhat clumsily dressed, his cravat was at an angle, several buttons on his sleeves were undone.

He stopped praying and put his hands down on to the table, managing to knock over a milk jug, and footmen scrambled to mop up the spilt liquid. He ignored the activity around him and looked directly towards her. His eyes were a very dark brown, almost black, and the sharp scrutiny of their gaze seemed at odds with his rather disordered appearance and behaviour.

She felt unable to look back at him and, for her part, stared intently at a triangle of toast on her plate. A clattering of knife and fork told her he was now eating and she surreptitiously glanced at him again and saw he was attacking a plate piled high with beef steak, eggs and bacon, with the same vigour he appeared to impart to everything.

"You remind me of Titian's paintings," he remarked bluntly.

His words and manner perplexed her. She had expected a more polite form of conversation. Her encounters with the Throgmorton nobility had always made her think of their talk as a sort of bird-like twittering, lacking substance, but very refined and correct. She also had no idea who Titian was and what his paintings consisted of, but thankfully did not receive the impression he was suggesting she was really a serving maid masquerading as Lady Sophie Throgmorton.

She nibbled at her toast and said nothing.

"Did your family know that my mother has not all her faculties?" he queried.

"Yes, your Grace," she murmured.

"You're very far from London society," he observed. "I would have thought a marriageable young lady......" he stopped speaking. "Are Lord Throgmorton's affairs going well?"

"Yes, I believe so," she replied softly.

"How do you spend your day?" he asked. "Do you make many visits?"

"No, no I don't," she had to admit.

"Well, how do you pass your time?" he persisted, an obvious curiosity in his eyes.

"I walk," she answered. "I enjoy walking."

He raised his eyebrows. "I know my experience is rather limited, but all the ladies I know only make social calls, or shop. I often ramble in the countryside. Perhaps you would care to accompany me some time?"

"Yes, I would like that," she replied, very disappointed that he did not appear to be about to return to France. She finished her toast and wondered when she could politely leave the table. She felt exhausted and was only too aware it was just a matter of time before she made a fatal error. She nervously drank her tea, but her hand was shaking so much she was forced to put down the dish.

She saw him again look very curiously at her and the colour rose in her cheeks. He slowed his rapid assault on his food and she had the impression he was making a conscious effort to eat more politely.

"I'm afraid I've been in the backwoods of Louisiana too long with just my men," he said. "I hope I'm not making you nervous. We had not intended to return so soon, but the Treaty of Paris was signed and the war came to an end." His face hardened with anger.

"It is good that the war is finished," she hazarded, hoping to be on safe ground as the subject bore no relevance to her own position and what happened in the far- off colonies had never been of any interest to her.

"It is true that it was a vicious fight, but France has now lost New France and all her land east and west of the Mississippi River." He now sounded furious and she wished she had not spoken. For a brief instant, she glimpsed the narrowness of her own life, the isolation of this northern part of Devon, and her days spent mainly in solitude or listening to the ramblings of an insane woman. It also seemed odd to her, and even traitorous, for someone to be talking so patriotically about France and not England.

"I have brought back many animals from my travels. I think you saw one of them last night. It has escaped for the moment, but I hope to find it soon." His tone lightened.

"The Algonquian people call it an aroughcun, which means 'he who scratches with his hands.' We have been calling it a raccoon. It is a very unusual creature and even washes its food before eating."

"And it can also climb trees," she added, very interested in what he was saying, in spite of her fear.

"How do you know it climbs trees? Have you seen it?" he queried.

"Oh no," she replied, blushing again, reluctant to be the cause of the raccoon's capture. "No, I haven't. I was just guessing because it reminded me of a cat."

At that moment, the grey-haired man she had noticed the previous night, entered the room and was introduced to her as Heinrich Scheyer. The terror that she had so far managed to keep under control now threatened to overwhelm her, as he scrutinised her with coldly critical, grey eyes, reminding her of the gimlet gaze of the buzzard always hunched predatorily on the highest trees in the wood. His face was lined with age, but his body was still that of a powerful man. A sense of strength and force emanated from him; even his name sounded sharp and strange to her, and she imagined that if the local people came across him, or his men, they would think that the threatened invasion had actually come about.

"I will leave you, your Grace," she said, his arrival having given her the opportunity to stand up, and she managed to give a demure curtsy before walking quickly across the floor, the lemon dress trailing behind her on the ground.

Jean Luc watched her as she left the room, then pensively strode to the window and looked to see which trees would be visible from her window. The horse chestnut was the nearest and as he peered towards it, a very distinctive, black and white tail could clearly be seen on one of the upper branches.

"Well, I'll be ….!" he exclaimed.

Back in her bedchamber, she felt faint. She had no idea if she had behaved correctly. Jean Luc de Delacroix did not remotely resemble any aristocrat she had ever seen. His face was burnt by the sun, he lacked a wig and she considered that the way he ate his food left much to be desired. The fondness with which she had always regarded his portrait had been destroyed by seeing him in the flesh and she flinched as she thought of the questioning way he had looked at her.

"It's unfortunate that he's right," she muttered. "It must seem very odd that Lady Sophie Throgmorton was sent away from her family to North Devon. And one seed of suspicion can quickly give rise to others."

She tried to regain her composure and concentrated on watching the seagulls flying inland from the sea. Just as she was feeling calmer, her gaze wandered to the horse chestnut tree and she blinked to see Jean Luc de Delacroix shinning up the trunk. He looked across and saw her and gave a cheery wave, then lost his hold and fell onto the ground, flattening two footmen as he did so. The raccoon suddenly shot downwards and streaked so fast towards the wood, she could only see a blur.

She saw him pick himself up, then she retreated back into the obscurity of her room, smiling at the unlikely scene she had just seen and apprehensively wondering what the rest of the day would bring.

She soon discovered she was not the only person displeased at the unexpected arrival of the visitors. The Duchess refused to speak and remained in her chair, sulking and petulant. Dinner had evidently been postponed until the evening and she was very grateful to find that they sat alone in the afternoon, forced to eat cold venison pie, as the cook and the kitchen maids were frantically preparing food for the large number of men now billeted in the west wing. Mrs Yelland's face looked as though she had swallowed a lemon and she was rushing backwards and forwards like a woman possessed by the devil, barking orders at the servants, who were cleaning away the ingrained layers of dirt and dust, which she suspected had accumulated since the last time the master of the house had made an appearance. The tranquil serenity of Wildercombe House had been destroyed by a whirlwind of activity and by the noise of men shouting and talking in a foreign language.

She wandered up and down the stairs and stood aimlessly in the library. She knew it would be far safer to closet herself in her bedchamber, but felt drawn to Jean Luc de Delacroix like a bird caught in the gaze of a cat. She was afraid, yet wanted to find out what he was doing and check that nothing untoward had happened concerning herself.

An acrid smell pervaded the hall and she wrinkled her nose. She realised he was in the room with the unusual glassware and jumped with fright as a series of small explosions shook the windows and door. Crackling noises could be heard and she braced herself for the extremely likely possibility that the whole of Wildercombe House was either about to come crashing down about her ears or be reduced to cinders.

Instead there was silence. She longed to rush over and open the door and discover what was happening, but did not dare. She was suddenly aware of the sound of horses' hooves faintly echoing through the quiet, and she peered in dismay through the library window to see three ladies perched side saddle on horses trotting up the drive.

"Who are they?" she muttered, more in exasperation than in fear. "What's happening?"

Finding John Buzzacott had been unsettling enough; the arrival of Jean Luc de Delacroix had terrified her; but although her small world had been rudely shaken, it had not yet collapsed. Now, however, the local gentry appeared to be making a social visit. She felt incapable of coping with any more threatening events and just as a footman was opening the front door she sprinted wildly across the hall. Her shoe became caught in the hem of her skirt and she fell sprawling at the bottom of the stairs. She scrambled to her feet and saw Jean Luc de Delacroix emerge from his room, a dirty smock over his shirt and breeches, his dark hair escaped from its ribbon and hanging untidily onto his shoulders. Blue smoke swirled out around him, suffusing the air with a smell of gunpowder.

"Did you fall? Are you harmed?" He ignored the arrival of the newcomers and spoke to her kindly and compassionately, in the way she had always imagined during the winter months sitting in front of the fire. His appearance, however, was not as she had visualised and she blinked in astonishment at his clothing which bore more resemblance to that worn by ploughmen tilling the soil.

"I'm fine, thank you," she replied breathlessly.

His eyes lingered a moment on her face, then he walked towards the visitors, leaving her to trail in his wake, fervently hoping that these people had never met Lady Sophie Throgmorton.

The three ladies entering the hall stopped short just past the threshold and were clearly disinclined to venture further. Their feathered hats nodded in unison, adding colour to drab, brown and green riding habits, and the pallor of their unnaturally white faces was offset by dashes of rouge. They looked familiar to her and she glanced at them, perplexed and worried.

"Mrs and Misses Vinnicombe," announced a footman and she now realised why she had thought she recognised them. They were all extremely tall, extra inches added on by their exotically plumed headgear and she saw that the attributes which made Captain Vinnicombe handsome, were not so attractive to her when found in his close female relations. His square-jawed chin and grey eyes were replicated in all three and his height and build was also shared by them, although on a slightly smaller scale.

"We had no idea you were in residence, your Grace," said Mrs Vinnicombe. "My son, Captain James Vinnicombe, was privileged to make the acquaintance of Lady Sophie yesterday and we have come to invite her to a musical gathering at our house in Ilfracombe on Saturday afternoon."

As she spoke, the Duchess, tricked out as a goddess in a loosely draped yellow curtain, a wreath of ivy on her head, was being carried through the hall on her chair by two footmen, one of whom had a broomstick hanging from his waist. Mother and son ignored each other and, as she passed regally by, she called out commandingly.

"You're with the wrong party, Princess Caroline! Come over to the fountains to see the king with me. And tell those men to go and rent a sword at the gate, if they want to enter the palace," she added, looking at the women.

The Vinnicombes stared. Jean Luc de Delacroix frowned. And Sarah would very much have liked to accompany her into their mutual fantasy world, which she knew from the broomstick-sword was taking place at Versailles, but felt constrained to remain where she was. A drunken-sounding, ragged chorus of a foreign song erupted from the garden and she caught the Vinnicombes exchanging sideways glances, as though to suggest that Wildercombe House and its inhabitants were extremely odd.

"I see you are not so much of a recluse as you led me to believe," he remarked. "I've hardly been in the house ten minutes and you already receive a social invitation."

At that moment, the Miss Vinnicombe nearest to Sarah opened her mouth in a strange, soundless shape and struggled to speak.

"Aagh!" she almost gurgled, in what appeared to be an abject state of horror. The other Miss Vinnicombe shrieked in a very high-pitched, piercing note and as Sarah glanced towards the source of their fright, she was amazed to see a brown snake poking its head out of the smock pocket of its owner, who quickly grabbed it and said with obvious relief,

"I thought it was dead. I hoped the heat from my body might revive it. It comes from a warm climate."

He held the thin body lovingly in his hands and, with an air of pride, displayed it to her. She smiled, entranced by a snake which she had never seen in her life before, while one of the Miss Vinnicombes collapsed on to the stone floor, muttering, "It's the sign of the devil!" and her mother threw herself down to comfort her, clutching at her hands.

47

He glanced angrily towards the women, cradled the snake in his hands and said brusquely to Sarah,

"Can you please attend to this, madam?" then strode off into his room and slammed the door.

She stood for a moment, nonplussed at unexpectedly finding herself the lady of the house, then called for hartshorn and cordials to revive the stricken Miss Vinnicombe, who made a remarkable recovery as soon as the snake had retired from her view.

"Thank you for your kind invitation. I would be delighted to attend your musical afternoon," said Sarah, thinking that she could perhaps avoid going, when the time came.

The Vinnicombes all beamed, then very quickly made their excuses and left, and as she stood on the steps, watching their horses trot sedately down the drive, she thought that it was almost as though evil spirits were conspiring against her.

" If only I had not gone to the wood, I would not have met James Vinnicombe," she murmured, and she tried to cheer herself with the idea that at least it was unlikely that anyone in Ilfracombe would know Sophie, as Devon was so far from London, it seemed like a different country.

The afternoon was growing late, storm clouds were blackly gathering on the far side of the wood, but she felt in desperate need of fresh air. She wanted to escape, even if only for a few hours, from her oppressive situation and not for the first time thought bitterly of how foolish she had been to put on Sophie's dress and jewellery in the coach.

"I knew it was ill-fated!" she murmured.

The freshening wind tugged at her cloak as she hurriedly crossed the lawns and Jean Luc, glancing out of his window, caught sight of a bright flash of blue and a glimpse of red hair for a moment before they were swallowed up by the wood. The horse chestnut tree outside the house was creaking and groaning like the timbers of the ship which had recently brought him across the Atlantic and he noticed cumulus clouds rolling ominously in from the coast. He felt uneasy that his young relation seemed to be walking into a storm, but after a few minutes fruitlessly watching, his attention was suddenly taken by the ground fragments of red sassafras wood he was heating to try and extract its yellow dye and which was beginning to spit and burn.

After weeks at sea it was a relief to be on dry land, although Wildercombe House was only a temporary rest to see his mother and inspect the North Devon estate. Preparations were already being made in Alsace for his wedding to Catherine de Montfort and he thought with satisfaction of the joining of the de Montfort lands to his own, already vast, estate. He attempted to picture the features of his fiancée, but was frustrated by his complete inability to do so. He knew that the truth was, that it would not be a marriage of love, but one of financial consideration, as was commonly the custom, and that he had been more occupied with the negotiations which had been taking place than with spending time with his future wife. He remembered the gold bonnet à bec on her head, sparkling with jewels, but her face remained stubbornly invisible. The more he tried to recall her, the more her shadowy figure retreated even further from him and in her place stood a woman in a white nightdress, a cloud of red hair blown by the wind. He saw her face opposite him at breakfast, the cream of her skin and the unusual colour of her eyes, which made him think of the mauve-blue of violets, and then he pushed her image away and concentrated again on the sassafras wood.

His one true passion was his love of science and many times in the last two years in the New World, he had longed to be back in his well-stocked work rooms in Alsace and Devon. He had missed his experiments, but had compensated by collecting hundreds of plants and animals and was now impatient to examine them properly. The aromatic scent of the sassafras filled the air, conjuring up the wonders he had seen in New France, in the land the Hurons called Canata. He imagined himself standing at Hochelaga, on the heights of Mont Royal, looking down at the brilliant blue of the Gulf of St Lawrence, the winding river flowing into it, the bands of smaller hills traversing the plain, and the mountains to the south east. The trees were a burst of colour; red, yellow and orange maples, golden aspens and birch and scarlet-berried rowans and he almost put out his hand to touch the purple leaves and red fruit of the bunchberry, the tall goldenrod and burnished yellow ferns, but they disappeared, to be replaced by the noise of battle and the screams of the injured. He could smell the smoke of death in the village which had been torched, and he clenched his fist with fury at the British victory and the loss of all the French possessions in the New World.

He thought with dislike of his mother, and the few times he had seen her since she had abandoned him on the death of his father, to be brought up alone in France whilst she returned to Devon. The strangeness of being here, with her, in his English manor house, was compounded by the unexpected presence of a young relation of whose existence he had been barely aware, and he involuntarily glanced again towards the trees where he had last seen her, even although the wind was now roaring and the rain falling so heavily, it was almost impossible to distinguish even the shape of the nearby horse chestnut tree.

8

Deep in thought, Sarah wandered along the woodland path. A dull bass booming reverberated through the trees as the wind increased in strength, then fell back to a whisper, moaning and whimpering, before rising again into a shrill keening, accompanied by cracks and thuds as branches broke and crashed to the ground. The eerie sound made her think of lost souls calling out for help and she was pleased to reach the open bareness of the slopes above the trees, even although the wind ferociously assaulted her, mushrooming out her cloak and dress and pushing her almost to the cliff edge. Far below, waves careered diagonally across the bay, breaking angrily onto the treacherous reefs John Buzzacott had told her were a ships' graveyard.

She laughed as the wind buffeted her. Her spirits lifted and she delighted in experiencing the power of nature. She forgot her problems and ran headlong across the spiky grass. Rain droplets were cold on her face and the sky was rapidly darkening. To the horizon, brilliant-white lightning forks seared the blackening clouds. A thunder clap deafened her and she rushed towards the shelter of a ruined church which stood, grey and squat, on the hillside overlooking Ilfracombe. As she reached its haven, the heavens opened and torrents of hail poured down, stinging her face and drenching her hair and clothes. She crept past the rotting remains of the door into the sombre interior and sank down in one of the pews. Her euphoria vanished. She felt afraid, alone in the derelict building, with water cascading down the steep roof and splashing in through narrow windows. She shivered, both from fear and from her cold, wet clothes. She waited and waited and still the violent storm continued. She had no idea how long she had been sitting there. The sky gradually lost all semblance of light and the uniform darkness of night took its place.

"I'm not going to be in time for dinner," she muttered, thinking that she had wanted to be as inconspicuous as possible and instead seemed destined to draw attention to herself.

Finally, she knew she could wait no longer. She was soaked to the skin and so frozen she had even stopped shivering. She peered out tentatively from the porch into the thick blackness. The howling gale tore at her and she shuddered at the idea of returning along the cliffs, in case she wandered, or was blown, over the edge. Bracing herself against the wind she trudged down the hill towards Ilfracombe, each step a struggle against the mud voraciously sucking at her feet and ankles. The track became a stream, rather than a path, and she splashed and stumbled over the stones, her legs and feet numb.

Hazy outlines of tumbledown cottages appeared through the sheets of rain and a tethered goat bleated pitifully. Cobbles mercifully replaced the hillside path and the clattering of her shoes was a musical sound which gave her the strength to carry on. The alleyway twisted and turned towards the harbour, then veered sharply up the hill, and she recognised the route the coach had taken so many months before. Fore Street, however, was deserted this time and she stood for a moment alone, swaying exhaustedly on her feet.

A brisk drumming of hooves blended with the beat of rain.

"Lady Sophie?" a foreign voice penetrated her dazed state. She tried to decipher the words, but was incapable of logical thought and gratefully allowed herself to be lifted up and handed to the man's companion who had remained on his horse. Her face was pressed against a leather jerkin, her head swam with dizziness, exacerbated by the swaying movement of the animal as it galloped off.

No one had realised Sarah was missing until dinner. Her seat at the table remained empty. A feast of pork, venison, swan, duck and pigeon lay ready to be eaten in silver serving dishes and had occasioned so much cooking that a second dog had been needed to turn the cage to rotate the spit, as the first had dropped dead from overwork.

Jean Luc tapped his fingers on the table.

"Please see if she is in her room," he told Mrs Yelland curtly. "Perhaps she is indisposed?"

The housekeeper returned with the news that the servants thought she had taken a walk.

"Where has she gone?" he asked, a measure of annoyance in his voice. "It's not safe to be roaming the countryside by herself in the night and in such weather. I think I saw her disappear into the wood shortly before the storm. Tell my men to saddle up and search for her. Inform them that she has red hair and is probably wearing a blue cloak."

A footman hurried off. Heinrich said the prayer and they both ate in silence. The storm raged outside. The mantelpiece clock ticked noisily and the Duchess sat sullenly drinking from a wine glass and refusing to eat. The fire smoke kept being blown into the room by the wind in the chimney and Jean Luc stared towards the invisible garden and shook his head, as though trying to physically erase a memory from his thoughts, when through the noise of the rain there came the sound of galloping horses.

In the hall a footman opened the door and Sarah was carried in to the house, barely conscious. Her sodden, mud-splattered clothes were torn, her hair was bedraggled and her face and hands were smeared with blood.

"Take her up to her bedchamber. Ride to Ilfracombe and ask the doctor to come immediately," Jean Luc ordered grimly.

Jenny ran out from the servants' quarters and followed the footman carrying Sarah up the stairs. Other servants also ran upstairs to help and when he reached her room, they were already taking off her cloak and shoes as she lay on the bed.

"Oh, my lady. Where 'ave ee been?" Jenny was saying. "Us 'ave been so worried."

Sarah opened her eyes. "I was caught by the storm," she murmured weakly.

After that, she was only dimly aware of what was happening. A dreamless sleep claimed her and she awoke to see a grey-haired old man standing next to the bed. She felt a sharp pain in her arm, then a feeling of warmth and the horrifying sight of blood, raspberry-bright against the whiteness of a china bowl. Sickness overwhelmed her, the room spun and she fainted.

....

Doctor Venner stood warming himself in front of the library fire.

"How is she?" asked Jean Luc.

"She'll survive. She's exhausted and has some cuts and bruises. I've bled her and given her a draught and I'll return in the morning to see how she is," he replied.

Jean Luc made a face, "I would have thought she had lost enough blood!"

The doctor bridled. "I suppose, sir, you are one of these modern men who think it's all quackery! Well, I can assure you that, in this case, without it, she would not have lived to morning. Perhaps, sir, you also entertain doubts about the efficacy of my potion? If so, may I seek to reassure you."

He withdrew a blue glass bottle from his pocket, uncorked it and proudly waved it in the air, introducing the stench of the midden to the book-lined room.

"What's this?" Jean Luc spluttered. "I fear I'm in danger of losing the dinner I've just eaten."

"Oh, just a recipe of my own, a bit of bat and toad and sheep droppings," the doctor assured him.

"And you've given this to Lady Sophie!" he exclaimed in horror.

"It'll do the trick, your Grace, you'll see!" the doctor confidently asserted and set off to Ilfracombe soon after, leaving Jean Luc hurriedly drinking several glasses of port. He stared into the fire and knew that on the other side of the ocean, hills and valleys lay heavy with snow, quivering stalactites of ice were festooning branches and lumbering bears were scouting for food, marking their trail with paw prints. His soul ached to be back there. He clenched his glass so hard the stem broke and fell to the floor with a tinkling, brittle sound.

His reverie also shattered. He turned his back on the burning logs and went upstairs to Sarah's bedchamber.

He did not knock, but just pushed open the door and came face to face with Jenny, who was brandishing a piece of wood in the air.

Startled, she hid the blackthorn wand in the folds of her skirt as he stared first at her, then at Sarah, who was lying pale and still on the bed, her eyes shut and her arm bandaged.

"Give that to me," he ordered, and with a defiant expression Jenny gave it to him, muttering, "It be only a stick."

"I'm having no accursed practices here!" he declared. "If Mr Scheyer caught you, he would whip you to an inch of your life!"

Jenny scowled at him and flounced out of the room, whereupon he walked silently to the bed and stood looking down at Sarah.

"Well, my lady, at least you still seem to be alive after the ministrations of the medical profession and local witchcraft!" he said. He stretched out his hand towards her red hair which was tumbling over the pillow, and hesitantly touched it, then he turned on his heels and quickly walked away.

Next morning, Sarah woke late. The sun was high in the sky and the bedchamber was honey-gold with warmth. The day seemed different; she ached from head to toe and could hardly move. She vaguely remembered the storm and the scramble down the hillside and her spirits sank as she struggled to recall what had happened. She had a memory of a stranger bringing her home on his horse, but what had occurred next was a blank.

'A grey-haired, old man,' she thought. 'And blood.' Her fingers strayed to the bandage on her arm and she knew that part had been true.

Jenny plumped the pillow behind her back and she sat in bed, disorientated to be there at such an unusual hour.

A knock at the door interrupted the morning quiet and she was very unhappy to see Jean Luc de Delacroix. He stood on the threshold, carrying two dishes; his hair was tied back and although he was finely dressed in a blue coat with gold trimmings, cream breeches and an ornately frilled cravat, she had the impression that his strong, powerful frame would be more suited to less elaborate clothing and that he would be happier in the countryside than in the house. His height and size did not help to reduce her fear of him and she wilted back against the covers.

"Madam. I hope I am not intruding. Are you feeling better?" he asked.

"Yes, thank you, your Grace," she mumbled, flushing scarlet to be in bed when there was a man present.

He seemed oblivious to any form of impropriety and strode towards her and rather awkwardly placed the dishes on the bedside cabinet. She shrank away from him, expecting at any minute to either be denounced as an imposter or to be sent back to her supposed family in London for having been the cause of so much trouble and not a suitable companion for his mother.

"I'm very sorry I was a nuisance," she murmured, clutching the bed covers to her.

He did not directly reply, but instead indicated a green jelly on one of the dishes. "I've brought you something to put on your cuts. I've made it myself."

In a flurry of embarrassment and realising he wanted her to sample it, she stuck her finger into the slimy substance and licked it.

"No, no!" he exclaimed, looking down at her. "It's to use on the grazes, not to eat!"

"Oh," she muttered, feeling both foolish and relieved, as its texture had reminded her strongly of one of her least favourite Devon dishes, the boiled seaweed called laver bread, only with the peculiar addition of cinnamon.

"You can eat this though!" he said, touching the other dish. She wondered what sort of Devil's concoction he was now offering her and as he had not thought to bring a spoon, was forced to stick her finger again into a golden, viscous liquid. This time, however, the sweet taste was delightful.

"It's from the tree of the maple. I've brought it back from the New World," he remarked.

"It's delicious," she said and saw him smile. It was clearly important to him that she liked it and she began to feel less nervous, realising that he was actually treating her as Lady Sophie Throgmorton.

He started to pace around the room and stopped in front of the arrangement of stones and shells on the dresser.

"What's this?" he asked. "Have you collected them? What an interesting range of local stone," and then he picked up her drawings, carefully scrutinising each one.

"They're beautiful! What detail you've achieved. What made you draw them?"

"I like flowers and plants. Until I came here I had never really noticed any." Her voice drifted away, she did not want to say anything about her previous life.

"And what happened yesterday, madam? Where did you go to?"

She noticed again the inflection of a foreign accent in his speech. His words and voice seemed to lull her; she could not explain the quiet contentment which suddenly possessed her and wondered if he had bewitched her with his potions. For a few seconds she was lost in a trance, before coming to her senses and replying to his question.

"I went for a walk along the cliffs and the storm caught me. I waited in the ruined church, until it became dark, and I walked down to Ilfracombe. It was black and....," her voice failed and she shuddered.

His eyes did not leave her face and she tried to reassure herself again that he had never met Sophie before.

He looked at her without speaking, for a moment, before saying, "In future, I would prefer you not to go for walks alone. It's not safe and it isn't seemly."

"Yes, your Grace," she acquiesced.

"Well, good day, madam. I will leave you to rest." He inclined his head towards her, then departed.

The rest of the day passed off very peacefully. She smeared the green jelly over her grazed hands, ate all the maple syrup and spent most of the time asleep, only awaking as dusk was robbing the garden of colour.

She was extremely pleased to find that no one visited her, except Dr. Venner at midday; and the nearest she came to encountering Jean Luc de Delacroix was when she tucked into a jugged hare for supper and discovered that he had been hunting and had said to Jenny to tell her that it had been caught by him.

9

The cock was crowing across the valley as she placed some clothes and Sophie's money in a leather bag. She carefully hid it behind the gowns hanging in her dressing room, then sat on the window seat, waiting for the sun to rise above the trees. If events took a turn for the worse she was determined to attempt to flee and if she was unable to do so, she had decided to throw herself from the cliffs into the sea.

"I will not be hung," she murmured. "I will be mistress of my own destiny."

The early morning was chill. Her legs and arms still ached and she was pleased when the dawn chorus began to be masked by sounds of people stirring within the household. A maid came to rake the ashes and make up a new fire in the grate and Jenny arrived to help her dress.

"Everyone says they'll be gone soon. Back to France. 'Is Grace and all they vurriners." She looked enquiringly at Sarah as she spoke, as though to obtain confirmation that what she was saying was correct.

"Is that so?" she commented, finding herself in the position of knowing far less than the servants and delighted by the news of an imminent departure. She could see that Jenny was cast down at the thought that the newcomers would shortly be leaving and had obviously taken great trouble with her appearance that morning. Her hair was laced with blue ribbons; she was dressed in Sophie's pink-striped gown that Sarah had given to her and she looked every inch the sort of aristocratic young lady Sarah was herself endeavouring to imitate. She felt envy at Jenny's uncomplicated life, which should have been her own, and wished she could be standing there now in her rightful place as Lady Sophie Throgmorton's maid, able to flirt and enjoy the company of a group of young men, without worrying that if she made an error, she risked death.

Rather sadly, she stiffly descended the stairs and made her way to the dining room, through whose open door she could already see a purple-coated figure, the sight of his dark hair still surprising her. He was eating from a heaped plate of ham and at the same time reading from a newspaper propped in front of him.

He looked up as she entered and politely stood and greeted her with a warmth she had not been expecting and with a similar expression to that when he was looking at his animals. She was amused to think that perhaps she had been elevated to the station of a raccoon and a snake and found herself almost smiling at him as she sat down and took a slice of buttered toast.

"Is that all you're eating?" he asked. "The wind could blow you away!"

She was stung by the implied criticism that she was too thin and it occurred to her again that his manners lacked the politeness she would normally have expected from a nobleman.

" I can see you're much recovered," he said. "Your face is...." He looked at her and repeated the words, "much recovered," as though he could not find anything more complimentary to say about her.

She presumed he was making a criticism of her lack of white powder and rouge and the fact that her hair was not in the top-heavy, bouffant style, generally affected by ladies in polite society, but was its own colour and reached her waist, and she was disconcerted to see that he continued to look at her.

"Are you still intending to call on the Vinnicombes today?" he enquired.

"Yes, I think so," she replied, having already decided that there was probably a greater risk in not going, as her behaviour would appear odd, and that it was extremely unlikely the Vinnicombes would ever have met the Throgmortons, who only moved in the higher echelons of London society.

"Perhaps we can ride there together?" he suggested. "I have affairs to see to in Ilfracombe today."

She did not know what to say and stayed silent.

"Does that not suit you madam?" he asked, a hint of amusement in his voice.

" I don't ride," she confessed, wondering if he might find it strange, although she could not remember Sophie ever riding a horse.

"You don't ride?" he queried, in an unbelieving tone.

"No," she replied.

"Well, we will take the carriage then. It can manage the rough ground here as it's extremely well sprung," he said firmly. "It's not as solid though as the Berlin I use for going to Rome. It's travelled over the Alps many times and the axle's not once broken."

She nibbled her toast. He was looking at her again and she tried to remain calm, glad she knew nothing of foreign places and so was unable to blunder into making an unsuitable reply.

"Did you have drawing lessons in London? he asked.

She gazed blankly at him.

"No," she replied, after a pause.

"What made you decide to draw?" he persisted.

"I saw pictures of plants in the library," she said, "and I wanted to do the same."

"You like reading?" he questioned.

She was feeling increasingly cornered, pulled down into a quagmire of her own making and felt annoyed with herself for mentioning the pictures. Her illiteracy was a source of immense shame to her, whereas Sophie had been able to read and write, as had most of the servants.

"Um, no," she said softly.

For a few minutes they sat in silence. She quickly finished her toast and tried to think of an excuse to leave the table. She pushed back her chair and caught a displeased expression on his face. She looked uncertainly at him and he said quickly, as though to keep her there, "You liked the snake, I believe. Perhaps you would also like these." He dug his hand into his pocket and brought out some oval stones.

"We call them wampum beads, but their real name is esnoguy. They're made from clam shells cultivated in the dead bodies of the Huron's enemies, placed in the river," he said and placed the beads on the table cloth

She wondered if she had heard him correctly and tried not to look startled.

"You are giving them to me?" she said slowly.

"Yes," he replied. " I would like you to have them."

She picked them up. "They're lovely," she exclaimed, touching their pearly sheen and ignoring their gruesome history. "Thank you."

The reserve between them seemed to fall away. She murmured again, "Thank you," hurriedly curtsied and left the room, clasping tightly the first present she had ever received.

"I'm too blunt and rough for her," Jean Luc muttered to himself. "I must behave with more finesse, then perhaps she will not be so cold towards me."

....

The carriage followed the stream along the lane towards Ilfracombe. Branches banged and scratched against the windows. The close proximity of the man seated opposite, his knees occasionally touching her dress every time the wheels lurched, combined with the memory of Sophie dying on the seat where she was now sitting, to make the sides of the coach seem to be claustrophobically pressing in on her.

She gazed out at the virginal leaves and daffodil banks, refusing to allow Sophie to appear amongst them.

"Have you known the Vinnicombes long?" he enquired.

"No, I don't know them at all," she replied.

"I thought I heard Mrs Vinnicombe say you knew her son?" he contradicted her.

"Oh yes, I met Captain Vinnicombe recently," she agreed.

"Where did you meet him?" he asked, disappointing her again by his obvious interest in her activities.

"In the wood," she replied.

"The wood? The wood on my estate?" he said in a surprised tone.

"Yes," she said, realising it was not the sort of social setting he had been expecting.

"What was he doing there?" he questioned sourly, his eyes black in the shade of the coach as he glanced first at her face and then at her hair.

"He was looking for smugglers with the Customs and Excise men," she replied.

He frowned. "The taxes on French wine and brandy are exorbitant and I've no objection to a bit of smuggling. My cellar's got more than a few bottles of excellent wine good King George has not managed to make me pay a penny on. I'll have to have a word with Captain Vinnicombe. I don't like people trespassing." He looked thoughtful for a moment, before remarking, "A crate of French brandy was very strangely left outside the house this morning."

Then he suddenly asked, "Did you, by any chance, see him the night of the storm?" and in a low voice she could hardly hear, muttered, "I expect you have half the county seeking you out."

She stared at him in amazement, anger flooding through her at the suggestion she had secretly kept an assignation with a man. Forgetting her intention not to draw attention to herself, she glared at him.

"How dare you! No, I certainly was not, sir!" she shrieked; not haughtily as Lady Sophie Throgmorton might have done, but more resembling the howls of her fellow kitchen servants when they lost their temper.

He was speechless. His mouth opened and shut as though he was a frog catching a fly.

She could feel the colour drain from her face. She was illegitimate – it was the only knowledge she had about her origins. She shuddered at the memory of the remorseless taunts and beatings she had received for the stigma caused by her birth. She knew that her own sense of self-worth had been almost nonexistent until her transformation into Lady Sophie Throgmorton, and his implied accusation that she had behaved with a lack of morals was not one she could deal with in a sensible manner. Her past suffering rose up in front of her eyes and she desperately sought to push it far away from her, into the darkest recesses of her mind.

'Whatever else I may be,' she thought with fury, ' I am not a slut!'

She tried to calm herself, knowing it was madness on her part to annoy a man who held such power over her and who was, moreover, a Duke, who had probably never been addressed rudely in his life. She bitterly regretted her outburst, but found herself almost choking with distress. A buzzard was circling high above the trees and she followed its graceful ellipses, visualising herself up there in the sky and attempting to distance herself emotionally from the shock of being unexpectedly reminded of her previous shame.

"I'm sorry. I didn't mean to say….." his voice trailed off guiltily.

"You just did!" she cried, her face white, her hands held taut together, and still unable to restrain herself.

They sat together in an uncomfortable silence, broken only by the grating noise of the iron-rimmed wheels striking stones. She continued to gaze out of the window, hardly seeing the primrose meadows and bluebell woods, and he sat without speaking, his face impassive.

The coach pulled up in front of a gabled house with latticed windows. He did not wait for the footman, but opened the door and jumped out, then stood, his face still expressionless. He held out his hand to her and she was forced to step down, her hand in his. She could feel the warmth of his skin and his firm grip and involuntarily snatched her hand away as soon as her feet touched the ground.

Four pillars enclosed an entrance porch almost entirely filled by Mrs Vinnicombe in a voluminous, purple and white striped gown, her hair teased high into stiff, powdered curls.

"I'm sure she's nowhere near as frightening as her clothes," she was astounded to hear murmured in her ear. He approached Mrs Vinnicombe, bowed and said, "I'm afraid you must forgive me, but I have business in Ilfracombe and will return later." He bowed again quickly in Sarah's direction, then he climbed back into the carriage, which sped off bumpily through an avenue of sycamores.

Her anger vanished with him and, with a sinking heart, she teetered on her high heels towards the formidable figure of her hostess.

The long drawing room was unexpectedly light and modern, its walls a delicate shade of blue, two glass chandeliers sparkling in the sunlight. A crowd of people thronged it, ladies sitting on slender, gilt chairs and men congregating in small huddles. There was a lull in the conversation as she entered and Jane and Elizabeth Vinnicombe came forward to greet her, their huge bosoms juddering like blancmanges, only very marginally contained by similar, green-frilled gowns; and she was escorted on a hectic round of introductions.

Faces seemed to pop up and down in front of her, white Jack-in-the-boxes, slashed with rouge and speckled with beauty spots. Lavender and rose perfume lay heavy on the air, overlaid by a smell of the farmyard, which emanated from a man with very red cheeks and mud-caked boots, whose idea of polite behaviour consisted of slapping the larger ladies on their bottoms as he passed by, an action which was greeted with screams of appreciation by his victims.

"Us be very glad to see ee, yer ladyship," he told her, as she firmly kept her back to the wall.

She had hoped that her imaginary social engagements with the Duchess would stand her in good stead, and that polite conversation with make-believe people would be the same as that with those of flesh and blood. Instead, it was the rough and tumble of kitchen life which more resembled the boisterous gathering surging around her.

Mrs Vinnicombe marched in a stately manner from guest to guest, her lips even twitching in a smile, as a succession of bawdy jokes was shouted out by two men across the room. Sarah found herself the only person not laughing, having absolutely no idea of the activities concerning sheep and pigs, which were being referred to, and was pleased when the conversation turned to the subject of a family of cannibals living at Clovelly, who had evidently just been caught and were being tried at Exeter Assises. She was able to shiver in horror along with everyone else, at the lurid account of their misdeeds, and began to feel that she was accepted without suspicion by the assembled company.

The soft Devon burr she heard all around her, with even richly dressed guests saying 'us' instead of 'we', increased her confidence and London and the Throgmortons seemed very far away.

"You're staying at Wildercombe House with the Duchess of Delacroix?" a heavily powdered and bewigged woman said. "Is she still in the land of the fairies?" and she pulled back her lips in a horsey grin, to reveal decaying brown teeth, which contrasted bizarrely with her decorated face and hair.

"No, she's quite well," Sarah lied, from a sense of loyalty to her benefactress. She was introduced to a Lord Bere Alston and immediately stiffened on hearing his title. Yet, once again, she felt that luck was smiling on her that day as she saw that he was an elderly man, who was effeminately fluttering a handkerchief, and who was clearly more preoccupied with a cherub-faced footman, than with herself.

A young African boy stood next to him, the blackness of his skin made even more striking by glittering jewels sewn onto his clothes and onto the turban covering his head. He was glowering at a coterie of ladies, who were fussing over him and giving him sweetmeats, and when he saw Sarah, he burst into laughter and jabbed a finger at her hair.

James Vinnicombe cut a striking figure in his uniform, his jacket a deep red, its brass buttons gleaming. He did not assault her with questions, like Jean Luc de Delacroix. Instead, he talked about himself and she was only too happy to listen. His grey eyes were friendly, his manners impeccably polite. He spoke at length about his recent military campaigns with the Devon and Dorsets in Germany and the room was hushed as he described the battle of Wilhelmstahl and the English superiority over the French.

"Women accompany the armies," he told her. "They help the quartermaster bring up the rations and are extremely useful."

"Is the Duke in France?" the woman with bad teeth suddenly asked her, an unpleasant expression in her eyes.

Mrs Vinnicombe hastily replied, "His Grace is in residence at Wildercombe House and will be arriving later," and she had the feeling she was forewarning the other guests. A middle-aged gentleman made a strange, harrumphing noise and various people were whispering to each other behind their hands. She heard the words, " the New World" and "France," mentioned and James Vinnicombe's face turned almost puce as he looked like he was trying to avoid saying something.

The afternoon quickly passed. No one came forward to denounce her as an impostor and she listened with enjoyment as Jane and Elizabeth sang with rich, vibrant voices, taking it in turns to accompany each other on the spinet.

"Would you care to sing for us, your ladyship?" asked Mrs Vinnicombe.

"No, no. I can't," she protested, but the warmth of the welcome she had been given that day made her wish to contribute to the entertainment and so she allowed James Vinnicombe to take her hand and lead her to the spinet. She felt unexpectedly delighted by her first foray into North Devon society and happily sat down, her cream dress spread out around her, her hair shining in the last rays of the wintry sun.

She sang with emotion. The songs she had watched Sophie struggle to master flowed liltingly from her heart. She lost herself completely in the music. The sea of faces in front of her, the drabness of men's wigs punctuated by the bright colours of feathers, ribbons and jewels on ladies' heads, seemed blurred and distant.

The last song finished, she became aware of a discordant note – the unsettling appearance of Jean Luc de Delacroix. He was standing near the door, looking different from the rest of the guests. His complexion was darker than that of anyone else, except the African boy. His clothes were richer and more strikingly decorated. His purple coat was lavishly trimmed with gold; he was the only man present to be wearing a sword and was bare-headed. He was openly staring at her and even when she had left the spinet she turned and saw that his eyes were still on her.

He made his way in her direction and she realised that a quiet had fallen on the room. Several people bowed or curtsied, but others turned away and there was a distinct coldness, and even hostility, in their behaviour.

She was pleased to find Captain Vinnicombe at her side.

"May I say how much I enjoyed your singing," he complimented her and smiled, a sensuous, warm smile, his eyes holding her eyes, making her knees feel weak. She smiled back, unaccustomed to the flattery of such an attractive man. The next minute, the novel sweetness of the moment was lost as Jean Luc de Delacroix joined them. He barely acknowledged James Vinnicombe. His manner was unfriendly, and her only consolation was that it appeared to be the captain who was the object of his attention, not herself.

She instinctively shrank away from him and stepped on one of her admirer's black-booted feet, making her lose her balance.

"I'm sorry," she apologised.

"The pleasure is all mine," he gallantly replied and held her arm to steady her.

"I believe, sir, you met Lady Sophie in the wood on my estate?" Jean Luc de Delacroix remarked sourly.

"Yes, she was out in the dark and I escorted her home," James Vinnicombe said, his tone almost equally icy. " It's not safe for a young lady to walk alone at night, even on your estate."

She noticed how the pattern of the polished wood floor, went first in one direction, then in another. Her stomach seemed to have become an empty pit and the afternoon was suddenly ruined. Smuggling alone had seemed to be a sore point with him, but she was now herself exposed as roaming the countryside on two nights, extremely strange behaviour for an aristocratic lady and perhaps giving the lie to her earlier protestations.

"Lady Sophie was walking in the wood at night?" he questioned.

"Well, we also met during the day, when we were searching for the smuggler we had shot," said James Vinnicombe.

Jean Luc de Delacroix's face was now looking thunderous, although whether it was in connection with people trying to catch smugglers on his land, or the smugglers themselves, or whether it was for some other reason, she was not able to judge. However, she was desperate to know that John Buzzacott had escaped and found herself asking if the smuggler had been caught.

"No, the demm villain gave us the slip," exclaimed James Vinnicombe crossly.

"Well, perhaps next time," she remarked consolingly.

....

The coach retraced its winding route by the River Wilder, its slow-flowing water eddying in deep pools by the bank, before tumbling down through weed-choked weirs towards the sea. She sat demurely, her mind feverishly occupied.

"Well, madam, perhaps we may continue our earlier conversation. Perhaps you would like to inform me now what you were doing out alone at night twice in the last few days? You seem to be afraid of the dark, so were you with someone?" he asked very quietly.

She said nothing. She glanced at him and with difficulty managed to hold his gaze, looking as innocent as she could.

"You're living in my house. You are my responsibility. I want to know what you were doing," he continued.

"I was just walking quite late in the evening and was caught out by the night. There's not a mystery," she said calmly, inwardly seething at the unfortunate turn of events. She did not regret helping John Buzzacott, but she knew that Sophie would not have done so. Nor would Sophie have wandered off alone over the cliffs into a storm.

" I don't believe you," he said flatly.

She flushed and was unable to think of a suitable reply and they sat in silence, as they had on the initial journey, until the coach finally stopped outside Wildercombe House.

"I would like to know what you were doing," he said forcefully. "We will remain here until you tell me, even if we have to stay all night."

A footman opened the door and unfolded the steps.

"Please wait," he was told.

She could see other footmen standing at the front door, waiting for them to descend. Her mind raced as she tried to think what Lady Sophie Throgmorton would have done. Should she throw a hysterical fit as ladies were reputed to do, although in her experience as a kitchen maid, it was not something she had ever encountered? Should she be angry with him, as she had been earlier?' Somehow she thought not. Knowing how much he liked animals made wild ideas, such as searching for bats and owls in the night, occur to her and she smiled.

"Oh, I can see it amuses you, madam!" he shouted, raising his voice for the first time.

She glanced apprehensively at him, thinking that he was very quick to anger. He was seated so close to her that she could see a thin scar above his eyebrow. She felt intimidated again by his size and remained very puzzled as to how she could extricate herself. She wondered how long he would be prepared to sit obstinately in the coach and looked with embarrassment at the servants patiently standing in the frosty air.

"I was caught in the storm, as I told you," she said finally, in exasperation. "I waited in the church and did not meet anyone."

"And the other night?" he enquired.

She took a deep breath and struggled to find the right words, to say as little as possible, while still telling the truth.

"I helped someone," she said at last.

"You helped someone? In the dark?" he queried, as though he did not believe her.

"I helped someone who was injured," she continued.

"What do you mean? Who was it?" he demanded.

"It was the smuggler who was shot," she murmured softly.

"The smuggler?" he repeated in amazement.

"I found the man they were searching for. His leg was bleeding and he was unable to walk by himself, so when night fell I went and helped him down the hill. And then, after I left him, I met Captain Vinnicombe and another man." She spoke nervously, realising John Buzzacott's life would be in danger if she revealed too much. She looked at him and thought she had never seen a man so taken aback. Words seemed to fail him; he just sat, staring at her and then shouted so loudly that all the servants could hear.

"You say you went back and helped him! You actually thought about it and then deliberately went and put yourself in danger helping someone engaged in a criminal act! He might have killed you, or the Customs and Excise men might have shot at you as well! What on earth were you thinking of?" He stopped shouting and said, more softly, "So when you said that "Perhaps he would catch the smuggler next time," that's not what you meant. You were mocking Captain Vinnicombe!" He grimaced, almost as though he was laughing.

"I think perhaps that the crate of brandy left on the doorstep this morning is yours," he continued. " However, you have put yourself at risk and, in fact, it all seems very strange!" He shook his head, as though he did not really believe her.

"After you, my lady minx!" he remarked, half-smiling, and indicated the door.

They walked together, without speaking, into the house, the mildew-redolent greyness of the hall seeming a welcome refuge to her.

She climbed the stairs and just as she reached the top step, she happened to look down and saw him still standing by the front door, watching her. His face was enigmatic and, with a strong sense of disquiet, she turned away and went into her bedchamber.

10

The next morning she lay in bed, enjoying the sight of the uppermost branches of the horse chestnut tree spread-eagled against a white-cloud sky. A decanter of brandy, specially sent to her from the dining room, still sat on the table, reminding her she had declined to attend the evening meal.

A tangled weave of emotions marked her recall of the previous day. Sadness, anger, pleasure and anxiety all intermingled and like a jackdaw carefully hoarding his treasure, she pored over every detail of what had happened.

"At least I did not let slip John Buzzacott's name!" she whispered to herself. Her face flushed as she thought of James Vinnicombe and his attention to her and she smiled, remembering her social success.

"They really thought I was Lady Sophie Throgmorton, in my fine clothes! I don't think a kitchen maid would have been quite so popular."

Then her mood blackened and the familiar mantra surfaced in her thoughts. 'What am I going to do? I can't stay here much longer. It's even more dangerous if I am courted as a marriageable young lady. I can obviously never marry anyone as there would be a wedding attended by the Throgmortons.'

She found it difficult to think of Jean Luc de Delacroix at all. His shadow loomed over her; the look on his face as he had stood in the hall had haunted her dreams and she tried to push her worries about him to the furthest recesses of her mind.

She dressed, and descended the stairs to breakfast, her natural optimism somewhat returned. There was no sign of him, but the door of his work room was flung open, revealing a complicated maze of glass tubes and metal containers on a long trestle by the window. She thought she could very strangely distinguish the autumn fragrance of blackberry and peered in to see if the snake was kept there. The room appeared empty, her inquisitiveness overcame her and she tiptoed towards a green liquid bubbling in a bowl held over glowing embers in a stone dish. Books and papers were scattered on the table and she noticed that many of the pages were covered in diagrams, not words.

'It's a magician's cave,' she thought. 'Is he making spells? He's French and a Catholic and people say they do terrible things.' She suddenly caught sight of the snake in a hutch at the far end of the room and quickly ran to it.

She stared, in wonderment, at a creature she had never seen in the Devon countryside. It was longer than she had realised. Its colour was a dull brown, enlivened with three orange stripes and it looked back at her with an unblinking gaze. She gingerly put her hand through the bars and felt the cool leatheriness of its skin.

"I feared it was dead, but it was still asleep for the winter. The thunder storm woke it up, just as people say." his voice carried clearly across the room.

She jumped and withdrew her hand, and turned to see him, dressed again in a long smock over his breeches, his hair escaping from its ribbon. He had evidently been standing behind the door, taking a book from the shelf, and had been watching her.

"You seem to be the only person in this household who is not afraid of it," he remarked. "Would you like to touch him again?" He walked towards her, unlatched the cage and picked up the snake.

She gently stroked it and they stood together, both completely absorbed by the reptile. Then he replaced it in its hutch, much to her disappointment.

"Perhaps you would care to help me for a few minutes?" he said, as he adjusted a glass pipe on the table.

"What are you making?" she asked curiously.

"I'm trying to discover what the air is made of," he replied solemnly.

She pinched herself to stop from laughing. It occurred to her that he was perhaps as mad as his mother, although in a different way.

"But you can see it's not made of anything!" she felt obliged to point out to him.

"Well that's where you're wrong," he said. "I believe it's composed of several things. Think about the wind. You can feel it's there, can't you?"

She regarded him dubiously, gracefully picked up her skirt and was on the point of departing when he said,

"Can you help me and read out this list, while I make up the mixture?" and he opened a large book. She stood in confusion, not knowing what to do, and glanced at the page. She felt her face, her whole body, go red with embarrassment, as he looked at her expectantly.

"I can't read," she whispered.

"You can't read," he repeated. "But you draw and sing so well. You must be able to read."

Her eyes filled with tears of shame and he quickly closed the book.

"I'll arrange for someone to come and teach you. Instead of sitting with my mother, you can spend the time learning to read. I don't agree with ladies being uneducated. In France, they discuss philosophy, as well as any man."

She had no idea what he was talking about, but very much liked his proposal.

"Thank you," she murmured.

"I've been asked if I would address a meeting in Barnstaple, this afternoon. Would you like to accompany me? I believe someone is going to speak about the local rocks, so you might find that interesting."

She tried to think of a good reason why she would in no way wish to do so, but her mind remained stubbornly blank.

"Thank you," she repeated unhappily and then, as the green liquid began to crackle and spit alarmingly, emitting clouds of smoke, she hurriedly left the room before any more suggestions were made, and before, as she put it to herself, 'I'm turned into a frog or some other sort of creature!'

They set off in the early afternoon. "Allez-y!" he shouted to two of his men, both strikingly blond and tall, who were waiting on horseback, guns and knives in their belts, next to the coach. She sat nervously, hoping she was not putting herself in danger by travelling, yet again, to an unknown place to meet strangers. He sat opposite her, but she did not feel as threatened by him as the previous day, as he was busy reading pages of writing and hardly looked at her.

A fine mist softened the landscape; the horses laboured as they pulled the coach along sunken tracks entombed in the gloom cast by the tall hedges; the wheels slipping and sliding in watery mud. The sun weakly shone at times, chasing away the lowering clouds and brightening a flat and open land, bounded by a broad stretch of blue water, dotted by sailing ships.

"That's the Taw," he said, indicating a river flowing into the estuary. The prosperous town of Barnstaple came into view, its houses built in pale stone, an ancient, many-arched bridge spanning a wide river. The coach stopped in front of a red brick building, next to a market where bleating sheep were being marshalled into wicker pens.

He opened the door, jumped down and held out his hand, as he had done at the Vinnicombe's. She placed her hand in his and could feel again the strength of his grip. She was suddenly very aware of him, then the

70

moment vanished and they were entering a room crowded with people, where rows of chairs had been arranged. Books lined three walls and the fourth enjoyed the provision of long sash windows, which framed a view of the fast-flowing Taw.

Everyone was talking animatedly and her attention was caught by an enormously fat woman, dressed in bilious yellow and holding forth in stentorian tones to Lord Bere Alston, who was accompanied again by the black child in his jewelled turban. Her voice carried like a bell across the room, clearly audible above the general hubbub.

"And Lady Throgmorton told me herself at the Xmas Ball, that the poor girl was so ugly, with her hair the colour of a carrot, that the only thing possible for her marriage prospects, was to bury her in the countryside, where she might find some sort of a turnip farmer!"

Sarah stopped dead, terror striking her. Panic welled up, she found it difficult to breathe and trembled violently.

'Has this woman ever seen Sophie? It does not sound like it,' she thought, frantically trying to calm herself.

Jean Luc also stopped short, his face thunderous.

The woman looked towards them, Lord Bere Alston muttered something to her and the woman blinked in obvious surprise as she stared at Sarah. She found herself shepherded quickly to a seat in the front row, and still shaking, she was only vaguely conscious of a whole procession of people who came to greet them.

'Will there be anyone else who knows the Throgmortons?' she worried incessantly; and as each new person spoke to them, the nightmare was enacted over and over again. Out of the corner of her eye she was suddenly aware of a movement of a large mass of yellow towards her; her heart stood still, the next minute she was granted a reprieve as the meeting commenced.

A Mr Charles Shebbear was introduced and talked at great length about the fair county of Devon. At some point, she was sure, he spoke about rocks, but quite when, she was not able to say. Only a few disjointed words made sense to her ears and he might have been speaking about the moon for all she knew or cared. In the middle of his speech, Jean Luc de Delacroix leaned towards her and said in a low voice, "I have a surprise for you later, which I think you'll enjoy."

She thought she was going to faint. The blood pounded in her head. She could not possibly conceive of any surprise which might please her and the chance it could put her life in jeopardy, was, she felt in the circumstances, extremely high. She regretted having been lulled into a false sense of security by her success at the Vinnicombes; it had been madness to expose herself to such a situation here, she decided, and just as she was wondering how to extricate herself politely from the meeting, the lecture on rocks finished and he stood up to deliver his speech.

He was introduced plainly as Jean Luc de Delacroix, a member of the Royal Society, whose studies were following in the path already trodden by Mark Catesby. She was aware of a ripple of anticipation going through the audience, which had become so numerous that people were having to stand at the back. She realised it was now too late to escape and sat in resignation, angry at her own recklessness.

His voice was strong and clear and, in spite of her agitation, she felt herself drawn almost hypnotically into the world he was describing; his years of travelling distilled into an eagle's eye view of a vast, river-scored land, lake-jewelled and mountain-ridged. A tree-quilted countryside; spruce, firs and pines, dark green against glittering ice and snow; woods of sweet gum, cedar, red oak, maple and walnut; red, white and black mangroves sinuously emerging from brackish, southern swamps; and everywhere embroidered with flowers, whose very names were colour-rich; black eyed Susans, purple fringed orchids and golden rod.

She saw flocks of passenger pigeons, so numerous they blackened the sky, blotting out the sun, making oak tree boughs break under their weight. She saw the wood bison in the Appalachian forests and felt the earth shudder beneath migrating herds of caribou. Exotically plumed birds flew around her and she marvelled at the Carolina parakeet and the pintera, a wood pecker with a beak like ivory. Rattlesnakes, copperheads, water moccasins, scorpions and tarantulas made her shiver, and the sing-song quality of native words like 'Cherokee,' 'Okeechobee' and 'Pahayokee,' all added to the beauty and strangeness of the picture in her mind.

He spoke quickly, almost without pausing for breath, often looking in her direction, and she noticed that his clothes appeared to have taken on a life of their own. His cravat was askew, his coat hung oddly, his hair had escaped from its tie and was hanging, dark and thick, onto his broad shoulders. She felt an over-riding urge to straighten his garments and present him, perfectly attired, to this gathering of sombrely dressed men, every one of whom was wearing the customary wig.

"And now may I show various specimens of plants to you from the New World, and one very special creature," he concluded his talk and watched as footmen carried in plants in tubs of earth and a small crate.

"Can I ask how many men died in your travels? Was it a very dangerous undertaking?" a man enquired.

"We did have to take many risks in the wilderness, it's true, but no one died as a result. Two men were killed in battle and another man died from the smallpox."

At the suggestion that he and his men had been engaged in fighting, she noticed that the room grew quiet. She could feel the hostility directed towards him that she had encountered at the Vinnicombe's and suddenly understood her naivety. He had been fighting on the wrong side, she realised. He was partly French and had been fighting against the English. She was horrified and her spirit was almost at one with the general sentiment in the room.

He, however, completely ignored any undercurrent in the gathering and walked over to her.

"Madam, I hope I have entertained you. May I now reveal my surprise."

He held out his arm and she was forced to accompany him to the wooden crate. He carefully opened the side and she looked in amazement at the largest spider she had ever seen. Its eyes were protruding, its segmented legs were long and hairy and it could only be described as indescribably ugly.

Speechless, she stared at the monster, which was about the size of a sparrow.

"Do you like it?" he asked, smiling like a father at his new-born child. "I thought you might."

"Yes," she murmured, unable to take her eyes off the fascinating creature. People crowded round, jostling and pushing. Gasps of astonishment could be heard, followed by a hushed silence.

She had a vision of Miss Vinnicombe and the snake, and in a moment of premonition knew exactly what was going to happen. The next second, several ladies, and one gentleman, screamed so piercingly that the windows rattled. Pandemonium ensued. Handkerchiefs were frantically flapped to give air to the hysterically affected ones and in all the commotion she saw the black boy sidle up to the crate, then poke its occupant with a jewelled pin he extracted from his turban.

"No!" she shrieked, but it was too late, as the spider was propelled out of his home and landed awkwardly on the floor. People dashed out of its way, opening a path for it, somewhat in the manner of Moses and the Red Sea.

Jean Luc lunged forwards, but it skittered sideways through peoples' legs, making a clattering noise as it ran over the wood floor.

She had never seen a room in such an uproar and she looked crossly at the black child, who had taken refuge behind his master. The obese lady had fallen to the ground and lay twitching, her canary-yellow stomach protruding like a mountain, high above the rest of her body.

She ran to the door as that had seemed to be the direction in which the spider had been heading. The air was cool and fresh on her face and she gulped it in gratefully. A quick scrabbling movement of black by the sheep pen attracted her attention and she thought she could see the spider. Then, to her amazement, one of the blond horsemen who had accompanied them and who was standing by the wicker fence, gave a strong kick with his booted foot and sent the object flying among the sheep.

She ran up to him. "What have you done!" she screamed, beside herself with anger. "How dare you!"

He looked insolently down at her and she realised that Jean Luc de Delacroix might well be the only person in his entourage who was happy to travel with snakes, spiders and raccoons. His iron-grey eyes looked familiar. His strong, large body blocked her view of the sheep pen and it suddenly came to her that she was looking at a younger version of Heinrich Scheyer. Her fear of him made her wary of challenging the man any further. She pushed past and with a complete disregard for her silk dress, plunged into the mud-caked, evil-smelling flock of sheep who scattered in panic and huddled against the far side of the pen.

In the earthen space now left bare, she could see the forlorn, trampled on body of the spider. It was clearly dead. Its legs were twisted oddly and it had lost an eye. She picked it up, cradling it in her hand and left the enclosure, glaring at the Alsatian soldier as she did so.

For the whole of the journey home she sat happily on the seat next to the body of the spider stretched out on an embroidered, linen handkerchief. The carriage was hot with the late afternoon sun and cirrus clouds trailed high across the blue sky.

"I enjoyed your talk very much," she told Jean Luc.

"Did you find Mr Shebbear's lecture interesting?" he asked.

"Yes, I did," she lied.

"There's several types of rock near Ilfracombe," he continued. "Have you noticed the grey shale in the cliffs?"

"Yes," she replied. "And in the caves by the headland there are lines of different colours of stone all jumbled together."

"You've not been exploring the caves?" he said reprovingly. "It's very treacherous in there. It's not a suitable place for you."

He sat looking at her for a few seconds, then said sharply, "Did you have servants with you ? The tide can come in very quickly and trap you. People have drowned there."

She remembered the sea often surprising her at the headland and knew he was speaking the truth.

"No, I was alone," she admitted.

He was now looking in annoyance at her and she felt disappointment that somehow she always managed to put herself on a wrong footing with him.

"You remind me of quicksilver, madam! You constantly astonish me."

She glanced at him and was suddenly not so sure he was cross, his tone seemed more one of concern, not anger, she thought. She would have liked to have drawn his attention to the fact that she had only explored a cave in Devon, whereas he had been engaged in far more dangerous acts in the New World, but sense prevailed and she resolved to reveal nothing more about her rather extensive rambles on his estate.

She sat quietly, thinking about the afternoon. She had, yet again, escaped a potentially threatening situation and the exciting vision of a wonderful country across the sea had awakened in her the hope that perhaps she too could visit it. She fingered the locket around her neck and dreamily mused about her future.

"Your hair is beautiful," he announced, breaking into her reverie. "Beautiful," he repeated the word. His voice was controlled and low, but there was a catch of emotion in it, which made her glance at him.

His side of the coach was plunged into shade and she could not easily see his face, whereas she sat exposed by the full glare of the sun. She blushed and nervously smoothed her dress, its silk sheen glinting in the brightness, its hem splattered with mud from the sheep pen. She did not know what to reply and absentmindedly stroked the dead spider. She knew he was referring to the remark of the woman in yellow and felt a disquiet as she recalled her fear, her annoyance at the unkind description of Sophie and the shock of unexpectedly encountering the malicious spirit of Lady Throgmorton, suddenly alive in a room in Barnstaple.

"Thank you," she acknowledged his compliment, taken aback by what he had said. She fingered her locket, very aware again of him, and blurted out nervously the first thing which came into her head,

"Do you not like wigs, sir?"

However, he did not appear at all affronted and answered in the straightforward manner she was beginning to associate with him.

"It impeded me when I was travelling. Why should I go around with part of a sheep on my head, when God has provided me with a perfectly decent head of hair. I threw all my wigs into the river and watched them float downstream."

She looked at him, not sure it had been the correct choice of action, but having to admit that he did, in fact, have a very attractive head of dark brown hair. She studied him in silence for a few minutes and then, emboldened, asked the question which had been constantly in her thoughts since his arrival.

"Will you be staying in Devon long, your Grace?"

His face darkened and she immediately regretted her words.

"I don't know. I'm committed to ….." he did not finish the sentence. It hung in the air, unsaid, and she presumed she had displeased him again. She bit her lip and looked down at the spider and did not see the uncertain, anguished look in his eyes. As she moved, the sun caught the gold of the locket round her neck, illuminating the design of the French royal fleur de lys. He stared at it, started to speak, then held his tongue. She saw him watching her and sank back into her seat, afraid that somehow, in spite of her best intentions, he found her very strange.

11

The early morning greyness of the next day was considerably enlivened by the arrival of Mr. Widdecombe, a curate from the Parish Church in Ilfracombe. She welcomed him as he stood in the library, anxiously fidgeting with the books he had brought with him in order to teach her to read and write.

They sat together at the desk in the window. His voice was low and he mumbled and swallowed his words so much, she had to strain to hear him. His face was the greasy white of candle tallow, beads of sweat kept breaking out on his forehead and her delight at the lesson was tempered by the thought that the nervous young man would make a bolt for freedom and her much longed-for education would be cut short. She was at a loss to explain his extreme anxiety and the more she smiled and tried to put him at ease, the more worried he seemed to become. She had seen Mrs Yelland coldly give him a substantial pile of coins, so she knew he was being paid very generously and wondered if otherwise he would not have come.

Outside on the lawns came the strident clash of metal against metal as Jean Luc de Delacroix and some of his men practised sword play. For her part, she was pleased to be able to see him safely engaging in an activity which had no bearing at all on her own situation. The curate, however, appeared in fear of his life as he glanced out of the window, and she began to be exasperated that he was paying so little attention to her.

She looked again towards the lawns and could appreciate that it was perhaps a more frightening spectacle to the curate than it was to her. The men were wearing black visors which partly covered their heads, giving each one a faceless appearance, and the swords were flashing and gleaming in the sun as they thrust and parried, moving in a crab-like fashion over the ground. Jean Luc de Delacroix was easily recognisable by his elaborately ruffled shirt and she noticed that he was the only one with dark hair; the others were overwhelmingly fair, although they were all tall and well-built. She knew that ordinary men were not allowed to use swords and it somehow did not surprise her that the law was being flouted. Between the noise of the blows, muffled shouts and exclamations could also be heard, sounding in a guttural way rather like English.

"Isch weis," she heard someone call and a strong desire welled up in her to learn other languages. She suddenly laughed out loud as she saw Jean Luc de Delacroix   chased backwards by his opponent and fall headlong into a bush. As he was extricating himself his more skilful adversary removed his visor and she recognised Heinrich Scheyer.

The curate gave a violent twitch as she laughed. He stood up and she was disappointed to see that the lesson had evidently come to an end. He mopped his brow one more time with a grubby piece of cloth, looked fearfully at the painting hanging on the far wall, of the Virgin Mary and her infant son, and almost ran to the front door, muttering "den of Popery," and escaping off down the drive, like a fox running from the hounds, his cassock flying out behind him.

A haunch of roast venison took pride of place on the dining table in the afternoon and she ate slowly and delicately from its sliced flesh. She was grateful that she had become accustomed over the months to sit at the long table and that she was very familiar with the ornate cutlery and crockery. She felt a confidence she had not enjoyed since before her acquaintance with the smugglers, and was even able to calmly observe the man seated opposite, who was dressed in a coat, waistcoat and shirt more frilled and flounced than any she had ever seen and whose hair was no longer tied back, but hung in dark curls over his shoulders and was adorned with a bow of blue satin. He looked exotically foreign and out of place in the English manor house with its solid, plain furniture and reminded her of the colourful birds he had spoken of in the New World.

'He's the stranger,' she thought, 'not me,' and smiled at the absurdity of such an idea.

The Duchess was also scrutinising her son, her painted mouth pursed in a moue of irritation.

"Princess Caroline was not allowed to visit me this morning," she complained. "I was walking by the fountains at Versailles but she was prevented from joining me!" Then she said with marked satisfaction, "I saw the enemy put to death. The Protestant was running away and the soldiers killed him with their swords!"

Sarah was taken aback at the venom in her voice and for one awful moment actually wondered if the curate had reached Ilfracombe alive, before remembering the world of fantasy lived in by the poor mad woman.

Jean Luc attacked the venison, ignoring his mother.

"What do you think of the wine?" he asked and she noticed the same pride in his eyes that she had observed when he was talking about his animals or plant specimens.

"It's very fine," she diplomatically answered. "I like it."

A look of pleasure crossed his face. "It's from my own vineyard in Alsace. We grow two sorts of grape and have been trying to sell the wine in France and the New World."

She had never heard of a nobleman in business before and glanced curiously at him. She remarked the wistfulness with which he spoke of Alsace and was reassured to realise that he wanted very much to return there.

"I hope you found the services of Mr Widdecombe suitable this morning," he continued. "I strongly believe that ladies should be educated."

He resumed eating, but kept looking across at her so often she flushed red with embarrassment and anxiety and could feel the fluttering sensation in her chest which often preceded her nervous attacks of panic. He seemed to be aware he was making her agitated and glanced around the room, as though searching for a topic of conversation. His eyes alighted gratefully on a white card propped up on the mantelpiece.

"Oh, yes," he said. "I forgot to say that Lord Bere Alston has sent an invitation to a ball at Berrynarbor Court. If you can read all the letters of the alphabet by the end of the week, you can attend it." His voice was light-hearted and teasing and he smiled broadly at her.

She looked guardedly at him, thinking he obviously had no conception of her hermit existence at Wildercombe House. She remembered Sophie's life in London. Every day had been a succession of tea parties, musical gatherings and balls. It was almost impossible for her to visualise herself at such events, wearing exquisite gowns and actually taking part, not just humming the tunes and dancing in the bareness of her attic. For a second, she was back in the squalid room, lit only by a skylight. Her head swam and she held onto the table for support.

'I have exchanged one sort of fear for another,' she thought bitterly. 'I am no longer beaten and exhausted, but I am living in a gilded cage, where I face the prospect of prison and hanging.' Her face was white, her eyes filled with tears.

"I didn't mean to distress you," he said quickly, looking very taken aback by her reaction. "I was only speaking in jest. Of course you can go to the ball. In my company, naturally," he added.

"I'm not upset," she protested.

He spoke quietly, as though afraid he might make the wrong remark.

"I would be delighted if I could enjoy the pleasure of your company again this afternoon. There's a new invention taking place at Hillsborough, in Ilfracombe."

"Thank you. I would like to come," she murmured, realising it would be safer not to go, but completely unable to resist the excitement of such a trip.

An hour later they sat together again in the coach, a bitterly cold wind buffeting it as the wheels trundled along the track towards Ilfracombe.

"May I ask what is this invention?" she enquired, wrapping her thick cloak more closely around her.

"Wait and see," he said mysteriously.

"Did you have a French acquaintance in London?" he suddenly asked.

She was baffled by the question and saw him glance at her locket.

"No," she replied, knowing that no one French had ever visited Sophie. It occurred to her that, strangely, the locket was the only connection she still possessed to her past and although she could not see any risk to herself in that, she felt a twinge of unease.

The coach followed the River Wilder, winding its way through beech and oak copses and bright primrose meadows. They reached a farm house and a few large houses on the edge of the town, then left behind the stream as it splayed out across the pebbles of a seaweed-strewn beach. They passed the harbour and she saw again the steep hill, at whose summit stood the ancient chapel, which she had first seen in the twilight on her arrival. The flat mud was crowded with fishing boats and sailing ships, and the huge bulk of Hillsborough, its eroded cliffs silhouetted against the sea and the sky, guarded the harbour entrance.

The coach stopped on a grassy slope. He jumped down and gave her his hand and she felt again the familiar shiver run through her as she touched him, and for the first time wondered if he also had the same feeling.

A festive crowd had already gathered. A juggler was throwing balls in the air. Children were bobbing for apples and the tang of the fresh salt air was overlaid by the smell of a suckling pig being roasted. At the far side of the meadow a fire was blazing fiercely and above it, swaying in the air, was an enormous balloon, patriotically striped red, white and blue. Strong ropes tethered it to the ground and it was gradually inflating, swelling out and straining to escape into the sky.

"What on earth is it?" she exclaimed.

" If it works, it's going to rise up and fly, but I hadn't realised there would be such a crush," he said frowning. "I would prefer it if you stayed here with Mr Scheyer. You will be able to see it almost as well from the coach and I want to get nearer to find out what material it's made of."

She had not realised Heinrich Scheyer had accompanied them on horseback behind the coach and was acutely disappointed to not only be kept so far from the exciting contraption at the end of the field, but to have to remain with a man who looked at her with mistrust.

Jean Luc spoke briefly to him, then was off like a bullet from a musket, elbowing his way through the crowds.

She ignored his instructions and ran impulsively after him, following his broad back through a surging, rank-smelling mass of bodies.

"It's the Duke of Delacroix!" she heard someone say and a path opened up in front of him. A few people appeared surly and hostile, she thought, but he took no notice and quickly reached the fire.

A large wicker basket, bouncing and wobbling on the ground, was attached to the ropes of the balloon, and a man wearing a coat and tricorn hat in the same red, white and blue colours, was busily adjusting its straps. Jean Luc approached closer and she stood timidly at the edge of the crowd, feeling very exposed to public view and beginning to regret what she had done. Her red hair was caught by the strong wind, her green cloak flared out and people were staring at her almost as much as at the spectacle.

"What a beauty," she heard someone say.

Jean Luc turned to see the reason for the comment and a look of surprise, followed by cold anger, crossed his face. The next minute, the man in the striped coat climbed into the basket, the ropes were cut and the giant balloon ascended towards the clouds.

"Ooh!" went up the cry and the onlookers stampeded en masse trying to follow, as the wind caught it. People were screaming, shouting and violently pushing. She lost her footing and as she fell, Jean Luc leapt towards her, putting his arms around her to hold her steady. She clung to him, grateful for his sturdy build, and then suddenly they were left alone on a deserted patch of muddy ground, the baying crowd ebbing and flowing erratically over the meadow in pursuit of its quarry.

He held her close for a few seconds more, before stepping back and letting her go.

"I'm your servant, madam," he said grimly.

She was trembling and tried to regain her composure. It was the first time a man had ever held her in his arms and she was still shocked by

81

the feeling of his body against hers. She always shrank from close, physical contact with anyone, afraid of being hurt, preferring to be alone, dependant only on herself, but now she felt almost as though she was on fire, a passionate longing for him to embrace her again, coursed through her. She was finding it difficult to catch her breath and knew she would have been trampled underfoot if it had not been for him. She was aware that she had not emerged toughened by her experiences in the kitchen and that she was frail. She looked shyly towards him, expecting to see annoyance, but instead, as their eyes met, he bent his head towards her and for one very strange moment she thought he was going to kiss her. Then he took a step backwards.

"Would you like to return home?" he asked, "or..." and they both glanced expectantly in the direction of the balloon and saw that the crowd was still wheeling and turning, and with good reason, for the basket with its unfortunate occupant was swinging violently just above their heads. The fabric had torn and now resembled a reduced, emasculated version of its former self. The proud colours were no longer distinct stripes, and people were scattering in all directions, unsure where it would land. It finally crashed on to the very edge of the cliff and men rushed to pull the balloonist clear, just as the whole contraption slithered down towards the sea. It was all over in a matter of seconds and the man lay on the grass moaning with pain.

"It needed tougher material," said Jean Luc. "I would like to build such a balloon. It would be a wonderful way to travel. You could see the countryside beneath you."

She saw that he was serious. "It's not safe!" she exclaimed in horror. "He is lucky to be alive!"

It strangely upset her that he should put himself at such risk. ' I only want him to leave Devon,' she justified her anxiety, ' not kill himself by falling out of the sky from a great height.'

"We're not meant to fly like birds!" she murmured reprovingly.

"It's progress!" he replied. "We've built ships to travel over the sea and coaches to go fast on land and the air will be mastered next. Perhaps one day someone will fly to the moon."

She giggled, and could see he meant it.

He grinned. "I think your fright is disappearing and that is perhaps not good. Let's take a turn around the harbour and see the ships, ma Belle.

"Take my hand," he said solicitously, each time they came to a difficult part of the steep path and sometimes when it was not difficult at all, she thought. She tried to keep her face from showing her emotional

82

state and had to restrain herself from looking at him as he walked beside her, his blue and silver coat glinting in the sun, the scabbard of his sword sparkling with rubies and diamonds. She lowered her eyes and moved away from him, her pleasure in his company evaporating. She felt that their relationship had changed that afternoon. There was a warmth between them now, a warmth which should not, could not, exist. She knew she had to remain distant from him and that only when he left would she be more safe.

On the cobbled harbour jetty a drab, brown, baby seagull was squawking aggressively, trailing after his grey and white-feathered mother. He was considerably larger than she was and was trying to bully her into feeding him. She laughed at the sight of the harassed bird and her demanding offspring, and as she turned to Jean Luc she found him watching her, not looking at the birds or the harbour.

They passed by lime-washed cottages, festooned with fishing nets hanging from windows and suddenly she saw John Buzzacott in a doorway. He was standing awkwardly and had a crutch under one arm, but he was definitely very much alive.

He knuckled his head as she came near. "Good day, me lady."

"I'm glad to see you've recovered from your accident," she told him as they walked by.

Jean Luc glanced at her. "How do you know that fellow?"

"He catches crabs and fish at the beach just past the woods," she replied.

"Do you often speak with him," he enquired.

" No, not often," she said.

They slowly continued their promenade, looking at the fishing boats leaning on the sand on their sides. Men were busily digging for worms, or mending nets; seagulls screeched, and there was an almost overpowering stench of fish.

At the end of the harbour wall was a jetty, at right angles to the quay. Wicker pots inhabited by barnacled lobsters were stacked against a wall, and in the outer reaches of the harbour, the tide was flooding across the mud, white waves washing over the grey. Sunlit patches of sea sparkled brilliantly against the graduating shades of blue, pale near the land, then deepening to a navy far out in the Channel. She glanced across the water and saw John Buzzacott hobbling painfully towards a fishing boat with a red and white sail. He looked in her direction and paused for a moment.

" Is there some sort of secret between you and that man? Is he your friend, the smuggler?" Jean Luc asked, guessing correctly.

She regarded him innocently, her fair skin slightly flushed from the south-westerly wind.

"No," she lied.

He stared at her suspiciously and when they passed near John Buzzacott, on their return walk to the coach, he glared angrily towards him.

On reaching Hillsborough they found that the crowd had not dispersed but was still excitedly milling around, and James and Elizabeth Vinnicombe could be seen, walking purposefully towards them.

"Good afternoon your Grace, your Ladyship," James Vinnicombe said and bowed. "I passed by Wildercombe House this afternoon, but you had already come here. My sisters and I are going on an excursion tomorrow to Combe Martin and we wondered if Lady Sophie would care to join our party?"

"If she wishes to attend, then she can," replied Jean Luc in a dismissive manner and the thought passed through her mind that the two men complemented each other, one very fair, the other, very dark.

"Yes, I would like to accompany you," she replied, unable to make any other response.

"Our carriage will come for you tomorrow afternoon then," James Vinnicombe said. He remained standing as they climbed into the coach, and as it gathered speed across the meadow she glanced out of the window and saw that he was still there. He caught her eye and politely raised his hat and she felt the trap tightening ever closer about her.

12

The following afternoon the sky was the colour of dull pewter and the biting wind was still blowing from the south west. She sat patiently on the settle in the hall, dressed again in her thick cloak and wearing her walking shoes.

The bleakness of the weather seemed to reflect not only her own worries about her increasing social contact with Captain James Vinnicombe and his amorous intentions to her, but also the general spirit of bad temper which had prevailed in the household that day.

It had been disappointing, but not completely unexpected, to find that Mr Widdecombe did not arrive for her lesson and she had spent several hours waiting in the library, practising what he had taught her. The Duchess had therefore been deprived of the range of multiple personalities she usually enacted for her every morning and had expressed her displeasure very forcibly at luncheon, sulking one minute, shouting the next. There had seemed to be a marked deterioration in the state of her mind recently, she thought. She was far more querulous, flitting rapidly between different eras of her life and different people she had known, leaving Sarah unable to adequately play the imaginary games.

Jean Luc had briefly come to the dining room, but had taken one look at the antics of his mother and had decamped to eat with his men and she could hear him now in his work room, making various banging and grinding noises. She suddenly jumped as the tinkling of shattering glass sounded, followed by angry shouting in French.

'It's more stormy indoors than out,' she thought wryly, then looked apprehensively across the hall as his door was flung open and he appeared, calling for a footman. She was startled to see that he was splattered with a vivid green liquid which was running down his face and had stained his smock.

"What are you doing sitting there in your outdoor clothes?" he exclaimed crossly. "These people can wait for you to get ready!"

She blushed. It had not occurred to her that it was inappropriate behaviour for Lady Sophie Throgmorton.

'Even now,' she thought, 'I still have the mentality of a servant. I can't escape from it.'

"It's very windy and a storm might be coming. Perhaps it would be better not to go with the Vinnicombes. I don't want a repetition of the other night," he said coldly.

His obvious displeasure was unsettling her, but was due, she presumed, to the accident which had just happened in the work room, rather than to her own behaviour. Coach wheels sounded on the gravel outside and she realised it was now too late to withdraw from the invitation and fervently wished the opportunity had been given to her earlier.

"I think they're arriving," she murmured.

They stood together unhappily for a few seconds. A footman pulled open the front door and the two Miss Vinnicombes could be seen standing in the drive, on either side of their brother.

He accompanied her down the steps, his green shirt flapping in the wind, his face streaked with the same colour. He icily acknowledged James Vinnicombe and the dislike between the two men was again very apparent to her. No one mentioned his strange appearance, and far from finding it amusing, as she had feared, she could see that Elizabeth and Jane were looking at him as though he terrified them.

"Two footmen will accompany you on horseback," he said. "And your maid can sit with you in the carriage."

"No, no," protested Captain Vinnicombe. "Lady Sophie has no need to bring any servants with her. We already have our own," and he indicated the men on the carriage.

"Then she will not be coming," Jean Luc said bluntly. "I hear Combe Martin can be a dangerous place," and with that he rudely turned his back and strode off in the direction of the stables.

She climbed up into the small coach, acutely aware that two magpies were chattering in the horse chestnut tree and that she was unable to greet them in front of the Vinnicombes, as folk lore demanded. She muttered "Hello" under her breath, hoping it would ward off any ill luck, and just as she was thinking to herself how bad the omens seemed for the trip, a loud wailing came caterwauling across the garden from the room of the Duchess. Elizabeth whispered softly to Jane and Sarah heard the word 'Bedlam,' which she knew was where people in London were taken who were insane, and then they were off down the drive, the coachman whipping the horses as though a swarm of hornets was after him.

"His Grace is French," remarked Jane.

"Yes," agreed Sarah, not sure if she was just stating the fact, or trying to explain why he was covered in green.

"It must be very quiet for you here in Devon after London," said Elizabeth.

"Somewhat," she replied rather shortly, not wishing to encourage any talk about her previous life.

The journey to Combe Martin seemed to take an eternity. She was wedged tightly between Jenny and Elizabeth and her bones were so shaken, she kept wondering if the coach possessed any springs at all. The iron wheels cut deep into the muddy ground and twice everyone had to clamber out in order to lighten the vehicle as the horses struggled to pull it through water-filled ruts.

The conversation mainly centred on Captain Vinnicombe's army exploits, a topic both he and his sisters were only too happy to relate and she gradually became less tense; the military vocabulary permeating her mind to the extent that every time she glanced out of the window she saw armies of rabbits bobbing over the hillsides, a buzzard swooping down to kill and even the sea appeared to be attacking the rocks.

'Perhaps madness is catching,' she thought to herself again and was relieved when the oddly-shaped cliff came into view and nothing connected with soldiers or armies occurred to her.

"That's the Camel's Head," announced James Vinnicombe and she wondered what a camel was and presumed it was some sort of an animal.

"There's an entrance to an old mine near there. They say that the silver from it paid for the English victory at the Battle of Agincourt."

"Oh," said Sarah, feigning interest, never having heard of such a battle and presuming it was a recent event. She was finding James Vinnicombe's manner pleasant and friendly as usual and was becoming more and more enamoured of him as the journey continued. He smiled and made jokes and even although she knew he was deliberately flattering her, it was difficult to avoid liking him.

The coach stopped by a wide shingle cove. Towards Ilfracombe the skies were a rain-heavy grey, but the valley of Combe Martin was radiant with sunshine, a diamond-sparkling sea sweeping into shore, the waves tearing at limp huddles of seaweed, then rushing back, hissing through the pebbles. A stream muddied by earth flowed along one side of the beach, before branching out into numerous rivulets, and women in caps and aprons were washing clothes, beating them against flat stones. There was the same pervasive smell of fish and crabs as at Ilfracombe; lobster pots were balanced in columns on a cobbled walkway and fishing nets were draped from poles.

"This hill is called Little Hangman and that one is Great Hangman," said James Vinnicombe, pointing.

The name 'Hangman' sharply cut through her enjoyment of the scene. The sunlight grew cold. She looked upwards and there, black against the sun, was a gibbet. It stood, gaunt and grotesque. A corpse was hanging in its wire cage and as she stared in horror, she could see a tarred body twisting and turning in the wind, its face macabrely grinning.

"And that's where the smugglers will end their days when I catch them," she heard James Vinnicombe say.

She felt faint. In her mind she saw Sophie; the white of the shroud, the red of her hair. Far away in the distance, she could hear James Vinnicombe's voice, but the words had become meaningless, a jumble of sounds.

'My wickedness will find me out,' the thought screamed at her, 'and I'll be hanged!'

She longed to be back at Wildercombe House, in her familiar room, alone with her drawings. The day was spoiled.

She followed James Vinnicombe and his sisters up the smaller of the two hills, past a flock of grazing sheep. In places, the path looked directly down to the sea and she found herself becoming hypnotised by the rocking motion of the water, as it rose and fell over razor-sharp rocks.

' It would be so easy to pretend to slip and fall. My wretched life would be finished,' she thought.

"No, ma belle, no," she heard a voice say inside her head. A voice which was soft and low and gentle. A woman's voice which spoke to her with the same accent and the same words Jean Luc de Delacroix had used at Hillsborough. She tried to put a face to the voice, but could only recall his body, and his arms.

'So madness is definitely catching,' she thought, but even so, pondering the words for a few seconds had meant that the moment had passed. She was no longer prey to a compulsion to drown herself in the sea.

'No,' she told herself. ' It's not time for that. It would be better to leave Wildercombe House now and take my chance with what life will offer, however bitter that might be.'

She walked between Jane and Elizabeth, her mind a long way from the wind-blown cliff and James Vinnicombe's efforts to court her.

"What are you thinking of?" he asked. "A penny for them."

" It would be better not to know my thoughts, sir," she replied, and thinking to herself that even if the real Lady Sophie Throgmorton was standing there, she would be unlikely to be allowed to marry him, as his financial and social position was far inferior.

'Although perhaps the Throgmortons would not actually care,' she mused, 'as they banished Sophie to North Devon.'

The obese lady's words at Barnstaple came back to her, " Where she might find some sort of a turnip farmer!" and she wondered if perhaps James Vinnicombe would, in fact, be considered very suitable.

She clumsily slipped on loose stones. He put out a hand to steady her and she realised that she felt nothing at his touch, and for the second time that afternoon the image of Jean Luc de Delacroix came into her mind, as he stood, green and bad-tempered, in the hall.

They descended the hill and she turned her face so that she could not see the corpse, while Jane and Elizabeth continued to chatter, seemingly unaffected by the ghastly sight. She was grateful that the afternoon had almost come to an end and her spirits finally lifted somewhat when the coach passed near Ilfracombe harbour and she saw the ships and fishing boats, pitching jerkily at anchor. The coach passed through the town, and arrived at the track leading to the Delacroix estate.

The drumming of hooves abruptly sounded as horsemen cantered past, making the coach driver veer into the hedge, and she recognised the wide-brimmed hats of the Alsatian men. Their fair hair was very distinctive and their large, stocky build set them apart from the local people. They were shouting to each other as they rode and it occurred to her that their language no longer sounded so strange to her. She had become used to hearing it as she passed them in the house or garden and she recalled the night of the storm and being carried home on horseback, and found the presence of the riders reassuring.

"Damned ruffians!" James Vinnicombe exploded with anger, his handsome face contorted. She glanced at him, surprised. Elizabeth and Jane looked embarrassed.

"Why has the Duke so many foreign soldiers with him?" he questioned, speaking more calmly and attempting to tone down his outburst, but she could still see his resentment and annoyance.

She was not offended, as she understood that people might well be afraid of armed Frenchmen riding through their countryside. A hatred of foreigners was common everywhere and even she had heard of scares of invasion. However, she did not know what reply to make and there was an awkward silence in the carriage as they entered the estate, finally halting in front of Wildercombe House.

"Mama would like to invite you to a tea party on Saturday," said Elizabeth.

"That's very kind. I would like to come," she replied, knowing she would not attend.

She stood on the steps and waved goodbye, then ran upstairs to her room. She sat on the window seat and glanced at the lake, a mirror image of the watery blue sky and soft rain clouds. She imagined the cold depths drawing her down, the weeds caressing her, her body yielding to the water's pull.

'It's like a living being,' she thought. 'It moves, it changes. It even has a face.'

She was oblivious to Jean Luc as he crossed the lawn, on his way back from the chapel in the west wing. He stopped momentarily as he saw her in the window, then continued walking slowly, his face turned towards her.

She looked across at the wood, visualising its shadowy stillness, where only weak rays of sunlight ever managed to filter through the branches and leaves. She could almost smell the damp of the lichen and hear the steady trickle of water finding its way down over stones and earth.

'I have to leave,' she reflected. 'Even although I know no one and will probably starve, it's too dangerous to remain here. Now that I have started to meet people and Jean Luc de Delacroix has arrived, the chance is so high that I will be exposed.'

She thought of the gibbet and the hanged man and her blood ran cold. She tried to think how to disappear without an enormous hue and cry going up for Lady Sophie Throgmorton.

Finally she decided. Tomorrow morning at dawn, she would leave a pile of Sophie's clothes on the beach above the high water mark.

'Hopefully everyone will think I've drowned. I'll walk to Barnstaple and then on to the next large town.'

She packed her old servant clothes, her favourite stones, her pile of drawings and the wampum beads, into the shabby bag she had brought with her from London. For the last time she dressed herself in Sophie's blue, silk and lace dress. She descended the stairs to dinner, hoping her face did not betray the emotions surging within her. She tried to tell herself that it would be a wonderful relief to finally remove herself from an intolerable situation, but the intended crumbs of comfort were swamped by an aching sadness at having to abandon her new life and the place she now thought of as home. The next day stretched before her as a vision of unimaginable terror and she crept into the dining room, subdued and anxious, her spirits even more downcast as she saw Heinrich Scheyer was joining them for the meal.

Jean Luc de Delacroix was dressed flamboyantly in a bright purple and silver coat and breeches, a style which she had to admit she was beginning to like.

"You look very pale," he remarked as soon as he saw her. "I should not have let you go. It was too cold and windy."

His concern took her by surprise and she blinked to stop her tears.

"Did you visit Exmoor?"

"No," she replied. "We walked in a village called Combe Martin."

"That's right on the edge of Exmoor," he replied. "I want to visit the moor to collect plants before I return to Alsace. Perhaps we can go together?"

"Yes, I would like that very much," she replied and realised that she had spoken the truth. There was nothing she would like more than to ramble in the countryside, collecting plants with him.

Her thoughts were interrupted by the rattling of the windows as the wind blew stormily outside. The candlelight flickered.

"The spirits are abroad tonight!" shrieked the Duchess, who was dressed in a brilliantly pink gown, an elaborate confection of pearls and bright feathers in her powdered hair, a black satin heart on her wrinkled cheek.

She saw Heinrich glance uneasily at the old woman and cross himself as she talked of the supernatural. The expression on his face made her think that he considered her a vain, foolish woman and it was very apparent that he did not like her.

She shivered. 'Perhaps the spirits are abroad. Perhaps they know about me.'

The Duchess peered at her as though she had never seen her before, then proclaimed loudly. " You're dead! What are you doing here?"

She felt the blood drain from her face. She sat in shock. 'Does she mean that she knows Sophie is dead?' a voice screamed in her head.

"Ignore her! She doesn't know what she is saying!" Jean Luc said angrily.

His mother cowered in her chair. "Yes, I do!" she whimpered plaintively, clearly afraid to cross him.

"What did you see at Combe Martin?" he asked again.

"I saw a...." and she stopped, too shaken to continue. Her memory of the afternoon was of a man hanging in a gibbet cage, his face and body tarred.

"Yes," he said encouragingly.

"I saw…" she started again and tried to talk about the beach and the cliffs. Both men were now staring at her. Her hand shook, she dropped her knife on the table and it clattered against the plate. A wild terror was suffocating her; she would one day be hanged like that man and people would walk by in their best clothes, chattering about trivia as she swung disgraced, and disfigured, from the wooden arm.

"Oh. Oh." she shuddered, her whole body trembling.

"What is it?" Jean Luc jumped to his feet in alarm. "What's the matter? What did you see?"

"A man was hung," she cried, and rushed in tears from the room and up the stairs to her bedchamber.

"Tell Jenny to go and look after Lady Sophie," he told a footman. " And take her to her room to eat dinner there!" he said, inclining his head at his mother, who was carried out unceremoniously on her chair by two footmen.

Jean Luc and Heinrich sat in silence, eating. The house was quiet and they could hear the distant sound of Sarah sobbing. Jean Luc stood up and went to the hall, then returned and glumly continued to dine, drinking heavily from his estate's wine.

"I would have thought the English would be used to seeing people hang," Heinrich remarked. "Everywhere you go, there's gibbets and dead bodies. I've killed many men, but I don't like what happens here in England."

"She's very sensitive," remarked Jean Luc.

In her bedchamber, Sarah gradually managed to calm herself.

"If anyone ever asks you," she said to Jenny, choosing her words carefully. " I have been wonderfully happy here at Wildercombe House and I could not have wished to be anywhere else."

She expected to sleep badly, with the constant vision of the gibbet in front of her, but as soon as her head touched the pillow she fell into a sound sleep and only awoke at sunrise.

13

She jumped out of bed and dressed herself in her old clothes, choking back a sob as she saw her image in the mirror. It was as though the intervening months at Wildercombe House had never happened and she was Sarah Durrant again.

'Courage." she told her reflection. "You have no choice."

She quietly opened the door, crept along the landing, and stealthily stole down the stairs. The ticking of the library clock echoed loudly through the stillness as she fumbled with the heavy bolts of the front door as quickly as she could, to avoid being caught in such a compromising situation. She slipped out of the house and scurried across the gardens, but could not resist turning round to take one last look at the ancient, manor house. Blinded by tears, she hurried through the dew-damp twilight of the wood, to emerge into the brightness of early morning on the grass slopes above the cliff.

She shot like a frightened rabbit down the winding path, past the butterfly bush, and stood breathless on the white sand of the beach. She placed Sophie's dress and cloak just above the high water mark, then retraced her steps, running through the grounds until she reached the main gate. Her breath was coming in gasps and her chest and side hurt, but she carried on down the lane and it was only when she finally reached the track to Barnstaple that she allowed herself the luxury of a rest on a low stone wall. She had rarely ventured alone in Devon anywhere other than the estate and was grateful the sun had not long risen and only a few emaciated cows were there to see her.

She felt in a state of extreme nervousness, her senses heightened to any indication of danger. The countryside now seemed a threatening, terrifying place. Huge wolfhounds bounded up to her, yelping and whining, as she walked through a hamlet, and a hunchbacked woman at the door of an ivy-clad cottage, called out abusively as she rushed hastily by. She knew she was back on the bottom rung of society, poor and wretched, and her life as Lady Sophie Throgmorton was fast seeming a fanciful dream.

Streams trickled across the path, ruining her shoes and making her feet wet. Thickets of trees and bushes reared high on either side of the sunken lane and she kept glancing anxiously into their darkness. Strange noises sent her scuttling even faster along the track; an unearthly, knocking sound made her think of the spirit world and she was very relieved when she turned a corner and saw it came from a man with a wooden plough, which was juddering against stones in the earth.

The sun climbed in the sky and she tried to ignore her growing hunger. She had not eaten breakfast and had also eaten almost nothing of the previous night's dinner. She was following the same road she had taken in the coach with Jean Luc de Delacroix and she smiled as she thought of him giving his speech, his clothes hanging untidily, his voice and face impassioned with his account of the New World. Tears flowed down her cheeks. It seemed strange to now be so completely alone, without him and without Jenny, or any of the other servants.

"I must be strong," she said to herself. "I have to do this. I risked being hung if I had stayed," and she thought bitterly that he had been the main reason for her having to leave before she had intended.

A scarecrow made of dead crows creaked in the freshening wind and she pulled up the hood of her thin cloak to cover her hair. She tramped on steadily through the morning, not allowing herself to think of what was happening back at Wildercombe House when it was discovered she had disappeared, and knowing she had to quickly get as far away as possible.

"Come and sit yere by us," called out a ruddy-cheeked, young man, a Devon burr in his speech, as he trundled by in a donkey-drawn cart filled with hens. She kept her eyes on the ground, ignoring his lewd comments, and was thankful when he and his cargo stopped outside a mill house and pond and she was left in peace again.

The sun was high by the time she reached Barnstaple and the town looked very different, as she walked along, than it had appeared from the carriage. Pigs squealed and scattered in front of her and she had to keep stepping over trails of manure steaming on the cobbles. She came to the same market square she had seen before, only this time the pens were empty.

"Where is the road out of town?" she asked an old man with one leg and a wooden block for the other.

He pointed towards the river. " Tis by tha Taw," he said gruffly and she thanked him and continued on her way.

She did not want anyone to see she was carrying Sophie's bag of coins. 'I'll wait till later to open it and buy food,' she thought. 'I don't want to be robbed.' She tried to ignore her hunger and marched on, her feet now quite sore.

At Wildercombe House, Jenny was surprised to find that her mistress was nowhere to be seen when she knocked at her usual time. She went downstairs and passed Jean Luc standing in the hall.

"Is Lady Sophie coming down for breakfast?" he asked. "I hope she's feeling better today?"

"I don't know, yer Grace. She's not in 'er room," she replied.

He went into the dining room and absentmindedly drank a cup of coffee and fiddled with the knife and plate in front of him. He took some slices of ham and ate them with bread, then stood up and looked out at the garden.

"Would you see if you can find Lady Sophie?" he asked a footman, " and tell her I would like to eat with her."

An hour later, Sarah had not been discovered. He gave orders to Mrs Yelland to send servants to scour the grounds and to see if she had gone to the Vinnicombes. Shortly afterwards, a footman who had ventured as far as the coast, returned with the news that he had found her clothes, and he had immediately mounted his horse and galloped there, accompanied by Heinrich and a posse of servants.

The small pile lay neatly folded, the silk and lace dress and velvet cloak incongruously placed next to a heap of slimy seaweed. He picked up the clothes and looked around at the beach, frowning. The sea was a tranquil blue, the sand littered with streamers of bladder wrack and cuttlefish bones and sacs, but there was no sign of her.

"Sophie!" he bellowed, the shout carrying to the headland, ricocheting from cliff to cliff and causing the seagulls to rise screaming into the air.

"Search the caves," he told the footmen, then he strode across the sand at the edge of the incoming tide, ranging backwards and forwards, clenching his fists in frustration and fearfully looking to see if her body was floating in the water.

"I should have spoken to her after dinner," he muttered regretfully.

"Why should she take off her clothes?" he shouted to Heinrich.

Black smoke drifted across the beach from a fire on the headland where men were burning an animal carcass. He swore softly, his pessimism becoming more pronounced.

"The smoke of death," he murmured.

Heinrich put his hand on his arm.

"Seigneur, there's no connection. It's a coincidence."

"The Iroquois chief, Deganwida, bore the loss of his wife and children in the fire with stoicism and courage. I don't think I would be so brave," he said.

Heinrich looked sharply at him, a puzzled expression on his face.

Jean Luc glanced again towards the sea, which stretched with a flat innocence to the horizon, and watched the servants scrambling over the rocks by the cliffs.

"There's a lot of footprints," Heinrich commented, sceptically regarding the sand. " Whose are they? There have been no women on the beach, except for Lady Sophie, so all the other prints are from men. But see, these marks are very small and they lead here, then go away again. She's abandoned her clothes and gone back up the path. She wanted us to think she had drowned."

"Why would she do that?" asked Jean Luc in bewilderment.

"Perhaps she wanted to leave and thought she would not be allowed to. Perhaps she has eloped with someone. Women do that." Heinrich shrugged his shoulders.

Jean Luc scowled and wandered back towards the butterfly bush. He mounted his horse and cantered up the hillside and through the wood to the gates of the estate and then galloped back to Wildercombe House.

In Sarah's bedchamber Jenny became the unfortunate victim of his attentions.

"She must have taken some clothes!" he shouted. "You must be wrong when you say there's nothing missing. I know it's a madhouse here, but I don't believe your mistress is running round the countryside naked!"

Jenny searched the cupboards of the dressing room again, this time rummaging in the boxes on the floor.

"Yess, there be some old, poor clothes missing!" she exclaimed. "But she never wears them. They were in this box and they be gone now."

He prowled round the room, where the fragrance of Sarah's perfume still lingered, mingled with the smell of beeswax.

"The drawings have disappeared," he remarked and went to look at the collection of stones. "The unusual blue one isn't here. Is there any jewellery missing?"

"No, yer Grace," said Jenny, opening the jewellery box. "Everything's 'ere. Except, of course, the locket, which she always wears. And those beads."

"Do you think she might have eloped with someone?" he asked slowly, as though the words were being reluctantly dragged out of him.

"No. No, I don't think so," she replied.

"Who does she see socially?" he asked.

"No one, yer Grace. The first time she visited anyone was to the Vinnicombes the other day."

"What! No social visits at all!" he exclaimed.

"No, yer Grace. She keeps 'erself to 'erself and just walks round, picking up stones and flowers."

"But that's incredible! She's so...".he said, almost choking on the words.

"I know, but until you came, that's what she did and was very 'appy. And I forgot, but last night she told me that if anyone ever asked, that she 'ad loved being 'ere at Wildercombe House and that you and the Duchess 'ad been more kind than anyone 'ad ever been."

"She said that?" he queried, speaking with difficulty. "She was very upset about the man she saw hanged at Combe Martin. Is that why she's gone?"

"I don't know, yer Grace. I think," and she hesitated. "Sometimes I think...."

"What? Tell me!" he demanded curtly.

"Sometimes I think she's afeared, I can't say why, it be just what I feel."

"Afraid?" he said in surprise. "Could it be connected with the smuggling that goes on round here? I know she helped someone who was injured the other day."

Jenny flushed with embarrassment. "Half of Ilfracombe knows that, I be sorry to say. People talk. She's the kindest person I've ever met. That's why she 'elped 'im."

" Do you think she's trying to go back to London, to her family?" he questioned.

No," she answered.

"Surely it would be natural to want to do so?" he asked.

She hesitated again, "No.... I think she 'ated it there.' She said she was beaten every day and when I 'elped 'er dress, I've seen 'er scars."

He stared at her. "Your mistress has scars from being beaten?"

"Yess, yer Grace," she replied.

He took six pence from his pocket and gave it to her. "Thank you, Jenny. You've been very helpful."

He pensively tapped his fingers on the dresser and then went back downstairs to talk with Heinrich.

"She's taken some old clothes, her drawings, the wampum beads and a stone," he said.

"That's an odd collection of objects to take if you're running away," Heinrich observed dryly.

"I don't see why," replied Jean Luc. "I myself have brought back ten crates of snakes, insects and plants from the New World."

"Yes," said Heinrich somewhat sourly, then continued, "If she's on a horse or in a carriage, she's probably too far away by now. If she's walking she can still be found."

" You're right," exclaimed Jean Luc. "Send some men towards Exmoor and we'll go to Barnstaple. There's not many paths she would take and they would be the most obvious."

He set off on horseback with Heinrich and six of his men, galloping at a steady pace along the winding tracks and reaching Barnstaple just after midday, even although they had kept stopping to ask if anyone had seen a red-haired girl.

"We had better split up," he said. "The road goes in three directions, to South Molton, Bideford and Exeter."

He passed the building where he had given his speech and reined in his horse to call to a blacksmith shoeing a horse at his forge.

"Have you seen a woman with red hair pass by?"

"I cawn't zay I ave," he replied.

He asked two other people the same question, his voice carrying to the one-legged man still sitting outside the inn.

"Iss. An urd 'aired maid was yere this vorenoon," he said, spitting at the ground and knocking his pipe against the wall.

"Where did she go ?" he demanded.

"I told 'er tha raud fer Exeter," the man replied.

"When was this?" he asked.

" I dannow. I cawn't spaik fer zure," he said, coughing and hunching his shoulders.

"Thank you, my man," Jean Luc shouted, throwing him a coin.

"We won't bother with the two other roads. We'll try the Exeter one first," he said and they cantered off, the horses' hooves clattering on the cobbles.

"I don't think she could have walked this far," said Heinrich, as Barnstaple vanished to a haze of houses and chimney smoke in the distance. "She does not look very strong to me."

" Yes, she is very delicate," agreed Jean Luc dispiritedly. "I wonder if that man duped me to pass over money."

They reached the brow of a hill and caught sight of a small group of people further down the lane and, at the back, was the distinctive sight of a woman with long red hair.

"Slow," said Jean Luc and they reined in the horses and steadily approached. The soft ground masked the sound of the horses and they came right up behind the travellers, without anyone noticing their presence. He swung down from his horse and strode quickly towards Sarah. She suddenly glanced round, aware of someone just behind her and stood stock-still in fright, her eyes wide with disbelief as she saw him.

"It's a long way to Exeter!" he said, in a pleasant, almost conversational tone. His face, however, looked white with fury, his mouth was set in a clenched, thin line, his dark eyes glared angrily at her. She retreated backwards, in a state of sheer terror, staring at him as though he was a ghost.

He said nothing more, just stepped closer and roughly picked her up. She screamed as her feet left the ground and struggled against him, but he ignored her and carried her towards the horses.

"Laive 'er! Er's our prize!" a dirty, shambling bear of a man growled, raising a wooden stave threateningly.

Heinrich's hand touched a knife at his belt, before appearing to think better of it and bringing his fist sharply down onto the man's face, knocking the would-be thief off his feet and into a hawthorn bush. His raggedly dressed companions took one look at the guns and knives held by Heinrich's men, then abandoned their friend, still pinioned in the middle of the prickly hawthorn, and fled down the path, an exceedingly fat woman waddling after them, calling out, "Us shouldn't 'ave waited til dimpsie, to rob 'er."

"Hold her." Jean Luc said, and Sarah was bundled into the arms of Hans, before being given back to him, now seated astride his horse. He gripped her tightly with one arm, threw her bag to Hans with the other, and then turned his horse and galloped off in the direction of Ilfracombe. She felt herself shaking from head to toe and was not able to see, as her face was pressed against the soft cloth of his coat. She tried to sit more upright, but could not, his arm was like a vice, and she lay helplessly, breathing in the smell of his body and feeling his heart beat. She attempted to think clearly, but found it impossible, she was so exhausted and hungry. Her feet hurt, her body ached and she felt shocked that she had been caught so easily by a man who looked more angry than any she had ever seen. She knew her position was now far more dangerous and difficult than it had been before and desperately tried to think of a convincing explanation for her actions.

It had been much more frightening walking alone on the road than she had imagined. Kitchen life had been brutal, but even so, she was ill prepared for the rude and unpleasant people she had met and the covetous looks given to her bag and her gold locket. She had wished she had thought of bringing a knife from the kitchen to defend herself and had wondered where she would spend the night, imagining that the dark and its strange creatures would be even more distressing to her than the day and its human flotsam tramping with her through the spring countryside.

She gradually stopped trembling; the steady rhythm of the horse was calming; she slowly became drowsy and fell asleep.

She awoke as she was being set down onto a chair in the library and immediately had the presence of mind to pull her cloak about her so that it was not apparent she was wearing a poor brown dress. Her clothes were covered with dust from the road and she wondered if her face and hair were similarly dirty.

"Shut the door!" Jean Luc barked at a footman and she saw from his face that the long ride home did not appear to have diminished his fury.

"What in God's name possessed you to pretend to have drowned, then run off, with no one knowing what's happened to you!" he shouted.

She had no answer to make and sat silently biting her lip, trying to seem as poised as was possible in the circumstances.

"If you want to leave my household you only have to ask and you will travel in a coach with servants!" he shouted again.

She braced herself for the blows that must surely follow and glanced at him, her eyes brilliant with unshed tears, as he stared back at her in exasperation.

"Were you going to meet someone?" he asked more quietly, his eyes searching her face.

"No," she murmured and saw him visibly become less angry. His expression softened.

"A man?" he queried again, coldly, as though she had lied.

"No," she said.

He drew in his breath and continued to regard her so intently she found it impossible to meet his gaze and looked down at the floor.

"Do you want to return to London, to your family?" he asked, in a way that seemed to her almost as if he already knew the answer.

"No, no, I don't," she replied vehemently and this time she was sure by his expression he had expected her reply.

"Well, where were you going?" he questioned, sounding extremely puzzled.

"I don't know," she mumbled sheepishly.

"You didn't know where you were going?" he exclaimed, his anger exploding again, his eyes not leaving her face. "You could have been murdered! You would not have survived the night! Have you any idea how rough and violent it is for a woman alone! A woman like you!"

"Please tell me what you were doing?" he continued, more gently. "Were you afraid of being hung because you helped the smuggler?"

She almost blinked in astonishment, wondering why he had suggested that and realising he had given her a reason for her action. A reason which might make her appear foolish and silly, but was one which he looked as though he would believe.

"I was afraid," she muttered truthfully, her old fear of being hung suddenly surfacing with all its terror and she started to tremble.

"No, no, my dear. Don't worry about such things. You're here under my protection. Nothing will happen to you."

He had stopped shouting and was obviously perplexed about what she had done, but there was no suggestion she was anyone other than Sophie. Her fear ebbed away. She looked crossly down at her dirty, shabby clothes and felt resentful at the ghastliness of the day and the undignified way she had been brought home.

"Have you eaten?" he enquired.

"No," she replied, pleased to be able to be truthful about something.

"You can dine here in the library, when you are ready," he said and pulled the bell rope on the wall to summon a servant to accompany her upstairs.

The scent of beeswax greeted her as she entered her bedchamber and she sank with a sob onto the feather bed and gazed contentedly across the gardens to the wood. For a few minutes she lay in exhaustion, breathing in the room's familiarity, before standing up, and with the help of Jenny, despatched Sarah Durrant back into her old box and became Lady Sophie Throgmorton once more. Her tangled, windswept hair was brushed until it gleamed and she happily chose the lemon gown to wear.

Her self-esteem now somewhat restored from the low ebb it had reached during the day, and hunger quickening her weary feet, she descended to the hall. She ignored the curious looks of the servants and the strange sight of two Alsatian men stationed at the front door and then stopped near the library on hearing Heinrich Scheyer's voice raised in anger. She at first presumed he was talking about her, but was puzzled when the name 'de Montfort' was said several times and it seemed odd to her that a man who was a servant and was in charge of the soldiers should have the effrontery to speak to his master like that.

She stood, not knowing what to do, and at that point Heinrich came out of the room. He looked coldly and suspiciously at her and she was very thankful that she had not been questioned by him.

She walked into the library where Jean Luc was quietly standing by the window, a troubled expression on his face.

He indicated plates of pies and tarts laid out on the oak table and waited for her to sit down, then seated himself opposite her, bent his head and prayed.

"Thank you dear God for keeping Sophie from harm today and helping find her. May you bless our meal."

It was the most perfunctory prayer she had ever heard him make. She was too hungry, however, to concern herself with anything other than her pressing need for food and immediately started eating a large slice of Starry Gazer pie.

He ate nothing. He drank a glass of red wine, then another, and the only sound in the room was the loud ticking of the same clock which had broken the silence of the early morning.

It seemed strange to be eating when he was not, but even although she had already consumed far more than she needed, a final plate of apple tart and cream tempted her. She tasted the sweet lusciousness of the fruit, savouring it in her mouth and was only then suddenly aware that he was enjoying watching her eat. She was unsettled by the look on his face, which almost seemed like a strange mixture of desire and possessiveness and involuntarily held her hand against the curve of her breasts, revealingly displayed by the low-cut gown.

She could see by his eyes that he knew she had guessed. He made no attempt to conceal what he was thinking and continued to let his eyes travel over her body. She took one last piece of tart and as she raised it on a spoon to her mouth, he startled her by reaching across the table and grabbing her hand.

"You've rejected my house and you've rejected me today," he said. "I don't know where the truth is. I don't understand you. I've had to chase you like a common criminal across the countryside." He squeezed her hand violently and she tried to draw back from him.

"If you have any worries about smugglers, or God knows what else, come and tell me. And if there is anyone courting you, I want to know about it." He glared at her and let go her hand and they sat staring at each other.

She glanced towards the window and saw that the sky was rapidly darkening and knew that somewhere out there, on the road to Barnstaple, a scarecrow made of dead crows was swinging and creaking in a desolate field. It epitomised the wretchedness of the day and it occurred to her that the only thing worse than being caught would be not to have been caught at all.

14

Her delight next day in waking up in her own bed, instead of finding herself alone and frightened on the road to Exeter, was tempered by her abject failure to have resolved her situation. The Duchess's words, "You're dead!" still rang in her ears and she dreaded seeing the old woman. The bright sunshine was overshadowed by her anxiety and she opened her locket and gazed at its picture, drawing comfort from the much loved face, which, more than ever, now appeared to resemble her own.

"I will see as little of him as possible until his departure and not draw attention to myself," she muttered, reverting gloomily to her previous plan, which seemed, as it had before, a pitifully inadequate strategy. She shut her eyes and, for a second, allowed her senses to be overwhelmed by the sensation of his strong, muscular body taut against her on the horse, his hand gripping her at the table, his eyes dark and passionate, and his anger, which had surprised her by being so controlled and restrained. She blushed as she thought of her own behaviour, which must have seemed incomprehensible and stupid to him.

His words, " like a common criminal", hammered repeatedly through her mind and she threw herself face down onto the coverlet and sobbed.

At breakfast he was studiously polite. He greeted her very formally, before continuing to eat a plate of ham and eggs, so enormous, she could not help thinking it would have fed the Blackmore family for a week.

She drank her tea and ate toast and listened to him talk about the weather, the garden and then back to the weather again and the usefulness of rain if you were trying to dig out a badger from his sett.

She nearly laughed at the oddness of his last topic of conversation, as he was so obviously trying to speak about subjects which would not prove at all contentious. She could see he wanted her to speak to him, that he was trying to draw her out and she would have been happy to oblige, but digging for unfortunate badgers was not a subject with which she was in any way familiar.

He made no mention of the previous day, but it lay unspoken between them, a rawness which it was not possible to gloss over easily with superficial talk.

"You're very quiet," he commented. "Are you alright?"

It was his first, rather oblique reference to what had happened and she assured him that she was fine. His expression was enigmatic and she wished he was like Captain Vinnicombe, an uncomplicated man, whose intentions were clearly evident.

"Oh, the tea party at the Vinnicombes this afternoon! I nearly forgot!" she blurted out, suddenly recalling the invitation as she thought of the captain.

"That's out of the question today. I will send a message to say that you're indisposed," he said brusquely.

The rawness of yesterday was exposed once more. She wondered if he believed James Vinnicombe was implicated in her flight, but presumed he did not trust her and imagined she might take it into her head to run off again.

"Have you ever tried coffee?" he asked, amusing her again by a new conversational gambit.

"No," she replied.

He poured out a cup himself and as he gave it to her, she noticed the circles under his eyes and that he appeared very tired.

She pulled a face as she tasted its bitterness.

"I prefer the tea," she remarked somewhat aloofly, knowing that both Lady Throgmorton and Sophie would have regarded it as little less than a crime to be denied their social visiting and to be restricted to the house.

"It's perhaps too strong for you," he said, ignoring her disdain. "I was hoping, madam, that we might spend the day becoming better acquainted. I am writing an essay for the Royal Society and as your drawing skills are greatly superior to mine, I was wondering if you would mind illustrating various plants for me this morning. And this afternoon, although I could not, of course, be such entertaining company as you would have enjoyed at the Vinnicombes, I would be pleased if you would do me the honour of...." It was patently obvious to her that he had absolutely no idea what to propose and that he had spoken on the spur of the moment, "escorting me to the beach," he successfully concluded.

She looked at him unhappily. He stood up and waited, and she knew she was not in a position to cross him.

"Well, perhaps the drawing," she replied, rather gracelessly, and ten minutes later, found herself sitting at the long bench in his workroom while he busily carried in a plant in a tub of earth, and arranged sheets of absorbent paper, containing dried leaves and flowers, on the table.

She sketched delicately, faithfully replicating the cardinal flower, black eyed Susan, bogbean gentian and purple fringed orchis set out in front of her. The withered petals only hinted at their original colour, but she could imagine them, fresh and bright, in meadows on the other side of the ocean. The blueberries on a twig were wizened and the leaves grey and mottled, but she depicted them plump and juicy.

"I picked that on the banks of the Ottawa River," he told her. "They grow everywhere and are particularly common near pools that beavers have abandoned. There's also a red berry which is very plentiful and it can be dried and eaten, like the blueberry, in the cold winter months. This plant grows in mangrove swamps in the south. It's not from the northern lands," and he pointed to a reddish, elongated bundle of stems, whose spindly tops branched out into clusters of leaves " Everything's venomous where they are. There's all sorts of snakes and spiders and many of the plants are poisonous – even the oak and the ivy."

The awkwardness of having him sit next to her, writing, faded away as she lost herself in the delight of drawing such unusual plants; his intermittent comments were fascinating and she began to look forward to his interruptions.

"Where do ships set sail from to go to the New World?" she asked him.

"Brist…" he truncated the word and she saw suspicion in his eyes. "It's a long way away, madam," he said. "Our ship put in at Ilfracombe, but that's quite rare."

The events of the previous day rose up again like a spectre between them and he quickly started speaking about another topic.

"In 1724, some people from the Otos tribe were brought from where they lived on the Missouri River, to France and were taken to see King Louis XV. When they returned home, it is reported that they said the ladies at the royal court smelled like alligators."

With that, he opened a book and showed her an engraving of a ferocious, long-bodied alligator skulking in a steaming lagoon.

"Oh!" she clapped her hands to her mouth, scandalised for a moment, and then shrieked with laughter. He grinned at her amusement and they sat happily again together.

Halfway through the morning, Heinrich Scheyer came into the room. She saw him quickly cross himself as he looked at the bubbling, green liquid, the weirdly shaped glassware and the caged snake, which everyone, except Jean Luc de Delacroix, believed was the sign of the

Devil. He looked sourly towards her, quickly placed a piece of paper on the table, muttered, "Seigneur," then retreated to the hall.

She had saved the plant she had thought looked the most boring, for last, and finally started drawing it. The stem was long, with a dark flower head, from which pale stamens stuck out.

" It's like a fairy brush. I've seen it growing here in Devon," she commented.

"Yes, you're right," he replied. "It's a plantain and was not originally found in the New World. I'm writing about it because it springs up everywhere that Europeans tread, so it's called 'whiteman's foot'.

She pondered his words for a moment.

"Do the people who already live there, mind that so many strangers come to their country?" she asked curiously.

"Well, it's an enormous land," he replied. "The French mainly trade. They buy furs and men called coureurs de bois travel deep into the wilderness, in canoes. The English, on the other hand, generally grow crops. They cut down trees, make fields and roads and build homes."

" I don't think that would be very popular if foreigners came and did that in Devon" she commented.

"It's progress," he replied, reminding her of his remarks about the hot air balloon and not directly replying to her.

"Your illustrations are excellent," he said, as he examined her drawings. "Shall we take drawing materials to the beach in case you want to sketch there?"

She had not intended to spend the afternoon with him; she had thought of being as 'indisposed' as she had evidently been for the Vinnicombes, but seeing the pleasure in his face as he praised her sketches and having just enjoyed a very agreeable morning with him, without any problems occurring, she decided to throw caution to the wind and changed her mind.

Two hours later, they walked together through the wood. The gloom closed in around them and she felt subdued as she trod the same path she had run along the previous day. He glanced at her and said nothing and she began to wonder if his wish to visit the beach with her was not so hastily conceived as she had imagined.

A sea wind stirred the trees and the sun shone as they stood on the grassy slope above the cliff. She clutched at her blue-ribboned straw hat and followed him down the winding path and past the butterfly bush. She stepped tensely onto the white sand, her eyes drawn to the place above the seaweed contour of high tide where she had left her clothes. His face was set in stone and she blushed with guilt and embarrassment. He still said nothing, but gripped her arm tightly, as though afraid she might escape, and marched her across the sand to the reefs near the headland.

Hundreds of pools lay trapped in the eroded rocks; miniature worlds within a world. Even the smallest crevice held water and enjoyed a variety of life commensurate with its size. He bared his arm and, rather bravely, she thought, thrust his hand down into the translucent blue-green depths in a long, narrow gully. He rummaged around beneath the stones and fished out a reddish-brown crab, with short, stumpy claws and long, hairy spider legs.

"Ooh", she shrieked in delight and he redoubled his efforts to find another interesting creature.

She could taste the saltiness of the sea on her lips. The wind was freshening and she tied the ribbons of her hat around her neck and let it hang down her back. There was an ebb tide, but every so often a wave, larger than the others would crash heavily on to the reefs, sending a fine mist of spray into the air. She was surprised to experience the exhilaration she always felt when alone on the beach and scrambled over the rocks, often leaving Jean Luc behind. She excitedly showed him a tiny, transparent creature frenetically twitching its way across a pool.

"What is that strange thing called? I never know the names of anything" she asked.

"It's a prawn," he told her. "They only go red when they're boiled."

They sat together and watched brown blobs of anemones open to display a swirling mass of red tentacles, and small blennies dart to hiding places as she stirred the water with her hand.

"They've got some sort of skin over the top of their eyes," she said and scooped one out and showed it to him.

"I've not met a lady before who shared my interest in plants and animals," he remarked, regarding both her and the fish. "You're very unusual."

'More unusual than is apparent,' was her immediate thought and she blushed.

"Look, there's a starfish by that stone," he exclaimed. "Shall I catch it for your star-pie?"

"Where?" she asked. "I can't see anything."

He put his arm behind her back and turned her in the direction he was pointing. Her head came just below his shoulder and he held her close and murmured in her ear, "Can you see it now?"

She felt weak as he looked down at her. For a few seconds they stood together, and she was conscious only of him, before she moved determinedly away.

"It's made from pilchards," she rebuked, " not starfish!" partly teasing and partly trying to disguise her emotions.

He withdrew his arm, but she felt that the increasingly sensual nature of her feelings towards him added another unknown dimension to the difficulties she was already facing. Forces beyond her control seemed to be acting on her and more than ever she wanted him to return to Alsace.

They retraced their steps along the beach. She held a stone striped with white veins of quartz, which had taken her fancy, and he carried a length of brown, frilled seaweed and the long-legged spider crab. This time she hardly gave the place where she had left her clothes a second glance and they slowly climbed the path, before descending down through the woods to the gardens.

The cavernous hall of Wildercombe House was sombre and sunless and the voice of the Duchess could be heard coming from her room. She shuddered, her fear suddenly returned and she felt the blood drain from her face.

"Are you unwell?" he asked sharply.

"No, no," she said dismissively.

"My mother will not be joining us for dinner in future," he said, "I think her irrational behaviour is perhaps frightening for you and so I also do not want you to spend time with her."

Her spirits rose appreciably. The colour returned to her cheeks and she left him to hang the seaweed in the hall, to see if it would predict the weather, as she had been reliably informed by Jenny, her usual informant on folklore.

Out in the garden, near the stables, Heinrich had been standing with his nephew, Hans, as Jean Luc and Sarah approached the house.

"I think we'll need a few more pack horses if we stay here much longer," remarked Hans, as they both noticed the dangling crab and streamer of seaweed.

"Only the Seigneur would think of courting someone by taking her to look in rock pools," Heinrich muttered, adding, "Although I think he might have just found such a person."

"Courting!" exclaimed Hans. "But he's committed to the de Montforts."

Heinrich shrugged. "It would be very difficult to withdraw from it now," he said.

"They would see it as a moral outrage and it would also deprive him of becoming the wealthiest man in France."

"Has Lady Sophie's family any money?" asked Hans.

"Her father is evidently as poor as a church mouse and that's why she is here," he replied.

"Catherine de Montfort's built like a cart horse," laughed Hans. "I know which one I would choose!"

"She will produce good strong sons for him," replied Heinrich. "Whereas this one looks as though a puff of wind would blow her away."

"Why did she run off?" asked Hans. "Jenny thinks she's afraid of something and the rest of the servants think she has a lover in Exeter."

"Jenny?" questioned Heinrich.

"Her maid," he replied, not looking at his uncle.

"I don't think she's afraid of very much," said Heinrich. "She's been nothing but trouble ever since we arrived. She needs to be reined in. She seems to run wild over the estate and do whatever she wants."

He looked fondly at his nephew.

"Don't go chasing that maid of hers too much," he continued. "Alsace is a long way from Devon."

"Yes, uncle," Hans said dutifully and they parted company; Heinrich to continue the preparations for the forthcoming journey and Hans to the orchard, where he had arranged to meet Jenny.

15

The greyness just before the dawn was disturbed by the steady hoof beats of a cantering horse. She jumped out of bed, ran to the window and found herself unexpectedly looking down at the black-clad figure of the priest.

He had been a very infrequent visitor to the house. She could not even remember his last visit and in any case she had not attended his service since the first week of her arrival. She had also never accompanied the rest of the household who all dutifully made their way to the parish church in Ilfracombe every Sunday, as the law demanded. She had initially felt guilty about her lack of religious observance, but after a few weeks it had no longer seemed important; she preferred to distance herself from God as she knew she was too sinful to enjoy the prospect of redemption and it seemed far easier to avoid the thorns and prickles of yet another burden on her conscience.

'What am I going to do today?' she asked herself. She wandered indecisively out on to the landing to see what was happening and discovered Jean Luc already in the hall, resplendently dressed in a gold embroidered coat and waistcoat, cream breeches and highly polished black boots. Most of his men were also there and they too were attired flamboyantly, many with bright red waistcoats, and coats decorated with numerous buttons.

Heinrich Scheyer came in the front door and Jean Luc embraced and kissed him to her immense surprise. She had never seen men do that before and noticed Mrs Yelland had a shocked expression on her face, which, for once, ,mirrored her own feelings. She stared down, waiting to see if he would embrace the priest and was relieved when he did not.

Realising she was still wearing her nightdress, she quickly returned to her room where, a few minutes later, Jenny arrived.

"'Is Grace says there be a service in the chapel when all the servants have left the house and would be delighted for you to come. If not, the carriage be ready to take you to the church in Ilfracombe."

The buzz of voices from the hall increased in volume as though more people had joined the throng.

"What are they doing?" Sarah asked.

"They be waiting to talk to the priest," Jenny replied. " Ee sees 'em one at a time and they confess their sins to 'im."

"Really?" said Sarah. "I would not like to confess my wrongdoings."

"Nor me," giggled Jenny "The poor man would 'ave to sit there all day for mine."

"Do you know if the Duchess will be there?" she enquired.

"No, she will be in her room," Jenny said. " Mrs Yelland asked for a special service for 'er. 'Is Grace thinks she be too mad to be with other folk."

"I will come to the chapel," said Sarah, the decision having now been made easier for her.

Jenny helped her dress. A footman brought tea and toast to her bedchamber, as the dining room was in use for the priest, and then she sat in her window seat and watched the heavens open and a straggling file of servants set off down the drive in pouring rain to go and worship in Ilfracombe. At the very back, walking by herself, she noticed Jenny, her black curls hidden under a jauntily arranged hat and wearing what appeared to be the green velvet cloak Sarah had left on the beach. She quickly became more detached from the group and suddenly darted off at a tangent into the shrubbery where she could be seen kissing one of the Alsatian men. She craned her neck to try and discover who she was with, but they disappeared into the shelter of a small arbour.

She had already guessed that Jenny's approach to churchgoing was as cavalier as her own, although for a different reason.

"My great, great grandmother was burnt as a witch at Bideford," she had whispered to Sarah.

"Look," she had said and pulled up her dress to reveal a brown mole on her plump, white bottom.

"That's 'ow they caught 'er! It's a mark they always searched for."

Jenny saw the world as a constant battle between supernatural elements and the forces of good and evil and thought that it was always necessary to be on one's guard. It had sounded like the teachings of the Church to Sarah, but Jenny seemed to think it was very different.

"It's the old religion," she had said. "You only find it in the countryside, in places like this."

Late in the morning, Mrs Yelland came to escort her to the chapel. Jean Luc met her at the door, his face solemn, and walked with her to a row of chairs in front of the crimson-clothed altar set with a gold cross. She sat down and he crossed himself, then sat next to her, and a few minutes later they were joined by Heinrich Scheyer, who also crossed himself, before sitting down. The rain drilled against the stained glass windows, as though a hundred woodpeckers were trying to enter. Candles were burning on every available surface, flowers were fragrant in oriental vases placed in the alcoves and incense perfumed the air.

The congregation comprised two servants from the household and the Alsatian soldiers and she looked round curiously to see if she could recognise the man who had met Jenny. She suddenly realised the man with grey eyes, called Hans, was not there, and at the same time it occurred to her that he was missing, she thought that Heinrich Scheyer had also noticed his absence. His expression hardened as he glanced round again and it struck her that the spider's untimely demise might well be avenged that day.

'In his eyes,' she thought, ' there is probably no greater crime than not to be here in the chapel.' Then she heard the door open and out of the corner of her eye she saw Jenny's companion enter. His hair was tousled, his cheeks were flushed and he gave every appearance of having been running.

She tried to concentrate on the service and the incomprehensible Latin words and noticed that the priest's face was very white and his hands were trembling as he held out the wafers and the wine. He spoke quickly, almost in a gabble, and when the last prayer had been said, insisted on immediately taking his leave and rode off into a dense curtain of rain, which quickly obscured him from view. She wondered if he had to visit other Catholic households in Devon, or just did not want to remain very long in one place, as what he was doing was against the law.

Jean Luc walked with her along the corridor leading from the chapel.

"It gave me great pleasure to be able to worship with you this morning," he said, in a serious tone.

"I hope it also gave you pleasure," he continued, as she did not volunteer a reply.

"Yes, it did," she murmured.

"You don't seem very attached to the Church of England if your attendance at their services is any indication," he remarked, a slight smile on his face. "Would you like to speak to the priest about the Catholic religion?"

She stared at him. "Well, I don't ...," she managed to say.

"I can see I've taken you by surprise. Perhaps you can think about it. It would be necessary for you to become Catholic," he said enigmatically.

She was baffled and wondered why it would be necessary; if she would only be allowed to remain in Wildercombe House if she followed his religion.

"I think you said you don't ride," he said, changing the subject.

"Yes," she hesitantly agreed.

"If it stops raining, I would like to teach you this afternoon."

She looked at him. "Well, I …." she said and was yet again lost for words.

That afternoon, a watery sun replaced the rain and she found herself for the first time alone on a horse; the side saddle was slippery and the ground appeared a long way down.

He rode beside her. "Pull gently on the rein. That's it. You're in control, not the horse." Together they slowly ambled backwards and forwards across the meadow. She found herself quickly adjusting to the animal's rhythm and began to enjoy herself, urging the old, piebald mare to go faster.

Towards the end of the afternoon Heinrich rode by on his way to the stables.

"She's doing well, isn't she?" said Jean Luc proudly.

Sarah had now completely lost her fear and was shrieking with laughter as she tried to make the sedate, elderly horse go faster. She was partly facing them, her red hair was caught by the wind and behind her was the dark outline of trees.

Heinrich watched, transfixed.

"She looks like…." He stared and did not finish the sentence.

"Who does she look like?" questioned Jean Luc.

Heinrich shook his head. "It's nothing," he said. "It's just my memory playing tricks about something I had completely forgotten. It was when I first came to the chateau and I was helping with a hunting party. The woodland was damp, like today, with a bit of sun, the boar was grunting in the undergrowth, and the lady on the horse was laughing. I remember she was half-turned towards me and her hair was red and flying out just like that." He paused for a moment, as though trying to remember.

" There was also something different about her, but I can't recall what it was. In fact, ever since we arrived here, there's something that's been niggling me about Lady Sophie."

"It's just a coincidence," said Jean Luc. "I know that the Throgmortons have no French blood on their side of the family."

"You're obviously right, Seigneur," Heinrich replied. "The lady was very reckless, I seem to recall and she sat astride the horse, like a man.

Well, I think I'll go before her ladyship falls off and breaks her neck," he commented dryly and cantered off towards the stables.

"That's enough for today," called out Jean Luc and about an hour later he had finally managed to persuade Sarah to abandon the horse.

"You always wear the necklace," he remarked, as they walked through the garden back to the house.

"Yes," she replied.

"Is it from an admirer?" he asked, in a flat, non- committal tone.

"No," she said, unhappy to be discussing her locket.

"Is it special to you?" he tried again.

"Yes," she replied, refusing to be drawn.

"You're very secretive, madam" he said and this time there was exasperation in his voice and she was sad that a cloud had fallen on such a wonderful afternoon.

That evening at dinner he was strangely quiet. She was relieved to see that the Duchess was not present, but, at the same time, was starting to wonder if she would be sent back to London, if she was no longer needed as her companion.

"This is a Riesling," he said, indicating a decanter filled with wine. "It's from my estate. Would you like to try it?"

He insisted on filling her glass to the brim himself and when she had drunk it he poured her another.

Her head was beginning to swim and she struggled to dissect the bones from the trout she was eating. She ate very slowly, as she always did, and tried to drink even more slowly. The footmen noticed her reluctance to finish the wine and seemed to be hovering almost at her elbows, every so often taking her glass and emptying its contents into the tappit hen, much to the annoyance of Jean Luc.

"I wonder if you would play the spinet for me after dinner?" he asked.

"If I have not drunk too much of your wine, I would certainly be glad to," she replied.

The fire in the music room had only recently been lit when they retired there after dinner and the cool air cleared her head. He sat on a chair, his legs stretched out in front of him, cradling a glass of port in his hand and she seated herself at the spinet. She sang, losing herself in the song as always. He was there, but she hardly noticed him. A contentment, a happiness, enveloped her, and as she played the last note, she looked at him and smiled tenderly, encompassing him in the love she felt towards the music.

He gazed at her, as though enraptured, and she came to her senses and hastily turned her attention to the sheets of music in front of her.

"If I sing, do you think you could accompany me?" he asked.

He hummed a song and she listened, then attempted to reproduce it. After a few false starts, she successfully copied the notes and he came and stood next to her and sang French and Alsatian songs while she played.

Next to the stables Hans and Werner were attending to their horses and they stopped and listened as the songs floated hauntingly through the night air, bringing a reminder of their distant homeland.

She played more tunes and he sang; the candles burned low and the evening was nearly gone.

"I think it's time to finish," she said. She stood up to tidy away the music and as she stretched out her arm, her sleeve slipped back to reveal long weals, a dusky pink against the cream of her skin. They both stood motionless, then he reached out and gently touched the raised scars. She jumped as though scalded, flinched in horror, and ran towards the door. He sprang towards her, blocking her path and putting his arms around her.

"Goodnight, sir," she cried, trying to free herself.

He held her close, cradling her to his chest.

"No. You're trembling. You're not leaving the room in a state. I'm not spending tomorrow searching the roads to Exeter! Come and sit by the fire and have a brandy."

He led her to the fireside chairs and she sat down rigidly, trying to control her tears. He poured out two glasses of brandy and gave one to her.

She held the glass which shook violently in her hand and rushed to drink it before it was spilt. The spirit burned her throat and she gasped for breath. He cupped his hand round the glass and pushed it to her mouth again.

"Drink some more. You'll feel better."

She reluctantly drank again, spluttering even more. He sat back and looked at her and she realised that if his intention was to make her drunk, he would very soon achieve his aim. Her head was still muzzy from the earlier wine and the brandy was the strongest she had ever tasted.

"I don't know what's happened in the past, but you're safe here. You have no need to worry about anything. " His voice was kind and she looked at him, her eyes held by his. The room was hushed and in shadow where the candles had already burnt to their base. The fire flickered in the grate, throwing sparks up into the blackened chimney.

116

She hated to think that he had seen her scars. She could still feel the pain and the shame which wounded her even now. She felt again the searing agony of the cuts on her back and arms and could see the cruel face of the man who had done it. Her face become almost deathly. She clenched her hands and tried to calm herself.

"It happens to everyone," he said. "I was often beaten. Although perhaps in my case it was justified as I was a very badly behaved child."

The brandy was affecting her now, her head swam dizzily and she flopped back against the chair, colour suddenly returning to her cheeks. He reached out and held her hands between his.

"Tell me what is worrying you. You're too beautiful to have any fears."

She attempted to focus her eyes on his face, but could only see a blur, and she laughed bitterly.

"I'm not beautiful! I'm so ugly, " and she shook her head.

"No, no, you're beautiful," he said, in a low voice, filled with emotion.

She stared at him drunkenly. "No," she said sadly, slurring her words. "I must see the Duchess."

"Why must you see her?" he questioned.

"I must be useful here," she replied.

"You have no need to be useful," he told her.

"Yes," she whispered. "You will soon be gone. I must be useful."

He stared at her, a puzzled expression on his face, and watched her drowsily close her eyes and fall asleep. He tenderly caressed her face with his hand and lightly placed his finger on her lips, then bent down, lifted her up and carried her to her bedchamber, where he laid her on the bed and summoned Jenny.

16

She drifted in and out of a restless sleep, occasionally waking in the moonlight-silvered room. Scarecrows made of dead birds chased her along winding, sunken lanes where monstrous trees and hedges arched together, devouring the light, their roots crawling towards her, entwining her clothes and trapping her in an endless nightmare. She awoke in the morning feeling as though she had not slept all night, her mouth dry.

Fragments of music were still playing in her mind, the notes sounding disjointedly in her head. A brandy-induced haze suffocated her memory of the evening and only snatches of words and images escaped to tantalise her.

Etched sharply against the general blur was the look of shock on his face as he saw her scars. She remembered with great clarity his hand on her bare skin, her silent shame.

"How could he?" she sobbed. "How could he bear to touch me?"

She buried herself under the coverlet, cocooning her body in the warm darkness, trying to shield herself from her misery.

She wondered what she had said; whether she had revealed anything; but the more she tried to recall what had happened, the more she found herself faced with a black void of nothingness.

"They think they've found that robber-fox !"

A soft Devon voice interrupted her thoughts and she peeked out from the covers to see that Jenny had come into the room and was excitedly looking at the lake.

"It be eating all the fish and 'is Grace says it be in the conker tree and it's got to be caught."

Jenny helped her dress and together they watched blue liveried footmen run in circles round the lake and they both shrieked with amusement to see a black and white creature dash towards the safety of the woods and escape its pursuers yet again.

She hurriedly made her way down to breakfast, knowing that he was safely hunting the raccoon, and was just finishing her toast when he finally appeared.

"Madam," he said, straight-faced, "I hope you slept well."

She stared at her plate, her face reddening, unable to look at him directly. She blamed him for her drunken state, but even so, felt utterly ashamed that, according to Jenny, he had carried her upstairs. And the knowledge that he had seen, let alone touched, her scars, was almost impossible for her to contemplate.

"Yes, thank you," she murmured indistinctly.

"I thought that we could ride together this afternoon," he continued.

"Perhaps," she muttered.

He settled himself at the table, prayed, then started eating and she stole a glance at him. He looked back at her, unsmiling, and as was so often the case with him, she found it impossible to gauge what he was thinking.

She made her excuses and left the table and spent the morning quietly occupied in her bedchamber, feeling ill and out of sorts. Jenny brought her a glass of mulled cider to clear her head, but it did not seem terribly efficacious and she had to lie on her bed after drinking it, as the room was swirling around her.

That afternoon she was somewhat restored to health. The piebald mare was led round to the front steps and she perched herself on the side saddle. Jean Luc mounted his own horse and they slowly trotted together down the drive.

She had found his face stern as she had come out of the house. He was still singularly unsmiling, a sombreness about him, which matched her own feelings. That morning, for the first time, it had suddenly occurred to her that she had been unfairly treated in her childhood. It was a cathartic revelation, an opening of her eyes. She had always carried the stigma of being illegitimate and had always thought she had been at fault, that she had perhaps behaved badly, that she was a very wicked person. Now she realised she had never acted wrongly. She wondered why she had always been singled out to be punished and she felt as though an enormous wave had taken her, throwing her up on an unknown shore.

That afternoon was the first of many they spent riding over the estate. Preparations were being made for the return journey to Alsace and she knew that, as he would soon be gone, she had nearly been successful in her deception. The fear she had experienced since his arrival, lifted, and she laughed and smiled with him, surprising even herself. Never before had she appreciated life so fully and she found herself flirting almost shamelessly, enjoying the sensation of seeing his eyes linger on her ankles as she clambered on to the horse, or gazing at her hair as the wind caught it.

One evening, after dinner, he went to his workroom and she sat by herself in front of a blazing fire in the library. A south westerly breeze whistled by the windows, banging the glass; the candles on the branched candelabra next to her burned brightly, illuminating the flower illustrations she was looking at, and without thinking she placed her opened locket on the table in front of her, as she had always done when alone. She looked at the familiar face of the woman, then glanced at the painting on the wall of the man she now knew was Jean Luc de Delacroix.

The wind was increasing in strength, howling in the darkness, driving the rain violently against the windows and making her feel in awe, as usual, at the force of these elements of nature which were far beyond the control of man. She had hardly noticed the wind and rain in London, but loved the way this wild Devon coast was so often battered by storms sweeping in from the sea. She drowsily turned the pages of the book, grateful to be warm and dry, and gradually fell asleep in the comfort of the chair.

Suddenly the window rattled more loudly than before and she jumped awake. For a moment she did not know where she was. The large room, its shelves heavy with books, the painted porcelain figurines on the marble mantelpiece, seemed completely unknown to her. Then she saw him seated in the chair by the fire and she remembered.

In his hand he was holding her locket. She drew in her breath sharply. Her body seemed turned to ice.

"She's very beautiful," he said, glancing at the miniature. " She resembles you strongly. Was she your mother?"

The implied suggestion that she was also beautiful, startled her, and she stared at him, her wits failing. As she was Lady Sophie Throgmorton, she did not feel she could say the portrait was of her mother, afraid she might somehow be caught out in a lie. At the same time, although she was not actually sure the portrait was of her mother, she could not disavow her, having loved her image for so many years. She stayed silent.

"Was she your mother?" he asked again.

"She was a relation," she replied and held out her hand for the locket. He gave it to her, then sat back, smiling happily, 'like a cat which has stolen the cream,' she thought and could not understand why he was so pleased.

"The design is the fleur de lys?" he said questioningly.

She said nothing, never having heard of the symbol.

"It's the emblem of the French royal family," he told her, "although it's also used in this country and was, I believe, on the flag of England."

120

She had not realised the pattern was anything other than a simple decorative marking and glanced uneasily at it. He looked thoughtfully at both her and the locket and she covered it with her hand so that he could not see it.

"Are you happy here?" he asked. "If there's anything at all that you would like, I will obtain it for you."

She found it difficult to look at him. It sounded as though he was about to leave and wanted to give her a present before he left. She pushed the thought away, as she always did, that he would soon depart. She knew she would only be more safe when he had gone, but it was very bitter to think of a life where she would never see him again.

The candles were burning low, the embers of the fire were glowing red. She wished him goodnight and went upstairs to her bedchamber.

When she had gone, he stared into the dying fire and reflected on what he was going to do. He knew he desired her more than any woman he had ever wanted. His longing for her had increased, rather than diminished, as he had come to know her better. His whole body ached for her.

"I can't delay returning to Alsace any longer. Am I going to reject the de Montfort lands after all the negotiations and the commitment I have given? Before I set foot here in Devon the idea would have seemed preposterous."

He could still smell her perfume and it conjured up the image of her oval face and blue eyes.

"I love you," he said, finally deciding. "You're the most beautiful woman I have ever met. You're going to be mine. I will renounce the de Montfort fortune and will not leave you here to be courted by others. I hate to think of you alone. You could suddenly take it into your head to continue your walk to Exeter and when I came back for you, I would find you gone."

Her face was fading from his mind and he made a conscious effort to visualise her again, but could only picture her riding away from him and disappearing into the darkness of the woods. He frowned, fearing it was a bad omen, and spoke determinedly to countermand any malevolent spirit.

" I can't tell you how I feel until I have disentangled myself from the proposed marriage, but I will take you with me to Alsace and when it's been annulled I will ask your father if I can marry you."

He discontinued his declaration to her absent figure and quietly reflected, feeling a slight unease about her intentions, as it was far from clear to him that she reciprocated his passion.

"That's not a problem," he reassured himself. "I'm very wealthy, with a large estate, and we're distantly related. There's no reason for her family to refuse and there will be plenty of time for me to win her love after we're married."

He drank his brandy and followed Sarah's example by going to bed, and failed to notice the wind was blowing the last faint whispers of smoke from the charred logs back down the chimney and into the room.

17

"It'll be quiet when 'is Grace be gone to France," said Jenny in a sad little voice to Sarah, who was holding on to one of the bed posts as her stays were being laced tight. "Yes," she agreed, guessing she was dreading to be parted from her Alsatian friend.

"Do you think it will be soon?" Jenny asked.

"I don't know," she replied, trying to decide which dress to wear, whether it should be the blue satin, the pale lemon or the cream. Her mind was not on the conversation and it was with a shock she heard "'Is Grace's wedding."

"Wedding?" she enquired, the dresses forgotten, her attention riveted on Jenny.

"Hans says 'ee's going back to be married," she volunteered, looking surprised that her mistress seemed to know nothing about it.

"Oh," said Sarah dismissively, trying to make it appear as though she had not the least interest in such a matter. She held grimly on to the wooden post to keep upright, her heart raced, the blood pounded in her temples and head.

'Why shouldn't he marry,' she said to herself. 'It would be very strange if he didn't.'

She attempted to put out of her mind the thought of him talking and laughing and being with another woman, but the spectre refused to retreat, disturbing her usual good nature.

Jenny seemed similarly upset, wielding the brush so violently that Sarah feared her hair would be pulled out by the roots.

" Why am I so blessed to have hair this colour?" she exclaimed in exasperation, her recently acquired confidence suddenly in tatters. She crept down the stairs to breakfast and sat, silent and withdrawn, at the table.

"Is anything wrong?" Jean Luc asked uneasily.

"No," she replied shortly.

" I have to see the estate today, so I'm afraid we won't be able to ride this afternoon, " he said. "I don't want you to go out without me, but hopefully we can do so tomorrow."

"Perhaps," she replied.

He looked uncertainly at her as he hastily ate ham and eggs, then departed on horseback with Heinrich and she was left to her own devices.

She spent the morning drifting aimlessly round the rooms. In the afternoon, she stood on the stone steps in front of the house and looked out over the gardens. It was a day of typical spring weather, blustery with a hint of chill in the air. A bevy of gardeners was hoeing and digging the flower beds, and the mirror-lake shivered in the breeze, its tree reflections staying constant against moving eddies of white clouds. She thought of the soot-blackened kitchen where she had spent most of her life and breathed deeply in the sweet, fresh, country air. The house today seemed both oppressive and also, somehow, empty; her spirits remained subdued and she felt an irresistible longing to collect more rocks and shells, wanting to distance herself from contact with people and to be by herself, surrounded by the woods, the beach and the sea.

His words sounded in her ears, "It isn't seemly to walk alone in the countryside."

'Well, I'm not a very seemly person,' she thought, and at the same time, although she knew it was illogical, she felt extremely angry at the way she had been deceived by his attention to her. She made a half-hearted attempt to look for Jenny, but she was nowhere to be found, and as she had no intention of ruining her walk with anyone else, guiltily slipped out of the house, carrying a leather bag for collecting her treasures.

'I won't be long,' she said to herself. 'He won't even know I've gone and, in any case, he obviously has more important things to think about than me.'

She wandered along the beach, scuffing her shoes against the sand and rummaging in the slimy mounds of bladder wrack with its crackling air bubbles. She fingered the elongated bodies of dead cuttlefish and became more cheerful on discovering a pink shell which resembled a witch's hat. She forgot the time and was gradually drawn further and further along the coast until she reached the patch of sand of the neighbouring cove. The tide had deposited mounds of seaweed and driftwood which straggled higgledy- piggledy and she sifted through them, unearthing shells patterned with silver whorls which glittered in the weak sun.

She tried to keep an eye on the sea, knowing how quickly it flooded over the beach, but her mind was elsewhere, and she looked up to see it was already lapping the nearby pebbles. She started to scramble back over the reefs, but realised she had left it too late.

With a sinking heart, she sat on a jagged spine of rock and watched a wide tongue of sea pour frenziedly into a deep chasm separating her from the next cove. Every so often a wave drenched her with spray and

124

she feared she would be beaten against the rocks if she attempted to swim. The strong current was dragging seaweed and sand past her and she tentatively held on fast to the rock and put her foot into the water. A wave broke over her and she clung on like a limpet, terrified by the force which snatched at her, before it surged back with a mighty roar, leaving her with a few seconds to throw herself onto the sand and run to the bottom of the cliff. The waves chased her, a hollow, booming noise was deafening and she clung to the rocks to avoid being swept away, as she stared up at the perpendicular shale wall.

She was not afraid. She was in such a state of dejection that it seemed unimportant to her whether the sea claimed her or not. She pulled off her dress and stuffed it into her bag, along with her shoes, then scrabbled upwards on the loose debris as quickly as she could. The first few feet there was almost a path and she inched her way along, dreading reaching the smooth expanse of cliff higher up, where she feared she would not find anywhere to grip. Then as she came closer to its sheer, grey face, she noticed iron rings hammered fast into the rock.

'Who's made this?' she wondered. 'Is it a path for smugglers?' and strengthened by the knowledge that someone else had been there before her, she steadily climbed, clinging to the cold metal. At one point she made the mistake of glancing down, the ensuing vertigo made the world go dark and she had to cling to the bare rock, pressing her face into a clump of spiky, pink flowers and wait until her head cleared.

On the opposite headland, Jean Luc and Heinrich reined in their horses and surveyed the cold blue beneath them, the waves whipped white by a strongly gusting wind.

"Too much sea for me!" muttered Heinrich, "I prefer the mountains of the Vosges, not this treacherous water." He looked down towards the far beach, his gaze caught by a red-haired woman in a blue dress, who was picking up objects and putting them in her bag.

"Seigneur, is that Lady Sophie?" he asked.

"No. It's not her," said Jean Luc dismissively. "She's at the house. She wouldn't be alone down here."

As Heinrich raised his eyebrows, Jean Luc stared in dismay at the miniscule figure, now clearly recognisable.

"What's she doing ?" he shouted. "The tide's coming in fast. She can't get back."

Even as they watched, they saw the sea surge and cut off the beach from the neighbouring cove.

125

"She's trapped!" he exclaimed. " She can't climb the cliff. It's too steep! It'll take too long to get a boat there! She'll drown!"

"No! Stop!" he shouted, his words carried away by the wind, as she took off her dress and started to climb. He swore furiously, dug his heels into his horse and galloped at breakneck speed down from the headland, closely followed by Heinrich.

Sarah quickly ascended the cliff. She ignored the wind tearing at her and by the time she reached the last broken layers of quartz and slate was almost enjoying herself and was even beginning to feel thrilled by the odd sensation of being balanced halfway between the sea and the sky.

She slithered over the final, jutting slab of rock and smiled with pleasure as she found herself standing on the grass at the top. She dressed, but could only find one shoe, so abandoned it in her bag which she placed next to a large boulder, in order to rapidly run home without its encumbrance. She was surprised to see her feet were bleeding, as she had felt nothing on the climb, but she ignored them and ran swiftly across the grass to a narrow track.

Hoof beats were thundering towards her, just round the corner, and as she did not want to be seen by anyone in such a dishevelled state, she crouched behind a hedge and waited until two horses had passed her. She hurried on, her feet now very painful, and hobbled as fast as she could through the wood and the gardens to the house.

At the headland, Jean Luc and Heinrich looked down the almost vertical cliff face, but could see no sign of Sarah. His face bloodless, Jean Luc scoured the sea for a tell-tale, white petticoat, but the water was a uniform blue, secretly concealing everything in its depths.

"She's fallen!" he exclaimed. "She must have drowned!"

"She was climbing very strongly," Heinrich said with his usual calm. "She was more than half way when we last saw her."

Jean Luc ran to another part of the cliff and peered over again.

"Sophie!" he called, desperation in his voice.

It was obvious they were alone. The headland was bare. There were no bushes or trees, just sheep-cropped grass. The sky was a threatening grey, empty except for a dark bird, with a distinctive diamond-shaped tail, which was circling high above a mossy boulder.

"A raven!" Jean Luc muttered. "They feast on dead bodies!"

He ran to the rock and discovered the bag, wedged at the side.

"Thank God! She didn't fall! She's safe!" and he involuntarily smiled as he saw the stones and shells.

"But where is she?" Henrich asked. "We didn't pass her."

126

" I don't know," he said, "but she's obviously reached the top." He glanced down again at the waves, but this time his face had lost its anguish. "Let's go back to the house."

He mounted his horse, clutching the bag, and trotted slowly down the hill, carefully looking around him.

Sarah had just reached the steps at the entrance to Wildercombe House when she looked back and saw two horsemen emerging from the wood. A second glance enabled her to recognise them and she immediately realised who had passed her on the path. She limped quickly into the house and entered her bedchamber just as she heard the front door open.

Jean Luc ran across the hall and up the stairs and banged repeatedly on her door.

"Yess, yer Grace," Jenny said sweetly as she opened it.

"Where's your mistress? I would like to speak to her," he said, peering into the room.

"She be indisposed," she replied.

"Indisposed? She's just this minute come in!" he shouted.

" She be in 'er dressing room changing," she said.

"Would you tell her I would like to see her in the drawing room as soon as possible," he said curtly, then turned on his heels. Half an hour later he was still waiting and sent a footman to ask her to come down .

"Her ladyship says that she is busy for the present and will attend dinner," he was told, whereupon he strode off to his workroom and slammed shut the door.

Sarah sat in her dressing room, her badly gashed feet soaking in a china bowl. She and Jenny had been trying to pick out grit and earth from the cuts and it had proved an almost impossible task.

She lifted her feet from the blood-red water and Jenny bandaged them and then helped her to dress for dinner. She wondered about remaining in her room, but remembering the bad-tempered conversation which had reached her ears and the peremptory insistence that she should come to the drawing room, she decided to eat with him.

'He can't have known what I was doing,' she reassured herself.
' He can't have seen me on the beach or the cliff. It was just chance that he and Heinrich Scheyer passed me.' She proudly recalled her ascent of the cliff and looked regretfully at her swollen feet.

It seemed to take nearly as long to go down the stairs as it had taken her to climb the cliff, but she finally managed it and sat waiting at the table, earlier than usual, nervously fiddling with her pearl earrings.

When Jean Luc walked into the room she stood up and held onto the table as she greeted him.

"You are no longer indisposed, I see, madam," he remarked.

He sat down opposite her and instead of saying the prayer, openly stared at her. She was beginning to recognise that he had an explosive temper, which very quickly cooled, and presumed he was just annoyed that she had not seen him earlier. She waited for him to calm and they both sat in silence as footmen carried in dishes of roast meat.

The prayer was forgotten for the first time since she had known him and she was disturbed to see he only toyed with his food, instead of eating in his customary, voracious manner. She, on the other hand, found herself with a healthy appetite from her exertions in the fresh air and was on her third dish of flummery with clotted cream, when he asked in a low voice , "What did you do today?"

"I walked in the garden," she replied.

"Oh, did you go anywhere else?" he asked politely.

"Well, perhaps the wood," she said quietly.

"And did you, perhaps, take a servant with you, as I told you," he asked, and she was dismayed to hear the coldness in his voice and see the anger in his eye.

"No, I'm afraid I forgot," she muttered.

"Did you go anywhere else?" he enquired, placing his knife on the table, his eyes not leaving her face.

She wondered what to say, very reluctant to admit anything about her afternoon's activities, and so settled on a complete avoidance of the truth.

"No," she said.

Even as she spoke, she knew she had chosen wrongly. He glared at her.

"So, madam, you did not go to the beach!" he shouted, so loudly it would have disturbed someone up in the attics.

She looked at him, blushing slightly. He stared furiously at her, jumped to his feet and went to a corner of the room where she was horrified to see her bag. He picked it up and emptied its contents onto the table, and stones, shells and one shoe cascaded over the damask cloth, narrowly missing the remains of the roast venison on its silver platter.

"So, madam, would you like to repeat what you just said!" he shouted again.

She felt near to tears. Her feet were starting to throb, she was beginning to feel hot and shivery and had been caught out in a lie.

"I went to the beach," she admitted.

"And?" he queried grimly.

She wondered what he wanted, as he could not possibly have known she had climbed the cliff. She looked at him and saw his expression soften as he looked back at her.

"I can't allow you to wander alone on beaches and scale a vertical rock face." His voice seemed to break and for a strange moment she thought he was going to cry.

"The tide caught me and it was the only way to save myself," she said quietly.

"Yes, I know," he replied frowning. " But you could have fallen. You could have drowned."

"I had to. I had no choice," she pointed out again.

"You should not have been there in the first place. You must always take a servant with you as I said. I cannot allow you to put yourself at risk."

They continued the dinner in an unhappy silence, after the stones, shells and shoe had been quickly removed by the footmen who appeared to be consumed by frequent fits of spluttering and coughing. He drank wine and ate almost nothing and when the meal was finally finished stood up, waiting for her. She hesitated, slowly putting her weight on her feet as she rose. It did not seem so painful as she had feared and she took a step forward.

The excruciating agony which followed, made her scream, and she staggered against the table. He ran to her. "What is it?" he cried, putting his hand under her arm to support her.

"I cut my feet on the cliff," she said. "I don't know what's happened, but I don't think I can walk."

She sat back down heavily onto her chair. She was starting to feel sick and wished she had not eaten so much, and as she glanced down, saw that her satin shoes were blotched red.

His face was white as he also saw the blood.

"Get the doctor," he said to a footman. Then he changed his mind. "No, he's a charlatan. He'll just bleed you and try and sell me some sort of poison. Ask Mr Scheyer if he would mind coming here immediately."

"No," she cried. "No, I don't want him."

"He deals with all our wounds. He will be much better than the doctor," he said firmly.

Jenny was summoned to help her take off her shoes and stockings and he went out to the hall to wait for Heinrich.

The next hour was one she would prefer to forget. Heinrich took one look at her feet and went to collect his box of medical instruments.

"The cuts are very deep," he informed her. "I will need to clean them."

Jenny held a candle for him as he gripped Sarah's ankle, using metal tweezers to extract the dirt.

"My daughters help their mother in the house and don't wander over the countryside," he said, by way of conversation.

Jenny looked horrified at his rudeness but Sarah kept her gaze on the floor, trying not to flinch and not wanting to meet his eyes.

Finally he said, "I have done the best I can. I will look again tomorrow."

He took one foot in his hand and liberally poured whisky over it. She found herself screaming in a voice that sounded as though it belonged to someone else. A glass on the table shattered into pieces, but Heinrich seemed impervious to the disturbance and did the same with the other foot, then bandaged them both.

"I have done what I can in this light," he told her.

He left the room and she could hear him talking in the hall. She gingerly placed her feet on the floor and attempted to stand.

"No, don't do that," said Jean Luc, as he entered. "Heinrich says it's best not to walk."

She looked at him. She knew her face was white and tear-streaked. She smelled of whisky, her feet were bandaged and there was blood on her dress. She remembered he was going home to be married and felt an intense jealousy towards an unknown woman who, she was sure, would not only be beautiful, but perfectly dressed and behaved at all times.

"Are you alright?" he asked in a kind tone.

"Yes, thank you," she replied, her voice shaking.

"Heinrich extracted a musket bullet from me once and I lived, as you can see," he said cheerfully. "You will be fine. It strikes me you would be more suited to the backwoods of the New World than English society. If you can climb a cliff, you can survive cuts on your feet." He smiled at her, but she burst into loud sobs and covered her face with her hands, knowing that he had partly guessed her deception.

"Don't cry. Please don't cry. You were so brave to climb the cliff," he said, looking almost as upset as she was. " Let me carry you " and without waiting for a reply, lifted her up in his strong arms and carried her to her bedchamber where he carefully put her on a chair.

"Goodnight, ma belle," he said, his voice sounding taut and strained.

As he descended the stairs he met Jenny and hastily fished several coins out of his pocket and gave them to her.

"Please come and tell me if there are any problems," he said. "Or if you have any cause for concern."

"Are you sure ee's going to be married?" she asked Hans later. "Er ladyship ' as 'im tied round 'er little finger. I've never seen a man so besotted."

Hans looked at her, clearly not understanding a word she had said and chased her into the scullery, where their lack of a common language did not seem to hinder their relationship in any way.

18

The cockerel across the valley had hardly stopped crowing when Heinrich Scheyer arrived to see her feet. Jenny appeared as intimidated by him as she was, and scuttled about the room arranging chairs and bringing in a bowl of warm water, pausing only to mutter in her ear, "What ungodly hour is this to come calling?"

She suspected that it was, in fact, a very 'godly hour,' knowing that he always prayed in the chapel before daybreak and presuming that he had just come from there. Everything about him reminded her of the colour grey; his hair, his eyes, the pallor of his skin and even the severity of his expression, and it seemed perfectly appropriate that he should choose to visit her in the early morning gloom.

He carefully scrutinised each foot, then tied linen cloth around them.

"It's good," he said and glanced shrewdly at her. "You climbed the rocks very quickly. Have you done it before?"

She could see Jenny bridling at his tone, but she had no intention of antagonising him and replied politely.

"There are metal rings to hold on to," she explained. "It's not as difficult as it looks."

" How many times have you climbed it?" he asked again.

" I have never done so before, Mr Scheyer," she said.

"Why did you run away? Do you not like it here?" he asked, introducing a new dimension to his questioning.

"Thank you, Mr Scheyer, for treating my cuts," she said firmly, refusing to be interrogated in this way by a man who was the least deferential servant she had ever met.

He looked at her, without any sign that he was discomfited by her tone and leaving her with the distinct impression that, of the two of them, he held by far the more dominant position. She tried not to show she was afraid of him, but as she held his gaze she knew he had recognised her fear and, worse than that, could feel he was suspicious of her.

"Do not walk much," he told her. " I will look again this evening." He inclined his head almost imperceptibly towards her and left the room.

Jenny scowled at his retreating back. " Ee's told Hans to stop seeing me, because I'm English and would not be a good wife," she complained. "Ee's 'is uncle."

She spent the next week confined to her room, as she shuffled painfully on bandaged feet. Her life seemed to have slowed to a halt, whilst all around her there was a frenzy of activity as preparations were being made for the journey to Alsace. Strings of pack horses, tied head to tail, sullenly filed past the house to the stables, and roasting and baking were taking place in the kitchens until late into the night, allowing deliciously mouth-watering aromas to seep into every corner, disguising the more familiar smell of damp and mildew. Even Jenny seemed to be infected with the general excitement and spent hours in Sarah's dressing room, sewing and sorting the clothes.

"I'm not going anywhere," she told her repeatedly, but Jenny just looked at her strangely and persisted in her work and in the end she shut the door to the dressing room and tried to ignore all the commotion.

She saw hardly anything of Jean Luc, who appeared as busy as everyone else and who had instructed that all her meals should be brought to her room, so that she had to walk as little as possible. The arrangement suited her. "I have no wish to see you, sir," she told herself.

Finally, Heinrich Scheyer pronounced the cuts healed well enough for her to leave her bedchamber.

"Your wings have been clipped," he remarked. "Perhaps it would be wise not to fly too high from now on."

She thanked him politely for his skill and was pleased to think he would soon be gone and she would no longer have to see him. She descended to breakfast for the first time in days and found Jean Luc reading his newspaper.

"Mr Scheyer says the cuts have healed," she told him. "But I can't walk too far."

He looked thoughtful for a moment, then remarked, "There have been a few problems at the main gate and with some of the horses, so you must stay in the garden, unless I am with you." He did not elaborate and she wondered if it was just a polite way of telling her she was not allowed to roam the estate.

"I'm intending to visit Exmoor today to search for plants," he continued. "Would you like to come? You can sit in the carriage if walking is difficult."

"I would enjoy that," she replied, somewhat frostily.

"What problems have there been at the main gate?" she asked Jenny, a short time later.

"Words 'ave been written there," she replied enigmatically.

"What words?" Sarah asked.

"Popish traitors," she said bluntly.

"Why would people write that? Is it because the Delacroix family is foreign and Catholic?" she said.

"Yess," Jenny declared in a forthright tone, looking as though she was in complete agreement with the criticism.

"And what happened to the horses?" she asked.

"Some of um were attacked in the field and cut with a cross and the old black and white 'as 'ad to be killed," replied Jenny.

"How cruel!" she exclaimed, realising it was the piebald mare she had ridden. "Why on earth would someone want to hurt a horse?"

She put on her outdoor clothes and went down to the carriage which was waiting in the drive. The coachman was already high on his perch; two servants were clambering onto the back and a postillion was mounting one of the lead horses, revealing his bare bottom when the flaps on his long coat parted as he jumped astride the animal. Heinrich Scheyer was standing by the steps and seemed to be remonstrating with Jean Luc, and she had the impression he wanted soldiers to ride with him, as he kept indicating Hans and Werther, who were walking towards the kitchens.

Jean Luc was waving his hands dismissively and she climbed up into the coach as a footman placed several pistols in a locker under the seat. He climbed in and they set off and her last sight, as she glanced back at the house, was that of Heinrich Scheyer, who was still standing on the steps, a morose expression on his face.

The coach slewed to a halt half-way down the drive and she saw that the postillion had fallen off the horse and was lying on the ground. He struggled to his feet, his face bleeding, and Jean Luc jumped down to see how he was. He exchanged a few words with him and told one of the men to help him back to the house.

They set off again, this time travelling more slowly, and she felt a slight twinge of unease that their numbers had been reduced by two. They passed through the stone pillars at the entrance to the estate which footmen were scrubbing and cleaning. Anger crossed Jean Luc's face but he said nothing.

She had not expected to ever sit in a coach with him again and she certainly had not expected that she would visit Exmoor with him. She stole a few glances at his face, then remembered his marriage and retreated back into herself, for once hardly noticing the countryside. Suddenly she saw that they had reached the head-shaped rock overlooking the beach at Combe Martin.

"Did you know there's old silver mines here and the money was used to pay for the English win at a battle called Agincourt?" she said, repeating James Vinnicombe's remarks.

He grimaced, "The English are always fighting everywhere. They are a very war-like nation."

She was taken aback and regarded him unhappily. She had never heard disapproval of the English fighting spirit before and, like everyone else, was intensely proud of British victories. However, he seemed oblivious to her displeasure and even moved to sit next to her, pointing out the different trees in the copses, and it was not until they reached the second cluster of houses by the church and he sat back opposite her again, that she realised she had not seen the gibbet on Little Hangman as he had blocked her view of it.

Combe Martin was soon left behind and the coach followed the winding, high-hedged track which led up to the moor. The trees became increasingly stunted and sparse until finally there were only the bare hills and wind-sculpted bushes. She noticed a raven, which Jenny had told her was the harbinger of death, alight on the body of a lamb with its eyes pecked out, and she could hear the aggressive cries of crows, high up in the sky, harrying a buzzard.

She had prepared herself mentally for seeing the moor again. She had known it would be difficult and she dug her nails into her hands, so that the pain kept her very much in the present.

She looked across at Jean Luc and knew that the happiness she felt in this last outing with him would be revisited for the rest of her life. She was aware his attentions had flattered her and given her a false impression of his feelings, but however tarnished her image of their relationship had become, she recognised it meant more to her than even the portrait of her mother.

She touched the locket and knew she was strong. The timid creature who had cowered in this coach, on this same, desolate land, had gone. She made herself think of Sophie lying on the kitchen table in the woollen shroud, and guilt and terror no longer assailed her.

She awoke from her reverie to find his eyes on her. She could not fathom his thoughts. She never could. And she knew that the faceless woman who seemed to hover near him whenever she allowed herself to think of his marriage, would be the one who would know his love and his passion. As she looked into his face, the desire she felt was strangely transmuted into his eyes, and she turned away, towards the melancholy countryside, to conceal what she was thinking.

"I hope to go down the gorge to Lynmouth," he said. "It's beautiful. You'll like it"

In spite of herself she shuddered.

"Lynmouth?" she queried. "I thought we were searching for plants on the moor?"

"That's so," he replied, "but I want to see Lynmouth first. Does that not suit you?"

"Yes," she said, speaking slowly. "Yes it does."

He stared at her. "Are you cold? You're very pale."

"No, I'm fine," she replied.

In the distance the hamlet of Lynton was now visible and her vow to visit Sophie's grave hung heavily on her. She would have preferred never to see it again. It was too uncomfortable a reminder of a past life which had been unbearable, and a reminder of the deceit on which her present life was built. It was, however, as though fate had brought her to the spot, and as it had been Sophie who had placed her on the path she was now taking, she felt that if she turned aside from this last, final communion with her, evil might result. And that evil, she was afraid, might not happen to her, but to someone else, someone who would shortly be embarking on a long and dangerous journey back to his home.

She wished she had brought a flower with a yellow corolla as a safeguard and looked unhappily out at the flowerless, wretched mire of mud, bracken and furze they were passing through.

"Would you mind if I visit the churchyard, just for a few minutes?" she said.

"You want to visit the churchyard?" he repeated in surprise. "You've been here before?"

"Yes," she replied. "When I first came to Wildercombe House, my servant died at Lynmouth and she's buried at Lynton." The words nearly stuck in her throat, but she managed to say them.

"Well, of course you can," he said. "I had no idea. How did she die?"

"She had an illness which suddenly became worse," she replied guardedly.

He called to the coachman to stop. They drew to a halt by a stone wall and she recognised the church. The yew tree still stood and the wind was blowing in gusts, not unlike the day Sophie had been buried.

"I would like to go alone" she told him, partly in case she was compromised in some way, and partly because she wanted to keep her old and new lives very separate. 'Sophie's grave is my grave too,' she thought.

' Sarah Durrant has also departed this life and will never, I hope, be resurrected.'

"Well, if you want to," he said very reluctantly, and she could see he was, for once, unsure what to do. They descended from the coach and he waited with an impatient air as she walked towards the lych gate and then round the side of the ancient building.

The grave was marked by the original wooden cross and not by the marble headstone she had paid for. A damp mist of rain was starting to fall, blending the subdued colours of the earth and grass and grey stone into a drabness which depressed her spirits. She tried to think of Sophie as she used to be, but she was only too familiar with the sight of decomposing corpses on gibbets and in public places as a warning to others, to know the sad reality which lay beneath the ground.

She sank to her knees in prayer, but it was a mechanical reaction; her emotions were bound up with life and hope and love, however hurt and angry she might feel when experiencing them; and not with the dead. She had embraced the vibrant nature of parts of Jenny's pagan religion, and folk superstitions had replaced a church which had never helped her and which offered only damnation to her soul for her present wickedness.

Dandelions were growing by the cross and she uprooted several, staining her hands with the milky liquid in their stems. Heavy footsteps sounded on the gravel and she turned round to see Jean Luc approaching, his familiar, large shape making her smile in the depressing gloom of the churchyard.

She stood up and with hardly a backward glance, fled from the grave and returned with him to the coach.

"I wanted a marble headstone, not a wooden cross. I paid for it in Lynmouth," she remarked, as the coach started on the steep descent to Lynmouth.

"Did you? Well, we'll go and see what happened to it!" he said.

"Did your servant die in Lynton?"

"No, in Lynmouth, in the coach," she replied.

"What! This coach!" he exclaimed.

"Yes. She had coughed all through the winter. She became much worse on the journey and died in my arms as we arrived," she said and it seemed wonderful to be able to tell him what had happened, even if it was only a small part of the hidden secret she carried with her.

'It doesn't matter,' she thought. 'He'll soon be gone. He won't even remember me, let alone something unimportant I say about a servant.'

" She was called Sarah Durrant?" he queried. " I saw her name on the cross."

"Yes," she replied, her name sounding strange when she heard it spoken by him.

"Was she old or young?" he asked curiously.

"She was quite young," she said, unwilling to say any more, knowing his sharp mind.

"Did she ramble in the countryside with you?" he enquired.

"Oh no. She never accompanied me," she said. " She hated walking or playing the spinet."

"She played the spinet?" he questioned. "That's unusual for a servant."

"Yes," she agreed and looked out of the window to curtail the conversation.

The coach drove over the cobbled street of Lynmouth and she saw the river again, this time not swollen by a storm. The dull thunder of waves cannoning against the shore could be heard and as they passed the inn she glanced away.

"Do you know where the stone mason lives?" he asked.

"No," she replied.

He jumped down from the carriage and told the footman to locate the nearest stonemason and tell him to make a gravestone in the name of Sarah Durrant, to replace a wooden cross in the churchyard at Lynton.

"It will be properly made and erected," he told her. "Now let us take a turn on the beach."

"Thank you," she said, his concern and kindness for an unknown person making her tearful, and instead of the reserve she had intended to show him, she consented to hold his arm as they took a turn along the harbour path. The terror she had expected to feel on seeing Lynmouth again did not claim her and she found herself delighting in the taste of the salt sea wind blowing against them and in looking with him at the hogs' back cliffs tumbling into an angry sea, and at the lime kiln by the huddle of houses near the beach. He skimmed pebbles into the waves and they both lost their footing as they scrambled up a shifting shingle ridge and she shrieked with laughter as he hauled her to the top.

Then they set off in the coach again, following the treacherous track snaking along the steep, wooded gorge.

On the moor, the rain clouds were gathering once more. He searched for plants and she ambled beside him, finding it difficult to walk on the tufted grass. Her feet were beginning to hurt and she felt disquiet at the barren openness of the land, relieved only by a few skeletal trees. A brown, crested skylark rose vertically from a patch of bracken in front of her, its warbling echoing eerily across the emptiness and making her jump in fright.

The peat-brown waters of a brook wandered across the floor of a small combe; the sky was rapidly turning black towards the horizon and the first drops of rain fell cold against her face, scoring the surface of the stream.

" We'd better go!" he exclaimed and she was pleased as they retraced their steps, her anxiety lessening as they drew nearer to the waiting coach. The moor was too lonely for her liking and thoughts of highwaymen and brigands had been preying on her mind since the start of the walk. The guns had been left in the carriage and she had felt unprotected in the rolling expanse of heather and bracken, bounded by the threatening sky.

The coach travelled quickly over the moor-land track, then descended, bouncing and swaying, into woodland. Trees overhung the route, their uppermost branches with new young leaves twining together above the path. The jolting movement suddenly shot her forwards and she landed laughing in his lap. He put out his hands to catch her and, for a second, she was held by him as he looked at her upturned face. He pulled her more closely to him, bent down and kissed her on the mouth. She was shocked to feel a bristling roughness against her cheeks and the strange sensation of his mouth on hers and then he abruptly stopped and placed her back on her seat.

She stared at him, speechless, her whole body on fire.

"Forgive me! I apologise! I should not have done that!" he said, but she did not think he appeared at all apologetic. Far from that, he was looking at her as though he was on the point of doing it again.

"I'm sorry. I didn't mean to behave badly." He seemed more contrite now, she thought, her cheeks burning. The next minute, the coach came to a halt outside a thatched, half-timbered inn.

The footman opened the door and he stepped down, then gave her his hand. She coldly accepted it, knowing that her flushed face, however, suggested a more accurate guide to her feelings.

They entered the inn and found a low-ceilinged room, traversed by blackened beams and filled with the odour of smoke, roasting venison and the human company that was there. A hubbub of voices and clattering from plates and knives greeted them, and the landlord, his face half-hidden by the very rare sight of a thick grey beard, ushered them to a table by a fire spitting out burning wood on to the hearth.

She was pleased to be among people again after the bleakness of the moor. She was also pleased to be among people instead of sitting alone in the intimacy of a small coach, with a man who had just kissed her. She could still feel his lips on hers and felt weak as she thought of his arms around her, his face touching her face, and of being held against his body, and was furious with herself for being so overwhelmed.

'It was just an accident,' she told herself. 'A fleeting moment which has no significance. If I hadn't been thrown across the coach, it would never have happened. He's going to be married and I'm nothing to him.'

Her gaze wandered to the stags' heads nailed as trophies on the walls and then, finally, she found the confidence to glance at him.

He was looking at her intently, she was horrified to see, at the same time as vigorously eating the roast trout which had been placed in front of him. She sliced her own fish, her hands shaking slightly, and felt emotionally distraught, tears filling her eyes.

' You foolish woman!' she told herself. ' He has behaved in a way he should not have done.'

"We will eat and then I'll show you the ravine which leads to the sea," he said, gazing at her.

He seemed oblivious to the bustling inn around him, but she gradually became aware of a group of men, dressed in hunting clothes, loudly and drunkenly discussing the colonies. She saw them stare aggressively in their direction and began to feel worried. He still showed no sign of having noticed them at all and continued to look at her in a way which, for once, very obviously expressed what he was thinking.

Out of the corner of her eye, she saw one of the men weaving unsteadily through the throng of people. He staggered as he approached their table and made an exaggerated bow, spilling the cider from a tankard he was holding.

"Squire Edgecombe, at your service!" he said, his face red and sweating, a greasy wig on his head, his brown coat caked with mud.

"The Duke of Delacroix, I believe," he said, slurring his words. "Pleased to make your acquaintance. My friends here tell me you're a lover of the Pope and a traitor to our fair land. To prove this is not so, join me in a toast to George, England and the Church!" and he lifted his tankard.

Jean Luc hardly bothered to glance at him.

"Go away, sir, You're drunk!" he exclaimed in a peremptory tone, his expression annoyed.

"So you refuse, you blackguard!" the man shouted.

"No one tells me what to do!" Jean Luc replied, in his usual strong voice.

The man's companions rushed to join him, jostling and pushing round the small table. They smelt strongly of ale and cider and were all holding tankards, and her first thought was that they would ruin her clothes by spilling their drink on her. She frowned and looked coldly at them. People were stampeding from the room and she suddenly realised the extreme gravity of the situation. One of the men was holding a large, hunting knife, covered in blood, and she sat transfixed with horror; their two servants were outside with the coach and they were alone, faced by a pack of baying, country idiots.

'Give them the toast!' she prayed to herself. ' Just give them the toast!'

Squire Edgecombe pulled a knife from his coat and pointed it threateningly, his face contorted with loathing.

"Take him away!" Jean Luc said in disgust.

"Traitor! Popish spy!" they jeered and shouted.

He slowly rose to his feet, unsheathing his sword. "Get behind me, Sophie!" he ordered, keeping his eyes on the men.

A woman screamed and then there was complete silence. The men circled, weighing him up. She was relieved to see that he was bigger than they were and that his sword glinted menacingly, but the memory of him falling into a bush when duelling with Heinrich Scheyer was suddenly in her mind and she despairingly saw that he was very outnumbered and that the men looked intent on harming him. She picked up a sharp knife from the table.

'If they touch him, I'll stab one. I'm not watching him murdered in front of my eyes!' she thought.

He glanced at her. "Get behind me Sophie!" he shouted, in a voice which normally would have terrified her, but she ignored him and stood her ground.

Two of the men quickly lunged forward at him. He jabbed with his sword and caught the nearest in the chest, blood spurting everywhere as the man fell. She slashed the cheek of the other, who howled in pain, and he quickly pulled his sword from the first and pierced the second, who screamed in agony. The others fell back, terror on their faces, and at that moment the footman appeared at the door holding a gun from the coach.

141

There was a silence, broken by what sounded like a death rattle, and Jean Luc violently pushed her in front of him towards the door, his sword dragging across the floor.

She ran across the courtyard and threw herself into the coach, as he closely followed. The coachman and footman jumped onto the top, and she heard the whip crack as the horses galloped off down the muddy track. He sat back heavily onto the seat, still holding his sword which was smeared with blood; the icy calm she had felt during the attack now deserted her and she shook with fright, at any moment expecting the men to appear on horses. She glanced at him, anticipating anger at her disobedience, but was horrified to see that his shirt was rapidly staining with blood and his purple sleeve was now almost black. He slumped back against the seat, his sword clattering onto the floor.

"You're hurt!" she shrieked in panic.

She flung herself next to him and tried to take off his clothes to see the wound. He lay back, white-faced, only semi-conscious, and after many minutes she finally managed to remove his coat and shirt in the swaying carriage.

He moaned and tried to speak, but could not form the words and she saw that he had been badly slashed on the arm. Blood was streaming from the gash, her hands and clothes were red.

She hastily tore the shirt into strips and tied the bandages as tightly as she could round the wound, then knelt by him, keeping her hand pressed down on the cloth, to try and stem the flow.

'He will bleed to death before we're home!' the terrifying thought struck her, and with her other hand she covered him with his coat to keep him warm, and then sat next to him, his head on her shoulder.

The coach creaked alarmingly and she feared that at any minute a wheel would break or the axle would snap. She listened for sounds of pursuit, but could only hear the breaking of twigs and branches as the coach sheered against the hedges, its wheels clattering against stones. He was endeavouring to speak and she heard him say "Sophie."

"Don't talk. Save your strength." she murmured and held him more closely to her.

The nightmare drive seemed to take for ever and she could feel him gradually becoming colder and colder, although she succeeded in staunching the blood to some extent, as it was no longer dripping onto the floor. The coach careered through Ilfracombe, people scattering as the horses raced dangerously along the narrow road. At last the tree-lined drive of Wildercombe House was reached and she began to have hope that he would not die before they reached home.

The coach shuddered to a halt and she stayed seated, still cradling him in her aching arms. A footmen opened the door.

"His Grace is badly injured!" he shouted in horror and then servants came running. He was carried up the steps and across the hall to his room, the movement making the blood drip onto the flagstones. They laid him on his bed, and Heinrich ran in, alerted to what had happened. He quickly undid the makeshift bandages and frowned as he saw the raggedly gaping wound.

"Are you hurt?" he turned to ask.

"No, no, I'm not," she said, her voice shaking.

"Are people chasing you?" he questioned.

"No, I don't think so. We were attacked hours ago on Exmoor!" she struggled to reply.

Mrs Yelland arrived at the door and he told her, "I want animal's blood heated up with wine. Hans will tell the cook what to do."

She sourly pursed her mouth and started to leave the room. "And I want the priest to be sent for!" he called after her.

'He must think he's going to die!' she thought, as she looked at Jean Luc lying unconscious on the bed, and the tears she had been holding back for the whole of the ghastly journey flooded down her cheeks.

"Would you help Lady Sophie to her room," Heinrich said to a servant.

"No, I want to stay!" she said firmly. Ignoring her, he started taking off Jean Luc's breeches to see if he had any other injury, whereupon she fled from the room.

In her bedchamber she watched the water in the basin turn pink, then red, as she washed.

"It's his blood!" she murmured and, for a moment, a strong feeling possessed her that he was now linked to her, and she felt again his kiss on her lips.

She trembled from exhaustion and slowly sipped a glass of brandy that Jenny brought her. When she had somewhat recovered, she stood on the landing looking down at the servants coming and going in the hall below. Two Alsatian soldiers were stationed outside his door and two more at the front door. They were well armed with knives and guns and she wondered if Heinrich feared a further attack. She was afraid to intrude and waited patiently for some time, breathing in an acrid smell of burning herbs and wine, and then descended the stairs and knocked on the door, which was opened by Heinrich.

"Can I see him?" she asked.

"It is not suitable at the moment," he replied.

She peered past him into a room dimly lit by only a few candles. He was lying in an ornately carved, four-poster bed. His eyes were shut and his face looked as white as the bed covers, his chest was bare and his arm heavily bandaged. The air was strongly suffused with the aroma of herbs, and a glass filled with a red liquid was on a table by the bed.

"It's best to leave him to sleep," Heinrich said curtly. He looked down at her and his abrasive manner softened.

"You did very well to bandage his arm in the carriage. Go to bed now. I think it has been very frightening for you today."

She acquiesced and with leaden feet climbed the stairs again.

"At least he's alive," she said to herself, as she sat in her window seat and looked out at the cold darkness. Her arms hurt from holding him and a chaotic welter of images flooded her mind. She turned away from the star-bright blackness and gratefully buried herself in her soft feather bed. She lay under the coverlet and tried to forget the trauma of the attack, picturing only the waves breaking on a pebble shore and a man with dark hair and eyes, laughing and pulling her to the top of a shingle ridge.

She knew that today she had at last left Sarah Durrant completely behind. She had known it earlier at Lynton and she had known it even more strongly holding the knife in the inn. She had sloughed off the chrysalis of her old life and had become a confident woman, who had slashed a man's cheek because he was threatening someone she had wished to protect. She experienced a momentary elation in her new pride at her ability to control her life and at being herself even if she no longer seemed to have a name, but then despair and anguish reclaimed her and she fell asleep dreaming of blood droplets falling like rain over Wildercombe House.

19

She woke next morning and idly watched the sun dapple the room with shifting flecks of light. A background hum of noise rose and fell, disturbing the usual country peace and taking her a few minutes to realise it should not be there. She sat bolt upright and could distinctly hear shouting, as though from a long way off. She jumped out of bed and rushed to the window. Nothing moved. The garden was a tranquil expanse of lawns and shrubbery, the lake a flat, silk-grey. The sound was reminiscent of the buzzing of angry bees, an insistent whine, and came from the direction of the main entrance. She pulled on the bell and a short time later Jenny came hurrying in.

"There be a mob at the gates!" she said breathlessly. " They be shouting and throwing stones!"

"Why?" asked Sarah, although, instinctively, she already knew the reason.

"It's because of 'is Grace! They be saying that ee's killed two men and want him hung! And that ee's a Catholic and an enemy of England!"

"Do you know how he is this morning?" she asked, quickly trying to dress.

"I know ee's alive," replied Jenny, " but that be all."

The clip-clop of hooves made them turn towards the window again and looking out, they could see a double file of red-coated soldiers on horseback; a man in a dark coat, wearing a curled, grey wig, leading them.

"What's happening?" exclaimed Sarah, shocked to see men in military uniform. The man in the dark coat stiffly dismounted and climbed the steps, accompanied by two soldiers. A slow, heavy knocking reverberated through the house, then raised voices could be heard, one of which was clearly Heinrich Scheyer's.

She rushed out onto the landing, just in time to see the man and several soldiers enter Jean Luc's room. Fearful about what was happening, she ran down the stairs and across the hall to his bedchamber.

He was sitting in bed, propped up by two large bolsters, his arm bandaged, a shirt loosely round his shoulders. His face was extremely pale, but he was obviously much recovered from his previous, unconscious state, and even the threatening words of the dark-coated man failed to depress her spirits.

"The Duke of Delacroix? I am the Lord Lieutenant of Devon and I'm arresting you for the murder of two men at Heddon yesterday. You will have the right to be tried by a jury of your peers!"

Heinrich was standing by the bed, his hand on a knife at his belt, and Dietrich and Werner, armed with both guns and knives, were at the door. She heard running feet outside the window and noticed several of Heinrich's men taking up positions outside the house and wondered if the Lord Lieutenant had realised that his soldiers would be heavily outnumbered.

Jean Luc spoke in a weak, angry voice, "How dare you come here and invade my privacy!"

Heinrich moved nearer to the Lord Lieutenant, his hand still on his knife, the look in his grey eyes unflinching and hard, as though he was a hunter stalking his prey.

"There's a rioting mob at your gates and they're baying for your blood!" the Lord Lieutenant continued. "I was in Barnstaple when I heard about the disturbance and Squire Edgecombe came to me asking for justice for his friends."

"That man should be locked up for inciting violence!" Jean Luc said. "We were attacked as we ate our meal."

"You were with someone?" the Lord Lieutenant enquired.

"Yes. I was with him!" replied Sarah.

Their faces turned towards her and she realised no one had noticed her arrival.

"And who might you be?" he asked.

"Lady Sophie Throgmorton," she replied with dignity.

" Please leave us madam. This does not concern you." warned Jean Luc, looking at her, his voice hardly audible.

The Lord Lieutenant seemed to be taken by surprise. His deep-set eyes, almost hidden by bushy eyebrows, squinted at her.

"Squire Edgecombe reported that a red-haired harridan, a harpie, had attacked one of his companions with a knife," he said ponderously, looking very puzzled.

"Squire Edgecombe and his friends set upon us as we were eating in the inn. If his Grace had not defended me, I do not think I would be here today," she said, in as refined a manner as she could manage. She could see Heinrich glaring at her and knew he was angry she had remained in the room and that he was probably expecting a violent struggle and did not want her in the way. Her resolve hardened to do what she could and she forced herself to look again at the Lord Lieutenant, her dislike of him increasing as she noticed the vivid slash across his cheek, which distorted his mouth, intensifying his already cruel expression.

"Would you by any chance be related to Lord William Throgmorton?" he asked, his scar twitching rhythmically.

"Yes, he's my father," she replied. She realised it was unlikely he would ever have seen Sophie, but was shaken by his acquaintance with the Throgmorton family. An expression of uncertainty passed over his face and she had the impression he was more reluctant to act.

"Froggy Morton's a demmed good card player and a true patriot," he remarked pointedly. "Why is his daughter here in this nest of French Catholicism?"

"His Grace is a relation," she sweetly replied, taken aback by the extreme rudeness of his words.

She glanced at Jean Luc and saw he was lying against the bolster, his face very drawn, as though he was trying not to call out in pain.

"Your reputation is widely known here in Devon and the mob want your blood!" he said bluntly, addressing Jean Luc again. "If I arrest you, you will be safe and under my protection. I can't say what might happen here otherwise!"

He seemed unsure what to do and glanced at the Alsatian soldiers outside the house.

"There's no need to concern yourself on my behalf!" said Jean Luc coldly, "My idea of safety does not include a spell in Exeter Prison."

The shouting outside was now reaching a crescendo and she was surprised the rioters had remained at the gates.

'They're afraid!' she suddenly realised. 'They know there are many armed men here and don't want to risk their lives. They just want him arrested.'

The Lord Lieutenant looked distastefully at Jean Luc and then stared hard at her.

"Surely I've seen you somewhere before?" he said, a tic seizing his features and contorting his face. "There's something wrong here, but I can't put my finger on it!"

He continued to stare. Her head swam and she felt faint as the whole room became blotted out. Only his scarred face loomed large in her vision and she had an image of herself in chains, being led out past the mob. The clock on the mantelpiece ticked in the silence a hundred times more slowly than her heart, and her face became as white as Jean Luc's.

She saw that Heinrich had noticed her faintness and her fear, and then, the next minute, the Lord Lieutenant shook his head and, as though from a far-off distance, she heard him say coldly, "I'll go now, sir!" disappointment very evident in his voice. He bowed politely in her direction and left the room accompanied by his soldiers.

Heinrich went to the front door and watched them leave. The noise of the mob suddenly abated, then roared even more angrily when they saw their quarry had not been arrested.

"Let's hope they haven't turned on the old fool!" said Jean Luc, as Heinrich returned. "That would cause a few problems."

A shot echoed through the garden, followed by a stillness.

"Send two men to see what has happened," he said weakly, "and have all the men stationed round the house."

"They're dispersing!" Heinrich said. "They realise there will be no arrest today."

He went to a decanter on a mahogany dresser and poured a glass of port. "Seigneur," he said, giving it to him.

Jean Luc drank slowly, holding it in his good hand, which was shaking, and she noticed spots of blood starting to appear on the bandages. The wine spilt as his hand trembled more violently, and without thinking she went to the bed, cupped her hand round the glass and helped him hold it to his mouth. He did not protest and gulped it down, then lay back with his eyes closed. She could feel the coldness of his skin and pulled up the coverlet to keep him warm. The spring sun was shining directly into the room and she went over and drew the curtains, and as she glanced at Heinrich for the first time she thought she saw friendliness in his look.

"Do not go to the main gates," he said to her. "Stay in the house."

"Yes," she agreed and left the room.

Heinrich regarded Jean Luc, who was now fast asleep, breathing evenly and regularly.

"You've been in far more dangerous situations than this, Seigneur," he muttered. "You're not going to be killed by drunken idiots in an inn on Exmoor. It's time to go home and we will hunt the wild boar again together in the forest," and he made the sign of the cross.

20

The April sun shone warmly into the house. She sat in her room and puzzled over the Lord Lieutenant's words, but suspected the riddle was not within her knowledge to unravel. She knew she had never seen him before in her life; that twisted, scarred face would surely have stayed in her memory, so he had therefore never seen her as a servant. It was possible, however, he had met Sophie at a social gathering, as he obviously knew her father.

"Although luckily we are not dissimilar in looks," she murmured, glancing at her reflection in the mirror, "and surely he would not have paid much attention to a young girl."

But the morning remained tainted by fear and she packed her bag with clothes, drawings and money, in case she needed to hurriedly leave.

'If he returns I will go and hide in the cave by the beach,' she decided and kept a wary eye on the drive.

The door to Jean Luc's room remained obstinately shut, but at midday she saw a servant carrying away a plate of cold meat and potatoes which had not been touched.

"Has he eaten anything?" she asked.

"No, your ladyship," the footman replied, " He is too badly injured."

She remembered the chicken broths the cook in the London mansion had prepared when the Throgmorton family were ill. The fragrant smell had lingered for days and the glutinous stew had been easy to digest.

She descended to the kitchen. The flagstones had been recently scrubbed and were still wet, a task with which she had once been well acquainted. She breathed in the familiar odours of a simmering stock and hanging, aromatic, herb bundles, and found herself looking to see if the cooking pots were clean. The bright kitchen pleased her, partly because it was so different from the dismal surroundings where she had spent most of her life and partly because the servants were used to seeing her obtain food for the Blackmore family and were always very friendly.

"I would like some chicken, onions, carrots, parsley, sage and thyme," she requested the cook. The ingredients were placed on the wooden table and she quickly chopped and sliced, ignoring any curious stares and preparing the vegetables with a dexterity she had forgotten she had possessed. Footsteps suddenly sounded on the flagstones and she glanced up to see Heinrich Scheyer.

He stared at her, then at what she was doing, and appeared lost for words, whilst the cook bustled round, heating up his daily mulled wine and lifting the lid of a jar to show him that the cabbage it contained was being suitably marinated for the choucroute he had described to her.

She placed the ingredients in a pot, gave orders as to how it should be cooked and left the kitchen. She would have preferred Heinrich Scheyer not to have seen her, as only the most impoverished aristocrat would have any idea how to prepare food, and even then, she reflected, they would probably prefer to starve before doing such menial work. However, she thought that he was probably only a minor worry in comparison with whatever suspicions the Lord Lieutenant seemed to possess.

She returned several times to check on the broth and the cook ladled it into a bowl for her when it was ready. A footman carried it on a tray and she accompanied him along the corridors to Jean Luc's room.

One of the Alsatian men was standing guard and as soon as he saw her, he opened the door and she unexpectedly found herself welcomed in by Heinrich. She looked towards the bed and was horrified to see the pitiable state of Jean Luc, who was propped up on a bolster, his face haggard, his unshaven chin covered in stubble, his lips pinched thin. The bandages on his arm were spotted with blood and his nightshirt was draped oddly over his chest and one arm. His hair hung down in matted curls on to his shoulders and it was only his eyes which cheered her by retaining their usual look of alertness, even though deep shadows were beneath them.

Her enthusiasm for her chicken soup waned. She realised she had been over-optimistic in expecting him to be able to eat and stood indecisively as Heinrich indicated a chair by the bed for her, and when she did not move was amazed to find herself propelled towards it by his hand on her back.

Jean Luc did not take his eyes off her as the tray was placed in front of him.

" Heinrich said you made the soup yourself," he said in a very weak voice.

"Yes, I did," she admitted.

His hand trembled and he tried to raise the spoon to his mouth, but only succeeded in spilling its contents.

"Let me help you," she said.

"No, no leave me," he muttered, in obvious embarrassment, but she ignored him, took the spoon, refilled it and held it to his mouth. He swallowed it with difficulty and she waited, then fed him another spoonful.

"Make sure Lady Sophie has everything she needs," Heinrich said to a servant and left the room.

"I want to see Mrs Yelland in the library," she heard him say, and shortly after could hear his voice, loud and angry.

"Where is the priest? I don't think you have sent for him!"

Jean Luc stopped eating. "What's that?"

"I think that Mr Scheyer is cross with a servant," she replied.

"Shut the door," she told Werner, but even with two doors between them, she could still make out his irate tones. She had noticed his profound dislike of Mrs Yelland and, for the first time, appreciated the strength of his character and felt very relieved that he was here in the house if the Lord Lieutenant should return.

She fed Jean Luc a few more spoonfuls, then he lay back, his eyes shut, and she could see he was incapable of eating any more. The strangeness of being in his room, seated by his bed, allied to the rapid series of traumatic events which had taken place since they had set off to Exmoor the previous day, made her feel as though she was in a dream and would suddenly awake to find preparations still being made for the journey to Alsace and that nothing untoward had happened.

"Thank you, my beloved," he murmured. His head slumped on to the bolster and he fell into a deep sleep.

She looked at his face for a few minutes and then crept quietly from the room, forcing herself to confront the reality of Heinrich's insistence on calling for a priest.

That afternoon she took the bag she had packed, and walked confidently past the men guarding the front door. The rioters did not frighten her.

"They will not venture in to the estate if they haven't done so already," she told herself. "In any case, the noise has stopped and they were evidently dispersing."

It seemed almost like a summer's day as she walked through the woods to the cliff top, then down the path to the beach and the cave. She lodged the bag high up in a crevice, out of reach of the high tide, and left the seaweed-smelling cavern, its rock walls slimy with water trickling from the ground above, and emerged back into the sunshine. She wandered along the beach, scuffing her shoes against the rounded pebbles; the hot sun on her face and the blue of the sea making her feel vibrantly alive, in spite of the anxieties possessing her.

She had not swum since the autumn, but the temptation to do so now was proving irresistible and she flung off her dress and shoes and waded into the icy water in her petticoat. She dived down to the sea bed, then came up and let herself be tossed in the waves.

The bitter cold enveloped her as usual, cleansing away the violence she had seen at Heddon and the ugliness of a rioting mob. She forgot the scarred face of the Lord Lieutenant and swam backwards and forwards in the cove, her mind only on the present.

Finally, shivering, and with chattering teeth, she ran up the beach, threw her dress over her wet petticoat and retraced her path home, just as the sun was sinking low in the sky. She ran up the steps and into the hall and came face to face with Heinrich, who stared at her sodden hair and rather damp appearance.

" Have you fallen in the lake?" he asked.

"No," she replied shortly and began to walk towards the stairs, but he gripped her arm.

"What are you doing?" he asked. "Where have you been?"

"It's none of your business, Mr Scheyer," she told him bluntly.

An expression of fury on his face made her shrink away from him. He held her arm more tightly and said, " The Seigneur is very badly hurt and I do not wish you to cause any problems. Where have you been?"

She looked at him and in a moment of devilry decided to say the truth.

"I've been swimming in the sea."

He glared at her. " Are you mad?"

At that moment, an odd cackling and singing erupted from the Duchess's quarters and she suddenly realised that since her son's injury she had heard frequent sounds of jollity coming from her room.

Heinrich grimaced.

"It's a popular pastime in England," she said.

"Well, it is not here!" he retorted and finally let her go and she took the opportunity to run quickly up the stairs to her room.

21

The following day he was much stronger. She prepared chicken soup, but this time he was able to feed himself, somewhat to her disappointment. She would also have liked to have been called 'my beloved' again, even although she knew he had not been aware of what he was saying, but she was disappointed in that, as well.

His face remained unnaturally white, but his old spirit had returned and he sat in bed looking at her, she thought, in a rather similar manner to the way he had in the inn.

"You stopped me bleeding to death," he said, "and you put yourself in great danger. I didn't want you to." He stared at her. "I didn't want you to," he repeated, more forcefully. "You're ..." his voice trailed off, as though he did not wish to reveal what he thought of her.

"They were going to kill you," she said tearfully. "There were so many of them."

"We're safe here, even if the Lord Lieutenant is trying to put me in prison," he replied, smiling faintly. "You mustn't worry. Heinrich will look after us."

She could hardly hear his weakened voice and saw his eyes gradually close. She watched him sleep and sat for a long time looking at every inch of his face, trying to commit it to her memory.

Next morning, she visited him after breakfast, her spirits high in anticipation that he would be even stronger. The room was quiet. A slight draught from the window was lifting up the curtain and she noticed an odd smell in the air, an odour of decay, and wrinkled her nose slightly. She greeted him and sat down on the chair next to the bed and saw he was flushed and his eyes seemed unusually bright.

Heinrich entered the room, his manner subdued, she thought, although as he always appeared so dour, she found it difficult to tell. He went over to the hearth and riddled the logs vigorously with a poker, making them blaze more fiercely.

'Why is he now behaving like an ordinary servant and attending to the fire?' she wondered, thinking that he seemed to go from one extreme to the other and that she was still very uncertain of his position in the household. He looked at her and for once the clear grey of his eyes held a troubled expression.

"I would like you to choose some flowers for me," said Jean Luc unexpectedly. "Would you be so kind as to go to the orangery?"

"Yes, certainly," she replied, surprised by the request and unhappy to be sent on an errand almost as soon as she had arrived. She stood up regretfully and for the first time, as the two men exchanged glances, noticed the strong affection which existed between them and thought they seemed more like father and son, than servant and master, and suddenly realised the extent of Heinrich's power.

She walked desultorily through the vegetable garden to the orangery, which was situated on its far side. The westerly wind tweaked the new potato shoots sprouting in the earth, and caught her hair, making it fly out around her. She pushed open the door and found herself in a different world. A slow fire was burning in a pit in the floor and the air was hot and humid, like a July day before a thunderstorm. The large windows set in wooden frames allowed light to fall over a serried thicket of giant ferns, broad-leaved tobacco plants, myrtles and fuchsias. Pear and peach trees twined up through espaliers, vines snaked along a roof trellis and orange trees stood in square boxes, their waxy leaves glistening. A cascade of blooms trailed fragrantly from baskets suspended on wall staging and the red, pink and yellow of begonias and roses in pots were bright against a green curtain of leaves, the flower scent combining with a mustiness of wet soil to make her head swim.

She first chose arum lilies before remembering the folk lore linking white flowers and death, if brought into a house, and after much deliberation asked the gardener to cut pink roses for her.

A cry abruptly jarred the warm stillness of the air. It sounded hardly human, its sharpness muffled by the glass windows and thick vegetation. Another cry followed, a bellow of agony which so startled the gardener that he cut his finger on a thorn and drops of blood fell on to a rose petal.

She jumped in horror at the noise and the ominous sight of the spoiled flower, then rushed outside, fearful that rioters were attacking the house or that the Lord Lieutenant had returned. She looked across the vegetable garden but the only movement she could see was that of a long-tailed field mouse running through the onion plants, and she hurriedly gathered up her roses and rushed back along the path.

The hall was quiet, but the muted fragrance from the orangery clinging to her clothes and hair was suddenly obscured by an unpleasant smell of scorched flesh. Her mind seemed to work in slow motion, whilst her feet carried her swiftly across the flagstones to the door of Jean Luc's room.

154

She tried to push the memory of Heinrich stoking the fire from her memory and felt sick with nausea at the realisation that the wound had become infected and he had cauterised it. The day which had started so well had become a nightmare and she flung the roses away from her on to the ground.

Two of the men barred her way and as she stood impotently in front of them, her ears caught a slight, almost whimpering, sound and she fled in distress to the library.

She stared out of the window, blind to the view, her senses attuned to what has happening in the nearby room. The moaning stopped briefly, then resumed and she clenched her knuckles to her mouth. She heard the door open and the soft murmur of voices, then Heinrich came in to the library, looking more severe than she had ever seen him.

"You cannot visit the Seigneur today," he said. "It is not suitable."

"I want to see him," she said.

"I am sorry," he replied and she could see compassion in his eyes and realised how much more awful the morning had been for him, than for her. He turned and left the room and she listened to the sound of his steps on the stone floor, gradually fading away into the distance, towards the direction of the kitchen.

She waited until she could no longer hear him, then ran outside and stood looking at the balcony in front of the ground floor window. She clambered over the stonework, pushed up the sash and wriggled through the gap. The curtains were half pulled, most of the room was in shadow and he was alone, lying flat on his back, his arm outstretched on a square of white linen.

She crept quietly to the chair by the bed and sat down, trying to control her nausea at the odour of singed flesh, her gaze held by the curved rawness of burned skin on his upper arm. He moaned, twisting his body towards her, whilst keeping his arm straight on the linen sheet. The material of her dress rustled as she moved and he opened his eyes and looked at her.

She expected him to tell her to go, but instead he lay there, clenching his teeth so that he did not cry out. They stayed in silence for some minutes and then he moved his hand towards her dress and grasped the satin. Sweat was beading his forehead, trickling down into his eyes and she picked up a damp cloth hanging from the edge of a porcelain bowl filled with water, set on a table, and gently wiped his face.

She heard the door open behind her and guessed Heinrich had come in. She did not turn round, but placed her hand on Jean Luc's hand and saw him visibly relax.

"You're not to touch the wound," Heinrich's voice said gruffly in her ear and she nodded her head in acquiescence, very content that she was obviously not going to be evicted. He walked over and closed the window and busied himself in the room, whilst she continued to sit with Jean Luc, wiping his face, giving him sips of water from a glass and holding his hand.

The evening proved worse than the afternoon. He became hotter and hotter, his face brick-red. He moaned and shivered uncontrollably, constantly turning his body on the bed, trying not to jar the burned arm. He fell asleep at midnight and she went wearily to her own bed. She had no idea if he would live; she felt so low and dispirited it was as though her whole world had reverted to the greyness of her childhood. The candles lighting her room hardly seemed to touch the blackness of the night, which epitomised her own despair.

The next few days possessed a timeless quality, not marked by hours and minutes, but only by whether he was delirious, or not delirious. He raved like a madman, his mind often in the New World across the sea, his body trapped in pain in the confines of a manor house in Devon. Just as she had delighted in hearing his interesting descriptions about life in the unknown land, so now she discovered a dark side to his experiences there. He had filtered out the horror and the tragedy he had witnessed and had only presented her with a partial picture.

Torture appeared to be commonplace amongst the native people. Agreements were made to allow a defeated English garrison to surrender peacefully and as they left the fort they were hacked to shreds, their scalps slashed off their heads; women and children were burnt to death in their cabins. She hated to hear details of the gruesome and vivid pictures which had lingered in his memory after witnessing the atrocities; and to hear him mutter, or shriek out, about what he had seen, at the same time as having to watch him suffer with his own ghastly injury, sometimes proved too much for her to bear and she would have to abandon her post and go and breathe the clean air of the garden, or play the spinet.

Heinrich appeared stolidly unmoved by everything, she noticed.

"They were savages," he told her one day, and she could see he did not share his master's enchantment with the strange country across the sea.

She had never been so close to a man before who was lying in bed and without his usual clothes. She supervised the servants who helped care for him and made sure the room was freshly aired and a fire kept burning. Mrs Yelland was rarely seen and she was unsure if it was because Heinrich was so often in the room and she resented him, or whether she was taking the opportunity to indulge her love of the gin bottle.

To Heinrich's anger, the priest not only did not appear, but never even came on Sundays. He compensated by often praying with his men in the chapel and she did not know whether it was by the force of prayer or by Heinrich's exceptional medical skills, that Jean Luc gradually became stronger, the wound healed and lucidity replaced his incoherence.

As he recovered he became a very demanding patient. Footmen were constantly running backwards and forwards and nothing seemed to be suitable. Food was too hot or too cold and his impatience at his weakness often boiled over into anger. He was much better behaved when she was in the room and servants appeared to breath a sigh of relief when they saw her.

Preparations were again being made for the journey to Alsace and she realised that Heinrich was determined to leave as soon as possible. She knew that Jean Luc would quickly be gone and that he would soon be married. She deliberately forced herself to think of both these events and pictured herself as a hermit crab, who had pushed its head out from its shell, exposing itself to the world around it, but now needed to draw back again, to try and safeguard herself from the suffering which would surely follow. Accordingly, she drastically reduced the time she spent in his bed chamber and only allowed him the very minimum number of visits in a day. It was not a popular action, either in his eyes or in those of the servants, and even Heinrich looked questioningly at her, but she was so frightened of the abyss looming before her when she would never see him again, she knew she had to harden herself before his departure and try not to think of the closeness which had grown up between them and the way he looked at her. She had surreptitiously cut off a lock of his hair when he had been asleep and had also made a sketch of him, and these treasures were now safely stored in a locked box in her bedroom for her to keep for the rest of her life.

'At least he will never know I have deceived him,' she consoled herself. 'He will never know my wickedness.'

One afternoon, she was sitting alone at the dining table, finishing her meal and was so lost in reverie she did not notice the sound of a horse in the drive and it was only when a footman came to say that Captain

Vinnicombe was visiting and would be grateful to see her, that she discovered someone had arrived.

She hurried to the drawing room, nearly having forgotten the Vinnicombes.

"My lady," he said, bowing very low. "You have not answered my invitations and so I have come in person to see you."

"I'm sorry, sir, I did not know of any invitations," she said apologetically, suddenly wondering about a pile of ripped cards she had found in the desk drawer in the library, and pleased to see the captain, who, she thought, looked handsome, as always, in his army uniform.

"I'm returning to my regiment, the Devon and Dorset's," he said, "and I wanted very much to see you before I leave. I am sorry to hear that his Grace has been injured,"

"I am afraid he is still confined to his room," she told him.

"Is that so?" he replied, with interest. " Well, perhaps we could walk in the garden?"

She agreed, happy to walk in the fresh air after so much time spent indoors.

In his room, Jean Luc was impatiently waiting for Sarah to finish her meal and join him and halfway through the afternoon he was still waiting.

"I think I've been abandoned! Now that I've recovered, she pays me no attention," he complained semi-jokingly to Heinrich, who looked suspiciously towards the beach and sent a servant to find where she was.

"Her ladyship is entertaining in the drawing room," said the footman, on his return.

"Oh?" remarked Jean Luc sourly, "and who is she entertaining?"

"Captain Vinnicombe, I believe, your Grace," said the footman.

"What!" he exploded in anger. "Why didn't someone tell me? Would you kindly go and tell Lady Sophie that I desire the pleasure of her company immediately."

The footman left the room, then returned to say that they were no longer in the drawing room and it was thought they were walking in the garden.

"I want her found!" he shouted. "I don't want her walking in the garden with Captain Vinnicombe! Where's my clothes? I wish to get dressed," and he lurched out of bed and staggered to his feet.

"I'll go myself and look for her," said Heinrich calmly.

He stood at the top of the steps by the front door, but could see no sign of anyone. He ordered his men to scour the grounds and beach and then went to search for himself. Finally he found a gardener who had seen them near to the rose garden and he strode rapidly there, entering the enclosed courtyard just as James Vinnicombe had fallen to his knees and was professing his undying love to a rather startled Sarah.

The noise of Heinrich's shoes crunching on the gravel made them both turn towards him and Captain Vinnicombe hastily jumped to his feet, his face furious.

"How dare you intrude!" he shouted.

"My lady, the Seigneur wishes to see you," Heinrich said and she was horrified to see him put a hand to his knife and look aggressively at Captain Vinnicombe in his English military uniform.

James Vinnicombe, however, did not appear in any way intimidated and bowed low to her, saying softly,

"Good day, my lady. I hope to see you again when his Grace has left and you are more free."

Her heart sank, not only at the sadness of Jean Luc's imminent departure, but that the emptiness of her life would be exacerbated by the amorous intentions of Captain Vinnicombe.

Heinrich put his fingers to his mouth and gave a piercing whistle and several of his men almost immediately appeared in response.

"Your horse will be brought!" he said.

She was accustomed to his rudeness and stayed rooted to the spot, not wishing to leave her unwelcome admirer to the tender mercies of Heinrich, and her estimation of him rose as she saw again that he was not afraid.

"My lady, I will take you back to the house," Heinrich said curtly.

"No, I'm waiting here until Captain Vinnicombe has gone," she told him and refused to move, and they all stood together in an uneasy silence until a servant came leading a roan mare. James Vinnicombe mounted, inclined his head towards Sarah and called out, " Goodbye my sweet lady." Then he looked insolently at Heinrich, before cantering off on his horse through the rose garden.

Heinrich accompanied her back to the house, his face expressionless. He escorted her to Jean Luc's room where she was surprised to find him not in bed, but sitting on a chair in the window, dressed in a coat and breeches. She was also surprised to see the annoyance on his face and wished her cheeks did not feel so flushed, as he stared suspiciously at her.

"I had no idea Captain Vinnicombe was paying a call. In future I would like to be told of the arrival of any visitor," he said coldly, " in case I don't wish them to be here."

"Where did you find them?" he asked Heinrich in Alsatian.

"In the rose garden," he replied in his native tongue.

" What were they doing in the rose garden?" Jean Luc continued, in Alsatian. "There are not any flowers there yet."

"He was kneeling on the ground in front of Lady Sophie," said Heinrich. "There is no question of a duel," he added hastily. "He was behaving perfectly correctly, although, if I may say so, rather strangely."

"What was she doing?" asked Jean Luc, and even although Sarah could not understand the words, she was shocked to hear the venom in his voice.

"She was standing there," replied Heinrich, shrugging his shoulders.

"Have you chased him off the estate?" shouted Jean Luc.

"Yes, Seigneur. His horse was brought and he left."

"I would have preferred him to have been given a few blows to help him on his way!" replied Jean Luc hotly.

"I realise that Seigneur, but Lady Sophie insisted on waiting until he left and I did not feel it was suitable to do so in front of her," Heinrich said. "Also, this is England, not France, and there have already been enough problems on Exmoor."

Jean Luc pulled a face. "Thank you," he said. "You have behaved correctly, as always."

"Would you like to sit with me, madam?" he asked, as Heinrich left the room. "Or would you find it too boring after your romantic afternoon in the rose garden?"

She glanced apprehensively at him. He seemed to be very petulant, she thought and presumed it was because she had been spending her afternoon with someone else and not that he was in any way jealous of Captain's Vinnicombe's attentions to her. She looked at his dark eyes and serious face and wondered again if he was sulking. She nearly giggled, but managed to restrain herself, very content to be in the now familiar surroundings of his bedchamber and very content that he was so much improved he could sit opposite her and even indulge in some sort of sulking fit.

He dismissed the two footmen remaining in the room, and he and Sarah sat alone. She maintained a dignified silence, knowing that he was quick to anger, but that his temper just as quickly died away.

"I think I'll return to bed," he remarked, his voice sounding shaky.

"Shall I call a footman?" she asked.

"No, I can manage," he snapped and walked across to the bed, on which he collapsed heavily. She bent down to pull the coverlet over him and as she did so he put his good arm around her and held her to him.

"What are you doing?" she said in alarm.

He tightened his grip and pulled her roughly on to his lap, his face a few inches from her own .

"So, what were you doing with Captain Vinnicombe?" he demanded.

"I was doing nothing, sir," she replied crossly. "Let me go!"

"He did not kiss you?" he asked, his eyes devouring her.

"No, he certainly did not!" she retorted, struggling to free herself and thinking he was obviously not so weak after all, as she could not manage it.

"More fool him!" he muttered and kissed her passionately on her lips.

She shut her eyes and felt the same exquisite sensation she had experienced before in the carriage, and so many times in her dreams. He finally stopped kissing her on the mouth, only to kiss her repeatedly on her face and hair and breasts.

You're so beautiful and so kind and sweet. My darling Sophie," he murmured as he let her go and she escaped to the chair by the bed.

Her whole body was aroused and at the same time, she felt a rush of bitterness towards him that he should behave so improperly towards her when he was about to return home to be married. The afternoon had been emotionally extremely demanding and she shrank from revealing to him her true feelings, knowing that in order to survive the bleak days to come she had to protect herself from any extra distress. Her love of him meant she could not be trifled with, like a toy, and abandoned when he left. She found herself incapable of believing his words and looked agitatedly at him, her face flushed, her bodice slightly undone.

I'm sorry. I took advantage of you," he said, "Can I hope that you have some affection for me?"

She did not reply, just gazed at him.

" I've shocked you, I can see, but there's no hurry. I have some matters to take care of first," he said, his voice calming her, as it always did.

"I think you are feeling somewhat better," she murmured.

"Yes, I think so," he said, smiling. " I would like a glass of wine. Would it be possible to pour me one?" and he indicated the decanter and glass on the table.

She looked at him, mistrusting his motives and suspecting it was an excuse to bring her within his reach again, to kiss her. She stood up and went to the hall and returned with Elsie, who was reputed to be the only lady prize fighter in England.

"Would you please pour a drink for his Grace," she said, then curtsied and left the room, leaving Jean Luc staring after her in disappointment.

22

The next day revealed the unpredictable vagaries of the spring weather. The warm sunshine was replaced by a biting north wind, which brought flurries of snow and sleet. The house was quiet and still, and huge fires blazed in every hearth. Jean Luc paced weakly around his room and even ventured across the hall, and she could see he was much improved.

The wild and windy weather delighted her. The tempestuous North Devon climate entranced her almost as much as the craggy cliffs and coves. She chafed at being denied her walks for so long and ached to see the beach and the wood, caught in the grip of the last cold clutches of the year.

"Would you mind if I walk to the sea?" she asked Jean Luc. " I will take someone with me."

"It looks as though the snow will get worse," he replied unhappily.

"I'll only be gone a short time," she said. "I feel the need for fresh air."

"Well, as long as you take two servants, and come straight back if it worsens," he agreed reluctantly, "and when I'm better we can explore the countryside together."

Clutching their thick cloaks, she and Jenny trod carefully over slippery ice, as they wandered upwards through the wood, closely followed by a footman. Snowflakes fluttered like lost birds down through the narrow chinks between the trees, alighting on frozen clusters of primroses and poker-stiff daffodils, 'lent lilies,' according to Jenny, who playfully shook them and reached out and pulled at catkins trembling on drooping twigs.

"Look at these little lamb's tails," she called.

Wind cadences rose and fell across the trees, breathing movement into inert bodies, making them dance in stiff harmony, orchestrated by the growing storm.

They emerged from the ghostly white of the wood to meet the full force of the wind on the exposed headland and found themselves almost blown down the steep descent to the beach. The butterfly bush was dusted with snow and piles of limpet-covered seaweed were rapidly being transformed into weirdly beautiful shapes. Breakers roared onto the pebbles and the sea was a devil's cauldron of bubbling surf, beneath a glowering sky of hunched black clouds.

"We'd better return," said Sarah. "The weather's worsening."

She looked towards the far headland and for a moment thought she saw a flag and a mast. She blinked and it was gone.

"What was that over there?" she said, pointing.

Jenny and John, the footman, gazed in the same direction. Then, suddenly, in the middle of mountainous seas, a ship could be seen, being tossed about helplessly, its masts dipping so low they almost touched the water.

"They're trying to reach the harbour at Ilfracombe," said John.

The ship was lost to view, then abruptly reappeared, skating madly along the crest of a wave.

"It's running against the sea!" he exclaimed. "It would do better to turn and try and go back down the coast. If it doesn't make it into harbour quickly it'll be one for the wreckers!"

"The wreckers?" she asked curiously. " Who are they?"

"If a ship is wrecked, people can go and help themselves to what comes ashore, as long as everyone is dead," he replied. "Sometimes wreckers walk along the cliffs with lanterns to make out it's a safe haven. They lure the ship onto the rocks and kill anyone who reaches land, so that they can have all the goods."

Her eyes widened.

"How cruel!" she exclaimed. "Do smugglers do that?" her opinion of John Buzzacott starting to tumble.

"No," he said. "Smugglers are quite different. They're bringing in wine and spirits and don't want to pay the duty. The wreckers are wicked. They kill innocent people. Sailors hate them, as they know they could be the ones who are being brought onto the rocks. There's been a lot of wrecks round here. The reefs off this beach are really dangerous."

She looked again towards the sea and prayed that the ship adrift on the terrifying waves would reach the harbour safely. She felt sad thinking of the people onboard and it soured her enjoyment in her icy fairy-land. She turned away from the beach and climbed back up the cliff path, against the wind, the sound of the breakers booming in her ears until the shelter of the woods was reached.

At Wildercombe House, Jean Luc was sitting in the chair by the window, watching the gardens, and he smiled as he saw Sarah and her companions hurrying across the lawns.

"She's coming back!" he said to Heinrich. "The snow's falling more heavily."

"Yes, Seigneur, she's returning," he replied reassuringly.

A few minutes later, Sarah came smiling into the room, carrying branches with catkins hanging from them.

"A present!" she said to Jean Luc, her face glowing from the exertion of walking in the cold.

"Thank you," he said, looking at them with pleasure, whilst she thought Heinrich seemed to be trying to keep a straight face.

"I've never seen the sea so rough!" she exclaimed. " There's a ship by the headland which looks in danger of sinking. Is it possible to help them?"

"I'm afraid not," he replied. "There's nothing we can do. It needs to shelter in a harbour somewhere. It's in the hand of God!"

She went upstairs to change her clothes and he resumed his walk backwards and forwards in his room and across the hall, and that evening, for the first time since his injury, he ate at the dining table. Outside the window, the north wind was steadily increasing in strength, a dull roar howling through the trees and the garden. The flurries of sleet and snow were now a thickly falling blizzard and sent her scurrying from window to window, watching in excitement.

23

That night she lay in her warm bed, listening to the gale battering the house, saddened by the thought of the ship at the mercy of the waves.

'May the poor wretches on board find a harbour,' she prayed and drifted off to a sleep which was frequently disturbed by the violence of the storm raging outside.

In the early hours of the morning she awoke. The darkness was soft around her; a lull in the wind made the room seem strangely quiet and she was drowsily closing her eyes when she caught the sound of people speaking on the landing. Surprised, she strained to make out the words and could hear a woman say, "Be careful, his Grace is still here and some of his men..." The curt, irritable tone sounded like Mrs Yelland, but she could not be sure. Snippets of a man's conversation followed, "We'll put any stuff... when he's gone... I'll keep.."

She tried to listen as the voices faded away into the distance and felt uneasy. It was very odd to hear anyone talking in the middle of the night and Mrs Yelland's sour and unfriendly manner always unnerved her.

She crept to the door, gingerly turned the handle and peered out. The landing was deserted. She tiptoed along the carpet in her bare feet and noticed in the gloom that the door to the attics was ajar. She remembered her fright when she had stepped back into the housekeeper when exploring the house and was not anxious to repeat the experience.

She stood, undecided, shivering from the cold draught of air blowing down the stairs. She listened intently, but could hear nothing and wondered if the people had come from upstairs and were now somewhere below her, and she waited by the banisters to see if anyone appeared in the hall below. Minutes passed and she was just on the point of returning to bed, when she heard footsteps again and the sound of a door creaking shut near the servants' quarters. She looked through the banister rails and saw two shadowy figures walking quietly across the stone flags. One resembled Mrs Yelland, the other was a thick-set, burly man who appeared to be carrying a lantern.

'It's from the attic,' she thought. 'What are they doing?'

John's words on the beach came back to her. "The wreckers use lanterns to draw the ship inshore."

She saw again the room packed with unusually carved furniture and rich trinkets.

' No,' she said to herself. 'No. Mrs Yelland would not be involved with wreckers.'

But the seed of suspicion was implanted in her mind and she watched the couple as they disappeared into the far wing of the house.

'I wonder if they're going to the cliffs ?'she thought. ' I can't disturb anyone in the middle of the night and, in any case, Mrs Yelland is probably doing nothing wrong. What should I do?'

The harrowing picture of the ship, dangerously close to the reefs, was still with her and she impulsively decided to follow them and see what was happening. She darted back to her bedchamber, slipped on her outdoor shoes, threw a shawl over her shoulders, then ran downstairs to the hall. She slid back the stiff iron bolt on the front door and stepped out into a suddenly raging wind, showering snowflakes onto her face and clothes.

It was impossible to see the garden or the figures in the storm and the darkness, and the ground near to her shone eerily white, but she did not hesitate, knowing that if they were wreckers, they would head to the cliffs. She floundered across the lawn, her shoes sinking into a clinging wetness, and stumbled blindly up the path through the woods, the bitter cold penetrating her shawl, her sodden night dress flapping unpleasantly against her legs. She brushed the snow from her face and realised her hands and feet were numb, but inured to physical discomfort from her life in the kitchen she carried on up the hill, not even considering that she should return.

She reached the cliff top and could again hear voices, not just one but several, sounding as though a group of men was very close by.

"Swing it, Ben! Higher! Come on!"

'What am I going to do? I can't stop them,' she thought, knowing that it was too late to go back to the house for help.

She could see the lantern now, twinkling like a firefly through the blackness. Flurries of snow obscured it, then it flickered as the snow lessened. She stared towards the sea, which she knew was in front of her, but although she could hear waves crashing and breaking, she could see nothing. The ship, if it was there, was invisible.

'Perhaps it's reached Ilfracombe,' she hoped, then bent down to look for a large stone, thinking that she might be able to break the lantern.

At Wildercombe House, her departure had not gone unnoticed. No one had seen the man and woman leave by the kitchen entrance, but the unbolting of the front door had been heard by the two men Heinrich had stationed as lookouts on the second floor, in case the Lord Lieutenant returned or rioters attacked the house. Sarah had not known they were there and Hans and Gunther were sleepily downing their tankards of ale when the noise startled them and they looked out of the window, just in time to see her run across the lawns. They had stared in disbelief, then Gunther had rushed to the west wing to rouse Heinrich, who hurriedly threw on his clothes and ran out cursing into the storm.

Hans woke Jean Luc who struggled to make sense of what he was saying, then leaped, horrified, out of bed and quickly dressed before making his way across the garden towards the wood.

....

It was difficult to find a stone. Her hands were frozen and clumsy as she scrabbled in the snow, her nightdress and shawl clinging in ice-cold folds to her shivering body, the wind screaming round her ears.

Heinrich and Gunther came out of the wood and immediately saw her. Her clothes blended almost perfectly with the surrounding white, but her red hair was visible almost directly in front of them and Heinrich ran soundlessly towards her, the snow muffling his steps.

She screamed as a man roughly hauled her up from the ground, his hand almost crushing her arm. She staggered and as she fell towards him, realised that it was Heinrich.

"They've got a lantern and they're trying to wreck the ship!" she shouted, her words blown away by the wind. He ignored what she was saying, picked her up and threw her over his shoulder, then raced back down the path. She shrieked and thumped his back with her hand.

"Stop! They're trying to wreck the ship!" she kept calling. "Stop!"

He paid no attention and ran sure-footedly down the hill, as though very accustomed to snowy terrain. At the bottom of the path he met Jean Luc and Hans, but did not slow and kept running until he reached the house, striding swiftly to the drawing room and dumping her on the settle in front of a glowing fire.

Jean Luc hurried in, breathless, his face white. He pulled the bell sharply to summon servants, then knelt on the floor next to her, looking shocked as he felt her wet night dress and touched her frozen hands.

She struggled to speak, "They've got a lantern, to wreck the ship. We must help them." Her voice faltered and she lay shivering and shaking, her hair bright against the extreme pallor of her face.

"A lantern?" he queried.

She tried again. "They're going to wreck the ship!" she said through chattering teeth.

"Bring dry clothes immediately," he ordered, " and covers. Shall I send for the doctor at Ilfracombe?" he asked Heinrich.

"No, she needs to be warmed slowly now. It'll be too late if we wait for him. Heat some wine," he told a servant.

"Please help the people," begged Sarah.

He glanced at her, then at Heinrich.

"Did you see any sign of a lantern"? he asked in French.

"No, Seigneur, only Lady Sophie," Heinrich replied, also in French.

"And the ship? Was it still there?"

"I don't know. It was so dark and it was snowing. I couldn't see anything. I don't want to risk the men's lives Perhaps it's a trap to make us leave the house. If not, I expect it's only the imagination of Lady Sophie," he continued, in the same language.

Sarah was furious to hear him say that.

"It's not true! It's not my imagination! I'm not lying!" she cried out, speaking fluently in French.

The two men stared at her.

"I'm not lying!" she shrieked hysterically, her head throbbing, tears pouring down her cheeks. The words were familiar, she remembered saying them a very long time ago. She remembered the pain which had followed them, the beating. Jean Luc moved nearer, his dark eyes riveted on her face.

"Don't hit me! Don't hit me" she screamed again in French, then covered her face with her hands and shrank back against the settle.

"Cherie. I'm not going to hit you! Not ever!" He grasped her hands and Sarah, exhausted, sobbed uncontrollably.

"Change your mistress's clothes," he said grimly to Jenny. "I'll wait outside" and he left the room, followed by Heinrich, who remarked,

" I did not know that Lady Sophie spoke French."

" Neither did I," he replied, in evident surprise.

When they returned to the drawing room, logs had been put on the fire and it was blazing more fiercely. Sarah was shivering violently in the covers which Jenny had wrapped around her and Heinrich knelt down and vigorously rubbed her feet. A servant came in with a glass of hot wine and she gratefully gulped the liquid, then lay back in a daze.

Heinrich finished warming her feet and wrapped them in the coverlet, then did the same with her hands. The indignity of being slung over his shoulder, like a sack of potatoes, and now having him rub her feet and hands, whilst knowing that it had all been in vain and that she had failed to stop the wreckers, made her tears flow again.

"Calm, ma cherie, Calm. It's God who will decide what will happen to the boat!" said Jean Luc, sitting down heavily on a chair, his face bloodless.

His words seemed to be coming from a long way off. They sounded strange to her and it was difficult to understand what he was saying. Her brain felt on fire, her hands and feet were stinging so painfully, it was as though she had been walking through beds of nettles, not the numbing cold of snow. She closed her eyes to try and stop the fever which was seizing her mind, and slumped into an exhausted sleep which was unpleasantly filled with abstract ideas of fear and abandonment, hurt and love, all mingling together as she ran her finger across hoar frost gleaming on a window.

"Is she alright?" Jean Luc asked in concern to Heinrich.

" Yes, Seigneur. She's alright now." He continued to rub her hands and then her arms, pushing up one of the sleeves of her nightdress, and stopped for a moment as he saw long red weals marking her fair skin. He looked questioningly at Jean Luc, then pushed up the other sleeve to reveal similar scars.

"She's been very badly beaten!" he exclaimed.

"I think so," Jean Luc replied angrily.

Heinrich gently placed the covers over Sarah.

"She will be fine now" he said. "A little later and the cold would have killed her." He stood up and Jean Luc also rose and embraced him.

"I'm tired of Devon" he said. "We will return home soon."

"Yes, Seigneur," replied Heinrich and returned gratefully to his bed.

Jean Luc sat back on the chair and watched Sarah as she slept, then fell asleep himself, whilst servants crept in and out of the room from time to time, making up the fire.

He woke in the early hours of the morning just as the light was beginning to show at the edges of the curtains. He looked at Sarah, who was still sleeping soundly on the settle, one arm flung out from the covers, her face very pale. He stared at her for a few minutes, then quietly rose to his feet and left the room.

"Please sit with her," he told a servant. " On no account is she to leave the house or be left alone."

He breakfasted, then went to his work room for the first time since his injury, a pleased expression on his face as he saw some of the crates of specimens he had collected and renewed his acquaintance with the garter snake.

He left the door open and kept an eye on the drawing room and was rewarded by suddenly seeing Sarah emerge in her night dress, her feet bare, clutching the coverlet around her. She ran across the hall, but he came quickly out of his room and stood in her path.

"Are you better, madam?" he asked.

"Yes, thank you," she mumbled sheepishly, looking more at the flagstones than at him.

"Would you like to change and join me for breakfast?" he asked, in a polite, controlled voice.

"Yes," she murmured, and he stood aside to let her climb the stairs.

She rapidly dressed, refusing to answer Jenny's questions, then reluctantly descended to the dining room and, as she entered, saw that he was speaking to Mrs Yelland at the far end of the room in the window bay. She stopped in the doorway and turned to go back into the hall, but he had already seen her.

"No, come in. I've nearly finished," he said. "Please start without me."

She sat unhappily at the table and took a piece of toast and waited while a footman poured her a dish of tea. She did not look towards him. She did not need to. She had come to know him so well over the past few weeks that she knew he would be furious with her. She glanced instead with distaste at Mrs Yelland's long, angular face, her sallow complexion, her black hair almost hidden by her lace mob cap.

'Was she the person she had seen last night?' she wondered. The voice had sounded like her. The figure had been a similar size and shape. However, she was still not completely sure.

"When I have gone, I would like my mother to be taken on short walks in the garden. It's not good for her to remain sitting in the house every day," he was saying, very clearly putting his affairs in order before his departure.

"Yes, your Grace, replied Mrs Yelland meekly.

He sounded like his old self, she thought and noticed that he was standing without any hint of weakness. It made her so incredibly happy to see him alive and restored to health that it seemed immaterial to her that he would be angry with her.

Somewhere, deep inside her, were terrible feelings and emotions she knew she was unable to control or understand. Once she allowed them

171

to surface it would be like Pandora's box opening and she would be incapable of acting in a rational, normal way. She nibbled her toast and tried to push every thought, every recollection, that hurt her, away into the farthest recess of her mind, refusing to acknowledge their presence.

Tears stung her eyes and she concentrated on looking angrily at Mrs Yelland, but somehow, unbidden and unwanted, came all the awful memories of being abandoned by someone she had loved and who had cared for her. It was so long ago she was not even sure it had really happened. There was just a hollow bitterness inside her and she knew that when she had been savagely beaten, there had been nobody to protect her. She suddenly remembered Sophie dying in her arms and then, try as she might to stop it, came the awful realisation that she was about to be abandoned again.

She attempted to reason with herself. 'He must go before he finds me out,' but knew, in reality, that what was in her best interest was not necessarily what she desired. She tried to think about his future marriage, but only found herself becoming more distressed.

"That's all for now, Mrs Yelland," she heard him say and discovered she was nibbling absentmindedly at her fingers, having finished the toast.

The housekeeper walked out of the room without glancing at her, and she frowned unhappily at her retreating back.

"Don't you like Mrs Yelland?" Jean Luc asked when she was out of earshot.

She did not answer, just looked at him.

"Silence speaks louder than words is the English expression," he remarked.

She had avoided looking out at the gardens, as it evoked the previous night too painfully, but as he seated himself at the table, her eye was drawn to the glistening, white landscape and she wondered if the ship had made it to harbour, or if the wreckers had succeeded.

'The purity of the snow contrasts with the evil of men,' she reflected sombrely.

She was surprised to find that he still appeared remarkably calm. She had expected his usual, explosive anger and wondered if he thought she was so foolish it was not worth his while to even become annoyed with her.

He said a short prayer, helped himself to several rashers of bacon and started eating, then looked questioningly at her.

"Can you even begin to tell me why you decided to run out alone into a blizzard in the middle of the night in your nightdress?" he asked, in a tone of exasperation.

"I saw two people leave the house with a lantern and I thought perhaps they were wreckers. I didn't have time to properly dress and I didn't want to wake you."

He chewed his food while continuing to look at her.

"If Heinrich had not caught you, you would have died!"

"I didn't know it was snowing like that," she said. "Then it was too late and I didn't realise it would be so cold."

"You deliberately disobeyed me!" he shouted. "You knew I would never let you do such a thing. You also thought I would not help this wretched ship! So you took it upon yourself to do as you wished, as you always do!" He stood up and glared at her.

"I'm sorry," she murmured.

"I think I've heard that before," he shouted. "Who were these people? God knows what you thought you saw."

She hesitated. "I did not know the man, but..."

"Yes," he said impatiently.

"I thought the woman was Mrs Yelland, but I can't be sure," she whispered so that the two footmen could not hear.

"Mrs Yelland?" he exclaimed. "You think my housekeeper is a wrecker!"

"I don't know," she replied. "At the top of the woods there were more people and I was looking for a stone to smash the lantern. Then Heinrich came."

He stared at her in horror. "You were going to break the lantern!" he bellowed, so loudly that the cook dropped the cake she was making in the kitchen.

She could not completely catch his muttered reply, but thought he was wondering if he should marry someone called Catherine de Montfort.

'You must know who you're marrying, sir,' she reflected tartly to herself.

"You've got more lives than a cat!" he bellowed again. "If it hadn't been for Heinrich you would be dead, either from the cold or from attacking a group of men!" His shouting, however, did not frighten her at all, and she started to worry that being so angry would harm his recovery.

"Please, sir, calm yourself!" she said. "It was very stupid of me! I didn't think!"

He came and sat on the chair next to her and tentatively touched her hair with his hand.

" I don't know what I've done to be given you back, yet again, madam, but I intend never to let you out of my sight!" his voice sounded choked with emotion. She did not know what to make of his words and just looked at him.

"You're not to leave this house, unless you ask me first," he said, more quietly. "You're not to even go into the garden without asking me!"

"But," she protested, and he cut her words short, saying bluntly, "I don't want to hear anything more."

" Do you know what happened to the ship?" she enquired, in the long silence that followed.

"I know nothing of the boat," he said crossly, but pulled the bell and a nervous-looking footman entered.

"Please send someone to the cliffs to see what's happened to the ship that was there yesterday," he said.

"May I ask when you are departing?" she asked, wanting very much to know the answer and emboldened because she could see that, as usual, his temper had exhausted itself quickly.

"You want me to be gone?" he enquired, surprising her by the jealous sound to his voice.

"No," she replied softly, struggling not to cry, her nerves stretched to breaking point by the trauma of the night and the present, rather demanding conversation.

"Will you miss me when I'm not here?" he asked.

She looked at him, keeping her face and eyes expressionless, trying not to reveal any of the maelstrom of emotions which were sweeping through her.

"You want me to be gone?" he asked again, very curtly, almost as though he was desperate to hear her say she did not, for her to show him she would be very unhappy if he left.

She continued to stare at him. His face was becoming a blur. The room was spinning. A roaring noise echoed in her ears and she slumped to the floor.

He shouted out in horror, "No!" and tried to catch her as she fell. But he was too late and she lay on the floor, her eyelids fluttering. He ran to the door shouting for help and then ran back to her and knelt on the floor, repeatedly touching her face and hands.

"Sophie! Sophie! Please… My darling!"

She could hear him, as though from a very long way off and struggled to sit up, but her limbs seemed paralysed and she had no idea how long she lay there. She was unable to see; she felt herself being carried and knew she was lying on the couch. Vaguely she knew he was there. She could feel a hand touch her face and could distantly hear voices. Then the faintness passed and she could see clearly again.

She raised herself into a sitting position and saw with annoyance that Heinrich was also there. He might have saved her life in the night, but she had not wanted him to do so and felt that he had treated her very rudely, as always. He saw her look sourly at him and he looked equally sourly back at her.

"I am sorry I shouted," said Jean Luc. "Are you recovered?"

"Yes, thank you," she replied.

"Good day, my lady" said Heinrich and walked very briskly from the room, followed by servants carrying the assortment of hartshorn, cordials and water which had been brought in for her revival.

Jean Luc came to sit next to her on the couch and said solemnly,

"I was teasing you. I should not have done and it was very wrong of me when you were not feeling well. I would be very pleased if you would accompany me to France."

She stared at him, blinking in amazement and so astonished she found it difficult to breathe.

"You will, of course, be able to bring your own maid who will travel in the coach with you. Many people visit the continent these days and it will be good for your education. You can learn French. But I was forgetting, you already speak it."

"No, I don't," she said, wondering what he was talking about.

"Yes, as you wish, my dear," he quickly replied, with a puzzled expression, as though not wishing to contradict or upset her in any way.

"I don't want to leave you here alone," he continued. "I don't feel it's suitable."

'He's getting married,' she thought in confusion. 'Why does he want to take me with him?' She was so astonished and so overwhelmed by his suggestion, that she could feel the faintness starting to possess her again.

"Have I surprised you?" he asked.

"Yes," she replied, hardly able to speak.

"Do you go to London on the way?" she asked, realising the impossible situation she would find herself in if he wanted to visit the Throgmortons en route.

"No, I'm afraid we're not going to London and Dover, like most travellers. I have arranged to set sail from South Devon, from the village of Babbacombe, near Torre Quay, and a French ship will take us to St Malo. I've had to pay dearly for it, as the French don't like venturing too near the English coast, even though the war is now over."

"Yes," she replied, light-headed with shock and acutely conscious that the only sensible decision would be to say no. "I would be delighted to accompany you."

He seemed to breathe a sigh of relief, as though he had thought it would be very difficult to persuade her. "That's settled then," he said. "Perhaps you could start arranging your packing. I know it's very short notice, but when we arrive at my home in Alsace, you can have whatever you want or need. It doesn't matter if you're not adequately prepared."

At that moment, the sound of running footsteps could be heard in the hall and the footman who had been sent to the beach appeared, out of breath.

"Your Grace! " he exclaimed. "The ship!"

"Yes, what is it?" asked Jean Luc.

"It's been wrecked on the headland. There's bodies everywhere and bits of the ship! There's hundreds of people from Ilfracombe looking for valuables. There's not a soul left alive!"

"Oh!" gasped Sarah. "Oh no!"

"Keep calm, my dear," said Jean Luc, placing his hand on hers. "I'd better go and see, but you're to stay here! It won't be a pretty sight. Do you understand? You're not to disobey me."

He walked towards the door and across the hall and she went to the window and watched as a servant brought his horse to the front steps. He mounted it with difficulty, holding his arm awkwardly, and rode off in the direction of the cliffs, accompanied by Heinrich, also on horseback. The snow's pristine beauty was tainted for her by the knowledge of the unfortunate ship and the poor wretches who had been on board, now lying dead on the beach, and she went sadly up to her bedchamber and asked Jenny to start packing her clothes for a long trip.

24

The beach was a scene of complete devastation. Shattered planks and debris lay strewn across the sand. On the jagged reefs, partly exposed above the water, the bare-timbered skeleton of the ship was grating backwards and forwards against the rocks as the waves shifted it. Naked bodies, spread-eagled over pebbles and seaweed, were being trampled on, or ignored by, the hundreds of people who had converged on the cove and who were fighting and jostling to retrieve any valuables they could find. The living and the dead were incongruously juxtaposed together in a bright tableau of blue sea and sky and snow-flecked sand, tipsily stained port-red with blood in places. When Jean Luc appeared on the cliff top the frenzied looting abruptly halted and there was silence.

"Carry on!" he shouted down. "You can take what you want!"

The gruesome foraging was resumed and he and Heinrich dismounted and walked down the steep path. By the butterfly bush lay the body of a young woman, clutching a baby. Her skull had been smashed, her face was unrecognisable. A little girl lay a few steps away, her fair hair streaked with blood, her features terribly disfigured. Jean Luc stood and looked at them, anger on his face.

"They're way above the tide line," he said to Heinrich "They had escaped the shipwreck and were climbing the path when they were attacked. There were wreckers here last night! Thank God you found Sophie. They would have killed her as well!"

He and Heinrich walked along the beach, but it was very apparent that no one had survived. They had either drowned or been brutally slaughtered. They returned to Wildercombe House and carts were sent to take the corpses to the graveyard in Ilfracombe for a decent Christian burial and then they stood in the drawing room, drinking a glass of mulled wine, and as Sarah came down the stairs she could smell the spicy fragrance and hear them talking quietly.

They stopped speaking as she entered the room.

"Was anyone saved?" she asked.

"No," said Jean Luc shortly, clearly not wishing to elaborate.

"Lady Sophie is accompanying us to France," he told Heinrich.

"I will make arrangements for more pack horses," Heinrich muttered, frowning, and left the room.

"Can you remember anything more about the two people you saw? They were carrying a lantern, you said?" His expression was very severe and she realised what a ghastly sight it must have been on the beach and that now he believed her.

"No, I don't think so," she murmured, after a slight moment of hesitation.

"Do you know something else?" he questioned again, looking suspiciously at her.

She stood pensively for a few seconds, then said, "The attic room had a lantern in it. The attic room where there is all the unusual furniture and jewellery."

"What attic is that?" he asked. "Do you mean here in this house?"

"Yes," she said. "Mrs Yelland told me not to go in it ever again."

"Did she?" he exclaimed in annoyance. "Will you show me?"

"Yes," said Sarah and they walked together across the hall and up the stairs to the landing. She pushed open the small door and then climbed the dark wooden steps leading to the top floor, the musty air no longer smelling of exotic fragrances. She was very aware of him so close to her in the confined space and knew instinctively that he felt the same.

"I've never been up here before," he said, looking round with interest as she opened the door of the attic to reveal a completely empty room.

"It's all gone!" she exclaimed, as somehow she had already expected. "It was filled with furniture and painting and jewellery and there was a large lantern here," and she touched the wall next to her.

"I find it strange to think of you here in the house, while I had no idea of your existence," he remarked, and went back on to the landing and opened the door to the parapet. He stepped out into the wind and the cold, and gazed at the snowy gardens and the blue ribbon of sea in the distance. She remembered her fear of the height and stayed in the shelter of the doorway, whilst he peered over the parapet and looked across at the flat roof adjacent to their ledge.

"There's a ladder over there," he remarked. "Why's that?"

He hung over the wall and exclaimed, "There's another ladder, but you can't see it. It's set back into the stone," and then terrified her by sitting astride it, swinging his leg over and lowering himself down.

"What are you doing? Stop!" she cried.

"Don't worry! It's quite safe! There's a proper ladder here," he called out.

He climbed down, jumped onto the flat roof and walked across it, calling out that he had found another ladder behind the next parapet. He

178

disappeared and she was left alone, clinging onto the doorjamb for support and preferring not to look down.

After what seemed like an eternity, he suddenly appeared in the garden below, waving and shouting. She did not dare approach the edge and felt afraid, left alone in the dingy corridor, redolent of decay, the wide expanse of leaden sky in front of her. She hastily ran back down the stairs and reached the hall just as he was coming in the front door.

"I think it was intended for a priest to be able to hide, or flee. All the old houses owned by Catholics, have escape routes. The ladders are set back, so that no one can see them, either from below or above, and link up to a tunnel under the garden. It is still against the law to have priests celebrate a mass, but it is not generally enforced."

She had no idea about the persecution of Catholics, but could see he was excited about finding the ladders and reaching the ground by the outside of the house.

"Ask Mrs Yelland to come to the library," he told a servant.

She retreated to the drawing room, guiltily worried about what was going to happen and still not sure that Mrs Yelland was one of the wreckers.

She saw her walk across the hall and into the library and heard Jean Luc say coldly,

"Where were you last night, Mrs Yelland? The other servants answered the bell when Lady Sophie was 'indisposed'."

"I'm afraid I was asleep, your Grace and did not hear it," she replied confidently.

"Can you tell me about the attic room which was filled with furniture and which is now bare?" he asked.

"There's no mystery there. The furniture has been used in different rooms of the house," she said.

"Why did you tell Lady Sophie not to go up there?" he enquired.

"I was afraid she might hurt herself, sir, roaming all over the house in odd corners."

"I must say this to you, Mrs Yelland. I'm not happy with your behaviour. A woman was seen escorting a man with a lantern from this house shortly before the shipwreck and she closely resembled you. I'm in two minds as to whether to dismiss you!"

"Please, your Grace, I've not done anything wrong. I take every care with the Duchess," Sarah was upset to hear her plead.

"Yes, I must say that you do," he conceded.

"Please, I beg of you, don't dismiss me!" she begged, sobbing.

Sarah now felt distraught and could not bear to think she had caused anyone to suffer, even the unpleasant housekeeper.

"I'm leaving in three days' time, so I will give you the benefit of the doubt in this instance. But be warned, Mrs Yelland, if there is ever any suspicion again towards you in this matter, you'll be dismissed!" he said angrily.

The housekeeper walked back across the hall and glanced into the drawing room as she passed. Her eyes met those of Sarah, frightening her by the hatred she saw there. She shuddered and felt relieved that she appeared to be leaving soon and would, at least, not be left alone with her.

'I have now made an enemy,' she thought. 'She knows it was me who saw her,' and she shuddered again.

She ran up to her bedchamber and sat at her writing desk in the window, contemplating both the view and the undreamt-of prospect of travelling to France. The snow was starting to thaw, green patches were emerging on the lawns, droplets were quivering on ice tendrils hanging above the window, and the lake, as it so often did, mirrored both the greyness of the day and her anxiety.

" No one has discovered my secret here. What's going to happen to me now? I'm as mad as the Duchess," she rebuked herself. "How can I possibly think of going to France? What I need to do is stop being Lady Sophie Throgmorton and somehow become the person I was before." She touched the rich softness of her dress. "I've become used to this," she mused. "I don't want to be a kitchen maid again."

She opened her locket and gazed thoughtfully at the picture.

"I don't think you abandoned me. Someone did, but I don't think it was you." Then Jean Luc's face came into her mind. "And why, sir, are you taking me to France with you? You are marrying someone. Why burden yourself with me?"

She pictured his dark eyes and hair and sturdy build and was surprised to find herself still thinking about him as the sun shone low above the trees, yellowing the sky in a pale imitation of a summer sunset. She pinched herself, to put an end to such thoughts, and summoned Jenny, who came in with an expression more suitable for a funeral.

"I can take a servant with me," said Sarah, guessing why she was so miserable. "Would you like to come?" and was gratified by her subsequent shrieks of delight.

"I'll go and ask his Grace," she said, her spirits lightening at the idea of the lively Jenny being with her in a foreign land, and she descended to the hall, managing to avoid glancing at Mrs Yelland standing at the front door.

Jean Luc was busy writing in front of the fire in the library and smiled as she came into the room.

"Have you arranged for your packing?" he asked

"Yes," she replied. "Is it possible for Jenny to accompany me? You said I could have a servant."

"Yes, that's fine. You can have whoever you want. Except for Mrs Yelland," he added wryly. "By the way, I've a surprise for you tomorrow."

Her heart sank as she waited to hear his words.

"I want you to wear your blue dress and your diamond earrings and necklace, as I've arranged for an artist to come and make preparations for a painting of you." He seemed to enjoy seeing the look of amazement on her face and continued, "I believe ladies enjoy having their portrait painted."

' A painting of me? What on earth is he thinking about? We're about to embark on a long trip and he's making arrangements for a painting. Why would he do that?' she thought, very taken aback and disliking the idea of a portrait of herself, painted in the name of Lady Sophie Throgmorton, for everyone to see.

He made no attempt to explain and just looked at her, somewhat uncertainly, realising that she was not overjoyed.

"I would like you painted in the blue dress," he said again firmly.

"As you wish," she replied, at a complete loss to understand him. She stood for a moment, not wanting to interrupt his writing, but knowing she could not go away and abandon the Blackmore family.

"Yes?" he asked, looking at her.

"There is often food wasted in the kitchen, particularly on Sunday," she said.

"Is there?" he replied, rather bemused. "I will have a word with Mrs Yelland about it."

"What I mean is that sometimes I've taken some of it," she said.

"You can eat whatever you want! In fact, you could do with a bit of fattening up! Please feel free to do as you wish," and he grinned again, clearly at a loss to know what she was talking about.

"I sometimes take food to a family who live nearby, who are often hungry," she said. "I'm going with you to France and I would like to give them some food before I go. Have I your permission to do so?"

He looked at her. "You take food from the kitchen and give it away?" he said in surprise.

"Yes," she replied.

"Is this family on my estate?" he asked.

"No, they live just outside the grounds," she admitted. "Mrs Blackmore's husband died in an accident and since then they've struggled to make a living and have nearly had to be put in Woodbine Cottage, the Poor House in Ilfracombe." She spoke quietly, afraid he was going to be furious that she had taken food to give to strangers.

"So I'm feeding half of Ilfracombe, as well as my own servants," he said, with mock displeasure.

"They're only a very small family and the food is often wasted here."

"Is it? I didn't know that," he replied and looked thoughtfully at her for a moment before saying, " Yes, you can, of course, take what you want and give it to them before you go."

"Thank you," she said and started to leave the room.

"I need some fresh air," he added. "Prepare the food and I'll accompany you."

"Oh no, I don' t think...." she said.

"Well then, no food!" he replied flatly.

She looked at him. 'How could he visit the hovel that was Mrs Blackmore's cottage?'

"I don't think," she remonstrated again.

"It's not for you to think what I do!" he rejoined. "Give your orders to the servants, then we'll go together." He pulled the bell and a servant entered.

"Her ladyship would like to have some food prepared," he said, looking at her curiously, as though wanting to see what she did, and she was forced to list what she needed.

"Do you carry it there by yourself?" he asked.

"Yes," she admitted.

"We had better go soon. It's still very cold outside and nearly sunset," he said and a short time later he and Sarah walked slowly down the drive, accompanied by two footmen carrying baskets. The air was chill and the melting snow and darkening sky gave the scene a forlorn aspect and she wished she had been able to go by herself.

'What's he going to think of the cottage?' she wondered as she cast a sidelong glance at his rich clothes and could not imagine him standing in Mrs Blackmore's wretchedly dirty home. She suspected he was cross with her and looked at his face, but she could not see a sign of any emotion on it, except that of extreme tiredness.

She pushed open the gate and followed by Jean Luc and the footmen, walked up the path to the tumbledown building, whose thatch sagged and enjoyed a gaping hole on one side. Two of the windows were boarded up and the two remaining had rags strung across them. There was no sound from within and she waited anxiously in the cold.

"There isn't any smoke from the chimney," she remarked. "Perhaps they're not here."

The next minute, the door swung open and a raggedly clothed urchin peered out at them.

"Hello, Charlie," said Sarah smiling. The little boy beamed in recognition of her and held out his grubby hands.

"'ello Sophie," he said. She put out her hand and held his. "Is your mother in?" she asked.

"Yess, us is in bed," he replied, looking surprised at the three unknown men standing behind her and he shyly retreated backwards into the dark room.

She followed him and as her eyes became accustomed to the lack of light, saw that Mrs Blackmore was in a low bed against one side of the wall, with her other three children. She was coughing violently, the sound very much reminding her of the way Sophie had coughed.

Mrs Blackmore's eyes widened with astonishment, to see not only Sarah, but the Duke of Delacroix and two footmen enter her cottage.

"Oh my goodness, your Grace!" she exclaimed and clutching a grimy cover around her, stood up and tried to give a curtsy.

"Your Grace," she said again, very flustered, her fair hair hanging dishevelled onto her shoulders.

The room was dirty and in disorder and Sarah could hear an animal scratching in the corner and hoped it was not a rat. She had a terrible fear of the creatures after dozens of them had swarmed around her one day in the summer, as she walked by a newly harvested wheat field. She had noticed the men working in the fields were all wearing strips tied around their ankles and had not realised it was to stop the rats running up their legs.

"I don't wish to disturb you," said Jean Luc politely. "Lady Sophie is bringing you some food."

"Thank ee," she exclaimed. " Ye're so kind to us. Us wouldn't 'ave got through tha winter without ee."

Sarah was embarrassed, both at being thanked and because she had clearly often taken food to give to the family. Charlie clung to her dress and she gently touched his shock of fair hair.

183

"Can I put some more wood on the fire?" she asked, looking at the dying embers. "It's so cold."

"Us as no wood. I've been took bad and cawn't get none."

Mrs Blackmore looked as though she could hardly stand and she was shocked to see how emaciated she had become since the last time she had seen her. The children also sat, pale and silent, not running round as they usually did.

She busied herself taking the food from the baskets and placing it on the rough table. She took out bread, cheese and ham and gave a piece each to the children, who ravenously tore at it with dirty hands.

"Only give them a little now," interrupted Jean Luc. "If they haven't eaten for some time, it will give them pains to eat too much."

"Please get back into bed, Mrs Blackmore," she said. "Shall I look for some wood?" and she unlatched the back door and peered out to see if there were any remaining twigs in the shelter but it was empty. She turned to Jean Luc, "Have you a knife? I can quickly go and cut some branches."

"I think we can manage without you cutting down trees this afternoon," he remarked and turned to the footmen and said, "Would you go back to the house and bring enough logs for the fire to last a week."

"You have no husband?" he enquired of Mrs Blackmore.

"No,'ees did a year ago, zur, and since then us 'ave lived from ' and to mouth," she replied.

Sarah put the food into a cupboard and when she had finished, he said, "We'll go now. The servants will make up the fire when they return. Good day, Mrs Blackmore. When you're feeling better, come to the house and ask my housekeeper if there's any work which can be found for you."

"Thank ye, your Grace, thank ye," she muttered, as a rattling cough shook her body.

"Good day," he said and then as Sarah looked reluctant to leave, took her firmly by the arm and remarked, "After you, madam."

The little boy followed them to the gate. "Go in, Charlie, you'll catch cold," Sarah said, smiling fondly at him.

As they walked back up the lane he told her, "I'll arrange for food to be taken to Mrs Blackmore in our absence. I remember when the crop failed in the Nordgau a few summers ago, from lack of rain. It was necessary to take food to the starving families then."

"Her cough was very bad," mused Sarah. "It reminds me of..." and she stopped.

"Yes?" he queried and she felt obliged to continue.

"It reminds me of my," she hesitated, then said, "my servant, who died at Lynmouth. Her cough sounded just like that, before she....," she could not finish the words and bit her lip.

"Have you any other families you visit?" he asked quickly, as though he wanted to help her avoid the subject of the death of her servant and also to know what she had been doing.

"No, I've only visited Mrs Blackmore," she replied.

His gaze lingered on her face. "I hope the artist will produce a good likeness of you. He is well known for his skill," he said, suddenly changing the subject.

Slush had replaced the snow and dripping water fell from leaves and twigs into puddles. The sun was now dropped so low, only a faint glow tinged the western sky and the deepening twilight obscured the desire plainly evident on Jean Luc's face as he escorted Sarah towards the house.

25

The next two days passed in a contradictory very slow/very fast time. She listened to the endless ticking of the mantelpiece clock, as she sat fidgeting for the preparation of the picture which was going to be painted in her absence. Mr Reynolds, the artist, was a lively man, who constantly chatted as he darted round looking at her from different angles, then sketched rapidly, while she tried to sit as still as she could.

'When I disappear one day,' she thought. 'I certainly do not want a portrait left behind, which shows me as Lady Sophie Throgmorton' and she looked unhappily at Jean Luc as he put his head round the door to see how it was going.

"You'll be pleased with the result, I dare say, madam," he said ironically, smiling at her glum expression, and went off whistling to his workroom. She felt a sense of foreboding. Events were moving too quickly for her and she wanted to cling on to the familiarity of Wildercombe House.

When Mr Reynolds had departed, she sat on her window seat in the bedchamber, staring out at a garden obscured by drizzling rain, which only served to depress her spirits further as she thought about Jenny, who had fallen seriously ill with measles.

"You can chose another servant to accompany you," said Jean Luc. But it appeared that no one else wished to venture to the unknown and frightening country of France and so she had said she would manage without a servant, rather than force anyone to come. He had reluctantly agreed and told her that a maid would be obtained for her when they arrived in Bretagne, and Heinrich, for once, looked positively joyful at the news that Jenny could not travel.

On the last evening she wanted to say goodbye to her favourite haunts, the beach and the wood, and went to see Jean Luc in his workroom to ask his permission for the walk.

"No, not now," he said hurriedly. "I've got a problem here. I've mixed two substances by mistake, which will explode in a minute!"

"I would like to see the beach," she insisted.

"No, my dear, I would prefer not," he said. "I fear you will be distressed to see the ship."

"I want very much to see the beach," she insisted again.

Heinrich was supervising the removal of the boxes and frowned in annoyance both at her and at the increasingly strident noise that the mixture bubbling in a metal dish over the fire was making.

"I can't stop now," muttered Jean Luc.

"Are the bodies all removed from the beach?" he hurriedly asked Heinrich in Alsatian.

"Yes, Seigneur," he replied.

"Well, take Hans and Werner and only go to the coast. I have to stop this somehow or I'll blow up the house!" he shouted to her above the din.

She quickly rushed out of the house while she could and almost ran across the gardens and through the wood, Hans and Werner following morosely behind. A misty rain was falling, dimpling the remnants of snow softening the gaunt, rocky outcrops along the cliff top and path, and she was shocked to see the broken hulk of the ship fast on the reefs, its figurehead and splintered masts trailing in the sea. A few people were combing through scraps of cloth and wooden spars on the sand and she was displeased to share her last visit to the beach with strangers.

She picked her way across the cove, the men she passed knuckling their foreheads. Then she noticed John Buzzacott who was standing near the cave, his boat pulled up beside him.

"You're better?" she asked him, smiling.

" Yess, me lady. Thank ee," he said, smiling broadly back at her.

"Have you found anything?" she asked.

"Naw, I came 'ere fer crabs and lobsters he said and pointed to two wicker pots in the bottom of his boat. He glanced over at the wreck, " Tis turrible what 'appened," he said angrily. "Twas wreckers what were yere. Those poor zouls niver stood a chance!"

"I know," said Sarah sadly.

"There be bad goings on!" he said and he looked in the direction of Wildercombe House.

"What do you mean?" she asked.

"That Mrs Yelland's a bad 'un! Ee's a vurriner, vrum Clovelly, not from yere! Ee's deul's nointed!" he replied.

"Devil's anointed? she queried. "Oh you mean she's wicked, she's in league with the wreckers?"

"Tis not for me to spake, me lady," and he fell silent, his face angry.

"I am going to France with his Grace for some time," she said, the words sounding very strange in her ears.

"If I can ever do aut fur yer, milady, just ax. I'll never ferget what thee did for us," he said.

"Thank you," she said, "I'll remember that," then picking up her skirts, bade him goodbye and left the beach without a backward glance, tears stinging her eyes and feeling very sad for the people who had died. For the first time she thought about her own journey and the sea crossing she was about to undertake, as she walked swiftly back to Wildercombe House.

Later that night, a maid snuffed out the candles in her bedchamber. The door closed and she lay in the four poster bed, remembering her fear when she had first arrived.

"This part of my life is finishing," she mused. "I wondered then what the future would bring. What strange path am I now following?" and she felt again that forces beyond her control were acting on her. She clutched her locket to her and fell fast asleep.

PART TWO

26

As the first rays of sun lightened the darkness, Sarah sat shivering in the carriage. The sound of men's voices and the scraping of hooves on the gravel rasped across the melodious, morning chorus.

"Let's go," shouted Jean Luc, astride his horse, and the coach, riders and a long string of pack horses burdened by crates, set off down the drive. She turned to look for the last time at the grey stone manor house, and glanced at the Duchess's window, to see if she was watching her son's departure; but remembering her short meeting with her the previous day, was not surprised to see the curtains still firmly closed. The Duchess had become the Queen of England and most of her remarks had featured threatened beheadings, particularly of a disreputable knave, called Jean Luc, whom she considered had all the failings of his father.

Just as she was about to glance away, her attention was suddenly taken by a figure in black standing on the parapet in front of the attic corridor. With a shock, she realised it was Mrs Yelland, and even at this distance, could feel her spiteful gaze. Her superstitious nature made her wish she had not seen the woman, particularly as it was almost as though, by standing so near the room which had held the treasure and the lantern, she was reminding her of the part she had played with the wreckers. She shuddered, then gathered her cloak and hood closely about her and drifted off into a fitful sleep, huddled against the boxes piled next to her.

A violent lurching of the coach awakened her and she jumped, blinking in the bright sunshine. She saw that the tall Devon hedges had vanished and a winding river was glittering with light. A grey and white heron was standing motionless, on one leg, on a sandy islet, and a family of brown moorhens was nodding jerkily, like a group of clockwork toys, beneath overhanging clumps of reeds. The road was traversing a flood plain, imitating, from a distance, the river's curves, and the coach was crazily weaving round bends and bouncing over deep ruts. Then the hedges grew tall again, a dense intertwining of hawthorn and hazel, overhanging the track and obscuring the sun and sky.

The day passed slowly. Pot-holes very frequently pitted the ground, the horses were flagging and Heinrich's annoyance became more marked, his shouting louder.

They stopped the night at an inn and she was so exhausted from the tedious travelling she fell asleep almost as soon as her head touched the rough, straw-smelling bed.

They set off again early next morning, a dank greyness chilling the air. Ribbons of pale cloud floated like ghostly spirits over the valley floor, wreathing the trees in swirling banners of white. Even at this hour, other travellers were already on the road and phantasmagorical figures of men and horses loomed out of the dark, distorted by the eerie mist. A rising sun gradually brought colour to the fields, chasing away the phantoms, and they continued, painfully slowly, on their way.

"Nous n'arriverons jamais," she heard Heinrich say angrily and knew he was complaining about the snail's pace. She realised he saw her and the carriage as an encumbrance and wondered again about his master's motives in bringing her; very afraid of the fateful day when he would find out she had duped him and that his solicitous attention towards a relation was, in reality, directed towards a former kitchen maid who had stolen her identity.

At that moment, the carriage stopped. She looked out and saw a pack horse just in front, weighed down by a heavy wooden yoke and carrying coal, which had met a truckamuck with four oxen coming from the other direction, dragging tree trunks roped together, on which were two enormous stones. The path was completely blocked and none of the animals could move.

She could hear Heinrich complaining again, but was no longer surprised by the position of influence he so obviously enjoyed. She idly wondered if Jean Luc de Delacroix was not wealthy, like the Throgmortons, as his Devon estate was not very extensive and the manor house would not perhaps be regarded as the usual residence of someone who was a Duke. She smiled to herself, remembering Lady Throgmorton's words again, "He's a savage!"

"Back up!" she heard him shout to the coachman, "and turn into the field." Then he leaned across and pulled open the door, "It's best to descend, in case the coach overturns, as the ground is steep."

She looked at the muddy road, very reluctant to step down into the slime.

"Get onto my horse," he said and held out his arm. "Come on. We've not got all day," he said impatiently, as she hesitated.

She clung to his hand and he pulled her up, holding her with one arm as she sat across the saddle, the reins in his other hand, and then made a detour into the field, followed by the coach.

"Put your arms around me, so you don't fall," he murmured in her ear, his face touching her hair. She awkwardly did so, experiencing, as always by his close physical presence, a strong sense of reassurance and also a sudden, very unwanted, sensation of desire.

The land sloped away in a series of steep ridges and the coachman struggled to keep the coach upright. He kept cracking his whip to encourage the horses to go quickly along by the hedge and the coach wobbled, nearly toppling over. He finally reached an open gate and drove back onto the track, just past the immobile oxen pulling the truckamuck.

"Well done, man!" Jean Luc called out and reined in his horse, pulled open the coach door and deposited her back inside.

By midday they reached Exeter, its narrow streets crowded with people who stared very curiously at the coach and its retinue of foreign-looking men. They crossed a bridge over a wide river and left behind the town and its great cathedral, travelling at a good pace now, even although some of the hills seemed as steep as those on Exmoor. They halted briefly in a clearing ringed by yellow furze and she ravenously ate the bread, cheese and meat given to her.

"I don't want to stop at an inn," he explained. "We've got to reach Babbacombe, near Torre Quay, by late afternoon. The English fleet often anchors in Torre Bay and the captain will not want to stay long for us. We are French and well-armed and I don't want to risk any trouble, and there will be no moon tonight, so it would be difficult to travel after dark."

"You will have to use the bushes for any…needs," he continued, grinning and for the first time in her life, she had to embarrassingly squat behind the cover of the prickly furze in order to relieve herself. Even this ordeal did not dampen her spirits and she stood looking with interest at the unusual red colour of the earth, exhilarated to be en route with him to France instead of suffering the anguish of being abandoned in North Devon.

"You can eat more in the coach if you're still hungry," he said and she reluctantly returned to the carriage she was sharing with an assortment of North American wild life crammed into boxes.

She nodded off to sleep, only awaking when the carriage came to a halt, and was immediately delighted by the lack of movement and the sudden quiet. A seagull screamed and she saw a dark blue sea, bordered by a coast indented with sandy coves and wooded hillsides. She opened the door and stepped down onto the ground.

Heinrich and Jean Luc were deep in conversation, looking towards the horizon, and she realised she was standing on top of a cliff; far below was a pale brown strip of sand, scallop-edged with driftwood at the base of the rocks. The cliffs reminded her of the soil she had seen; they were crumbling and boulders had fallen onto the beach, staining the sea water with elongated fingers of redness projecting out into the bay. Waves were rolling in across the shingle, barely audible from such a height, and a fierce wind was blowing from the east.

The men were looking seawards and as she followed their gaze she could discern a fast-moving, white speck. She turned to watch Jean Luc, who was talking rapidly in French. He used his body more expressively when he spoke it, she noticed; he shrugged his shoulders and waved his hands, whilst Heinrich remained the same, whether he spoke English, French or Alsatian, his face remained impassive and he was always very much in control of himself.

The ship was quickly approaching, the wind pushing it towards them, its masts in full sail, its bow rising and falling.

"We're going to the beach," called Jean Luc to her. " It's very steep. Get on my horse again."

She stood on the top step of the coach and let him pull her onto his saddle. Then, pressed against his body, they left behind the warm sunshine of the cliff-top, descending into a leaf-shaded twilight as the horse delicately picked its way down the path zigzagging towards the beach. The hillside was nearly perpendicular and saplings and mature trees jostled together above banks of wild garlic and green hart's tongue fern; an occasional lavender bush clinging to bare outcrops of rock, the fragrant mauve flowers adding a sweetness to the garlic. The sun found it difficult to pierce the tree canopy and infrequent puddles of brightness splashed the sombre vegetation.

"Put your arm round me. It's easier for you," he said, as though it was for her benefit, not his, and then, all too soon, they reached the shingle and he lifted her down.

The ship was coming in fast now, its sails filled by the strong wind. She could see sailors on the deck and did not recognise the black and white flag on the mainsail.

"It's lucky that we've arrived. I don't think he will wait long," Jean Luc said. "He's afraid of the English. We must hurry."

She found it very strange to be standing on this unknown beach, its red cliffs and sea putting her in mind of a picture she had once seen of Hell, with a fiery coast and fire-breathing sea monsters, and hoped it was not a bad omen. The ship dropped anchor, rattling chains could be heard plunging into the blood-coloured depths and gigs could be seen being lowered.

"It's the 'Antoinette'," remarked Heinrich.

She turned to him, thinking he had spoken to her.

"Yes?" she said. Then she realised he was saying the name of the ship. Her face flushed.

'What made me do that?' she wondered in bewilderment. 'I thought he was calling me.'

She stood on the rounded pebbles, lost in thought, suddenly a long way from the Devon beach. She was standing in front of a fire and someone was saying to her in a low, kind voice, "Antoinette."

"Is that one of your names?" Jean Luc asked, noticing she had answered to it.

"No, oh no," she said dismissively, realising with horror she did not know Sophie's other names and briskly walked away from him to the water's edge. She watched the sea lap the sand and tried to recall the memory, but it had vanished, a fleeting moment, now forgotten. She looked back and saw him curiously watching her, and felt her previous contentment destroyed by her awareness again of the danger he posed to her.

The gigs ferried the men and boxes across the water, before she, Jean Luc and Heinrich were taken to the ship. She clambered with difficulty in her dress up the ladder hanging over the side and they all stood together on the deck, looking at the shore as the sailors rushed to adjust the sails and pull up the anchor. The chain rattled again through the water, the deck groaned and the ship ponderously turned seawards. She glimpsed the horses filing back up through the trees before her attention was taken by an island of rocky limestone, occupied by a colony of large, black birds, their wings outstretched as if they were hanging washing to dry.

"Those are cormorants. They can swim underwater," Jean Luc told her.

They passed a succession of coves, wooded hillsides and cliffs and she saw that they were in a wide bay and had set sail from somewhere near its centre, each arm of the coast indistinct. As she watched, the sailors were running nervously backwards and forwards, shouting to each other in a strange language, which did not sound French.

"They speak Breton," said Jean Luc. "We are sailing to Bretagne. I don't understand their speech."

"Doesn't everyone speak French in France?" she asked.

"No, it's quite different to England. There's several languages and there's also patois. People from one area often speak a French which can't be understood by people from somewhere else. Heinrich and the men speak a different language again."

She stood watching the coastline until it disappeared, her hand touching the familiarity of the locket round her neck, and wondering if she would return.

The ship heaved up and down, its wooden planks creaking, the wind filling its sails. It raced through the water, a foaming wave in its wake, screamed over by seagulls wheeling and swooping. She felt as though she was also flying. She had never dreamt of such a speed and clung onto the side, thrilled, watching the limpid blueness rush by, until the sun sank low in the sky.

"When I die, I want to be buried in the sea," she exclaimed. "Not in the ground."

"That's a very morbid thought, my dear," Jean Luc replied unhappily and quickly changed the subject. "You are having the captain's cabin. Perhaps you would like to go down to it now?"

The captain was short and swarthy and had black curly hair and a beard. He reminded her of John Buzzacott and had the same twinkling eyes. He looked as anxious as his men while in sight of the shore, but once the coast was left behind, he relaxed and smiled and gesticulated to her to try and make her understand what he was saying.

"Come," he said in English and pointed to a door which led down below the deck. She followed him and found herself in a spacious cabin, whose narrow windows looked out onto the sea. It was difficult to stand, the deck was pitching backwards and forwards beneath her feet and she grabbed the door to keep herself upright. He waved his hands expressively to suggest that the cabin was hers, gave a bow and left her alone.

Jean Luc poked his head round the door. He was having the same trouble as she was in trying to stay on his feet and nearly fell as the ship lurched.

"Is it alright for you?" he asked. "My cabin is next door."

A sailor appeared, carrying steaming bowls of food, which he placed on a table, already set with plates and cutlery and several bottles of wine, held in wooden squares to keep them from shifting.

"Heinrich is eating with the men," Jean Luc said. "Would you like to sit down, madam? I'll be your servant," and with a flourish he pulled out a chair.

It seemed very odd to her to have left England behind and to be sitting in the smoky cabin, lit by candles in metal bowls, her ears filled by the sound of the creaking timbers, the water slapping against the hull and the wind screaming like fairy banshees announcing a death.

He ladled out a portion of a stew onto her plate, then helped himself. She gingerly tasted it, enjoying the flavour of the rich sauce. The taste surprised her by evoking a haunting sensation of well-being, a fleeting image of a far-off, dimly remembered time. She concentrated on trying to pierce the darkness of her memory for the second time that day, but it eluded her again, as it had on the beach, and she savoured each mouthful, withdrawing into herself.

He ate quickly and drank much wine. "Do you like the dish? It's a fricassée of chicken. It's different to English food. The meat is cut up into pieces, herbs are used and I think it's probably heated for longer."

She was surprised that he seemed to be so knowledgeable about cooking, but had come to accept that he had a lively interest in everything. She wondered if he would try and kiss her. She recognised the look in his eye and moved slightly on her chair, so that she was just out of his reach. He made no attempt to touch her, however and contented himself with letting his gaze wander over her. She reflected that, very strangely, she was the one who knew <u>his</u> body intimately, whatever his desire might be towards her. She thought of nursing him, when he was injured, and remembered her delight on seeing his naked skin and the dark hairs on his chest and arms. She blushed and felt caught in a entrancing, silken web, which was entangling her more as time passed.

'I'm adrift in more ways than one,' she reflected. 'You are going home to be married and should not be looking at me like that. And I have a secret which I cannot share and which I hope you will never know.'

He quickly drank one bottle of wine, then started on the next and for the first time since she had met him, except when he had been delirious and semi-comatose on brandy, she thought he was becoming drunk.

"Your hands are so small," he said. "Your hair is so beautiful."

They gazed at each other and she attempted to cool the passion that was only too evident from his expression, and less so, she hoped, from her own.

"I think, sir, I would like to go to bed now," and after she had said it, almost giggled at the unfortunate, double entendre.

"Yes, I think it's time for bed!" he replied, but without a hint of a smile.

She stood up, nearly falling into the dishes as the ship slewed suddenly. He leaned over to catch her, but was hopelessly intoxicated and only pulled her down with him onto the floor, both of them laughing helplessly. At that moment, Heinrich came into the cabin. She hurriedly got to her feet and Heinrich hauled him upright.

"Goodnight, my beloved Sophie," he said and raised her hand to his mouth and kissed it gently, then helped by Heinrich, managed to lurch to the door.

27

It was a long night. She tossed and turned in the unfamiliar bed and put the covers over her head to lessen the sound of the wind and the sea and the grinding of the wooden planks all around her. The ship rose and fell and she refused to think of the three-masted boat she had seen plunging up and down in the terrible waves, and which finally came to rest, its back broken on the reefs.

Towards the morning she awoke and watched the dark change to a pale brightness which lit the cabin with warmth as well as light. She dressed as quickly as she could in the swaying motion, then pressed her face to the window and peered out. Spray hit the glass, trickling down, and for a moment there was only a watery outline, before it cleared, revealing a low coast with bleached-white beaches and a sprinkling of islands.

She ran up onto the deck and watched the coast grow near. Houses were becoming visible and a wide river flowed into the sea, disgorging brown sediment into the blue.

A sailor gave her a piece of dry bread which she was dipping in a tankard of wine as Heinrich appeared and joined her.

"Nous sommes arrivés," he remarked.

Her thoughts on the approaching shore, she absentmindedly said, "Oui, nous sommes arrivés."

" You speak French well," he replied.

"No, no. I don't speak it at all," she hastened to say, suddenly realising she had somehow said a few words in French. "I think English and French must be similar, as I can sometimes understand what you're saying."

"No. They're not similar at all," he said. "You have had lessons, I think."

"Mmm," she mumbled, well aware she had never been taught French in her life. Somehow the language felt familiar to her. She was beginning to understand more and more of Jean Luc's conversation with Heinrich and it gave her the same warmth to hear it that she had felt at the name 'Antoinette' and on eating the meat stew. Perplexed, she dismissed it from her mind, her attention completely taken by the sight of a formidable town, enclosed by ramparts. She could see cannon protruding from slits in the walls and unfamiliar flags were flying on poles.

" It's St Malo," said Heinrich, and she could sense his hostility to her, although his words were polite, and she turned happily to greet Jean

Luc when he came onto the deck, wearing clothes which were even more ornate than she had seen in England. His coat and waistcoat were a rich plum and purple, trimmed with lace and gold, and his cravat was extremely frilled. Apart from his lack of a wig, he was impeccably and colourfully tailored and she felt almost shabby standing next to him in her dark green travelling dress and cloak, her only jewellery being her locket.

He greeted her, his face unusually white, and he too stared at the approaching town and put his arm on Heinrich's shoulder.

"Ca fait deux ans depuis notre départ de la France," he said. " Il est temps de retourner."

"Ce n'est pas vraiment la France," Heinrich replied. " C'est la Bretagne."

" C'est suffisament de la France pour moi," Jean Luc replied.

She could not completely understand the words, but knew again what they were saying. The language was like an echo from a distant time. She struggled to remember, but the memory eluded her.

The sails were lowered; the ship slowly came to a halt by a jetty, ropes were thrown onto the shore and made fast. She stared in awe at towering granite walls in front of tall houses with steep slate roofs and rows of dormer windows. The cobbled wharf swarmed with people in clothes she had never seen before. The women had white, coiffed headdresses, their dresses were mainly black, although several were brightly coloured and embroidered, and they all wore aprons. The men had baggy breeches and short jackets and many had clogs on their feet.

"Don't say anything when we leave the boat," said Jean Luc. "The English are hated here."

"But I thought many English people come to France," she protested.

"That may be," he replied. "But they usually go to Calais, then Paris and   south. We've landed in the far west, in Bretagne, and it's very different. The English destroyed the town of St Servan just over there a few years ago," and he pointed towards the east, " and they've tried to attack St Malo itself from the sea and failed. The only English visitor to these parts I'm afraid, wore a red coat and carried a musket."

Heinrich raised his arm and whistled to a group of men in the familiar Delacroix blue livery, who were standing with a coach and many horses. They came clattering across the cobbles towards the jetty and she wondered how long they had waited, as they could not have known when they would arrive. A gang plank was laid in place and he motioned her to walk over it, then followed close behind and stood on the quay, supervising the bringing ashore of the boxes.

A footman opened the coach door for her and she settled herself on the padded seat and was immediately besieged by people thrusting fruit and cakes at the windows for her to buy.

Finally, the heavily laden pack horses were ready. Jean Luc and Heinrich rode in front and they set off towards an arch in the walls, and then along narrow alleys, past tall houses, some built of the same granite as the rampart, whilst others were constructed of wood; and everywhere there seemed to be the distinctive smells of bread being baked and fish being grilled.

The cramped streets were soon left behind and only a few stone houses straggled along the dusty road. Women were working in the fields next to the men, and chickens and pigs roamed across the track, causing the coach to keep halting. Solid stone crosses were often erected at the roadside and slowed their travel even more, as Jean Luc, Heinrich and the men, dismounted and knelt and prayed at the foot of each one. She was shocked to see such religious devotion in the open air and was pleased when a particularly ornate one with sculpted figures, was reluctantly passed by without any religious observance.

" Presumably as they will never reach Alsace if they keep stopping every few miles," she muttered.

She was also shocked in another way. Men, and sometimes women too, were urinating in the fields. The first time she saw it, she gasped and was so embarrassed she had to wrap her cloak round her eyes so as not to see. No one else seemed to remark it at all, and it happened so frequently, that after a while her surprise faded and she hardly noticed.

By midday, the sun was shining down so hotly she removed her cloak. The sunken, pot-holed paths, with their thick hedges, closely resembled Devon lanes, and their progress was so slow, she thought she could probably walk more quickly than the coach was travelling. It jolted and bounced like a maniacal marionette and she was very relieved when they stopped in front of a low, stone building and she was able to stand on firm ground again.

"On va déjeuner à cet auberge," said Jean Luc to her, as though he was trying to ascertain the extent of her knowledge of French and she realised she understood all the words except 'auberge' which she guessed meant 'inn.'

'Perhaps someone spoke French to me when I was young,' she wondered.

A log fire burned in an open hearth; wooden trestles stood on a flagstoned floor and the landlord and his wife and daughters came running to help serve everyone. She sank gratefully onto a bench in the window, basking in the hot sun like a lizard.

Jean Luc smiled at her. "I hope you don't feel ill in the coach. The road's very bad."

She struggled to speak in French, sure that somehow she could. "Non, ça va," she finally managed, the words sounding strange, her tongue having trouble pronouncing them. They seemed to be there in her mind from long ago and if she tried hard somehow she felt she would remember them. He beamed at her, "Très bien," he said encouragingly.

A large bowl was placed in the middle of the table and she looked hopefully at it, hunger making her nauseous.

"Voulez-vous les déguster?" he asked, somewhat quizzically.

"Oui," she replied, her tongue again feeling odd with the word, and then stared aghast as a servant ladled what were clearly snails onto her plate.

"They're very tasty," he said and started noisily eating.

She remembered Mrs Blackmore and her family being forced to eat slugs and snails because they had no food and was rather disturbed to find that here they were regarded as proper food. However, she was extremely hungry and extracted one from the shell and put it in her mouth. The flavour was of a rich, garlic butter, but she found herself choking on the creature itself and spat it out onto the plate. Heinrich roared with laughter, the first time she had ever seen him so amused and she was relieved when grilled crayfish was brought to the table, followed by a rabbit stew.

"If we pass an inn in the afternoon I think we'll stop, even if it's early. I don't want to be caught out in the open tonight." Jean Luc glanced at her as he spoke and she wondered if, without her, they would have travelled late and slept in the countryside if need be. His obvious lack of concern for his own comfort surprised her and made her wonder again if he was somewhat impoverished.

"There, it's not so bad to be in France with me, is it?" he joked. "You're learning more French."

"Yes," she agreed.

"Perhaps you can return to England with a recipe for snails, as well as chicken soup!" She laughed with him and noticed Heinrich watching them thoughtfully.

"It's time to go," said Jean Luc, as flies buzzed over the remaining food and a calm settled in the room, and he took coins from his pocket which he gave to the inn keeper. She presumed he had been very generous as the man's face became wreathed in smiles and he repeatedly said, "Merci, Seigneur," in a strongly accented way.

The afternoon passed quickly. She was drowsy from food and wine and was entranced by the houses with their steep roofs and shuttered windows. The people often looked wretchedly poor, she was sad to see. Many had bare feet and were dressed in rags, and beggars constantly assailed them as they passed by.

The road became more and more pot-holed and Jean Luc leaned into the carriage from his horse and said, "When it rains, people have been known to drown in these holes! We're lucky it's dry!"

She wondered if he was joking, but his face was serious as he cantered off.

Dusk began to fade the colours of the countryside and they came to a halt in the cobbled courtyard of a small inn, its shutters creaking in a freshening wind.

Stiff and tired, she stepped nervously down from the coach as bats shot backwards and forwards in the evening gloom, their short, piercing squeaks contrasting with the low, mournful cry of an owl from the gable of a nearby barn. Heinrich was trying to communicate by gestures with a peasant woman in a black dress and wearing the Breton coif, and after a few minutes she beckoned them into a narrow room, reeking of onions and lit by a solitary candle. A battered cauldron hung over a log fire and children and hens were scrabbling together on the earth floor.

The woman led the way up rickety wooden stairs to a small room, whose only furniture was a bed and whose wall was blessed with a crucifix. She indicated to Sarah that this would be her bedchamber and Jean Luc and Heinrich were taken into adjacent rooms on the same landing.

The poor, bare room unpleasantly reminded her of her attic in London, but then a footman appeared, carrying one of her bags, and her spirits rose.

"Whatever the future will bring, I've left that life far behind," she murmured.

Dinner was a greasy stew of fatty meat, floating in an onion broth, which she found impossible to eat. Cheese, cold meat and wine supplemented the meal from the provisions brought with them and as soon as politeness allowed, she rose to her feet and retired upstairs.

She lay in the lumpy bed in the small Breton room, watching the moonlight filter through the sides of the shutters and reliving the day's images in her mind. She could hear Werner's voice outside and laughter, and fell into a peaceful sleep, not disturbed by Jean Luc and Heinrich walking unsteadily along the creaking corridor late in the evening.

A cock woke her at day break. She jumped out of bed and opened the shutters. Light flooded the room and she stood in her night gown, lifting her face to the sun, and feeling a vitality course through every part of her body. She looked into one of the bags Jenny had packed and pulled out a blue gown, scented with lavender, and quickly dressed, without her usual stays as she needed a maid to help fasten them, and then crept down the stairs. The woman from the night before, still in black, with the same grubby apron and coif, smiled broadly at her and carried in a tankard of milk, warm from the cow, and a slice of rye bread which she hungrily ate.

There was no sign of Jean Luc and she wandered to the door and looked out into the courtyard where the footmen were already packing boxes onto the carriage. She walked past them and came to a row of dilapidated houses, their courtyards filled with weeds. Emaciated children, with distended stomachs and hollow faces, looked at her as though she was invisible, as though they were so near death the current world did not exist for them. Two young men, half-naked in dirty rags were mending a plough, and as she passed one of them stared at her with such a look of smouldering hatred and envy that the warm spring sunshine was suddenly cold, and she retraced her steps, shame corroding her happiness that she should be dressed in such finery and they should be so destitute.

The horses were already harnessed to the coach when she returned, the hampers of food tied on to the back. She hastily undid the strap of the largest one, took out some cheese and cold meat and ran back down the road.

She thrust the food at one of the youths, who grabbed it, without even looking at her, and ran excitedly into the house, followed by the skeletal children who seemed to have miraculously come alive. She picked up her skirts and rushed as fast as she could back along the path, where she was disconcerted to be met by Jean Luc.

"I've only just realised you weren't here. You're not to go off alone," he said and held her arm, clearly in a temper. "Don't you understand that you could be robbed of your jewels and your throat cut."

He glared at her, his expression only softening as he saw her flush and her eyes fill with tears. He helped her in to the coach and she thought she heard him mutter, "My precious," but was not sure if he was referring to her or the snake which was in its box on the seat next to her. They set off once more and feeling very chastened she quietly gazed out at the countryside as the coach trundled along.

Peasants wearing clogs were already in the fields, ploughing with oxen or with horses, whose bones could often be seen through their skin. The curving furrows in the fields followed the contours of the land and flocks of birds swooped low in the wake of each plough. The land was sometimes flat with verdant water meadows dotted with flowers, and sometimes gently undulating, divided into fields of different shapes and sizes, which were contained within hedges or mounds of earth. She began to feel happier and sang softly to herself.

Suddenly the coach stopped. She looked out and saw that trees had fallen and that the road leading up to them was a morass of thick slime, dissected by streams. She heard Heinrich call to the coachman to pull the coach onto the side of the track in order not to have it bogged down in the mud. The coachman and footmen climbed down from their perch to go and help and she could hear everyone shouting as they pulled together to shift the obstacle.

One minute the sun was streaming into the carriage and she was luxuriating in its rays, the next, the door was flung open and two youths similarly dressed in dirty rags to the ones she had seen earlier, burst in. She was so taken aback, she was not afraid, only amazed that they should have the effrontery to steal from Jean Luc, when he and about twenty men were just down the road, armed with their usual weapons and each man about twice their size. One boy held a knife to her throat and was trembling so much she was afraid he would kill her by mistake. The other boy, his hair hanging in rat tails, opened one of the cupboards under the seat and grabbed a metal box before jumping nimbly from the coach.

A gang of youths joined him, gulping down the food they had stolen from the hampers and they all ran off together towards the trees. The boy remaining in the coach tore the gold locket from her neck and she froze in terror as he raised the knife as though about to stab her. His eyes met hers and for a second they stared at each other.

'He's only a child!' the thought flashed through her mind, as she saw his petrified expression and his puny body. Then he leapt to the ground and went running towards a rocky path winding upwards across a hillside of brambles and trees.

She sat in shock for a moment at the loss of her locket and was about to scream for help, when it occurred to her that the men would soon catch them and they would, in all probability, be killed or injured. She felt a strong sympathy towards the half-starved wretches who had just robbed her, even if the theft of her locket hurt her more than she could bear.

'I can't be part of any violence towards these children,' she thought. 'I will try and get my locket back myself,' and she pulled open the cupboard under the seat, where she knew weapons were kept. Her hand touched the cold steel of a sword and she pulled it out and jumped headlong from the coach in pursuit of the boys, her long dress hampering her running, her red hair flying out behind her.

At the corner of the road, Heinrich and Jean Luc stood watching the last tree being shifted to the side. Heinrich suddenly noticed the two footmen and the coachman and quickly glanced back along the road to the coach, just in time to see the last of the young thieves jump from it and run up the hill, followed by Sarah holding a sword.

"We've been tricked!" he bellowed angrily. "The trees were pulled down in front of the mud to ensure the coach stayed back."

Jean Luc heard him shout and also looked towards the coach, but Sarah had by now disappeared into the trees.

Heinrich ran through the mud, splattering his face and clothes, followed by Hans and Werner, who quickly overtook him, their legs easily covering the ground.

"Go up through the trees," he shouted to them as he and Jean Luc stopped at the coach. Jean Luc looked in horror at Sarah's empty seat and Heinrich looked equally horrified at the locker door hanging open and the strong box with all the money stolen.

Hans and Werner pounded up the path, rapidly gaining on Sarah. As they came up to her they could now see the youths in the distance, and could hear the twigs and branches crackling and snapping as they rushed frantically through the undergrowth, trying to escape. She turned to face them.

"No, no! Leave them!" she screamed. "They're only boys! Don't kill them!" knowing only too well that mercy was never shown to thieves in England, who were hung, even if they were children, and presuming the same would be true in France.

"No! No!" she screamed again and lifted the sword with both hands and held it out straight towards them.

"Stop!" she shouted.

They hesitated for a second, unsure what to do; the path was narrow with steep rock on either side and they were being threatened by a slight girl, very clearly adored by their master and wielding one of his extremely sharp swords. Then Jean Luc reached them and with a roar of rage, ran to her and prised the sword from her grasp.

"No! Please don't kill them! They're only young!" she screamed hysterically as he grabbed her arm and gave her to Hans.

"Take her to the coach, both of you!" he shouted, "and don't let her go!"

Hans gripped her arm and he and Werner escorted her down the hill, both looking very disappointed at not being able to continue the chase. The rest of the men followed Jean Luc and Heinrich and encircled the boys in a gloomy clearing, the sun filtering down through the trees and dappling their frightened faces. The young thieves stopped, terrified, and Heinrich snatched the strong box and Sarah's locket from their hands.

"What do you want me to do, Seigneur?" he asked.

Jean Luc thought for a moment, looking angrily at the children, who stood trembling, the smallest crying.

"Free them," he said.

Heinrich gave the biggest two a thump round their ears, then shouted, "Go!" and the boys fled to the safety of the trees without a backward glance.

"Back to the coach!" Jean Luc said tersely, his face like stone, as he pocketed the locket Heinrich gave him.

Sarah was standing in a state of utter misery next to Hans and Werner on the grass. Her locket, her beloved, and only link with her unknown mother, had gone, and now that the heat of the moment had passed, she almost wished that kindness had not allowed her reckless and headstrong nature, which she had never suspected she possessed until her impersonation of Sophie, to push her into a foolish action. She looked nervously at him as he strode up to her.

"What were you thinking of madam?" he shouted, almost spitting out the words. "Why didn't you come and tell us we had been robbed? What in God's name possessed you to chase them with my sword?"

He glared angrily at her and she retreated backwards. He roughly pulled her to him, sat on a fallen log, put her over his knee and vigorously spanked her. She screamed and struggled to get free but he was far stronger than she was.

"Well, his arm's obviously healed well," Heinrich remarked as he approached and caught sight of what was happening. Then Jean Luc seemed to come to his senses, the expression of fury on his face replaced by one of horror. He stood up and released her and as he did so she leapt at him, scratching his cheek with her finger nails and drawing blood, then punching him so hard in the face with her fist that he reeled backwards as she jumped into the coach and slammed shut the door.

The men stood watching, open-mouthed.

"Get on your horses!" shouted Heinrich in the sudden quiet.

Jean Luc glanced briefly into the carriage, where Sarah sat huddled in the corner, sobbing violently, then he grimly mounted his horse, rode to the front, and everyone set off.

Several hours later they stopped at a farm and Heinrich dismounted and asked a plump, red-cheeked woman if she could provide food for them. She scurried backwards and forwards with cider and cold rabbit pie, clearing the chicken she had been plucking, from the kitchen table, and the footmen brought in bottles of wine and the food from the hampers. Jean Luc went out to the carriage and opened the door and looked at Sarah who had wrapped her cloak tightly around her and was sitting ramrod-stiff, like a statue, in the corner.

"We're stopping at this farm," he said, his voice calm and controlled, as he glanced at her pale face and swollen eyes. "Would you care to eat?"

She did not even condescend to glance at him, but stared out of the window and said nothing.

"I lost my temper," he said humbly. "I'm sorry."

She gave no sign that she had even heard him, and he spoke again, "Would you like to eat in the carriage with me?"

She finally looked at him, her gaze lingering on the long scratches from his forehead to his chin.

"No," she said shortly, a glacial hatred in her eyes. "I never want to eat with you again," and turned her face away.

He stood quietly for a few minutes, very evidently discomfited and ill at ease. "I'll have something brought out to you," he muttered.

She was relieved to see him go. She knew his temper flared up very quickly, but had been shocked to her very soul that he could hit her. In an instant, her trust and confidence in him, which had taken so long to come about, had crumbled into a million fragments. The joy that she always felt on hearing his voice, on seeing his sturdy build and dark, serious eyes had been replaced by anger and an icy contempt. And where once she had thought of herself as worthless and always deserving of a beating, she was now self-assured and had a pride in herself, and sat vengefully and angrily in the coach.

"Take a plate of pie and some wine to her ladyship," he told a footman and frowned when, a few minutes later, it was returned uneaten.

206

Heinrich looked at the food and appeared considerably cheered, but said nothing, and they ate in silence and then resumed the journey. Jean Luc glanced briefly into the carriage as he rode by, but Sarah was still shrouded in her cloak, and he clearly thought better of speaking to her again.

The emotions sweeping through her mind were so blackly wretched she felt as though they were physically consuming her; her vision was blurring, a veil of darkness was obscuring her sight and an agonising pain throbbed in her head. Through her nausea she wondered what had happened to the boys and if they had been killed. She kept reliving the robbery, their wretched faces reminding her of how she had once been, and she could not bring herself to blame them for stealing her locket.

'I seem rich to them' she thought, 'and they have nothing.'

Its loss was, however, unbearable. It had always helped her to survive and she could not envisage a life without it.

She fell asleep and when she awoke the headache had passed and she was able to see clearly. The city of Rennes was visible in the distance and she saw that the road had improved and they were in the middle of a procession of carts, people and horses. The earthen track became cobbled streets with wooden houses. Officials at a customs post waved them through; the Delacroix ensignia was prominently displayed and the column of heavily armed men was a disincentive to any questioning.

They came to a halt at a granite hostelry. The innkeeper led Jean Luc to his best bedchamber, but he chose the smaller room next door for himself, then went rapidly out to the coach, where Sarah still sat, although the footman had opened the door.

"Madam. Your room is ready," he said.

She ignored him as she descended the steps and walked slowly to the inn, where the landlord escorted her to the bedchamber.

"Have you anyone who can act as a maid?" Jean Luc asked him.

"I'll see what I can do, Seigneur," he replied. "Would you like to eat now?"

"Yes," he said. "Is there somewhere we can dine quietly?"

"Yes, Seigneur," he replied and left the room.

They looked at each other and her anger was somewhat lessened as she saw again that his face was very badly scratched and a bruise was beginning to show below one eye.

"I'm sorry I behaved as I did," he said, a hint of annoyance sounding in his voice and lessening the apology. "I lost my temper, but the fault was not all mine. You were also to blame because you took it upon yourself to act in an extremely foolish way. You could have been killed!

You also threatened Hans and Werner, which is not acceptable, and if we had not caught the thieves they would have stolen all our money!"

She had not realised the box held money and felt somewhat guilty. However, she was unable to forgive him for what he had done and regarded him coldly.

"Would you like to change and then dine with me?" he asked.

"No! I don't wish to see you ever again!" she replied.

"Have you my locket?" she demanded, realising the boys had obviously been caught.

He did not reply, just looked at her.

"Please leave my room, sir," she said. "I don't wish to see you and I certainly do not wish to eat with you!"

"If you consent to dine with me, I will give you the locket back," he bargained.

"I would like the locket now!" she said imperiously.

"No, after dinner," he said calmly. "I will leave you to rest," and he bowed politely and left the room.

He gave instructions to one of his men to stand guard at the entrance and not let her leave the building and ruefully touched the scratch on his cheek.

"At least she was not killed," he said to himself. "I can suffer her anger. I could not have suffered her death."

He took out the locket, opened it and was looking at the picture of the woman when Heinrich entered the room.

"It's painted from an unusual viewpoint," Heinrich remarked. " Perhaps she has a scar on her face like the red-haired woman I saw years ago at the hunting party. That could be why her head is turned away."

"And you said you thought she was French?" Jean Luc asked.

"Yes. I think so," Heinrich replied.

"Then she can't be a relation to Sophie," he said. " I know that the Throgmortons have never married anyone French. I expect she just resembled her."

"I expect so, Seigneur," Heinrich agreed.

Jean Luc fiddled with the back of the locket to see if it would open, which Sarah had never thought of doing and, after a few minutes, managed to extricate the miniature. He turned it over and saw a name written almost illegibly on the back.

" 'La', he said. "Presumably 'Lady', but I can't see the rest," and he replaced the picture in the locket.

"Shall I put some whisky on your cuts?" asked Heinrich.

"No, don't bother. I'm dining with her ladyship in a minute. I'll probably have a few more injuries by the end of the meal!" he replied, grinning.

An hour later, he and Sarah were seated opposite each other at an oak table in the dining room and it was quickly apparent to her that his appetite did not seem to be in any way diminished by the emotional demands of the day, as he quickly consumed the whole of a rabbit, a duck and a chicken. She looked crossly at his seemingly cavalier approach to his wickedness and toyed with her own food.

"You ate nothing earlier. You must eat something," he reproached her.

A church bell pealed with a deep note nearby, blue wood smoke drifted past the window, and the noise of laughter and talking outside in the courtyard sharpened the sense of quiet in the room. She stared at the food on her plate, physically unable to swallow it and glanced at him.

"What happened to the boys? " she asked icily. "Were they hurt?"

"No, Heinrich cuffed them," he replied, looking pleased to be spoken to, even if the topic was rather sensitive. He sliced off a part of the chicken he was eating and placed it on her plate.

"Eat this," he said. "It's very good."

She tried to nibble it and managed to wash it down with gulps of wine, the anticipation of retrieving her locket allowing her in part to do what he wanted. Its strong herb flavour calmed her and drew her back into the past, as before, but her memory still failed her.

"Now, sir, can I have my locket?" she asked. "I would like to retire to my room."

He put his hand in his pocket and withdrew the locket. "Here you are," he said, looking at her intently. "I will have the chain mended for you."

She took it and without thanking, or acknowledging him, stood up and stalked out of the room, haughtily tossing her head.

28

They left early next morning and she felt the day started badly when he kissed her on both cheeks to greet her as she was about to step into the coach.

"I'm afraid that a maid could not be found at such short notice," he said, as though nothing untoward had happened.

His embrace distressed her. She frostily ignored his words and was horrified when he climbed in after her and sat down heavily on the seat opposite.

"I would like to enjoy your company today, madam," he remarked. "I hope that is acceptable to you."

"I would prefer to be alone, sir," she replied, the intervening night not having altered her perception of him; but he stayed seated, an air of determination about him, and out in the courtyard Hans muttered to Gunther, "He's going to be eating humble pie today."

The coach set off and she pulled her hood around her face, steadfastly ignoring him. However, he gave no sign that that he was in any way perturbed and proceeded to tell her about his travels in Europe and the New World.

"This coach is very strong," he remarked. "It's like a small house on wheels, it's so well equipped. I've gone all over Europe in it." He told her about Rome and Florence and Berlin and Vienna and the artistic masterpieces and churches that were found there, and described the stockade at Fort Ticonderoga, the fortifications at Quebec and the tranquillity of Lake Champlain.

She tried not to listen, but after an hour's travelling and his informative conversation, considered that she knew more about the world than any decent person would need to know in a life time.

He fell silent and watched her for a few minutes and then, his voice now sounding hoarse, talked about beavers. He described their rudder-like tails and the two- room houses they built in dams and, in spite of herself, she began to be interested in what he was saying and looked towards him somewhat more kindly as he proceeded to tell her in detail about other North American wild life, and several hours later, he had exhausted his knowledge of raccoons, skunks, beavers and every other animal he had ever seen, or heard of.

She was, in fact, beginning to relent. Each time they changed horses, he bought her sweetmeats, cakes or little gifts like ribbons, which she accepted. She even found herself laughing at his frequent jokes and her sudden hatred of France and the French person opposite, started to fade and she looked with interest again at the passing countryside.

She very much liked the mellowed stone and ornate woodwork of the houses, which often stood isolated, surrounded by raised dykes where trees grew. There were many villages and each seemed to possess its own fish pond and mill and a communal washing place where there were always women beating and scrubbing the clothes.

"The Seigneur enjoys many privileges. He generally owns the baking house and the peasants pay him dues to have the bread baked," he informed her. "It's very different here from England. At home, I even have the right to make people stop the frogs croaking on the marshland, so that I can sleep well. And peasants have to pay a lot of taxes, both to the king and to the land owner."

There were whole fields of daisies and poppies and very tall trees she had never seen before, with graceful upward-sweeping branches; and grand, turreted houses with vast gardens could also occasionally be observed from the road.

"They're called chateaux," he told her. " A lady's heart can sometimes be given to a man who owns such a house, even if she perhaps does not like its owner," and she noticed an odd glint in his eye as he spoke.

At times he left her on her own and rode on horseback next to the carriage and she even sometimes found herself wishing he would return. He had distressed her by what he had done but she knew that she could have been killed by the youths and she was very grateful to him for the return of her locket.

The sunken lanes of Brittany were left far behind and she lost count of how many days came to be spent in travelling.

" The main roads are good, but the small tracks are so atrocious that people generally make their wills before travelling a long way," he told her and again, as with the pot-holes in Brittany, she did not know whether to believe him.

The soft verges trapped and overturned many coaches, which lay marooned, wheels in the air or on the side, waiting to be pulled erect by oxen, but theirs seemed more blessed, or perhaps sturdier, and they made good progress.

He came and sat next to her and touched her hand as he pointed out an ancient abbey, cloistered by trees on a nearby hill. She felt her body stiffening and involuntarily flinched away from him and suddenly realised

211

that although she was able to appreciate, and even enjoy, his company, any sort of physical contact with him now reminded her of being beaten, both by him and by others. She tried to reason with herself, knowing that her own behaviour had been extremely foolish.

'He did not even hurt me,' she mused. 'A chemise, three petticoats, a dress and a cloak were ample protection. It was my dignity which was hurt.'

But however she thought about it, she remained deeply in shock that he had raised his hand to her and the confidence which she had only gradually come to feel with him had been destroyed.

She saw uncertainty on his face as he looked at her. He seemed to be thinking, wondering what to do, and she hoped his temper would not erupt again. She had never known him as patient as he had been since leaving Rennes and she knew what an effort he had been making.

He did not move towards her, but said quietly and deliberately,

"I would be very grateful if you would let me hold your hand until the next staging post."

She did not reply, just looked at him while he waited, his eyes on her face.

"Yes," she murmured, not finding it in her heart to refuse him.

He slowly put his hand on hers and she felt its warmth. She trembled, but made herself sit still and not push him away and they sat in silence. She was afraid he would demand more favours, but when the staging post was reached, he withdrew his hand and she breathed more easily and was able to enjoy the view from the window again.

The houses became more numerous and magnificent, the road increasingly crowded with carriages, carts, riders, foot travellers and long lines of horses, their tails tied together, and she longed for the journey to be over.

"We're nearing Paris," he said to her, late one afternoon.

Orchards of apple, pear and peach blossom appeared everywhere. Espaliers of fruit trees grew against houses and walls, some still flowering, others with young fruit, and woodland copses were replaced by vegetable fields.

They reached an impressive stone entrance to the city, but she was surprised to see that there was still more marshland, market gardens and abbeys with extensive estates.

An inquisitive customs official poked his nose into one of the crates and recoiled in horror when he saw a jumble of dead snakes and one large, green and black toad which spat at him. He quickly decided not to open anything else and they continued on their way.

A spider's web of streets drew them into ever more crowded and congested thoroughfares. Road arteries, feeding the life blood of the city, were veined by narrow alleys, from where people, carts and horses spilled out into the main routes, causing much confusion and shouting and reducing the speed of their carriage almost to a crawl. The houses were crammed together, tall and steep-roofed, some blindly shuttered against the sun, others with windows so wide-open she could catch tantalising glimpses of other peoples' lives; their pictures, furniture, caged birds and even their clothes hung out on washing lines strung from wrought-iron balconies. Aromatic cooking smells merged with the odour of rotting rubbish and horse dung and her senses reeled from the pungent pot pourri of humanity existing in such naked closeness.

A hot sun shone fiercely down; the glare from light-reflecting windows and pale flagstones accentuated by the sharply contrasting blackness of foetid alleys. Near the centre of the city, she saw the embankment of a wide river, spanned by high bridges lined with houses, and in the distance she could see two imposing cathedral spires. Jetties protruded into the water, people swarmed around market stalls on the riverside and a heavy traffic of horse-drawn barges and sailing boats was passing rapidly up and down, rippling brown waves against the banks.

The coach stopped outside a tall mansion with balconies in front of each window and she sprang to her feet, thoroughly disenchanted with the tedium of being cooped up, for days on end, like a pea rattling round a pod.

She stepped down on to the ground and he escorted her to the main door and she realised it was not an inn or a hotel, but a private house. Inside, in a vaulted hall of marble, stood a line of servants, all in dark blue, the women with white caps and aprons.

"My house is at your disposal, madam," he said formally, turning to her. It had not occurred to her that he would own a house in Paris and she stood gazing around her.

A servant showed her to a bedchamber, where the canopy of a bed and the walls were as richly decorated as those in the hall. A young maid helped her change and then, still feeling rather ill at ease, she descended the stairs to the dining room.

Hundreds of candles burned, lighting a dining room whose central feature was an extremely long table, gleaming with silver cutlery and tureens. The half-panelled walls were hung with oil paintings and richly woven tapestries, and blue-liveried footmen were waiting to serve the food.

He bowed, then kissed her hand. "My dear, please be seated," he said and then prayed.

She ate slowly, overawed by the splendour of her surroundings and sat quietly, glancing now and again at Jean Luc, who was attacking his food as he usually did, enjoying various bottles of wine and looking, she thought, extremely contented, like a hunter who had bagged a deer.

"I wish I could show you the city, or Versailles, tomorrow," he said, "but unfortunately I have business to take care of with Heinrich. We sell wine from the estate. When we were in the New World, we obtained many contracts and we want to try here in Paris."

He continued to talk enthusiastically about his ideas for expanding his vineyards in Alsace and she reflected again on how different he was to the Throgmortons. They would have been horrified at the thought of doing any sort of work and she wondered again if he was somewhat impoverished, although the sumptuous furnishings of his house seemed to indicate not. It also surprised her that he told her in detail about his plans. At the Throgmorton household, ladies had not been allowed to remain at the table after dinner with the men; they were despatched to another room to talk about more frivolous, female topics, and yet here, he was seriously talking to her about his business ideas.

Guilt and shame suddenly made her blush as she remembered she was not really Lady Sophie Throgmorton, his relation. She had become so used to being her, it seemed unreal now to think of herself being anyone else, and her former life seemed a figment of her imagination.

'I wonder if they hang people in France' she thought dejectedly, 'or perhaps they have some other ghastly method,' and she tried not to think of his terrible anger when he discovered she had deceived him. Jealousy of his future bride surfaced in her mind and she almost laughed out loud to think she could add yet another sin to the panoply she already possessed.

'I must be an extremely wicked person,' she thought.

Then, as she always did, in order to be able to cope, she firmly pushed all her fears to the back of her mind, and tried to concentrate on the advantages of bottles with elongated necks, and the different properties of corks, being described by the very enthusiastic wine producer sitting opposite her.

" You're looking very pale. I'm tiring you," he said. "It's thoughtless of me. It's been a long journey."

"Yes, I am rather tired," she replied truthfully, her bones aching from so many days of travel.

"I don't want you to leave the house tomorrow in my absence," he said. "Please make yourself at home here and ask the servants for anything you need."

She wearily stood up and he took her by surprise by gently embracing her and kissing her on both cheeks. His physical closeness distressed her and she pushed him away.

"Goodnight," he said, and then he more firmly embraced her, kissing her on each cheek a second time.

"Good night, sir," she said very coldly and retired to her new bedchamber, where she quickly fell asleep, dreaming about a faceless woman who was marrying him and who very much enjoyed being kissed by him.

She spent the next day alone in grateful idleness, reprieved from the jolting carriage. She wandered through the richly furnished rooms and spent a long time gazing at a painting of a chubby boy in velvet breeches and coat, standing with two spaniels. His dark eyes stared out at her and she longed to pick him up and smother him with kisses and cuddles.

The sound of trickling water enticed her out into a small, sun-baked garden and she passed most of the day in the shade beneath a rose bower, intending to think about her predicament and how to escape it, but, instead, spending her time sketching the garden's insect life. Water boatmen skating across a pond captivated her, as did a green rose chafer, buzzing through the air. Ants, beetles and a snail also found their way on to her drawing sheets, and the only regret she had at the end of the day was that she suddenly longed to see Wildercombe House and the wood and beach again. She ate dinner, feeling very lonely at the huge dining table, and had already gone to bed when she heard Jean Luc talking with Heinrich in the hall. Their voices echoed up the stairs, then faded away and she sank back into her soft bed and passed a second night dreaming about the faceless woman.

29

Dawn had only recently broken as they set off once more to Alsace and the distinctive smell of the city lingered in the carriage long after its streets were left far behind. She had a new companion, a young, dark-haired maid called Jeanne, who looked out of the window as excitedly as she did herself.

They travelled through fertile farmlands. Hamlets of stone houses clustered amongst vineyards, poplar trees stood in rows along the road and copses hugged low hills.

Then the land became bare and open. Huge wheat fields stretched to the horizon. There were no trees, just the occasional stunted elm and bushes of dogwood or blackthorn; the earth was parched and dry, without streams or springs, and the half-timbered houses often appeared poor.

"Say nothing to customs officials," he told her. "You haven't got a passport. There wasn't time to obtain one for you in Paris."

He remained on his horse and she rarely caught a glimpse of him, except at the staging posts, a situation which pleased her as she still felt in a state of emotional turmoil, sometimes hating him with a violence which astonished her and, at other times, longing to hear his voice and see his face.

They stopped at inns, some very comfortable, with flowers in window boxes and courtyards, whilst others reminded her of the flea-ridden place she had stayed at with Sophie in England, and her fair skin began to be marked by the redness of numerous bites. She always insisted on dining alone in her room, citing tiredness as the reason, and he let her do as she wished, although his face clearly expressed his displeasure.

She did not sit idly in the carriage and tried to improve what appeared to be her half-remembered grasp of the French language. She continually asked Jeanne the names of everything and by the end of the journey was able to speak far more fluently; and she now accepted she must have spoken it as a child, but where, and with whom, she still had absolutely no recollection.

After many days, the countryside appeared very wooded and the previous lack of water was replaced by an abundance of ponds and fast-flowing streams everywhere. Hills and valleys alternated; low, square houses were strung out on each side of broad streets, plum orchards at their back, wagons and steaming manure heaps at the front.

The hills became steeper and densely forested and there were occasionally whole encampments of beggars and vagabonds living in shacks made of branches and wattle and daub. Deep valleys could often be seen far below; blue lakes or muddy swamps lay at the foot of hillsides sometimes denuded of vegetation, and she unhappily saw similar red sandstone cliffs to those she had seen in Devon, the colour again reminding her of blood. The road became only a rutted track. The coach followed it with difficulty down the slopes and she was relieved that so many armed men accompanied them as the sinister howls of wolves frequently made her blood run cold. Finally, the hills were left behind and they were travelling across a flat plain, where clumps of woodland vied with vineyards and fields growing hemp, maize and tobacco and a multitude of vegetables and where for the first time she saw horses yoked together with oxen for ploughing.

Twilight was beginning to soften the outline of trees and bushes and she looked forward to escaping from her prison on wheels. Each evening since Paris, they had stopped at this time of day and she was disappointed to find they continued on their way, clattering through solidly built villages, the houses large and half-timbered; red flowers bright in window boxes. Even at this hour, it felt stiflingly hot, and she fanned herself repeatedly.

She was astonished to find that as the evening darkened, their speed actually increased and she looked out to see if there was a full moon, but only a slender crescent gleamed feebly in the sky. The last glimmer of light disappeared and she again prepared to leave the coach. Then, the next minute, flaming brands carried by men on horseback, surged out of the darkness and surrounded them; the coachman shouted to the horses and they continued on their way. Pinpricks of starlight shone brilliantly in the black heavens and when they passed through villages, people poured excitedly out of their houses to welcome them. Jean Luc rode level with the coach, the burning, smoking light flickering over his face; church bells were ringing loudly and she realised they must nearly be at their journey's end.

She peered out of the window, amazed that their arrival should provoke this deafening, flaming scene, and could see a large house and people running along the road. They swept through an arch in its middle and she realised that, in spite of its size, it was only a gate house, and the coach sped down a straight, oak-lined drive.

They came to a halt in front of an enormous chateau, three storeys high, with two smaller wings at right angles to the main building; its grey slate roof rounded and set with dormer windows. Fire brands were burning in metal holders on the front steps and in the courtyard, and thousands of candles were visible inside the house, lighting the rooms.

She descended from the carriage and saw a mass of servants, in the Delacroix livery, standing in the courtyard. People were embracing all around her, parents were welcoming back their sons, and girl friends and wives were kissing loved ones. Bells were still pealing and a burning smell tainted the warm night air as Jean Luc firmly took her arm, guiding her towards the flight of steps leading to the front door.

Bemused by the noise and the crowd, she accompanied him into the main hall, hung with glittering chandeliers, ablaze with candles. The ceiling was painted with scenes from antiquity, like the house in Paris, and gold and silver tapestries decorated the walls.

"Welcome to my home," he said, kissing her on both cheeks.

Hundreds of curious eyes looked at her and she felt almost as though she was one of his prized specimens, which he had brought home for them to view. She blushed and he said, "If you would care to change. When you are ready, I will come to your room and escort you to dinner," and as she followed a servant up the stair-case spiralling to the landing, she glanced down and saw him enthusiastically embracing and kissing people in the hall.

Her bedchamber was as opulent as the rest of the chateau appeared to be. A bed, its canopy woven with gold and silver thread, was against one wall, and snow-white covers were already invitingly turned back. The furniture was of a solid, dark wood, intricately carved, and she noticed with surprise that the bedside table was made of silver.

She prepared slowly for dinner, disorientated in the richness of her new surroundings and wished she was back at Wildercombe House, with the chipped stone birds at the entrance gate and the familiar smell of mildew in the rooms and knew he was escorting her down to dinner as he suspected she would otherwise find an excuse not to attend the meal.

'Why do you not leave me alone, sir?' she thought. 'You obviously don't need me at your dining table tonight. You have many others here who would fulfil the role far better.'

Thinking of him troubled her and she turned her thoughts to the very welcome realisation that the last English traveller they had seen, had been many days before, at an inn near Paris. He had been clutching a guide book and map and complaining bitterly about the food, the weather and the French.

"Alsace seems even more distant from London society, than North Devon," she reflected. "I need have no fears about the Throgmorton family for the moment."

Her spirits rose and she was able to greet him with a smile when he arrived at her door a short time later.

She saw him glance at her hair which was tightly curled, high on her head, and at her lace-ruffled, lilac silk gown, which she had never worn before, as it had always seemed too elaborate for Wildercombe House and was also far too long for her. This palatial chateau, however, seemed the right setting for it, but as she walked she caught her foot in the hem and stumbled, nearly falling down the vast flight of stairs.

"Please take my arm," he said courteously. "I don't want to lose you now we've finally arrived."

The dining room was filled with light. Candles burned in chandeliers, the walls were resplendent with mirrors and the table overflowed with silver dishes.

"May I say how beautiful you look, madam," he complimented her. "I hope you find my chateau to your satisfaction."

She gradually relaxed, a sensuous warmth creeping through her body, and watched with amusement as he valiantly despatched a bustard cooked with five other birds, one inside the other. She nibbled at the food on her plate, very aware of his eyes on her.

"Can I ask a favour?" he asked, as he finally reached the smallest bird, a warbler stuffed with an olive.

"Yes," she replied.

"Would you let down your hair?" he said. "I like it hanging long."

She stared at him, words failing her and taken aback by his rudeness.

'You don't wear a wig, sir,' she thought to herself. It also struck her as a very strange request for a man about to be married, that he should be interested in how she arranged her hair. She hesitated, not knowing what to do, whereupon he stood up and walked round the table and clumsily touched her hair and pulled out a hair pin.

"No!" she protested and to stop him proceeding further, quickly pulled out the pins herself.

"That's better," he remarked, as her hair fell down her back, and he gently touched it again, a look, almost of adoration, on his face, which she could not explain, his behaviour shocking her.

None of the servants standing in the room blinked an eye and he stood next to her for a moment, then returned to his place.

219

She was speechless. 'If he is like this with me, what is he like with the woman he loves?' she thought and was relieved to see he resumed his onslaught on his food.

They sat together, without speaking, enveloped by the sultry heat of an Alsatian summer evening. Suddenly something buzzed by her ear and she jumped.

"It's a mosquito," he said. "Don't let it bite you. They carry diseases. We're near to the River Rhine and its very low-lying here, with much marshland, and we're often plagued with them in summer."

A footman neatly killed the insect between his hands and she looked dubiously around her, hoping not to see any more.

"There's also a problem with insects called ticks," he continued. "Don't walk in the undergrowth of a wood or forest, or long grass, where there's animals. If ticks bite, they can give you a nasty illness. It's best to stay in the garden."

She stared at him, wondering if it was safe to venture out of doors at all and thinking that at least she seemed to be out of reach of the Throgmortons, even if not these insects.

He finished eating and slowly drank a glass of brandy.

"I'm intending to hold a ball at the chateau in a week's time. I'm hoping to celebrate an announcement I'm going to make," he said enigmatically.

She waited for him to elaborate, but he remained silent and she guessed sadly that he was talking about his marriage. She looked at his serious face, his eyes smudged dark with tiredness from all the travelling, his hair tied back, and she almost burst into tears. Then controlling herself, and suddenly so exhausted she could hardly stand, she bade him goodnight and retired to an unfamiliar room where she discovered she had to sleep under a muslin canopy to ward off the mosquitoes.

She awoke to an unfamiliar world of whiteness shifting in the window's gentle draught. For a second, she thought she was finally in the clouds of Heaven and then realised it was the drapes hanging from the bed's canopy and, very relieved, she pulled a bell to summon a servant.

When she had dressed, she descended to the hall and was disappointed to find he was about to depart with Heinrich. He was very formally dressed in a dark coat and breeches and, to her utter amazement, was wearing a long, grey wig.

"I've affairs to take care of at the de Montforts' chateau," he said grimly, and she knew he was going to see his future bride. She was puzzled to see that he looked like he was about to have a tooth pulled, rather than meeting his wife to be, and noticed that Heinrich also appeared even more dour than usual and that, he too, was wearing a wig.

Her pleasure in the day disappeared, and as he saw her downcast face he said quietly, "I also am sad at not being able to be with you today."

She choked back her tears, and attempting to look nonchalant, followed them out to the courtyard and watched them mount their horses before cantering off down the drive, accompanied by a retinue of servants.

She spent the morning wandering through the grounds, discovering that although immediately in front of the chateau there was a very formal arrangement of flower beds and rows of clipped orange trees in square boxes, behind it there was a rambling garden, its paths winding through trees towards a lake where a fountain was spraying a fine mist of water, rainbow-coloured by the sun's rays. The heat of the day was enervating and she lingered for a long time in the cool shade of trees, only returning at midday. The beauty of the chateau filled her with awe as she approached, its many windows sparkling in the sun, but her spirits remained stubbornly low and she spent the hot afternoon resting in her bedchamber, looking at the picture in her broken locket and trying not to think of him.

Towards evening she stood on the front steps, grateful for a cool breeze which was now blowing across the garden and smiled as she saw him returning. He cantered up and dismounted, looking extremely pleased with himself, she thought, a very different man to the one who had left that morning.

....

The meeting with the de Montforts had gone better than he had hoped, although he had been forced to part with a substantial amount of money to recompense them.

"She's waited two years for you!" her father had shouted. "She's no longer as young as she was! It will be more difficult to find another suitor!"

'That's certainly true!' he had thought, horrified to see his future bride after being used to Sarah's ethereal beauty.

'Did I see her in the dark when I came before?' he wondered and could not believe he had managed to engage himself to a woman who looked so ugly, and remembered being more interested in the land she was bringing with her than why she had been wearing a veil at the betrothing ceremony.

' I've changed,' he thought, 'since meeting Sophie.'

One of her brothers had wanted to fight a duel with him.

"Why?" he had shouted. "I never laid a finger on her." And he thanked God he had not consummated the betrothal, as he could have done.

"It was consummated in her mind!" her father had retorted. "Her honour has been besmirched!"

But after Heinrich had calmly negotiated how much money he thought he needed in order to save the family's good name, everyone had parted on surprisingly good terms and he had ridden home, at last free to marry his beloved.

He ran to Sarah, picked her up and embraced her, and this time she did not feel the slightest urge to push him away.

"Did your day go well?" she asked, nearly in tears to see he looked so contented after visiting his fiancée.

"Yes, it went extremely well. Come and tell me what you have been doing today," he replied and they went together in to the chateau.

30

The next seven days before the ball passed very quickly and if she had not known better, she might even have thought he was assiduously courting her. He showed her the gardens and they often sat by the lake, watching its chief denizen, a giant gold fish, sluggishly circling in the pale green water, while a turtle paddled backwards and forwards across its path, both seemingly oblivious to the other. The spray from the fountain drifted mercurially over the trees and the sun was so fierce the air shimmered in waves of heat. He frequently attempted to hold her hand, but she consistently rebuffed him, wondering why he was not holding the hand of Catherine de Montfort. She overheard him say to Heinrich that he did not feel he was advancing quite as quickly as he would have liked along the road to marriage and she remained very puzzled about his behaviour and his intentions to her.

Late one afternoon, they were wandering in the shade of the trees when an enormous, white bird, its wings tipped with black, landed gracefully by the side of the lake.

"What's that?" she exclaimed.

"It's a stork," he replied. "If they ever leave Alsace, it is said we will have bad luck. Haven't you noticed their nests on the chimneys?" And on their return to the chateau, he pointed out the untidy constructions perched ungainly on the roof.

She stared, fascinated, for several minutes.

"I never thought I could be jealous of a bird," he laughed, "I wish you would look at me like that!"

She felt much happier helping him unpack his specimens in his laboratory, than sitting with him in the gardens. She liked to kneel on the floor and carefully take out each creature or plant, then place it in a glass box and attach labels. She often found herself contentedly singing and was delighted when he showed her how to write letters and read a few words. She very much enjoyed being with him, but when he tried to be at all affectionate towards her, she stiffened with distress.

"I do confess, madam, you treated me more kindly when my arm was injured," he complained bitterly.

She spent part of each day with the seamstress, who was making a ball dress for her. She loved touching the soft fabric and watching the gown quickly take shape, feeling guilty about its obvious expense. The thought of attending the ball thrilled her, even although she presumed

Catherine de Montfort would be there; and she had attempted to remember the steps she had practised so long ago in the attic.

She now always talked French with Jean Luc and was speaking almost fluently.

"You've been well taught," he remarked and she said nothing, just blushed slightly. He worried her by making her practise writing 'Sophie Throgmorton ' and asked to know her other names but she teasingly refused to say.

"You're very mysterious, madam," was all he said and then, one afternoon, when she was engrossed in unpacking a large crate, he softly said, "Antoinette?"

She immediately turned towards him, but this time, instead of an empty hole in her memory, she suddenly recalled the woman who used to call her by that name. She remembered her hands – they were large and red, and then she remembered her long black dress and apron and being picked up and sitting on her lap. Emotion flooded through her. Her eyes were blind with tears. There had been so much kindness and love and suddenly it had gone, vanished, and she was abandoned to be beaten.

"I was alone!" she murmured. "I was all alone!" and in her mind she was back in the dark kitchen. Panic seized her and she struggled to breathe. Jean Luc shouted in alarm as she fell to the floor and she felt him holding her hand and water being sprinkled on her face and people flapping her with cloths.

"Perhaps it's the heat?" she heard someone say.

The attack subsided almost as quickly as it had come and with his arm around her, she stood and walked to the couch.

"I'm sorry," she lied. "I don't know what came over me."

She saw from his face that he did not believe her and that they both knew it was the name, 'Antoinette' which had caused her to faint.

"You always seem so fragile," he murmured and she could see he did not dare mention the name again.'

"I feel fine now," she said and stood up and returned to the boxes of specimens.

"Perhaps it would be better to rest?" he suggested.

"No," she said firmly. "I'm completely recovered," but as she quietly picked out the plants again, niggling away at her was the thought that he had called her Antoinette to see her reaction. Her heart raced frantically to think that he might have a suspicion she was not really Sophie, making her head swim with dizziness again.

At that moment, Heinrich came in to talk to him and she became less agitated as she saw his attention diverted. She took the opportunity to leave the room and went upstairs to her bedchamber and lay on the bed, her heart still beating erratically, trying desperately to recall more about the woman she now remembered and whether her own name had originally been Antoinette and not Sarah.

31

The day of the ball arrived. The fresh coolness of early morning rapidly changed to a dry, scorching heat and she was forced to abandon some of her petticoats, fearing she would collapse from suffocation before the evening festivities had even started.

She visited the ballroom to see what was happening and found panicking servants rushing backwards and forwards almost unsupervised, as the chateau's new housekeeper, a charming lady called Madame Schneider, the antithesis of Mrs Yelland, told her, in a state of near-hysteria, that she had never organised a ball in her life.

She was afraid she might make a fool of herself and reveal her scant knowledge of the dances that evening, but she was well-versed in the preparations needed for a ball from a servant's viewpoint and stood in the middle of the long, mirrored room, attempting to calm Madame Schneider and bring order to the chaos.

Halfway through the morning, Jean Luc arrived with Heinrich to check on the preparations. He looked surprised to find her confidently organising everyone and taken aback by the brief greeting she gave him, before she ran off to supervise the arrangement of the flowers, very pleased to be busy and not brood about his forthcoming marriage.

" She seems very much the mistress of the chateau already," he remarked with satisfaction to Heinrich, and then, looking unsettled in not enjoying her full attention, he went off to the library.

"I need to make preparations of my own," he told Heinrich. "I want to decide on the exact wording for my proposal this afternoon. I hope to be announcing my marriage tonight."

When they ate together in the afternoon, she found him quiet and contemplative and when they had finished enjoying a perch and tench from a river on the estate, washed down with its wine, he surprised her by asking her to come to the library. He told the servants he did not want to be disturbed and firmly shut the door.

She looked at him apprehensively. His manner was solemn and unsmiling and she hoped she had not annoyed him by helping in the ballroom.

"Would you like to sit in the window with me?" he asked, his voice sounding deeper than usual to her. Her heart began to race. 'Has he guessed my secret?' she wondered in terror.

As though to complement her fears, as she looked out over the garden, she saw the bright sunshine being devoured by monstrous, black, storm clouds surging across the sky. A strong wind gusted through the trees making the windows rattle. The first drops of rain pattered against the glass, then a torrential downpour lashed the parched ground and the wind rose to a howling, baying shriek.

"It's nothing," he said. "It often happens in the afternoon when it's been very hot. It will quickly pass. Would you like to sit with me for a moment. I've something to ask you."

She sat down, her heart fluttering. He sat on a chair next to her and took her hand, raised it to his lips and kissed it.

"What are you doing? Please stop this!" she pleaded.

"I love you. I adore you, my darling Sophie," his voice broke and he was so overcome with emotion he was hardly able to speak.

"Sir, please stop this! It's not right! It's not fair! You're going to be married to Catherine de Montfort!" she said tearfully.

"Catherine de Montfort! No, I'm not! How did you know about that?" he exclaimed. "I had no idea you knew about my proposed marriage."

"Jenny told me," she replied.

"And how did Jenny know?" he enquired, looking shocked to think she had believed him to be about to marry someone else when he was trying to court her.

"I don't know," she said, not wanting to betray Hans.

He appeared baffled and said, " I annulled the arranged marriage the day after we arrived here. I'm free to marry now. I didn't see any reason to tell you."

She stared at him, the seriousness of her situation beginning to sink in as she suddenly realised he had been trying to court her, not just playing with her affections or treating her kindly because she was a relation.

"I love you," he said, "I love you more than I can possibly say. I would like to ask you to marry me."

"You want to marry me?" she echoed unhappily, astonished by his words.

She saw his face cloud over at her less than enthusiastic response.

"I don't expect you to love me immediately," he said. " You can wait until we're married. I've enough love for both of us and you will never want for anything. I'm one of the wealthiest men in France."

She stared at him, nearly in tears. The man she loved was asking her to marry him and she had to refuse.

"I cannot," she said despairingly. "I cannot," and she covered her face with her hands and could not look at him.

He rose to his feet and stared down at her. "You're refusing me?" he said in an incredulous tone, clearly not having expected that she would reject him. "I'm not asking for a dowry. I do not expect any financial settlement from your family."

She stood up and started to bolt from the room, but he anticipated her flight and grabbed her tightly by the arms, pulling her to him.

"Why can't you marry me? Are your affections already given to another?" he demanded.

"No, they're not," she whispered, " but I can't marry you."

"Why can't you?" he repeated, ashen-faced.

She looked at him and was torn by different emotions. The delight of him holding her and saying he loved her, almost made her faint, and at the same time, she knew she could not possibly agree to a marriage as there would be contact with the Throgmortons. They would attend the wedding and she would be exposed and even if she managed to somehow avoid their being present at the ceremony, there was bound to be a time when they would meet. She felt bitterly disappointed and afraid.

" I cannot tell you," she whispered. "Please let me go."

He stopped holding her and strode up and down the room, his face white.

"Can I hope you have some affection for me?" he asked. "Might you reconsider your reply?"

She knew what she had to do. She had to make him abandon any plan to marry her and it broke her heart to have to do so.

"No, I cannot give you any such hope, sir," she said in as strong a voice as she could manage, trying desperately not to cry and not able to look at his beloved face.

For such a strong, tall man he seemed to almost crumple. He appeared so downcast she could not look at him any longer and she picked up her skirts and ran from the room.

He stood, gazing into space, in a mood of black dejection.

"I'm sure you love me as I love you," he muttered, his despair lifting somewhat. " What do you mean, "I cannot." Is there some problem preventing you or am I just clutching at straws? Are you in love with another man? Well if you are, he certainly isn't here. I have you and you will stay with me until I win you over.'

In her room, she sat and sobbed, until she could not cry any more. She found it difficult to believe that he loved her and had asked her to marry him and she found it even more difficult to believe that she could not possibly do so.

She wondered if there was any way she could marry him and not be found out. But she knew there was none. Sooner or later, and probably sooner rather than later, she thought, her deception would be revealed.

She knew she had really hurt him and her tears flowed again as she pictured his face.

She looked down at the garden and saw that the storm had passed and that a pale evening sun shone weakly. Her delight in the ball had evaporated and she now thought of it with dread. She feared seeing him again and wondered how he would behave towards her. She dried her eyes and tried to compose herself and summoned servants to help her with dressing.

The hairdresser arrived from Strasbourg and much discussion ensued about how best to arrange her hair. The gong sounded but she could neither spare the time to sit through a lengthy dinner, nor did she want to be alone with him. She sent a servant down to say that she would like to be excused, as she was busy preparing for the ball, and he sent the same servant back with a plate of food and a glass of wine.

32

She was finally ready as the sun faded from the sky and a round, full moon appeared high above the trees. 'They'll be able to see to go home safely,' she thought, as she realised why that evening had been chosen. She had already heard several carriages arrive and could faintly hear the sound of musicians tuning their instruments. A servant knocked on her door and told her that the Seigneur would be pleased if she would come down to greet the guests with him.

She took one last glance in the mirror and found it difficult to believe that she was looking at herself. Her dress was a fairy-tale confection of cream and blue silk, with lace frills on the sleeves and on the edges of the train, and more lace ruched on the bodice and hem; pearls gleamed round her throat and her hair was interlaced with pearls and ribbons. It seemed bittersweet to her to wear the gown now, as she finally understood why he had lavished so much time and money on her.

"I've been so blind," she murmured and for a moment let herself be carried away by the bliss of knowing that he loved her, then she brutally pushed the thought from her mind and ventured out onto the landing and looked down at the hall below, where people dressed in a rich extravanganza of clothes and jewellery were pouring through the main door.

Faces turned towards her and he paused as he welcomed the guests and also glanced upwards. They stared at each other, as they had the first night they had met, and then she nervously descended the stairs, the dress swirling out around her, the soft candlelight catching the gleaming red of her hair, her blue eyes strikingly bright in her oval face. He came to greet her and bowed,

"My lady," he said, "May I say that you look beautiful."

She looked uncertainly at him, pleased to see that he was handsomely dressed as always, in a maroon silk coat and breeches, a sword at his waist in a heavily jewelled scabbard. His face, however, was pale and unsmiling and she thought she could see a determined glint in his eye and suspected he was not about to relinquish her easily. She stood next to him and together they met the steadily increasing flow of guests, among whom, she was relieved to discover, no one appeared to be even remotely English, many of their names sounding so foreign to her ears that she was completely unable to even pronounce them.

Finally, the moment arrived that she had been both dreading and awaiting with delight. He took her hand in his and they went into the ballroom, where the musicians were playing a minuet.

"It's a long time since I danced," she murmured.

"Don't worry. I can never remember the sequences," he said and led her on to the dance floor. Her first steps were faltering, then her confidence increased and she copied other people when not knowing what to do. Her whole body thrilled to the music and the brilliance of the spectacle; the ladies with towering hair styles, bedecked in flowers, ribbons and jewels, the brightness of their swirling gowns; the silk coats of the men, the bejewelled swords and scabbards; the scent of the flowers decorating the room blending with the perfumes of the dancers, fragrantly suffusing the warm evening air.

When she touched Jean Luc's hand or arm during the dancing, she found it difficult to disguise her love and smiled radiantly at him, whereupon he whispered in her ear, "I think, madam, you are teasing me."

She longed to reassure and comfort him, but it was not in her power to do so, and as the evening wore on, she began to wish she knew the signs of his temper less well, as she seemed to be permanently surrounded by a host of young men who were almost queuing to speak to her or ask her for a dance and she could see he was becoming increasingly jealous and angry and she prayed that there would be no outburst from him.

At the far end of the room Heinrich was watching the proceedings with his wife.

"I think she's refused him!" he exclaimed in amazement, as he saw Jean Luc's glowering face and heard no announcement of marriage. "I thought she seemed almost as besotted with him as he is with her. Doesn't she want to be a Duchess and live in this chateau?"

....

.   Long after the ball had ended, she lay restlessly in her bed, unable to sleep, still hearing the music in her head and feeling the excitement of the dancing. The hot air pressed down claustrophobically and Jean Luc's face and words haunted her.

She had hardly fallen asleep when she awoke to brilliant sunshine stabbing through chinks in the dark mass of the shutters. She rapidly dressed, with the help of servants, and went downstairs where she found the dining room overflowing with guests who had stayed the night. He greeted her with a kiss on both cheeks and she sat next to him at the table, and drank a bowl of hot chocolate, which she had acquired a taste for since being in France, suddenly feeling very shy with him. She hardly noticed the guests; she only saw what he was doing; how he held his cup and smiled when he spoke; and how he put his arm on the back of her chair, in a proprietorial way, as though she was his. A longing for him surged through her body and she found it extremely difficult to concentrate on the lively discussion about hunting wild boar which was preoccupying everyone else.

When the last guest had finally departed, they stood on the steps together, watching the carriages speed off down the drive.

"I'm going to work on my new specimens," he said, in a matter of fact voice. "Would you like to help?"

She had intended to see as little of him as possible, but was completely unable to resist the attraction of being not only with him, but also with the exotic creatures and plants he had collected. At first, it seemed awkward being alone with him in his work room. His expression had in the past often baffled her, but now she knew very clearly what he was thinking and was only too aware of the passion in his eyes. She was very afraid he could also see her own desire for him and tried to conceal her thoughts.

They spent the day politely behaving as though his proposal had never happened. They laughed together and chatted and she drew pictures and practised copying the letters he wrote for her.

He watched her and waited, having resolved to act more slowly. He had wondered if the idea of marriage had just been too much for her, had perhaps even frightened her. He had recognised from the beginning her extreme naivety and lack of education, and then had been astonished at her ability to speak French. He was very curious about the problem with the name Antoinette and wondered why the Throgmortons had sent such a beautiful woman of marriageable age to North Devon and why she had been so badly treated.

He looked at her sitting on the floor, uncaring about her fine dress as she unpacked the last box, and had to restrain himself from rushing across the room and throwing his arms around her. She looked at him and, as their eyes met, he saw an unmistakeable desire for him, before she quickly glanced down again; but in that instant, he knew she loved him as much as he loved her.

She stood up, her face very flushed. "I think I'll go to my room now," she said and almost ran towards the door and he realised she was afraid to stay any longer in case he saw her true feelings towards him. He had never before felt so inadequate in knowing what to say or do.

'Why won't she admit her love?' he thought and then Jenny's words came back to him, "She's afraid."

'Yes,' he reflected. ' She seems afraid. But why? Is she afraid of me?'

He had wondered about asking her father for her hand in marriage, whether she agreed or not, but had decided for the moment to continue to court her, expecting that whatever the problem was, it was probably very slight and it was only her innocence and lack of knowledge of the world which had enlarged it out of all proportion.

Thinking of his conversation with Jenny made him recall her saying that her mistress had scars on her back, as well as on her arms, and he also remembered her denigrating herself when he had made her drunk.

'Perhaps she feels she's too ugly for me?' he suddenly thought, 'She seems to have no idea how beautiful she is. Perhaps it's only these scars which are the problem?' And the more he reflected on it, the more he was convinced he was right.

33

She attempted to be somewhat reserved towards him in the days that followed, to try and show she did not care for him at all, but found it very much an uphill task. When she looked in a disdainful or disinterested way at him, he would grin and make a joke or just seize her hand and take the opportunity to kiss it and say he was her faithful servant and she could behave towards him as she wanted.

He left her in no doubt that he realised she was play-acting and she felt increasingly trapped by the situation, and, at the same time, overwhelmed by her love for him and the knowledge that he also loved her. She found it difficult to sleep and the face which stared back at her from the mirror, looked white and anxious, dark circles below her eyes.

They wandered together along the grassy paths of the estate, following the waterways. Red poppies were bright in the fields and verges, and tall frames of delicate green vines formed alleys of coolness on the dusty earth. They rode through dense woodlands or along the banks of the fast-flowing Rhine, but the beauty of the countryside went almost unnoticed as they fell more and more deeply in love and only had eyes for each other. She lived from minute to minute, her resolve weakened, a terrifying fear of the future almost asphyxiating her, but unable to break free.

"My dear," he said to her one evening, as they sat quietly after dinner, in the library. He took her hand in his and with his other hand gently touched her face. "My beloved," he murmured, "I fear I've distressed you and I want to resolve the problem."

He looked down at the hand he was holding and then pushed up her sleeve to reveal the weals.

"No!" she gasped. "No!" and unsuccessfully tried to stop him.

He bent his head and kissed the marks. "You are beautiful, my darling. You're so beautiful," and then kissed her arm again as she trembled violently. He held her in his arms, kissing her hair and her face before kissing her passionately on her lips.

She murmured, "No," and half-heartedly tried to stop him again, but the delight of feeling his mouth on hers was so intense, she was almost dizzy with pleasure and spent the rest of the evening seated on his lap abandoning herself to being kissed repeatedly. He murmured endearments to her and caressed her and as she lay in his arms and the light finally faded from the sky, he kissed her ear and said softly, "Will you marry me?"

She immediately went rigid and he tightened his arms around her and looked at her face, so near to his own. He said nothing, his expression almost disbelieving.

"Will you marry me?" he repeated more forcefully.

"I cannot," she said tearfully.

"I know you have scars on your back. " he said. "It doesn't matter to me. I love you and you're the most beautiful woman I've ever seen."

Her face white, she said again, "I cannot," in so low a voice, he could hardly hear her.

He stood up and roughly placed her on the ground, then paced the room in a fury.

"And what have you spent your evening doing, madam?" he shouted. "Was it a game? Have you been mocking me?"

She wished the floor would swallow her up. His shouting did not frighten her. She understood his hurt and frustration. She longed to tell him what had happened. She longed to unburden herself to the man she loved, to tell him of the fear which had stalked her since that first day in the coach when Sophie had died. She had never felt so vulnerable and so alone as she did at that moment .

She bit her mouth to stop herself revealing her secret. Much as he obviously loved her, she could not envisage him wishing to marry a servant, let alone be happy that she had deceived him. She knew very well that Dukes always married within a small social circle and it was unusual for them to marry someone of even slightly lower rank.

She loved him with a passion the extent of which, she thought, he was almost completely unaware and she realised she probably had very little time left to be with him. She expected to be cast aside when he finally accepted there would be no marriage and she found it impossible to even contemplate being rejected by him. She knew her anguish would be unbearable and ever since she had seen the powerful river flowing to the east of his estate, the Rhine, had entertained the thought that she no longer wanted to live if she could not have him and would prefer to drown herself here in Alsace, his home, and would therefore always remain near to him. She would put an end, not only to her suffering, but also to his.

"Tell me why you won't have me!" he was shouting at her. "Am I not wealthy enough? What do I have to do to make you want me?"

For all his loudness, she thought he actually seemed about to cry. She timidly approached him and then, surprising herself, and certainly Jean Luc, she very gently put her arms around him.

"Please calm yourself. I am not worthy of you," she said.

He held her at arm's length and said, "If you can look at my eyes and say you don't love me, then I will stop asking you to marry me."

She knew that she had to say the words. He put his hand under her chin and forced her to look at him. Her eyes filled with tears which trickled down her cheeks.

"I don't love you," she said softly.

They stared at each other, his face completely unbelieving. His expression hardened.

"Goodnight, madam," he said curtly and turned and walked out of the room.

She waited, shaking, until she heard the door of his bedchamber close, then ran sobbing upstairs.

34

She stayed in her room for three days and sent a message to say that she was indisposed.

'He won't want me now,' the refrain beat constantly in her head. 'He won't bother to pursue someone who clearly does not love him.'

Her heart broken, she spent most of the time in bed, huddled under the bedclothes.

'If I don't see him, I can't retract what I said,' she told herself.

On the fourth day, her black mood of despair lifted and she felt a renewed vigour for life. She had not heard from him and none of the servants had mentioned him at all, so she presumed he had not even enquired how she was.

'It's for the best,' she thought, and even entertained the hope that if he was no longer enamoured of her, she could perhaps stay in his house as his relation and still see him. The drastic alternative mainly featured drowning herself in the River Rhine, a prospect which seemed distinctively less appealing as she happily dressed herself that morning in his favourite blue dress, fastened a diamond necklace around her neck and wondered about playing the harpsichord she had seen in the ballroom.

He had spent three days quietly reflecting and waiting. Love was not an emotion he had been well acquainted with until meeting Sarah, and although he was perplexed about what to do, he was determined that he would marry her, regardless of whether she decided she did, or did not, love him. His initial anger and hurt at her words had disappeared, almost as soon as he closed the door of his bedchamber and heard her crying as she ran up the stairs. He had followed her, but she had already gone into her room and he had then spent some time making sure that a servant was stationed at every exit from the house, as he had no intention of letting her run off into the Alsatian countryside. He had spent the last three days continually questioning her servants about what she was doing and had found it almost impossible to stay away from her.

He had been told that she was dressing and waited impatiently for her in the library. He realised his actions had provoked some sort of nervous crisis and hoped that now, by giving her time to come to terms with whatever the problem was, she would finally agree to marry him. He had absolutely no intention of holding to his promise not to pursue her when she said she did not love him. He had never wanted anyone, or anything, like he wanted her, and he knew there was nothing he would not do to achieve his desire, even to the extent of killing a rival for her.

He waited until he heard her footsteps on the hall floor and then came out to greet her and was immediately shocked by her appearance. Her face was completely without colour, her blue eyes brilliant against the pallor of her skin. She looked thinner and even more ethereal, but smiled as she glanced at him, her manner very calm and composed.

"You're feeling better?" he said and gently kissed her on both cheeks. She smiled with obvious delight at seeing him again, making him almost euphoric with joy, both to be with her and to see her pleasure in his company.

They spent the morning walking slowly through the grounds of the chateau. He offered his arm and she contentedly took it, and they both drew strength from feeling the closeness of each other's body. They hardly spoke, just existed solely in their own small, intimate world, and he took her to a stone seat, shaded by drooping willows, at the far end of the lake. They sat and watched dragonflies darting above the water, their fairy wings shimmering iridescently and a long-bodied rat marking the limpid green surface with v-shaped ripples.

"You're so pale," he said. "I should not have left you alone."

The sun caught the flame-red of her hair and he stared at her without smiling, making her blush. He let his eyes travel over her, but made no attempt to hold her hand or embrace her.

By the end of the day, she was almost relieved to escape and go to bed. The intensity of their mutual passion had exhausted her. She could see he was struggling not to touch or speak in any way that might offend or upset her, and also knew that whatever she said, it was more than apparent now that she loved him, and she could almost see his mind working to think what he had to do to make her say why she would not marry him.

By the end of the week he had abandoned the unequal struggle of not touching or holding her and she had completely abandoned the pretence that she did not love him, and they passed their evenings with her mainly seated on his lap, enjoying his caresses and kisses.

"Well, what am I going to do with you, my lady?" he asked, obliquely referring to her refusal to marry him. "Are you going to be my mistress?" he said jokingly.

She stared at him. It was not a solution she had thought of.

"Yes, I would like to be your mistress," she replied.

He was so taken aback, he stared at her almost open-mouthed. For the first time, he recognised that she was carrying such a terrible,

238

frightening secret, that she would happily be his mistress, not his wife, and forgo any claim to his chateau and wealth, either for herself, or for any children she might have.

They stared at each other, Sarah wondering why he looked so thunderstruck and not grasping his sudden realisation of the situation.

He held her close to him and looked down at her in amazement, whilst her heart beat faster in anxiety, as she could tell he had somehow come closer to guessing her secret.

"Good night, sir," she said, breaking free from him and even more worried as she saw his puzzled look. "I do not, of course, wish to be your mistress," she said, trying to right a situation which she still did not fully understand, but where she knew she had made an error.

"Are you already married?" he asked.

He took her by surprise and watched her curiously to see her think about the question and reluctant to answer immediately.

She toyed with the idea of saying yes, but realised that, in time, it would lead to even more problems. He would want to know to whom, and when, and might even question the Throgmortons.

"No, sir, " she said softly. "I'm not married."

"I didn't mean to offend you," he said, appearing extremely relieved, and as she left the room, he muttered to himself, " I know what I'm going to do."

35

The days passed and she quickly grew used to life in Alsace and encouraged by Jean Luc, helped Madame Schneider with some of the decisions needed to manage the household. She was surprised to discover that Heinrich was in charge of the Delacroix estates. He lived in one of the wings of the chateau and seemed to possess nearly as many servants as Jean Luc himself. He introduced her to his wife, a lively woman with black hair and dark brown eyes, and to his daughters, who all had blonde hair and blue eyes and often smiled, appearing completely dissimilar to their solemn, grey-haired, grey-eyed father.

Jean Luc did not mention marriage again and she wondered at times if she was becoming lulled into a false sense of security or if he had lost interest in her.

"I want to show you my hunting lodge in the Vosges mountains," he said one morning at breakfast. " If you would like to make preparations today, we can travel there tomorrow."

His face was unsmiling and she was slightly disconcerted to find that he wanted to leave his vineyards, where he seemed so busy, to take her on a trip.

The next morning, she sat in the carriage and waited for him. The sun was already climbing into a hot, cloudless sky and she watched a stork perch motionless, on a ramshackle arrangement of twigs and leaves on one of the tall chimneys.

He came down the steps in front of the chateau, dressed in a resplendent, blue and purple coat, his hair tied back. She noticed Heinrich standing at the foot of the steps and her glance idly travelled from him to Jean Luc and then back to Heinrich again, as she realised with a shock that he was furious. She had never seen him so annoyed and it was obvious there was some sort of disagreement between the two men.

Heinrich glanced towards her and his eyes looked troubled, but she did not feel that he was angry with her, whereas Jean Luc's face was grim and she had no doubt he was disregarding the older man's advice.

The next minute, he jumped into the carriage and sat down opposite her. The coach started off down the drive and, for the first time, she thought there was a strangeness about the way he glanced at her, almost a suggestion of guilt, it suddenly occurred to her.

The coach travelled slowly along roads that were often just grassy tracks. They crossed sluggish waterways and she wished she had brought her drawing paper to capture the images of the animals and birds she saw. The flatness of the plain was soon left behind and they ascended higher and higher up steep mountain sides. The carriage was tilted backwards and when she glanced out of the window, she was horrified to see an almost vertical descent beneath them. He smiled at her fright and said, "We're nearly there. The lodge was built to look over the clouds!"

He offered to hold her in his arms to calm her terror, but she laughingly declined and when the coach halted, jumped out first to stop him helping her down.

"I think you are teasing me today," he said good-naturedly, but as he looked at her, she was suddenly aware of the intensity of his desire and for a moment felt a sense of disquiet.

The stone lodge resembled a tiny castle and stood on a crag, surrounded by pine trees. She was delighted by her room which was filled with bouquets of roses on every shelf, reminding her poignantly of the enclosed garden at Wildercombe House. Sunlight streamed through an open window and she could hear the fluting notes of bird song, warbling and trilling.

She spent an idyllic time with him, wandering beneath the trees and standing on the parapet, enchanted by the panoramic view across the plain and, far beyond, to a range of distant, purple-tinted hills. The sky was a brilliant blue and storks circled, gracefully and slowly, caught in air currents carrying them up and down. They flew in swooping arcs, landing on huge nests which stuck out at odd angles on the towers and chimneys of the lodge. The day was etched forever into her memory as being a day of love, when she and Jean Luc existed only for each other, sensuously enjoying the intimacy of being together, on the forested summit of a hill, bounded by an azure sky and the wheeling storks.

With regret, as the sky darkened, she said goodnight to him; he kissed her hand and she retired to her rose-scented room, where silk sheets had been turned back on an enormous bed and an embroidered nightgown she had never seen before had been placed on it. Servants helped her undress and she was just snuffing out the candles they had mistakenly left burning, when the door suddenly opened. Jean Luc stood in the entrance in his nightshirt, his dark hair reaching his shoulders. He closed the door and came towards her.

"What are you doing?" she asked, astonished.

"I'm trying to find a solution to your problem," he answered. "I love you and I'm sure you love me." He put his hands round her waist and pulled her to him.

"Stop, sir," she exclaimed. "You should not be here."

"I know this is not the right way round," he replied, "but I intend to have our wedding night first and our wedding second. I hope that after tonight you will have no more worries and you will finally accept me."

"This is absurd!" she protested, hardly able to speak. He kissed her passionately on her lips and although she knew what they were doing was so extremely foolish she would probably regret it for the rest of her life, she also longed for him to continue. They could both feel each other's bodies through the thin material of their night clothes and she gradually gave herself up to his exploring hands and his mouth which became more and more demanding. He pushed up her sleeves and kissed her scars.

"I love you," he whispered and carried her to the bed and finally made love to the red-haired woman he had desired and adored since seeing her on the landing one cold February night in a far-off English manor house. They fell asleep in each other's arms, Sarah at last feeling freed from the horrors of her childhood, knowing that she was held by the man she loved.

He awoke first, as the sun lit the sky with a golden radiance, and gazed down at her as she lay against him. Her red hair fell over his arm and he watched her as she slowly opened her eyes, then he bent to kiss her on her mouth.

Later, as they drove back down the almost perpendicular road, she laughed with delight as the coach lurched and swayed over the rocky path, and felt weak from the love she felt for him, he asked the question she had been dreading.

"Will you marry me?"

She could see he no longer feared her reply. He smiled at her in anticipation of her acceptance, his expression changing to one of disbelief when she just looked at him, her face and eyes suddenly so miserable and sad as he stared at her uncomprehendingly. He grabbed her by the arms and held her to him.

"Why? Why won't you?" he shouted. "You love me!" and he gripped her so fiercely she thought she would suffocate.

"Are you promised to another and you don't think you can break your word?" he demanded.

"I can't say," she sobbed and clung in a black despair to him.

He thrust her away. "Tell me!" he ordered. "We are now man and wife in all but name. No one else will ever possess you. You're mine!" He thrust his face into the softness of her breasts and moaned with pleasure. "My love, my darling. You realise your reputation is now ruined. You

242

have to accept me!" His words became increasingly incoherent and he passed the rest of the journey alternating between kissing her repeatedly and furiously demanding to know why she would not marry him.

They finally arrived back at the chateau, Heinrich curtly acknowledging his master as he descended from the carriage. He glanced curiously at Jean Luc, whose face was flushed and who looked beside himself with fury, and then at Sarah, who had clearly been crying and who was gazing at Jean Luc almost in adoration.

On seeing Heinrich's anger, she realised for the first time, the extent to which Jean Luc had abandoned his strongly held religious and moral beliefs in order to win her love, and felt deep in her soul that the fateful journey which had started that morning as she stared out at the waves at Lynmouth, was now rushing headlong into a terrifying and ghastly conclusion, consuming him as well as herself.

36

The grapes grew large and black on the straggling vines. She tasted their sweetness and knew that soon they would be picked to make wine. She wandered between the rows, grateful for the shade.

She felt he watched her, like a cat watched a bird, and knew that in both their minds was the memory of their night in the lodge. She had abandoned herself to him and now was unable to suggest she did not love him. She was only able to stay obstinately silent as to why she would not marry.

He cajoled. He tried to persuade. He shouted and repeatedly lost his temper. But she remained deaf to every entreaty. Without telling her, he sent a messenger to the Throgmortons to ask for her hand in marriage and while he impatiently waited for the reply, he continued to court her.

She rode every day over the estate. She loved the thrill of galloping across the fields, her hair flying out behind her. The pounding of the horse's hooves and the wind in her face made her forget her worries. She realised that her only hope of easily extricating herself from her quandary was that he would finally tire of being rejected and abandon his pursuit. When that happened she did not know if she would have the strength to survive, and although she found her position increasingly difficult, in a strange way her love made her strong and enabled her to resist him, as she knew that if she told him the truth, she would then lose him. Each minute, each day that they continued as they were, was yet more time to spend with him. His anger did not trouble her. She hardly noticed his cold fury or his shouting. She saw beyond that to his frustration and his hurt, and remained calm and dignified, driving him almost to distraction as he gazed at her eyes and face.

He recalled making her quickly confess to helping the injured smuggler when he first met her and thought ruefully how she had changed since then. Her shyness and timidity had been replaced by a confidence which was impervious to any of his threats or pleadings. He no longer dismissed her obstinacy as based on naivety or ignorance. He appreciated her intelligent and sensitive nature and realised that what drove her to defy him was a secret which literally terrified her.

When his attempts at coercing her failed, he turned to more subtle ways to discover the truth. He tried to make her talk about her life before she knew him, endeavouring to know about other suitors. Captain Vinnicombe obsessed him and she longed to soothe his jealousy, but found herself floundering in difficult circumstances. He twice questioned her about Antoinette and she felt the blood leave her face.

Summer slowly passed. The messenger returned from the Throgmortons and he carefully opened the sealed letter, hardly daring to look. He saw that consent had been given to his proposal of marriage. Relief swept over him. He passed the whole day in an obvious state of contentment and Sarah looked suspiciously at him.

"You are very happy today sir," she said uneasily.

"Yes, I am," he replied enigmatically. "Perhaps two people can play at having secrets."

He waited until after dinner, then bluntly announced,

"I am very pleased to be able to tell you, my dear, that Lord Throgmorton has given his consent to our marriage."

He stared at her and she stared back at him, lost for words. He did not repeat the mistake of asking her to marry him. He could see that her father's agreement did not appear to have made her ecstatically happy.

"You will be my wife," he said flatly. He reached out and took her hand and kissed it.

She did not immediately contradict him, just continued to look at him. Then, her voice shaking, she said, "I do not wish to be married," and standing up, curtsied and left the room, leaving him staring blackly after her.

In her room she sat dazed. Contact with the Throgmortons had awakened her old fears and terrors. She knew she had very little time now left with him and desperately tried to think what she should do.

'Should she flee or should she drown herself in the River Rhine?' For a moment she even considered the possibility of telling him the truth, but the idea of that was so distressing, she preferred to contemplate suicide.

Her thoughts raced madly. She found it difficult to breathe, a coldness seized her in spite of the evening warmth. Servants bustled around, closing the shutters and lighting candles and she slowly undressed and changed for bed.

She lay in the dark, still unable to make a decision. She reached out and touched her locket on the silver table and found strength and reassurance in its familiar shape. For many weeks she had carried an additional burden, which she had tried to ignore, somehow hoping she was wrong, but now, for the first time, she forced herself to confront the frightening thought.

"I'm going to have his child," she murmured.

37

Autumn in Alsace seemed almost as hot as summer to Sarah. Jean Luc was very preoccupied with his vineyards and spent much of the day there, which pleased her, as she was finding it increasingly difficult concealing her swelling stomach, and the candle glow of evening was less revealing than the clarity of daylight. Strangely, she thought, although her problems were now much greater than before, a sort of contentment had settled on her and she drifted happily around the chateau and its gardens, putting off the terrible decision she ought to make.

"It suits you here," he remarked. "You're becoming plumper and you look even more beautiful."

He restricted their social life so that she could not meet any suitable young men and the most frequent visitors to dine with them were Heinrich and his wife.

She picked desultorily at her food one evening, finding it difficult to eat the many rich dishes brought to the table, and feeling queasy. Madame Scheyer watched her struggle, and with the intuition of a woman who had given birth to five children, said, "It's best to eat plain food. Like they say the English do."

"No it's not," retorted Jean Luc. "It's better to have it cooked with herbs and spices."

"Sometimes for ladies, plain food is best," she replied firmly and Sarah blushed as she realised her secret had been guessed.

Madame Scheyer smiled reassuringly at her and Heinrich, suddenly understanding his wife's remark, glanced critically at Sarah and rapidly downed a whole glass of brandy.

The next day he curtailed her horse riding. "It's not suitable in your condition," he said. " If you wish to take it up with the Seigneur, please do so, but in the meantime I do not wish you to ride any more," and then watched her walk crestfallenly back along the path.

"I think I saw her sitting astride the horse like a man the other day," he told his wife. "She's reckless and wild and still puts me in mind of that red-haired woman all those years ago. What on earth is she thinking of, to be pregnant and yet not accept the Seigneur?"

"For such a clever man, he seems to be extremely stupid where Lady Sophie Throgmorton is concerned," his wife remarked.

She could hardly make her dresses fit when the culling of the grapes began. The baby was beginning to kick and make its presence felt and her love for Jean Luc was now partly diverted to her unborn child. More than ever she wished to keep her pregnancy secret, so that the baby could continue to grow while she lived in comfort at the chateau. If she was found out she had no idea what the consequences might be, for the unborn child as well as for herself.

Sometimes she noticed the servants openly staring at her and wondered how much they had guessed. Heinrich also knew and she often felt his eyes critically looking at her. The only person who seemed oblivious to it all, appeared to be Jean Luc, who was spending nearly all his time in the vineyards.

She watched the season change to the strident colours of an Alsatian autumn. The leaves became vivid yellows, oranges and reds and she suddenly longed for the more pale, more delicate beauty, of an English woodland. The frenzied grape-picking finished, the wine-making was set in motion and Jean Luc finally turned his attention back to his reluctant bride-to-be.

"I want to go to North Devon," he told her. "My mother's health has evidently deteriorated."

"I've other reasons for returning," he informed Heinrich later. "I intend to visit the Throgmortons to see if that might shed some light on why she's refusing me, and if any other suitor is the obstacle to my marriage, perhaps I can deal with him by duelling."

So, to her disappointment, an unwilling Sarah found herself back in the same coach she had travelled in many months before. She had asked to remain in Alsace.

"You want to stay here without me?" he said dejectedly. "No, it's completely out of the question."

She pulled her cloak about her and tried to make herself comfortable, but no matter how she twisted and turned, her back hurt and she could not sit still.

The journey was a nightmare. Sleet-grey skies and a chill northern wind promised an early winter and the fiery leaves prematurely stripped from bare-boned trees, lay in dirty, bedraggled piles on the ground. The cold-steeped landscape found its echo in her spirits and each day's travelling was tinged more darkly with her fear and she could feel the invisible thread of fate twitching and jerking her ever nearer to her nemesis. Jean Luc always rode next to the coach and she ignored the passing countryside and bell-towered towns and only saw the sharp detail of his face and body against a background blur. Inside her, she felt the baby stir and kick, a physical reminder of their shared love.

She knew she had to break free, now not just for her sake, but also for her child, but how to do it and when, was almost too much for her mind even to contemplate, let alone find a solution.

The cold, dour Heinrich fussed about her at each stop to change the horses. He procured more cushions for her from an inn and insisted on often halting so that she could walk. Jean Luc looked surprised at his attention to her, but still remained in ignorance of the reason and she felt beset by guilt as she knew Heinrich was trying to ensure the survival of his master's heir, and he had no idea that whatever the future might bring to her child, it was not likely to include being the Duke de Delacroix.

She could see that he was becoming increasingly annoyed with Jean Luc for bringing about such an unfortunate situation and began to wonder if he doubted whether her pregnancy would survive the rigours of the trip, a question she was also asking herself. She knew that she was not strong and found herself often slumped disconsolately in the coach in complete exhaustion. To her relief, the wooden and granite houses of St Malo finally heralded the end of their gruelling and slow route from the eastern tip of France to one of its western outposts and she struggled up the stairs of the inn to her room and sat, out of breath, on an oak settle.

Outside in the courtyard, Heinrich spoke to Jean Luc, "Seigneur, do you think it would be better to remain here for a few days?"

"No, I would prefer to carry on," he replied. "I know Lady Sophie is feeling ill, but she will be able to recuperate when we reach North Devon."

"Do you think that's wise, Seigneur, in her condition?"

"In her condition? What do you mean?" he asked sharply, staring at Heinrich. He looked blankly at him for a moment, then, like a man possessed, ran across the cobbles, pounded up the stairs to her chamber in the inn and banged on the door, which was answered by her maid.

"Would you leave us?" he said and as the door shut behind her, strode over to Sarah who was still sitting on the settle, hastily trying to arrange her dress more loosely around her.

"My lady!" he said, for the first time catching her before she had time to disguise her pregnancy.

"You're….," He stopped, overcome with emotion. "You're going to have my child!"

"Yes," she murmured.

"Why didn't you tell me? My darling, my beloved. You <u>have</u> to marry me now," he said, looking almost beside himself with pride and joy.

"I will make you so happy. You <u>will</u> marry me now, Sophie," he said forcefully.

She just looked at him, afraid to contradict his words.

He seized her arm. "Say yes! You must say yes now!"

"I am not worthy of you," she stammered, her face devoid of colour and feeling so tired and ill, she was not capable of thinking logically.

"What do you mean? You are not worthy of me? What sort of talk is that?" he demanded.

"I have behaved badly. I cannot marry you." She spoke so softly, he could hardly hear her, and trembled violently, the words reluctantly forced out of her.

"What do you think you have done, my beloved? This is all in your mind. It's like your worry about the smuggler. You are naïve about the world. You imagine problems when there are none. I will look after you. Tell me what it is you fear," and he knelt down in front of her and clasped her hands in his.

But she bit her lip and refused to talk and could not stop herself shaking. He sat down next to her and held her in his arms and she sobbed, her face against his chest.

"Calm, my darling. Calm yourself for the sake of the child," he said and she gradually stopped crying and lay quietly in his arms.

He shared her room that night for the first time since the day at the hunting lodge. She had protested strongly, mainly from embarrassment at her less than slender shape, but he jumped into bed next to her, dressed in a shirt, and she abandoned herself, as she had before, to the sheer bliss of being loved by him.

The next few days were spent at the same inn.

"I bitterly regret having started the journey," he said. "But now we've come so far it's better to carry on to North Devon where you can recover."

He remained very kind and considerate towards her and she would have enjoyed his attentions more if she had been less worried. She expected him to persist with his marriage proposal, but instead he did not mention the subject, which unnerved her almost as much as if he had.

"I've decided to wait until our arrival to resolve the problem of marriage," he told Heinrich. "She becomes so distraught when I mention it, I fear for her own health and that of the baby. She seems so fragile, I'm afraid she'll die."

A physician came and pronounced her fit and well, just in need of rest. But he remained beset by worry.

"Don't worry, Seigneur. She once climbed a cliff!" Heinrich remarked cheerfully.

38

The Breton sky was a luminous blue, soft against the line of the horizon. The sea stretched flat and without waves, pale over the white sand, then in darker and darker bands of turquoise as it deepened.

Jean Luc and Sarah walked slowly towards the rock pools at the far end of the beach. The sand clung to their shoes and she smiled with pleasure, delighted to be in the fresh air after a day resting in bed.

"Don't worry," he said. "We're not far from Devon now. We'll travel gradually in short stages."

She was surprised at his anxiety about her pregnancy. In her experience, scullery maids had been expected to carry on working at hard and laborious tasks until they gave birth.

"I'm fine," she said. "Are we sailing on the same ship, the 'Antoinette'?" She made herself calmly say the word.

"Yes, we are," he replied and then, clearly taking advantage of the opportunity which had presented itself to him, tried to enquire more.

"Is Antoinette one of your names?"

"No, it isn't," she replied, somehow feeling guilty for her denial. "But I like it," she continued thoughtfully. "If I have a daughter I would like to call her Antoinette."

"Is Antoinette a friend?" he asked very curiously.

"No, she's not a friend," she replied.

" A relation perhaps?" he asked.

"No, she's not alive any more," she said, thinking that it was probably in some way, the truth. She looked at him seriously and could see him wanting her to say more.

She dug the toe of her shoe into the sand and watched the sand hoppers jump through the fine grains.

"She spoke French, I think," she said softly .

"She was a servant, at your house?" he said, guessing.

"Yes," she agreed. " She was a servant."

"Did she die at Lynmouth?" he asked.

"No, she did not," she replied firmly. "She died before that."

"Servants seem to die like flies in the Throgmorton household," she was surprised to hear him mutter irreverently to himself, and then he waited for her to say more, but she continued to scuff her shoes against the sand and said nothing.

She looked at him again. "If I should die, you will look after our child. You would not abandon him?"

"As we will be married, he will be the next Duke de Delacroix, so I hardly think I would abandon him!" he said sharply. "And in any case, you are not going to die!" He held her hands and kissed them and she instinctively knew that his own fear had been spoken aloud.

If you have a son what will be his name?" he enquired.

"Why, Jean Luc, of course," she said, for the first time saying his name.

"You like that name?" he teased her.

"Yes, I do," she admitted and giggled as she skipped off towards the sea, in spite of her rather stout shape. He strode after her and embraced her by the water's edge, kissing her, and then hand in hand they strolled back along the strand.

39

She enjoyed the sea crossing and with regret watched the Devon cliffs slowly approach. This time the water was a clear, translucent blue, not stained by the crumbling red sandstone. She was too superstitious to think of it as a good omen, but at least it did not remind her of blood as it had before.

The sunken lanes drew them deep into the countryside, weaving unevenly up and down the never-ending hills. The air was chill. The bird song seemed muted to her ears and she gazed forlornly at the sunless landscape, where the variegated green, brown, red and orange colours of the leaves and trees were tempered by lowering storm clouds. People looked miserable and poorly dressed and she briefly remembered a day of storks and a blue sky, before resolutely pushing it from her mind.

Her heart gave a leap as they passed the lichen-covered stone birds and then there was the crunching noise of the wheels on the drive and Wildercombe House appeared, grey and solid against the curve of the hill.

Servants ran out to form a row and Mrs Yelland, her body more stooped than before, stood at one side, a mask-like politeness freezing her features, but Sarah hardly noticed her, she was so intent on looking at the much-loved house and garden.

She descended from the carriage, suddenly ashamed to show people she knew well, that she was pregnant and unmarried. Her cheeks flushed and she saw Jean Luc realise why she was blushing.

"I'm not going to tell the servants that we will shortly be wed," he whispered in her ear. "Perhaps you will now realise the gravity of the situation for yourself and your child and stop being so obstinate, madam."

They entered the hall together, Jean Luc frowning and Sarah almost wishing the floor would swallow her up.

They stopped abruptly. She gasped in shock, the colour leaving her cheeks. In front of them on the wall, hung a life-size painting of herself. She had completely forgotten Mr Reynolds and his sketches before she left and she stood stock-still in amazement, clasping her hand to her mouth to stop herself crying out.

The painting was beautiful. It glowed with a luminosity that enhanced the perfect oval of her face, the blue of her eyes and the flaming curls reaching almost to her waist. The silk dress, with its layers of ruffled lace, clung to her bosom and flounced out around her and she glanced with amusement at the slender waist she had enjoyed then.

Jean Luc seemed almost as taken aback as she was to see the painting.

" He's caught you perfectly," he said and looked at her. "You like it, my beloved? It will be my wedding present to you."

"Yes," she murmured, almost inaudibly. " Yes, I like it."

She was looking not just at herself, but also at the woman in her locket. She had always recognised a strong resemblance between them both, but the painting reminded her even more of the familiar face she had always turned to for help and inspiration, than it did of her own, and she now knew, with certainty, the woman was her mother.

Her usual tendency to avoid thinking about the recklessness of her behaviour, was replaced by a sickening fear of what she had done, as hanging on the wall, for everyone to see, was Sarah Durrant, masquerading as Lady Sophie Throgmorton.

'How long will it be before I am found out,' she thought, and as she looked at   Jean Luc, she shrank in terror, fearing his fury and his rejection of her, when he knew the truth.

She was suddenly aware that Heinrich was also staring at the painting and thought she heard him say, 'It's her!' The next minute, the hall started to spin, she felt violently ill and Jean Luc caught her as she fell.

....

The wind howled across the garden, a fore-runner of the Atlantic storm rushing in towards the Exmoor hills. Rain pattered softly against the panes, the fire blazed in the hearth and Jean Luc glanced at Sarah, who was sitting up in bed, completely restored to health.

"Well, madam. You have managed to give us all a fright, as usual," he remarked. "The doctor says you're to stay in bed for the next few days. The journey's been too tiring for you."

She smiled at him, happy to be in her old bedchamber and was disappointed when he did not smile back, but strode up and down, still wearing his travelling clothes.

"How is your mother?" she asked, suddenly remembering the reason for the trip.

He shrugged. "She's not expected to live. The priest has been sent for."

He looked strangely at her as he said the last words and she felt uneasy. His coldness towards his mother also unsettled her and her eyes filled with tears at the thought of her imminent death.

She watched him, reflecting on how much she loved him, as he stood in the middle of the room, lost in thought. He started to speak, " Are you afr…?" then stopped, clearly thinking better of it.

She could see he wanted to question her, but dared not, and was relieved when he abandoned any attempt to do so and instead contented himself with kissing her passionately good night.

40

The Duchess hovered between life and death, her face and body so shrunken, she reminded Sarah of a wax doll. She lay without moving in her bed, her rheumy eyes peering suspiciously at the priest as he prayed for her soul.

Time passed slowly for Sarah. North Devon had once seemed her sanctuary, but now being there was spiked by jagged bursts of fear, and she longed for the distant haven of Alsace. She was used to living from day to day, pushing her wickedness to the back of her mind, but she had always enjoyed two, very clear plans of escape, either to flee or, rather more drastically, to kill herself. Now, heavily pregnant, the idea of fleeing was even less practical than it had been in the past and although she might have once contemplated killing herself, she would never harm her growing child.

Her health began to fail her more. She felt weak and ill and was increasingly confined to the house. She knew that if she had become pregnant while still a kitchen maid, she would not have managed to survive; she was only just coping, surrounded by all the luxury of Wildercombe House and she realised that the long hours, heavy work and unceasing brutality of her childhood had damaged her.

"She is very strong in spirit," Heinrich tried to reassure Jean Luc, "even if not in body."

A physician resided permanently in the house and Jean Luc kept begging her to tell him what was worrying her.

"It's an unnecessary burden for you to carry at such a time," he told her. "What are you afraid of?" but she continued to refuse to talk to him on the subject.

During the day she was calm and smiling, but at night her fears surfaced. Jean Luc now always shared her bed. She had pleaded with him not to, from embarrassment at the impropriety of it, but he had grinned and remarked, "It's hardly relevant, is it? I think our love is more than obvious."

She knew, however, that his religion was a bigger obstacle to him and that he spent many hours confessing his sins to the priest who was also living at Wildercombe House.

In bed she tossed restlessly. She would cry out with fear and panic and he would hold her close until the attack subsided. She rambled incoherently, although often saying " Antoinette," and one heart-rending night for Jean Luc, she seemed to be pleading not to be beaten and even spoke to herself, calling out "Sophie, don't leave me!"

In the morning, she was always pale, but composed, and he became almost as exhausted as she was, as he struggled to cope with the emotional demands being made on him for the first time in his life.

On Xmas Day, his mother died. Sarah was very sad and could not stop crying. She felt that the mad old woman had been her salvation, that she had been given the joy of living at Wildercombe House because there had been no one to question her when she had first arrived, naïve and vulnerable.

Jean Luc, however, did not appear at all moved and ate his Xmas goose with great relish, washed down with many glasses of claret.

The funeral was a simple affair, partly held in the chapel and partly in the small cemetery at the back of the house. The seamstress had made her a dress of black silk and as she stood wearing it at the grave, she suddenly remembered Sophie's blood-stained dress she had brought with her from Lynmouth and which she had completely forgotten.

As soon as the funeral was over, she rushed to the corner of her dressing room, where she had placed it in the locked drawer of a small cabinet, behind a rail of clothes. The wood was splintered. The lock had been broken and the drawer was empty. She stared in horror.

' Who would do that?' she wondered in distress. ' Surely none of the servants would dare to break open the furniture? Who would want Sophie's dress? It doesn't mean anything to anyone except me.'

She now wished she had disposed of the garment, but it had not seemed important. She had initially wanted to retain a link with Sophie and had then pushed it to the back of her mind, until that day.

The theft worried her and she anxiously searched the dressing room before giving up in despair. Then, a few days later, she again felt a shiver of disquiet when Jean Luc announced he was going on a journey, but would be returning as quickly as he could.

She was both displeased and upset at the news. His daily routine of hunting, working in his laboratory and spending the rest of the day with her, helped her remain calm. No visitors disturbed the peace and quiet of Wildercombe House. No unpleasant surprises, apart from the loss of the dress and the occasional, venomous glance from Mrs Yelland, disrupted the uneventful day and she had begun to feel safer. Now a sense of the unknown threatened her.

"Are you going far?" she asked.

"No, not far," he replied, unhelpfully. "Heinrich will remain here to look after you."

He did not like to worry her, but did not want to lie. He had decided to visit the Throgmortons and try and discover the source of her problem. It was clear to him from her nightmares that the terror which possessed her was somehow related to her previous life. Each night was becoming worse than the last and although she clung to him as he comforted her, he had several times caught her looking at him during the day with an expression that he could only describe as fear.

Her health was clearly suffering and the physician had several times expressed his worry at her weak state and he knew that in a few weeks he would not be able to leave, as the birth might be imminent. He did not dare to hope that the problem would be so well resolved that she would marry him when he returned, but the thought was very much in his mind. He had also decided that if he was unsuccessful, he would marry her against her will.

"Will you miss me?" he teased her.

"Yes," she replied tearfully, which considerably cheered him.

He left very early next morning on horseback, accompanied by several servants, and galloped as fast as he could towards London, carrying an image of her, still fast asleep, her red hair spread out across the covers.

41

He bowed low to Lord and Lady Throgmorton. He was travel-stained and weary and aware he was not as well dressed as he would have wished, for his first meeting with his future parents in law.

He had expected poverty. The dispatching of their marriageable eldest daughter to the remoteness of North Devon, to distant relations they hardly knew, had made him convinced that they must be impoverished, and he was unprepared for the splendour of the mansion.

He looked curiously at Lord Throgmorton, hoping to see a resemblance to Sophie, but was disappointed. The plump, florid man in front of him, with small, piggish eyes and a lugubrious expression, bore no similarity at all to his beloved. He knew that Lady Throgmorton was his second wife, so her pointed, witch-like features and bulging eyes, did not surprise him in their marked difference to her step-daughter's beautiful face.

He disliked her as soon as he saw her. Her haughty manner was unfriendly; her bouffant hair was arranged with jewels and with what appeared to be, to his eyes, a small bird peering out from foliage, and was complemented by two, bright red dabs of rouge on her cheeks and a black patch on her chin. He had always disliked the artificial look affected by aristocratic ladies and thought she was one of the worst examples he had ever been unlucky enough to see.

She, for her part, seemed equally disenchanted with the tall, dark - eyed man without a wig and streaked with dirt and dust from the road, standing in front of her.

"My house is at your disposal," said Lord Throgmorton. "I expect you have come to negotiate a dowry?"

He shrugged, not able to reveal why he was there and not having the slightest interest in any financial settlement, which he had never expected. He smiled as he thought of Sophie, as he had left her, asleep and expecting his child.

Lord Throgmorton offered a very large sum of money and he politely thanked him, thinking of Heinrich's pleasure when he returned.

"Is there a painting of Lady Sophie?" he asked, looking at the pictures on the walls.

"Why, yes," said Lord Throgmorton. "There she is as a young girl."

Jean Luc stared at a white-faced child with spiky, ginger hair, who bore no resemblance to Sarah at all.

"May I say how she has bloomed since then," he said. "In more ways than one," he murmured to himself.

Lord Throgmorton looked displeased. "The picture was well done," he remarked.

"Is there a painting of Lady Sophie's mother?" he enquired.

"No!" snapped Lady Throgmorton.

He thought he could see jealousy in her eyes and wondered if the portrait had been removed and if Sophie had suffered solely because she was the daughter of Lord Throgmorton's first wife. His temper flared as he thought of her being so badly beaten and he regarded the Throgmortons with hostility.

"You're getting a bargain, sir," exclaimed Lord Throgmorton, slapping him on the back. "I'm sure her looks will improve with age!" He appeared to be struggling to find a compliment to give his daughter, to Jean Luc's amazement, and finally managed, "She's well educated. She reads and writes beautifully. Her spinet playing...." and then seemed to fall diplomatically silent.

"Really?" remarked Jean Luc, knowing Sarah's complete lack of education when he first met her. "She certainly speaks French well and her singing and playing are excellent!" he added, suddenly wanting to annoy Lady Throgmorton, by praising her step-daughter, but instead, he was taken aback to see a look of extreme surprise cross her face.

More polite conversation followed, mainly concerning the extent of his Alsatian estates and the well-deserved victory of the English over the French in the New World, and Jean Luc, apart from experiencing a greater feeling of dislike at Lady Throgmorton's appearance and personality, did not think he was any nearer to finding out his beloved's problem and thought that the only strange note occurred when Lady Throgmorton asked him,

"What about the servant girl? Is she still there?"

"Do you mean Sarah Durrant, the maid who accompanied her to North Devon ?" he replied, remembering the name on the grave and amazed that the arrogant Lady Throgmorton should be enquiring after a mere servant.

"Yes!" she exclaimed curtly.

"Why, she's dead!" he replied. "She died on the journey! Didn't you know?"

Lady Throgmorton's eyes glinted and she smiled. He was horrified that she was pleased at someone's death and, at the same time, found her obvious delight very strange.

"How did she die?" she asked.

"I believe she died of an illness, a cough," he said coldly.

" A cough, you say?" she repeated, drawing in her breath sharply.

"I gather so," he replied.

Lady Throgmorton fell quiet and she said nothing more on the subject.

"How is the health of Lady Sophie?" she asked.

"She's well," he lied.

"Has she a cough?" she enquired.

"No, she has not," he replied and then, as he retired to his bedchamber, disappointed at his lack of success, he stopped in the doorway and stabbing in the dark, said, "May I ask who is Antoinette?"

If a thunderbolt had fallen through the ceiling into the room, Lord and Lady Throgmorton could not have looked more shocked, and they all three stood immobile, as though in a tableau. He waited. There was complete silence. Lord Throgmorton's florid face had reddened even further and his wife stared malevolently at Jean Luc with what he thought was hatred.

His spirits rose. There <u>was</u> some sort of mystery concerning Antoinette. He had been right.

"She is no one!" shrieked Lady Throgmorton, her manner betraying her words. "She is no one we know here! I think it is time for you to retire, sir!" and she turned to a footman and asked him to escort Jean Luc to his bedchamber.

He glanced at Lord Throgmorton, who was shuffling away towards the window, his eyes on the floor.

'This is a man who is not master in his own house!' he thought and bowed briefly to him and to Lady Throgmorton as he left the room.

He rested until dinner, and was hopeful he would discover more, but when he came down to the dining room, was disappointed to find that he was dining alone. Lord Throgmorton had evidently gone to his gaming club and Lady Throgmorton was said to be indisposed, but he was given a message to say that she would like to see him in four days' time at five o'clock in the drawing room, when he would learn something to his advantage.

He spent that evening and the next four days chafing at being so far from Sarah. He mistrusted Lady Throgmorton and suspected her of being spiteful and malicious, but he had come such a distance and wanted so desperately to resolve the problem, that against his better judgement he waited. Lord Throgmorton did not return from his card playing; Lady Throgmorton remained in her room; and he spent his time walking the malodorous city streets and asking the servants about Antoinette, none of whom had ever heard the name before.

Five o' clock on the final day arrived and he stood impatiently in the drawing room. Lady Throgmorton did not appear. Ice seized his heart and he felt a deep sense of foreboding.

He questioned the footmen, but no one seemed to know where their mistress was. He became increasingly angry and began to fear he had been duped, that she had made a fool of him. But why she would want him to waste his time waiting to see her, he could not comprehend.

Finally, a footman came bearing a message from the housekeeper, that Lady Throgmorton had left the house, shortly after his arrival, to travel in the carriage to Ilfracombe.

"Ilfracombe!" he exclaimed, realising he had been deliberately kept in London, presumably to enable her to reach Wildercombe House before he returned. He bellowed in rage, wondering what malice she was intending.

'Thank God I left Heinrich with Sophie!' he thought.

He and his servants set off as quickly as possible through the darkness, but by the time they reached the countryside, it was already as black as coal-tar. No stars shone. No moon hung in the cloud-covered sky and he was forced to abandon the journey and spend the night in an inn. He hardly slept, the face of Lady Throgmorton haunting him.

'I fear she has harmed my beloved in the past and I feel sure she means only evil now.'

He was ready before dawn and waited for the first rays of sunrise to light the fields. Then they set off again, changing the sweat-soaked horses as often as they could find staging posts.

42

Sarah heard the noise of a coach coming up the drive. She knew it was not Jean Luc as he had left on horseback, but still hoping it might be him, she eagerly looked out from her bedroom window.

She was shocked to see red-coated soldiers, and a carriage, come to a halt just below her. Her heart stood still, blood pounding in her ears, as she recognised the Lord Lieutenant. The carriage looked familiar, and puzzled, she peered down at the woman descending from it. The bouffant hair structure swayed in the biting winter wind; the heavily made-up face and bejewelled figure with its wide skirt, appeared incongruous in the North Devon countryside.

She turned to stone. She found it difficult to see. The room blurred, dizzily spinning around her. She clutched onto a chair and forced herself to breathe deeply. Then, her vision clearing, she ran in a panic out onto the landing from where she could already hear a thunderous knocking. Heinrich was standing in the hall and momentarily glanced up at her, as a footman pulled open the front door. Her legs had turned to jelly, but she forced her swollen body to dash towards the attic door, then scrambled up the narrow stairs and out onto the parapet.

An Arctic wind hit her and she flinched. In utter desperation, she clumsily clambered over the low wall and put her feet on the ladder which Jean Luc had found, so many months before. She clung to the rusted metal sides and climbed down, trying to look at the rungs in front of her, as otherwise she knew she would fall. She reached the ground, shaking, her hands bleeding, and found herself in a narrow enclosure, hidden from the front of the house by a wall, where a small tunnel, buttressed by wooden piles, disappeared into the ground. She squeezed into it with difficulty and crawled on hands and knees through its claustrophobic blackness, feeling her way along in the earth and completely unable to see. She finally emerged breathless at the edge of the wood and scurried as quickly as she could manage up the path towards the cliffs. She did not dare look back, and was all the time expecting to be caught by the soldiers, but to her surprise found herself, still alone, on the windswept grass beyond the trees.

She walked towards the very edge of the cliff and balanced herself, like a bird, on the flaking, grey, slate rock. A golden winter sun was low, illuminating the horizon and flooding the base of the cumulus clouds rolling in towards Exmoor. Below her was the sea, an eddying expanse of dark blue water, inviting her to jump and be free. For a second she braced herself to plummet sickeningly downwards, then the baby kicked inside her and she jerked away from an end which had, temptingly, seemed almost easy, and fell back again into her world of fear. Panic-stricken, she stumbled on, flat-footed, trying to balance her ungainliness so that she did not slip.

A pain wrenched at her side and she clasped the stone wall of the derelict church, pressing her face against its coldness. She was finding it difficult to breathe and reluctantly abandoned the building and hurried down the hill towards Ilfracombe, ice splintering under her feet, making her sink ankle deep into the mud. She knew it was useless to think of hiding in a cave or in the countryside. It was winter. She was dressed in thin clothing, her arms were bare and she had no food or money with her. There was only one person she could think of who might shelter her. She remembered his words on the beach, "If I can ever do aut fur ye." She knew he was prepared to flout the law and hastened her steps down the slope towards the harbour, not wanting to endanger him, but knowing that her situation was desperate.

She had no idea if Lady Throgmorton had come to North Devon having already guessed her deception, but it made no difference. As soon as she entered the house and saw the painting she would realise what she had done.

....

At Wildercombe House Heinrich regarded with hostility the Lord Lieutenant, the heavily armed soldiers and a shrieking Lady Throgmorton.

"That woman is an imposter!" she howled, jabbing her lace-covered finger at the painting. "That is not my step-daughter! She has killed her and taken her place!"

"It is true Sarah Durrant has taken your step-daughter's place, but it is not yet proven she has killed her, " the Lord Lieutenant remarked to her. "Although, of course, she will be hung for either crime."

" Where is she?" he demanded, turning to Heinrich, who remained silent.

Mrs Yelland was listening, open-mouthed at the news that Sarah was not Lady Sophie Throgmorton and almost before he had finished speaking, she called out, "Yes, she did kill her! I have the evidence!" and rushed to her bedchamber, returning with Sophie's blood-stained dress, which now possessed two, hastily made tears. She waved it as proof, a smile of happiness contorting her face.

"That's my step-daughter's dress! I recognise it! She stabbed her!" screeched Lady Throgmorton. "She's a murderess!"

"Search the house!" commanded the Lord Lieutenant to his men.

"I protest! You cannot do this!" shouted Heinrich furiously. "Stop!"

"Keep him under arrest until we have finished!" ordered the Lord Lieutenant and Heinrich was surrounded by four soldiers.

The whole house was turned upside down, but Sarah was not found, and the soldiers were then sent out in to the grounds. She still had not been discovered when Jean Luc arrived late in the afternoon, exhausted from the gruelling ride and galloping even more frantically along the drive as he caught sight of the red-coated intruders.

Heinrich had been freed after the search of the house and ran down the steps to meet him.

"Lady Throgmorton has arrived and says that Lady Sophie is really her servant, Sarah Durrant and that she has killed her! The Lord Lieutenant has come to arrest her!" he said, speaking very rapidly in Alsatian.

"What!" exclaimed Jean Luc, also in Alsatian, so shocked he could hardly speak, his face draining of blood. He swayed on the steps and Heinrich put out a hand to steady him.

"They are waiting in the drawing room, Seigneur."

" Where is she? Has she escaped?" he asked.

"She was in the house when they arrived, as I saw her on the landing, but they have not yet managed to find her," he replied.

"Have you told them she was in the house?" he asked.

"No, Seigneur," Heinrich replied. "They are beginning to think she is not here."

He ran up the steps and into the hall and strode into the drawing room, his face ashen.

"I want your soldiers to leave my house and grounds immediately!" he shouted angrily at the Lord Lieutenant. "I will deal with this problem. You can leave it in my hands."

"I am sorry, I cannot do that," he replied. "This servant has impersonated and killed Lady Sophie Throgmorton! She must be arrested and then she will be hung."

"She's expecting my child," Jean Luc said harshly. "I gather a pregnant woman cannot be hung in England."

Lady Throgmorton gasped. "She's with child!"

He glared angrily at her, "And you, madam, would you leave my house. I accept she has deceived me, but I do not accept she would ever kill anyone."

"Here is the evidence, sir, in front of your very own eyes!" and she pointed to the dress which Mrs Yelland was still holding. "Look at the slashes and blood on this dress of my step-daughter's, which your housekeeper has found!"

"Mrs Yelland! What the devil has she got to do with all this? I don't know anything about a dress, but I do know that Sophie," he corrected himself, "Sarah Durrant, would never harm anyone. She is the most sweet, gentle person I have ever met!" His voice broke and he struggled to compose himself, before continuing, "You knew your step-daughter was very ill. That's why you remarked on Sarah Durrant dying from a cough. You were suspicious. Why are you lying?"

"Why are you so frightened of the name Antoinette?" he shouted, more loudly. "Why was she beaten so badly? There's wickedness afoot here and I'm going to leave no stone unturned until I discover the truth!" He clenched his fists and Heinrich grabbed his arm to restrain him as Lady Throgmorton looked contemptuously at him, her white mask of a face immobile, but her eyes glittering with excitement, as though she was at a hunt and had arrived for the kill.

"Seigneur," he said and Jean Luc, grimacing with the effort, just managed to control his temper.

"Your sweet, gentle lady slashed a man with a knife at Heddon! I know that sir!" announced the Lord Lieutenant.

"She was defending me and if she had not done so, I would not be alive here today," he retorted. "Now get out, all of you!"

And you, Mrs Yelland," he said turning to her, "are dismissed immediately from my service and I never want to see you again."

"We will search Ilfracombe and the countryside round here tomorrow," announced the Lord Lieutenant. "The murderess has eluded us today!" He mockingly bowed towards Jean Luc, then walked towards the door followed by Lady Throgmorton who paused to say sneeringly, "You're a fool, Frenchman. She's ensnared you, like all the others. This time the child will not live and nor will she," and she swept out of the room like a ship in full sail.

Jean Luc waited as he watched the carriage speed down the drive, then ran back into the hall shouting out, "Sophie! Sarah! Where are you? They've gone," as he rushed frantically from room to room.

The door on the landing was ajar, cold fingers of winter air blew down from the attics and he stopped for a moment in thought, then ran up the stairs and onto the parapet and looked down at the ground.

" There's a priest's escape route over here, but surely she couldn't have done it!" he exclaimed to Heinrich. "She's too weak and ill." He shook his head in disbelief. " I think she had no choice," he said. "It was this or death!"

He threw himself over the wall and climbed down the ladder, followed by Heinrich. They crawled through the tunnel and when they came out into the wood, they both saw traces of blood on a stone, but neither mentioned it.

Twilight was beginning to obscure the trees and bushes and Jean Luc glanced despairingly around him and then with his last ounce of strength, ran up the path towards the coast. He stopped at the cliff top and looked down at the sea-covered beach, before carrying on to the ruined church.

"It's hopeless," he said, as the dark closed in on them. "She might not even have come along here. She's going to die if she's outside in the cold tonight! What was she wearing?"

"A dress," replied Heinrich shortly.

Servants were told to keep searching for her all night. Lanterns were brought and flickered faintly through the dusk. He slowly retraced his steps to the house and slumped, exhausted, onto the chair by the fire, his head in his hands.

"Why did she do it?" he asked Heinrich. "Why did she take her place? I know she didn't kill her, but why did she pretend to be her? My darling, my beloved!"

Heinrich poured out a generous helping of brandy and gave it to him and he gulped it down.

"I was in the hall under guard while they searched," said Heinrich " and Lady Throgmorton kept coming out from the drawing room to look at the painting. She seemed unable to stay away from it and at one point tried to slash it with her nails, but the Lord Lieutenant prevented her, as he said it was evidence."

"Well?" said Jean Luc. "What are you saying?"

Heinrich frowned. "She said something very strange. I was not even sure I heard correctly."

"What did she say?" asked Jean Luc.

"She said, 'I killed you once and I'll kill you again'."

"You must be mistaken," said Jean Luc. "How could she have possibly done that? It doesn't make sense."

"That's what I thought I heard," said Heinrich.

" And what did she mean when she left?" he continued. " Was she suggesting she had already had a child? That's not true. I know it's not."

He spent the night in the chair by the fire and ordered all the candles to be lit in the house and all the curtains open, so that she could see to return.

By the morning, he had given up all hope and had the painting moved to the library and gazed at her face, beside himself with grief.

43

The days passed and there was no sighting of Sarah. Lady Throgmorton was offering a reward for her capture and the Lord Lieutenant's soldiers had managed to frighten almost the whole of Ilfracombe, banging on doors and searching the houses. It was as though she had just disappeared into thin air. Jean Luc was afraid to hope she had survived and constantly feared that she had thrown herself into the sea and that her lifeless body would be found one day on the beach. He could not sleep or eat and spent his whole day in despair in the library.

He had discovered from the reward poster that she had been a kitchen maid.

"How many of our kitchen maids play the spinet and sing and behave in such a refined way? How could she have managed it?" he asked Heinrich.

"She was a very unusual person," he remarked.

" 'Is', not 'was!" Jean Luc shouted. "I don't care what she is! I want her back!"

He finally emerged from the library, only to spend all his time in her room, touching her clothes and sitting in the window where she had often sat. Her locket, still unmended, had been abandoned on the bedside table and he idly fingered it.

"The woman is clearly her mother," he said to Heinrich. "She looks exactly like her. But why would a kitchen maid have a mother dressed in such finery?" As he said the words, he suddenly stopped and looked at Heinrich. "Do you think Lady Throgmorton was talking about her mother? Or had come to believe that Sarah was her mother?"

Heinrich carefully opened the back and peered again at the partly legible letters, "It's impossible to decipher it."

Jean Luc took it from him. "I might have a powder which will reveal it better," he said. " It will probably ruin the picture though."

"You have the large painting, Seigneur," said Heinrich.

"Yes," he replied and for the first time since Sarah's disappearance he went to his laboratory and spent the morning endeavouring to make the letters legible.

Finally he succeeded. The words were faint, but could be read. He looked at them in amazement and gave the picture to Heinrich.

"La Princesse de Durante," Heinrich read out. They stared at each other.

" 'Durante' has been changed to 'Durrant'! What's going on here?" Jean Luc said. "And Antoinette's a French name. Perhaps she's really called Antoinette de Durante."

Heinrich slowly rubbed his face with his hand. "I think that's the name of the woman I saw all those years ago. Yes, I'm sure. La Princesse de Durante. She was with a hunting party of the King. I said I thought she looked exactly like her."

" And my mother!" Jean Luc exclaimed. " She often called her Princess Caroline. Perhaps that was her mother's name? Her confused mind might suddenly have made her remember that she had died and she thought she was seeing her spirit that night when she looked at Sarah at dinner. I'll have enquiries made about the Princess de Durante in France and I'll ask someone in London to find out more from the kitchen staff at the Throgmorton house."

He quickly wrote two letters to be despatched to London and Paris and thought for a moment, then exclaimed, "I'm a fool! I need to find out more about Sophie's death. I know she died at Lynmouth, which is only a very small village. I'll send someone there to ask at all the houses and see who laid her out after her death. That person will know if there were stab marks on her."

A few days later, Heinrich's sharp eyes noticed Jenny had disappeared. He enquired in the kitchen and no one seemed to have any idea where or why she had gone. He told Jean Luc, who asked a footman where she lived.

"Down by Rapparee Cove," he replied.

"That's an odd name!" he remarked.

"I think it be Irish and means wild man, or smuggler," the footman told him.

"Smuggler?" Jean Luc said. "I wonder if most of Ilfracombe's fishermen are connected to the smuggling going on around here and whether Jenny's family might be involved. Sarah helped the smuggler escape the Excise men. She saved his life and they owe her a debt."

He hurriedly galloped to Ilfracombe and knocked at the door of Jenny's cottage.

"I'm afraid ee be at Widecombe to look after 'er old aunt who be took ill," her mother told him.

"If Jenny can help Lady Sophie in any way, would you please give her this money," he said, taking out coins from his pocket and pressing them into her hand.

He left the neat, white-walled cottage and cantered slowly round the harbour, remembering the afternoon of the hot air balloon and Sarah speaking to a fisherman with dark curly hair. He sat on his horse, at the end of the cobbled jetty, watching the cottage where he thought the man had been standing, and noticing that the fishing boat with a red and white sail that the fisherman had limped towards, was not in the harbour. He dismounted and walked along the path towards the cottage door.

"They not be there," said an old woman, picking cabbages in the next garden. "They be out at zee."

"Thank you," he said thoughtfully and returned home.

"I think someone's hiding her," he told Heinrich. "I think she might have got away and that she hasn't killed herself."

The next day he received word from Lynmouth that when Sophie had died, there were no stab marks on her. Her skin had been smooth and unmarked. He instructed a servant to go and take a signed statement to that effect and then waited to see if the investigations in London and Paris proved in any way fruitful.

Finally, a letter arrived from London and he frantically tore it open.

"She was called Antoinette!" he exclaimed to Heinrich. " Lady Throgmorton herself changed it to Sarah Durrant. And she was illegitimate. Lady Throgmorton gave orders for her to be often whipped to punish her for the sins of her mother and of herself ."

His voice failed him, emotion clouded his eyes and he found it difficult continuing. "She was looked after by a French woman who married the butler. They went to live at Lord Brabant's estate in Yorkshire and the investigator has gone there to see if he can discover any more."

A week later, he received a second letter, this time from Paris.

"The Princess de Durante was called Caroline," he told Heinrich. "She was evidently considered very wild and caused a scandal when she eloped with her lover, Count Rouen, instead of marrying the Prince de Montpellier, to whom she had been betrothed. They fled to London, where he was killed in a duel, before they could marry, and she died after giving birth to her daughter, who is also said to have died, although that's obviously not true. So why did her family not know of the existence of her child? Why was Antoinette kept in London in the Throgmorton household?" He struggled to unravel a puzzle which had begun its momentum many years before.

Every day he rode his horse around Ilfracombe. He followed a circuitous route past the Parish Church, along a path winding across the

271

steep hills of the Torrs and then down to Crewkerne Cave and lastly the harbour, where he would look to see if the fishing boat with the red and white sail had returned. He had guessed that Sarah had probably escaped down the hill past the derelict church that first day and cursed himself for having abandoned the pursuit there and kept wishing he could turn back the clock. He knew very little of her activities before his arrival in North Devon and although Jenny had told him she had always stayed on the estate, he realised that this might not have been the case and that Ilfracombe was the nearest place she could have walked to. He had also initially wondered about Captain Vinnicombe, but had several times been surprised to see him enthusiastically searching for her with the soldiers and so had discounted any help for her from the Vinnicombe family. He also kept looking for any sighting of Jenny.

Finally, a further letter arrived from his investigator, who was now in Yorkshire and the last piece of the puzzle was revealed to him. He had tracked down the former maid to the Princess de Durante, who was still living at Brabant Hall with her husband, now the head butler there. She had told him that Lord Throgmorton had been a friend of Count Rouen and that he and the Princess had lived with him in his house when they first came to London. When the Count had been killed, Lord Throgmorton had become infatuated with her, even although she was pregnant and not in any way enamoured of him, and was grieving incessantly for her lover. His first wife had already died and he was betrothed to the present Lady Throgmorton, whom he jilted and who consequently hated her rival with an intensity of incredible ferocity.

" The Princess was found one morning smothered to death in her bed," he told Heinrich in shocked tones, "and her baby was discovered, miraculously unharmed, in a rubbish pile by the kitchen and was thought to have been thrown out of the window. It was never known who had done such a crime and Lord Throgmorton married his previous fiancée whose spite extended to the new-born child, who had the same red hair as her mother, and she wanted her abandoned in the street as a foundling. Lord Throgmorton, however, had insisted she be kept in his household, so she was placed in the kitchen. The maid initially cared for the baby and then she married and Lady Throgmorton refused to allow her to take Antoinette with her to Yorkshire."

" She has robbed Antoinette of her family, she has had her cruelly treated and now she is trying to ensure she is hung!" he shouted. "Her hatred towards the Princess has survived all these years and as Antoinette clearly resembles her mother, it is perhaps as though she is looking again at the Princess de Durante. It is even possible she was brought up from the kitchen to be a maid to her step-daughter, in order for Lady Throgmorton to gloat at her."

"I wonder why Antoinette became Lady Sophie Throgmorton?" he continued. "Do you think she had some inkling her birthright had been stolen from her and she was trying to redress the balance? If she did not, then what has happened is a strange quirk of fate."

"Where are you Antoinette? Where are you? Please God keep you safe until I find you!" he prayed, crossing himself.

44

He heard that the Lord Lieutenant was in Barnstaple and rode to see him, presenting him with the signed statement from Lynmouth.

"It is evident that Lady Sophie Throgmorton died from an illness! She was not stabbed!" he said. Then he related the story of Antoinette's birth and upbringing and made various suggestions as to what should happen to Lady Throgmorton, the least ghastly being that she should be dismembered and thrown to wolves.

The Lord Lieutenant looked with cold distaste at him.

"So she's French, this kitchen maid of yours!" he remarked sourly. "Is she Catholic as well?"

" She will be!" rejoined Jean Luc, " when she marries me!"

The Lord Lieutenant picked up the signed statement and tore it in half.

"Here is what I think of your deposition, sir! It's all a fake, a forgery! And if it's true that the Throgmortons have brought up an illegitimate orphan in their own household, then they must be thanked for their good Christian kindness!" He stared at Jean Luc, his scar twitching, his eyes hard.

"Lord Throgmorton is a true Englishman!" he shouted and Jean Luc realising that whatever he said would be useless, stormed out of the room. The Lord Lieutenant watched him go and leaned down out of the window as he mounted his horse in the courtyard below.

"Good riddance to you and your trollop, sir, who will soon be caught!" he called, a safe distance from Jean Luc and his sword. Then he returned to the delightful company of Lady Throgmorton, whose sophisticated hair style and dress had set the cream of Exeter society ablaze with attempts to imitate her, and who had accompanied him in his coach, as there had been a report of a sighting of Sarah Durrant in Ilfracombe, and she was hoping to be there when she was arrested.

As Jean Luc rode home, soldiers galloped past, riding towards Ilfracombe.

"I'm surprised to see them again," he said grimly to Heinrich riding next to him. " I thought the search had been given up. I wonder why the Lord Lieutenant is in Barnstaple? He seemed very sure Antoinette is going to be caught. Do you think there's been some word of her?"

"It's possible," he replied. "The reward is very large. A lot of people would turn in their own mother for that sum."

He decided to ride on to Ilfracombe and as they reached the outskirts of the town they saw more soldiers knocking on doors and entering into houses.

"They obviously don't know anything certain. They're just looking," he said with relief. They rode down to the harbour and he saw that the fishing boat with the red and white sail was moored to the side of the jetty.

"That's strange!" he remarked. "First the soldiers are back and now the boat's returned!"

He hurriedly dismounted and knocked at the door of the cottage near the harbour. John Buzzacott opened it and scowled as he saw the identity of his visitor.

"Do you know where she is?" Jean Luc asked bluntly.

"No, us ' ave no idea!" he replied, his tone unfriendly.

He peered into the small room, which reeked of the sea. Fishing nets hung from hooks in the ceiling, lobster pots were stacked against one wall and he could see that Sarah was not there. He turned to leave and then stopped short as Jenny came running along the path, frantically shouting,

" The soldiers are coming! Quick!"

She stumbled into the solid body of Heinrich, who blocked her way and grabbed her arm and pulled her into the cottage.

"Where is she?" he demanded.

There was a silence in the room. Then a baby cried plaintively from upstairs.

Jean Luc slowly walked across the beaten earth floor and lifted the latch of a door set back in the wall. He climbed the creaking stairs and with fumbling fingers unlatched another door and went into a low-ceilinged attic, filled with more pots and nets and again smelling strongly of the sea.

Facing him, in a rough wooden bed, cradling a baby in her arms, was Sarah. He stood, lost for words, just gazing at her. She looked back at him, her face white, her eyes smudged with dark circles, her red hair hanging lankly down.

They stared, entranced, at each other and then he slowly approached the bed and put out his hand and touched her face.

"I can't believe I've actually found you," he said.

Her eyes filled with tears. "I'm sorry. I'm so sorry for deceiving you."

"My darling! My love!" he murmured, embracing at the same time, both her and the tiny, red-haired baby she was holding.

275

"We must go now!" said Heinrich, close behind him. "The soldiers outnumber us! Take the infant, Jenny," and Sarah's eyes widened in surprise as she realised they were intending to try and save her.

"Can you take us to France in your boat?" Jean Luc asked John Buzzacott. "I will pay you handsomely, as well as rewarding you for the immense service you have already done me."

"Yess, yer Grace, the zee's high and there be a good wind blowing. Us can get ee out of the 'arbour quickly."

Jean Luc took off his coat and wrapped it round Sarah, then lifted her up and carried her downstairs and out into the street. They all hurried along the quayside and could see the soldiers directly opposite them, on the hillside, straggling in a disorderly fashion towards the strand.

"There they are!" the shout went up and John Buzzacott ran ahead and untied the ropes, which he threw hurriedly onto the deck. He climbed down the ladder attached to the quay, quickly hoisted the sail, and the boat was already starting to leave its mooring place as Jean Luc rapidly clambered down the ladder, holding Sarah with one arm. Jenny followed with the baby, and Heinrich jumped last onto the deck from the wall.

The boat moved rapidly across the water, the strong wind filling its sail. Soldiers were now running along the quay and the boat sailed past the entrance to the harbour, shuddering as it met the full force of the waves, then passed under the lee of Hillsborough and out into the Bristol Channel.

Muskets cracked sharply in the winter air, but they were too far away to cause damage. Jean Luc glanced back and could see a carriage come to a halt at the very end of the jetty. The Lord Lieutenant descended from it, followed by Lady Throgmorton, her fantastically sculpted hair caught by the fierce wind and blown around her head like so many waving snakes of Medusa. Even at this distance, he could feel her vindictive gaze, and stood defiant and proud on the deck, Sarah in his arms, her red hair bright in the sun, and next to him, his new-born child, held by Jenny, bellowing lustily in the cold air. He hurriedly took his small family to the greater safety of the bow and said to Sarah,

" I think the Princess de Durante can now rest peacefully!"

She looked at him, perplexed, and he said, "I'll tell you about her when we're further away from Ilfracombe."

He glanced at the screaming infant and continued, "And in the meantime, I might be a very new father, and no one has yet told me if I have a son or a daughter, but I think my child needs to be fed."

STRASBOURG

The bells pealed in ringing cadences, echoing across the steep, gabled roofs of the half-timbered houses. People thronged the cobbled square and sunlight struck dusky sandstone arches and pillars and the glowing rose window

Jean Luc stood on the steps of the cathedral and paused to kiss his new wife, her silver dress and train sparkling with thousands of pearls, her long hair gleaming with a brilliant redness. Wedding guests poured out behind them, several of whom possessed exactly the same colour hair as the bride. Devon accents could be heard, mingling with French and Alsatian.

The storks flew slowly across the blue sky, high above the flat, river-crossed land. Antoinette gave her hand to Jean Luc and a sudden, inexplicable image came into her mind of her chapped fingers tracing a pattern on a hoar-frosted window pane. She looked up at the birds, dark against the sun, and firmly placed the memory back in the cobwebs of the past. The future belonged to her and her husband and her daughter, untainted by malice or fear.

The storks soared high over the cathedral spire, above the shimmering sun-bright wedding, and gradually disappeared towards the distant mountains of the Vosges.